DESPERATE SURRENDER

"Don't touch me," Revel gasped between hard breaths.

He answered as he lowered his head toward hers. "You need to be touched."

His mouth ravaged hers. There was no sweetness, no tenderness in him, only the oblivion of plunder and, God help her, she welcomed it.

Revel had never felt anything like this. Before, kisses were brief, subdued experiences. There was nothing brief or subdued about Jake Reno. He tasted of something wild, untamed, primitive that fed on something equally untamed within her.

She had never confronted this kind of need before. Always it was the old need that drove her—the desperate desire for revenge. But this was far different. It was an emotion that unleashed a torrent of uncertainty, in which the only certainty was her response to this man.

Reason surrendered to the wind . . .

READERS ARE IN LOVE WITH ZEBRA LOVEGRAMS

TEMPTING TEXAS TREASURE   (3312, $4.50)
by Wanda Owen

With her dazzling beauty, Karita Montera aroused passion in every redblooded man who glanced her way. But the independent senorita had eyes only for Vincent Navarro, the wealthy cattle rancher she'd adored since childhood—who was also her family's sworn enemy. The Navarro and Montera clans had clashed for generations, but no past passions could compare with the fierce desire that swept through Vincent as he came across the near-naked Karita cooling herself beside the crystal waterfall on the riverbank. With just one scorching glance, he knew this raven-haired vixen must be his for eternity. After the first forbidden embrace, she had captured his heart—and enslaved his very soul!

MISSOURI FLAME   (3314, $4.50)
by Gwen Cleary

Missouri-bound Bevin O'Dea never even met the farmer she was journeying to wed, but she believed a marriage based on practicality rather than passion would suit her just fine . . . until she encountered the smoldering charisma of the brash Will Shoemaker, who just happened to be her fiance's step-brother.

Will Shoemaker couldn't believe a woman like Bevin, so full of hidden passion, could agree to marry his step-brother—a cold fish of a man who wanted a housekeeper more than he wanted a wife. He knew he should stay away from Bevin, but the passions were building in both of them, and once those passions were released, they would explode into a red-hot *Missouri Flame*.

BAYOU BRIDE   (3311, $4.50)
by Bobbi Smith

Wealthy Louisiana planter Dominic Kane was in a bind: according to his father's will, he must marry within six months or forfeit his inheritance. When he saw the beautiful bonded servant on the docks, he figured she'd do just fine. He would buy her papers and she would be his wife for six months—on paper, that is.

Spirited Jordan St. James hired on as an indenture servant in America because it was the best way to flee England. Her heart raced when she saw her handsome new master, and she swore she would do anything to become Dominic's bride. When his strong arms circled around her in a passionate embrace, she knew she would surrender to his thrilling kisses and lie in his arms for one long night of loving . . . no matter what the future might bring!

Available wherever paperbacks are sold, or order direct from the Publisher. Send cover price plus 50¢ per copy for mailing and handling to Zebra Books, Dept. 3506, 475 Park Avenue South, New York, N.Y. 10016. Residents of New York, New Jersey and Pennsylvania must include sales tax. DO NOT SEND CASH.

DESPERADO'S CARESS

CARLA SIMPSON

ZEBRA BOOKS
KENSINGTON PUBLISHING CORP.

ZEBRA BOOKS

are published by

Kensington Publishing Corp.
475 Park Avenue South
New York, NY 10016

First printing: September, 1991

Printed in the United States of America

Prologue

El Paso, Texas
June, 1881

The clean, spicy smell of fresh pine lumber pierced the late morning air. It was starkly out of place in this part of Texas, where trees grew sparsely or not at all. Rumor had it the lumber had to be shipped in from the railhead just for this occasion.

Heat built in waves and shimmered across the rutted street that ran through the heart of town. The sun climbed over the rooftops of adobe and clapboard buildings, radiating the blue sky to intense white. Hammers snapped a rhythmic staccato beat, then fell silent as the stark skeleton of the hangman's scaffold was completed.

Through the long hours of the morning, the crowd had gathered. Women herded small, curious children, while Mexican vaqueros idly drifted up from the rail yards where noisy cattle bawled listlessly in the dusty heat. Peasants, on their way to the open-air market at the far end of town, prodded donkeys laden with baskets filled with fresh vegetables. The storekeeper emerged from the front of the mercantile. And from inside the Lone Star Saloon came a slurred toast to "poor Quint Burdett."

"Bad luck!" came a roared response. "Hangin's bad

5

luck. Always steered clear of it myself," the same man boasted.

Big, raw-boned, Hannah Cantrell who ran the local boardinghouse stepped out onto the boardwalk in front of her place. She smoothed her work-roughened hands down over an apron stained with the remnants of breakfast as she proclaimed to the pinch-faced school-marm beside her, "Had to build a new scaffolding after the old one burnt. I could hear 'em hammerin' on it all night long. The marshal is real nervous. Some folks think some of Burdett's old gang will come fer him." At Miss Kate's alarmed gasp, she nodded with thinned lips, "You mark my words. There'll be trouble before they snap his neck."

Miss Kate, playing hookey like her students, listened with pale-faced disbelief.

El Paso was an odd mixture of cowboys, drifters, Mexican vaqueros, and peasants. Almost as one, fifty or more people who had slowly gathered throughout the long morning hours and had watched with mounting curiosity and impatience, turned and stared as the door to the local marshal's office slowly opened.

"Ten o'clock," Mr. Bodie of Bodie Hardware remarked as he snapped his watch closed. "I always thought they hung 'em at dawn." Beside him, Mrs. Bodie narrowed her gaze disapprovingly as she disgustedly turned on her heel. She rattled of something in a mixture of English and broken Spanish to the young Mexican girl who helped behind the counter. They retreated inside the store. The door slammed behind them.

Hannah Cantrell elbowed Miss Kate. "It's all because of her." She gave a horselike snort as she gestured to the young woman who stood nearby yet apart.

"Now what would a lady like that have to do with the likes of Quint Burdett? Been stayin' at my place, ya know. I tried to find out why she's here, but she wouldn't say nothin'. And the marshal ain't been real talkative either."

6

"Wouldn't say *anything*." Miss Kate corrected her effeciently as she turned to glance in the woman's direction.

"That's what I said." Hannah gave her a dark look.

The lady in question felt the penetrating gazes of the two women as the buzz of conversation around her died to a faint whisper. The heavily armed marshal and his deputies slowly escorted their prisoner to the hangman's scaffolding that waited across the street. The spectators slowly parted to let them pass.

Like the others, she moved closer, determined to watch.

The marshal and his prisoner approached the steps to the scaffold. Their way was blocked by a heavyset man. His clothes, hair, and beard suggested soap and water were low priorities. He thrust his face at the marshal.

"Damn fine hangin'!" he complimented as he staggered and weaved about uncertainly.

"We ain't hung 'im yet!" The marshal snapped as he gestured angrily to one of his men. "Get him outta here! Someplace where he can sleep it off!"

As the town drunk was removed by one of the deputies, the marshal gave each of his men a hard look. Then he gave Burdett a shove up the steps to the platform and called down, "Keep everyone back. I don't want trouble. Let's just get it over with." He glanced back over his shoulder and shouted, "Where's the priest?"

"*Aquí.* Here, *señor.*" The frocked priest emerged from the crowd. He was a short, portly man dressed in heavy brown robes. Sweat poured from his face and dripped down upon his vestments.

"Do your part, *Padre,*" the marshal instructed him.

The priest labored up the steps, holding the front of his robes with one hand, the Bible and a crucifix clutched in the other.

The ancient prayer of atonement, begging forgiveness and mercy, was made in Latin. But before the priest could

7

finish, Burdett jerked up his head and spit on the poor man.

"I don't want none of your holy words, priest. I don't believe none of it anyway. Save your jibberish for someone else."

The priest stared back at him in horror at this blasphemy and made the sign of the cross with trembling hands.

"May God have mercy on your soul," he whispered and shrank back. He shook his head gravely.

Burdett laughed, a chilling sound that whipped through the blazing heat as he taunted the priest, the marshal, and everyone who watched. The noose was jerked down and tightened about his neck.

The marshal stood back and nodded to the inconspicuous little man who waited at the far side of the scaffolding.

Burdett saw the gesture and sensed what was to come. His head snapped around, and those cold black eyes fixed on the lady. The mechanism was released. Just before the door beneath his feet dropped open and the rope cinched tight about his neck, he snarled at her, "I'll see you in hell, lady!"

She flinched as the door snapped open. Her natural instinct was to look away, but she fought it back. She'd come too far and waited too long to turn away now.

Quint Burdett was a large man. The rope had been shortened to accommodate his height and prevent him from dropping all the way through the door in the floor of the scaffolding. His eyes bulged from their sockets. His arms and legs spasmed.

The spectators, those who'd gathered throughout the morning to witness this moment, gasped at the sight of the gruesome death. Young Mexican women shielded the eyes of small children with their *rebozos* and muttered their prayers.

In front of the hardware store, Mr. Bodie wiped beads of cold sweat from his upper lip with the sleeve of his shirt. His face was a sickly shade of green.

"You satisfied?" his wife asked sharply as she reappeared. She seized him by the arm and jerked him inside the store.

"Well, I never woulda believed it," Hannah muttered with disappointment. "I thought sure we'd have us a gunfight on our hands."

Her gaze fixed briefly on the elegantly dressed young woman, and she inclined her head toward the ashen-faced schoolmarm. "Seein' a man hang sure don't seem to bother her none. I'd sure like to know what someone like her has to do with Burdett." Then her gnarled hands worked the fabric of the plain gingham dress stretched taut over her wide girth.

"That's a mighty fine dress she's wearin'," she added thoughtfully. "Guess that's what a *real* lady wears to a hangin'." She snorted again, but Miss Kate didn't share the humor. She pressed her handkerchief against her mouth as she stared horror-stricken at Burdett's lifeless body.

Seeing her distress, Hannah offered, "C'mon, honey. I got something over at my place that'll fix you right up. I swear you Eastern gals ain't got no backbone or stomach." She wrapped a large, hamlike arm about Miss Kate and pulled her toward the boardinghouse.

The marshal nodded to one of his men. "Tell Purdy we got a customer for him. Just a plain box will do. Let's get him buried—no marker. I don't want no trouble."

His deputies disbursed the remainder of the spectators and the marshal turned and walked toward the lady.

"Damn fine hangin'!" the drunk roared in vague approval from the doorway of the marshal's office as he was shoved to a cell in back.

The marshal stopped at the bottom step of the boardwalk that lined the storefronts at the side of the street. He squinted against the glare of the sun and adjusted his wide-brimmed hat as he looked up at her.

"You satisfied?"

He'd met her ten days ago when she had arrived in El Paso, and he still didn't know any more about her now then he had then.

He was fifty, balding, and weathered. He'd been a U.S. Federal Marshal in these parts for nearly twenty years. El Paso was a rough, border town. Every form of humanity—Indian, Mexican, and rawhide cowboy—could be found here. It was a wild town, not a place for women, but they came anyway. But not women like this one. A town like El Paso—a place like Texas—was hard, harder still on women. If they didn't break and run, they withered and dried up.

She didn't fit. From the polished leather high-top boots, glimpsed when she lifted her skirt carefully, to her deep blue silk gown with its immaculate, white lace collar and cuffs. A matching blue hat sat atop her thick coil of deep auburn hair, and brought out the color of eyes angled over high cheekbones. Her nose was straight and fine-boned above the curve of a full mouth.

At the marshal's comment, delicate brows of that same rich, auburn color knitted together.

He immediately regretted the harshness of his words and coughed uncomfortably as he lowered his gaze from the elegant, refined beauty of her face to the single strand of delicate pearls that encircled her long neck above the lace collar. Matching earbobs peeked from beneath the sweep of auburn wings of hair drawn back from either side of her face. Spotless white gloves encased her hands.

He'd never been one to pay much attention to women other than the kind Flossie kept over at the Lone Star, but everything about this woman suggested refinement, good breeding, and intelligence. All were rare in El Paso.

"Yes, Marshal. I'm satisfied," she said simply as she stared past him, watching as his men lowered Burdett's body.

For several long moments they simply stood there. The marshal's embarrassment grew as she continued to stare, lost in her own thoughts. He cleared his throat.

10

"There's paperwork to do. You'll need a signed affidavit about Burdett."

At first he thought she hadn't heard a word he'd said. "Miss?"

Those compelling blue eyes fastened on him once more, and the marshal realized she'd heard every word.

"Yes, of course," she said softly, almost as an afterthought.

He tried again. "And then, of course, there is the reward."

It was the first time he'd ever had to remind someone about reward money—in this case five thousand dollars. He thought back to his original impression when she'd first walked into his office over a week ago—that it was something more than merely supplying him with the location of Quint Burdett, more than seeing a man wanted for more than three years brought to justice, more than money.

"It's yours," he went on. "There was five thousand dollars offered on Burdett. You've got that comin' little lady."

"No!"

The anger set him back. It reminded him of something else he'd been immediately aware of when she'd first come to him about Burdett—that the elegance and reserve was all carefully controlled. He'd seen anger that day too—anger at his reluctance to go after Burdett. It had surprised him then, but more so now. Nobody he knew walked away from five thousand dollars.

As quickly as the anger came, it was gone—hidden behind an elegant smile. "I don't accept blood money, Marshal," she carefully explained, and then added, "It's against company policy." Then her smile deepened.

"I'm certain you can put that money to far better use right here in El Paso. Perhaps for the school, or to help the orphan's fund that the priest has started."

He frowned. He wasn't aware she knew so much about their town. Then her voice softened.

11

"The children must be taken care of." She laid a gloved hand on his, and he was reminded of how persuasive she had been a week ago.

"I'll leave the matter in your capable hands, Marshal." She turned toward the boardinghouse.

"You leavin', then?" he called after her, feeling an unexpected twinge of regret. Usually he was glad to see people like her go—except she wasn't like the others.

She turned briefly. "Yes, on this morning's train. My work is finished here."

"Just what sorta work . . . ?" the marshal started to ask, only to be cut off once more by that smile.

"Thank you, Marshal—for everything."

With that she turned and disappeared inside Hannah Cantrell's boardinghouse.

Upstairs, in the sparsely furnished room that over-looked the street, she packed and closed the small trunk. Her hairbrush, comb, bottle of lavender water, and scented powder were carefully wrapped and tucked inside a carpetbag. On top she packed the shirtwaist, petticoats, and delicate undergarments Hannah Cantrell had washed for her. She cleared stockings and handkerchiefs from the top drawer of the dressing table.

The only relief from the searing heat was the breeze that lifted the muslin curtains at the window. A badly wrinkled piece of paper gusted from the top of the dressing table to the floor.

She knelt and picked it up. Large, block print boldly spelled out the words WANTED—DEAD OR ALIVE across the top. Below them had once been the likenesses and names of four men, along with a chilling account of their crimes. The paper was torn, the images of two men ripped away. She stared down at it and then carefully tore away the likeness of Quint Burdett.

She smoothed the wrinkles from the paper as she stared down at the remaining likeness.

"And then there was only one," she whispered to herself.

The sound of the train whistle split through the late morning heat choking the small room. The westbound train had arrived. She folded the wanted poster and tucked it carefully inside the carpetbag. She glanced up briefly at the knock at the door.

"The train is here, *señorita*," a small voice informed her as she opened the door. The young orphan boy who worked for Hannah had come for her bags.

"I can take these for you, *señorita?*" he asked excitedly, in anticipation of the pesos to be earned.

"Yes, I'm ready." She smiled down at him as she stepped back from the door. His eyes beamed as he struggled under the weight of her trunk.

He disappeared through the doorway, and she returned to the dressing table. At the back of the side drawer her fingers brushed against cool steel. The pistol snugly fit her hand. She checked the small, short-barreled revolver to make certain it was loaded, then turned to leave but stopped at the window.

The scaffolding she'd watched the town's carpenters build through the long hours of the night stood abandoned, but she couldn't erase the image of Quint Burdett's body hanging from that rope. She didn't want to forget.

Her delight in the child was momentarily forgotten. She had only one thought—Quint Burdett had finally paid.

Revel Tyson gave the room one last sweeping glance to make certain nothing was left behind. Then she slipped the pistol into her reticule and closed the door behind her.

Chapter One

Tombstone, Arizona

Jake Reno was going to die.

He knew *where* he was going to die, he knew *how* he was going to die, and he knew *when* he was going to die.

It struck him with a sort of dark irony, what with the kind of life he'd led the last fifteen years—dodging countless bullets, facing down dozens of gunfighters, numerous sheriff's posses, federal marshals, and the U.S. Cavalry—that death had never been specific. It had always been a possibility, but only if he got careless or stupid . . . certainly not if he could help it.

Now, it was very specific. On August 28, 1881, at precisely twelve o'clock, noon, he was to be hanged by the neck until dead.

Long fingers, accustomed to the perfect balance of a gun, sliced back through a shaggy mane of dark hair. Several days' growth of beard shaded his lean face. Dark shadows haunted his green eyes. The sensual fullness of his mouth thinned.

It wasn't *where* that bothered him so much. He'd come to terms with that weeks ago, and when it came right down to it, maybe Tombstone wasn't such a bad place to die. The town already had a notorious reputation. He was joining an infamous brotherhood of gunfighters and outlaws who had died there and were buried at Boot Hill.

Jake figured it was certainly better to die in Tombstone than some piss-ant place no one had ever heard of, like Squirrel Crossing or Mudsling Hollow.

After countless arguments with hs cellmate, he'd even convinced himself that the *how* part of this latest predicament didn't bother him. After all dead was dead. It didn't matter how you got there, the results were all the same. And he had a sneaking suspicion that once a person was dead, he didn't much give a damn about how it happened anyway. What really bothered him, surprisingly enough, was the *when* part of this latest turn in his life.

He had always thought hanging took place at sunrise, at least that was what he'd heard—"Ned Pepper was hung at dawn," someone had once told him. "You shoulda seen it. He kicked and twitched, and then messed hisself. But I reckon he wasn't a mind to care much about that."

Or, according to another story he'd heard: "Yeah, I was there when they strung up ole Pete at sunrise. He didn't put up a fuss at first, jes' sat on that horse all quiet like. They put the rope around his neck, then slapped that horse out from under him. I heard his neck snap, like a tree branch comin' down in high wind. Trouble was, the rope snapped. There he was, lying on the ground, still alive, and couldn't move a lick on accounta his neck was broke. They had to haul him up and have another go at it. Took four fellas to get him back up on that horse. They propped him up, got a new rope, and hung him a second time. By then, he was cursin' a blue streak. Damnedest thing I ever seen."

Dawn, in Jake's estimation, was definitely preferable. The way he figured it, there were fewer people out that early in the morning. And the fewer people to witness his hanging, the better. But in his current situation, he didn't have much say in the matter.

His thoughts focused back on *how* he was going to die,

16

and he had to admit, hanging always seemed pretty damned uncivilized, like an animal being killed and then hoisted up and left for everyone to gawk at.

One of the other prisoners commented about what a fine scaffolding they had in Tombstone—a real fine piece of craftsmanship.

As his mood darkened, Jake wondered again what the hell difference it made. God, he hoped to hell the rope didn't break.

He jumped as a loud sound snapped through the stifling heat. It was like a single clap of thunder and came from beyond the steel bars at the window. It jerked him back to the present.

He swallowed back the hollow ache that had begun in the pit of his stomack just after sunrise when he'd first heard that sound—the unmistakable crack of a trapdoor dropping away from beneath a man's feet, followed by the stunned gasp of the crowd gathered to watch.

Jake heard that sound three more times throughout the long hours of the morning. It followed a precise pattern—the noise of the crowd took on a carnival-like atmosphere, then a hushed quiet descended as the prisoner was led up the steps of the gallows, and lastly there was that cannon-shot noise and the crowd's echoed shock, as if they were stunned by what they deliberately came to see. After a while, it all was repeated.

Six men were being hung today, and Jake had the dubious honor of being last. That gave him plenty of time to contemplate his situation, the circumstances that had brought him to it, and the opportunity to discuss it with his cellmate, Gus.

Gus was the strong silent type. And he was one ugly, nasty-faced son-of-a-bitch. There wasn't much to him, he was a small fella with a gnarled body that had obviously been battered about. When you were little like Gus, Jake supposed everyone came after you. But if pure ugliness was any salvation at all, it accounted for the fact that Gus had survived long enough to find his way into Jake's cell.

17

And he did have his redeeming qualities. He didn't crowd the place, he was neat, he didn't eat much, and he was a good listener.

The humor with which Jake tried to face all this slipped. He was going to hang; there was nothing he could do to stop it, and he had to face it.

"Charlie Trask deserved to die," he explained to Gus, not trying to convince him, but as a simple statement of fact.

"It took me a long time to find all of them." Jake shook his head. "Fifteen years. If only that old man hadn't got caught in the crossfire."

He regretted the old man's death, he had never meant for anyone else to die. From the angle at which the old man was hit, Jake knew it was a bullet from Charlie's gun that had killed him. Virgil Earp had agreed; a hysterical witness hadn't. It was all that was needed to send him to the gallows.

He lit a cigarette, his green eyes narrowing against the sting of smoke as he slowly exhaled. It was one of the "last privileges" he was allowed. He vaguely wondered about that *last meal* all condemned men were supposed to get. He'd had visions of a thick steak, fried potatoes, maybe a slice of fresh apple pie, and, if he was really lucky, a bottle of whiskey.

His last meal consisted of some kind of stew with suspicious chunks floating in a gravy that separated into pools of cold, gray grease. It was served with a slice of bread so stale and hard he considered using it as a weapon. The whiskey he'd hoped for turned out to be a cup of cold coffee.

Damn! He really could have used a good stiff drink.

Hell, he could have used a whole damn bottle of the stuff. He'd like nothing better than to be roaring, stinking, obliviously drunk.

The plate and cup sat on the floor, untouched except for the bread. Gus had nibbled around the edges, then had given up.

Jake had been thinking about everything that had happened the last few weeks—the trial, the sentencing, and the waiting. The irony he'd first felt hardened, turning the hollow ache into cold anger. If he had it all to do over, he'd do it exactly the same. Except, he thought with keen appreciation for his dilemma, he'd make certain he got away afterward. That had been his one mistake, and it was about to cost him dearly.

Any other man might have wondered if all those years spent chasing after Charlie Trask, Billy Sims, and Newt Dobbs were worth it all now. He'd been to hell and back to get the three of them for what they did. He figured what was in store for him now couldn't be much worse— that is, of course, unless he came up with a plan.

"You got any ideas how to get us out of here?" he asked Gus. The silence was a familiar answer.

"Me neither." Jake muttered as he stood and paced the thick-walled, adobe cell. His pacing brought him back to the window and a scene he wasn't quite ready to face yet.

"You know, you're not a great deal of help, Gus. I really should complain about having to share my accommodations with you," he muttered under his breath, the cigarette clamped firmly between his lips as he grasped the steel bars for the hundredth time and tested them. They held firm.

"I don't suppose you have any friends who could bust us out of here," he suggested as he came away from the window, disappointed. At Gus's continued silence, he leaned his head back against the wall of his cell, eyes closed. When he came away from the wall, the lines at the corners of his mouth deepened.

"Just as I thought, me neither. Let that be a lesson to both of us."

Jake felt a hard stab of regret that he hadn't ridden with a loyal band of outlaws. He could use someone to bust him out right about now.

Then it was gone. He'd made his choice a long time ago, when he went after Charlie Trask. That was also when he'd made his choice about life and death.

"You know something?" He gave Gus a long look. "You could be a little more cooperative. Your next cellmate might not be so generous with the meals around here," he pointed out, trying to block out the rising clamor of the excited crowd outside.

"Come to think of it, the next guy might not be so generous with the choice of beds either."

His comment brought only a blink of response from the large, black eyes that protruded at odd angles from Gus's head.

Jake threw down the cigarette disgustedly and ground it under his heel. "Sometimes, you're a real pain in the ass!" he muttered to his companion.

The noise of the crowd had him pacing again. Four men had been hanged. The marshal's deputies had come for another prisoner more than a half-hour ago. He wiped his arm across his forehead. Damn, but it was getting hot in the cell.

Jake had tried to plan an escape. He'd thought of rushing the deputies when they brought his meals in, but they always pushed the tray through the small opening at floor level. He'd considered starting a fire, but the jail was made of rock, mortar, and adobe. If the guards were deaf and blind, he might have dug his way out, but all he had was a bent metal spoon. The problem was, there was no way out of that jail cell.

"The least you could do is say a few kind words," he grumbled to Gus in growing disgust. "After all, you aren't the one about to be hanged. Is that too much to ask?"

Evidently it was. Gus merely stared back at him with an expression somewhere between faint boredom and sleep.

"You know, I had someone else besides you in mind as a companion for last night," Jake went on, a smile curving his mouth. "Someone like Cherry over at Crystal Palace." He shook his head with rueful appreciation.

"Now there is someone to make you forget life's little problems."

Cherry had been to see him several times, thanks to his friendship with Wyatt. He might not be able to get Jake out of jail, but he had made his stay just a little more comfortable.

The startled gasp of the crowd worked along Jake's nerve endings like salt in an open wound. He knew what came next, but still jumped at the sound of the trapdoor dropping open. He took a long, deep breath.

"Looks like we're in one helluva mess, Gus." At his cellmate's long speculative stare, he amended that observation, "All right, *I've* got *myself* in one helluva a mess."

His head came up at the distant clanging of a steel gate, reminding him that time was short.

He thought back—before that bloody morning fifteen years ago, before he wandered both sides of the law, before revenge had become more important than anything else.

Memories of the small spread up in Wyoming played across his mind. He could almost smell the sharp tang of winter on the wind, feel the expectancy in a leaden sky before first snowfall, see the wide, verdant valley. He thought of smoke-colored mares, almost invisible against the gray rim of the Wind River Mountains except for their brightly spotted rumps, and half-grown colts at their sides carrying the distinct mark of the Appaloosa.

He didn't feel fear, he felt regret—sharp, like a blade thrust between his ribs and twisted—for what might have been. He had returned only once, five years ago. When he'd left he'd taken an Appoloosa stallion from the herd friends watched over for him.

Regret deepened at the thought of the Appaloosa. He'd been sold off when Jake was sentenced to hang, along with everything else Jake owned.

"Reno!" The shout came from down the long passage of steel-barred cells. The guard, Brady, was heavily armed, the barrel of his Winchester rifle gleaming dully in the dimness. The key grated in the lock.

"You're early," Jake pointed out with thinly disguised sarcasm. "I'm not quite ready."

"Stand back from the bars, Reno," Brady ordered.

Jake's mouth tightened as he slowly stood up. "Well, Gus, looks like my time just ran out."

Overhearing the one-sided conversation, Brady gave him a puzzled look as he shifted a thick wad of chewing tobacco into his cheek. He looked about the cell and shrugged.

At the sudden intrusion, Gus stirred. He gave them both a disgruntled look, then turned and headed for the far wall. He leaped at it and clawed his way up to the barred window.

"Damn lizards!" Jake cursed with a mixture of disgust and envy as he watched his four-footed, scaly friend slip over the edge of the window and disappear with a swish of tail.

"It figures you'd run out!" he called after Gus. "Well, good riddance!"

"C'mon, Reno," Brady said gruffly, motioning with the tip of the rifle.

Jake fought down the clawing sensation in his stomach as he turned back around. He fixed an indignant expression on his face. "Don't I even get a priest?" he asked with mock incredulity.

"You interested in last-minute confessions, Reno?" Brady shot back with a grunt of laughter.

"Do you think it might help?"

Brady shook his head. "Not where you're going, Reno. Put yer hands behind yer back."

"I suppose you're right," Jack sighed as Brady bound his wrists with heavy rope. None of the other prisoners had been bound when they were led to the gallows.

"Is Marshal Earp worried I might try to escape?"

Brady fixed him with a sullen expression. "Are you trying to tell me you ain't thought of it?"

Jake shrugged. "There's sure no foolin' you, Brady. You know somethin'? You're smarter than you look."

Brady stepped back and gave Jake a dark look as if he thought he might have been insulted but wasn't quite certain. He backed out of the cell and waited for Jake to follow. Another guard stood at the door. Jake took in everything in one sweeping glance. He counted four more deputies in the outer office of the jail. There were undoubtedly more outside, as a precaution. Virgil Earp, marshal of Tombstone, was known to be careful.

Each deputy carried a holstered gun and a rifle. If he made just one wrong move, they'd kill him.

He'd been shot before. It wasn't pleasant. Of the two, hanging or being shot, Jake wasn't at all certain which was worse, having no prior experience with hanging.

Brady saw the hesitation, and his fingers tightened over the trigger of the Winchester. "I said move, Reno!" Jake slowly walked out of his cell and down the passage toward the door at the end.

Each of the other condemned men had been led out that door earlier in the morning. Jake took a deep breath to slow the hammering of his heart, and swallowed against the tight dryness in his throat. The only thing he could think was that he sure as hell hoped he didn't embarrass himself like old Ned Pepper. Then he almost burst out laughing. Hell, he'd be dead and wouldn't care.

Jake wondered what this moment would feel like, what his thoughts would be. Brady nudged him hard, and he stepped out into the glare of the midday sun.

Expectant silence immediately settled over the crowd. Only moments ago, Jake had thought he'd prefer being drunk when it came right down to the end, senses completely dulled so that he wouldn't know what was happening—wouldn't feel or see or care.

But he knew different now. He wanted to feel and see everything one last time.

23

The breeze was hot as the sun sliced down through a blazing blue-white sky. Clouds of dust and flies filled the air, along with the stench of horses from the livery stables nearby.

Empty-faced strangers gathered at the bottom of the gallows, along with inventive merchants who sold cool lemonade. Somewhere in the stark silence a baby cried. In the distance a dog barked. The wind gusted through the empty street behind the gallows, raising ladies' skirts so they looked like gingham clouds suddenly set adrift. Wood, leather, dust, the tangy pungent scent of sage—all mixed together to sharpen the images frozen in his memory along with the sharp pull of the emotions he'd felt earlier.

Jake thought of all the things he would never experience again—the cold bite of wind in his face, the hard-muscled power of the Appoloosa beneath him, the brilliance of a sunset over the desert. Memories, both good and bad, washed over him.

The ranch and the small herd of Appaloosas had been part of his dreams for the future. He had wanted to settle down, put down roots, and find some peace in his life. He had never thought far enough to consider sharing his life with someone.

There had been a lot of women—pretty women, older women, experienced women—who'd shared their time, their rooms, and their bodies for gold.

Then there were the women who had shared and asked nothing in return—a rancher's wife in Laredo; a minister's daughter in Abilene, the widow in Fort Laramie. But the only memory that remained crystal clear was of Rachel.

He fought back the wave of longing that surfaced. He'd carried it around so long, he was used to it. It hadn't been excised even when he'd had his revenge on Charlie Trask and the others. Now it was sharp and pulled at him insistently, forming in soft images behind his eyes in that dark void of the mind called memory—images of

24

Rachel, sweet Rachel.

As always her sweet face looked back at him with overwhelming love and complete trust. The next image shattered that sweetness. If he closed his eyes, he could see blood everywhere—Rachel was covered with it—and the only thing left was a deep wrenching sense of loss and the guilt that had scarred his soul for fifteen years.

He'd tried to forget—with each town he rode into, every saloon he got drunk in, every whore he bedded, each time he used a gun. But it was always there.

Even now, when most other men would have confronted a final accounting of their lives, Jake forced the memories back, until the vision of blood vanished once more into the dark void where all his emotions had been buried long ago. Only the sense of loss remained, as it always did—for the things he would *never* experience.

Brady gave him a hard shove. "Get a move on, Reno. Yer time's up."

Jake haltingly climbed the steps to the gallows. He had tried a thousand times to imagine what these last moments would be like. Now, with the hot wind in his face and the sun glaring down, everything came into sharp focus.

He was surprised that he wasn't afraid. In some small way, he would have welcomed fear, or any emotion that might have made him feel alive if only for a little while.

Brady turned him around to face the crowd of spectators. He heard some vague question about being blindfolded and knew he shook his head.

The rope around his wrists was tightened. Then he was jerked around. He faced Brady and looked up. He concentrated on the thick rope that hung only inches from his face—on the precise coils that bound the rope; the large, gaping loop; and the opposite end, secured over the crossframe overhead. Somewhere nearby, he knew, was the lever that would drop the trapdoor out from under him.

"Let's get on with this," Brady grumbled, and the

hangman stepped forward.

He slipped the noose over Jake's head, settling it about his neck. As he tightened the rope, Jake ignored him and stared fixedly ahead.

Now, at this final moment, the images he'd refused to confront whispered softly in his thoughts. If he was any other man, if he believed in the hereafter, he might have hoped to see Rachel once again. But he wasn't any other man, he was Jake Reno and he'd done enough sinning for ten men. If there was a heaven or hell, he knew which way he was headed.

"Ready?" the hangman asked.

Jake was vaguely aware of the mumbled agreement that passed between Brady and the other two deputies. The pressure of the rope increased as it was snugged around his neck.

He wasn't afraid to die; he had confronted death a long time ago. As the crowd grew quiet and the wind suddenly died in the hot morning air, he closed his eyes—and thought only of Rachel.

Jake Reno took one, last, deep breath.

Chapter Two

"Dammit! I gave you an order! Stop the hanging!"

The first thing Jake was aware of was the searing heat of the sun as it beat down on him. His eyes flew open and he stared in complete bewilderment at the equally confused deputy who stood beside the hangman.

He expected angels, but realized the way he'd lived the last fifteen years, the devil would have been more appropriate. What Jake didn't expect was the commotion, the ripple of speculation in the crowd, and the hangman's hoarsely muttered curse.

"What the hell is goin' on?" the deputy who had brought Jake from his cell shouted down to the one at the bottom of the gallows.

"Orders from the marshal. Bring the prisoner inside."

"Damn!" the hangman muttered again under his breath as he reached to loosen the noose from about Jake's neck. "And we almost had him hung too. That woulda been a record for me—six in one day." The disappointment was bitter in his voice.

He called down to his assistant who stood under the gallows in the small space where the bodies dropped through after the trapdoor was sprung out from under them. "Hold on, Emmett. Marshal's stopped the hangin'."

"Damn!" came the echoed sentiment. "And we almost had us a full half-dozen—the most we ever hung in one day."

27

"We might still get 'im yet; the marshal might change his mind. Jes' hold on down there."

Jake was numb. His mind had completely shut down except for his last thoughts of Rachel. He had needed something to hold on to, something that was completely removed from the horror of being hanged. Everything else ceased to exist. He wasn't even fully aware of the rope being removed, not until the deputy nudged him roughly.

"Come on, Reno. The marshal wants to see you. Seems you got a reprieve, at least for a few minutes." He laughed, giving Jake another hard shove toward the steps that led from the gallows.

His legs were weak, as if all the blood had drained out of them, and he almost pitched headfirst down the steps. He felt the cold trickle of sweat that seeped down between his shoulder blades. Instinctively, he tried to reach out to steady himself, but his hands were still bound behind his back. Not that they would have been much use to him if they were untied. They shook badly from clenching his fists so hard, and the muscles in his arms spasmed from the strain. The deputy grabbed him roughly by the shoulder.

"I said move!" he ordered, and then laughed again. "What's the matter, Reno? Disappointed? We'll bring you right back up. Won't be more than a few minutes. Face it, you're gonna hang."

Jake staggered against the railing as he willed his feet to take one step and then another. He dragged deep gulps of air into his lungs. Slowly his head began to clear, and one thought registered—they haven't hung me! Unless this is all some kinda bad dream.

The skin at his wrists was laid open beneath the cutting ropes that bound him tightly. The pain that caused was proof this was no dream. And as the cold nausea of the moments before finally disappeared, it was replaced by a rush of anger.

"What the hell is going on?" his voice was raw in his dry throat.

"Get on down, Reno. The marshal will explain."

As Jake reached the last step, the deputy pushed him with the butt of his rifle. Jake lunged forward, and the crowd that had gathered at the bottom of the gallows swelled away from them. A young mother grabbed her little boy and pulled him protectively behind her. Another boy, maybe thirteen or fourteen, stuck his face forward and complained.

"Hey! Ain't they gonna hang 'im?" By the expression on his young face, he was disappointed.

"Damn!" cursed an old woman standing nearby. "And I made a fresh batch of fried chicken especially for this. They said six of 'em was gonna hang." She wasn't merely disappointed, she was upset.

"Been waitin' most of the mornin'," she continued to grumble. "It'll be months before they get that many together again for a good hangin'. And a woman my age ain't got much time."

She moved off through the crowd, hitching up her wide-swaying skirts in one hand, a picnic basket in another.

"You sure disappointed 'em, Reno," the deputy drawled.

Jake's emotions were raw from weeks of waiting, from hearing the trapdoor sprung on five other men that morning, and knowing he would also hang. Now, curiosity seeped through his anger. He knew enough about hangings to realize there was very little that could stop one.

"What's happened?"

His only answer was another shove toward the back door of the marshal's office, where Brady and another heavily armed deputy waited.

"Hold it right there, Reno," Brady ordered.

Jake's head came up as he stopped. He shot a glance at Brady. What the hell were they doing now? Were they deliberately delaying the hanging just to see how much he could take?

"This way." The second guard motioned through the

doorway that led through to the marshal's office. A rifle was cradled in the crook of his left arm. He took two careful steps backward, his right hand sliding cautiously along the handle of the rifle.

Jake fought back the cold tangle of fear and rage that bubbled inside him. "What the hell for?"

"Nice and easy, Reno," the deputy warned, "we don't want no trouble."

As he walked into the front of the marshal's office, Jake was aware of the other guards' watchful gazes. Another deputy was positioned in the doorway. Beyond, two others stood at the front of the door. From outside, he could hear the agitated buzz of conversation on the crowded street as those gathered to watch the hangings became listless in the late morning heat.

The second guard nudged him with the barrel of the rifle, and Jake stepped inside Virgil Earp's office.

He hadn't known it was possible to burn up with sweat at the same time he ached with bone-chilling cold. He felt emotionally and physically drained, while at the same time he wanted to grab someone—anyone—by the neck and tear his head off. He had never been one to deny there were times he felt afraid. Now the fear and anger worked along every nerve ending.

"Dammit, Virgil! What the hell is goin' on!" Jake demanded as anger exploded into cold fury at the man behind the desk. He was vaguely aware Wyatt Earp sat in a second chair cocked back on two legs against the back wall.

"Close the door behind you," Virgil Earp instructed his deputy. At seeing the man hesitate, he gave him a sharp look.

"Wyatt and I are both armed. Just what the hell do you think he's gonna do? Now get the hell outta here until I call for you."

Jake was a bit surprised at the anger in Virgil Earp's voice. Ever since he'd brought Jake in he had maintained a noticeable distance, letting his deputies handle whatever contact was necessary with prisoners. Jake understood why, given their past friendship. Now, Virgil Earp, U.S. Federal Marshal, sat on the other side of the desk, frowning in silence.

"Get on with it, Virg," Wyatt spoke up. "He has a right to know."

The small office fell silent as Jake's wild gaze fastened first on Wyatt, then Virgil. At a nod from his brother, Wyatt leaned forward in the chair, rose, and crossed the small office. He untied the rope at Jake's wrists.

"Get him a drink," Virgil Earp suggested. "I think he could use one. I know I sure as hell could."

Jake blinked hard, the anger easing out of his taut body.

"What the hell is going on, Virgil?" he asked, his voice no more than an anguished whisper. He was having a difficult time grasping all this. One moment he was up on the gallows, the rope tight about his neck, just seconds away from that trapdoor dropping out from under him, and now he was sitting across from Virgil, about to share a drink like in old times. Except this wasn't exactly like old times. And he wanted to know what was going on.

Virgil motioned to the bottle Wyatt held out. Jake accepted the drink and quickly downed it. In spite of the hot day, the fire in the whiskey that went straight down to his belly was comforting. It helped steady him.

"There is someone here to see you." Virgil Earp slowly sipped his own drink, then went on, "It's important. And it's dangerous. Give it a lot of consideration before you accept."

Accept? Accept what? Was there some kind of choice in all this?

The anger returned, fueled by another whiskey. "Someone to see me? They sure as hell took their sweet time about it." He didn't even pause to take a deep breath.

"Who is it? Some fancy-pants newspaper reporter

31

trying to get himself the next exciting installment for one of those dime novels?"

"Take it easy, Jake. I don't wanna have to tie you back up."

The threat was effective, so Virgil Earp went on. "I'll admit it was cutting it a bit close," he conceded, reaching for the bottle of whiskey. "But this is important. It's a chance to save your neck."

Then he continued as he poured. "You know I haven't liked none of this, Jake. It gets under my skin, hangin' a man I consider a friend."

Jake's mouth twitched with a bitter smile. "I'm not real crazy about it myself."

The marshal rose from his chair and came around to sit on the corner of the desk. He poured Jake another drink. Jake ignored it as he came to his feet and paced across the office, his fingers driving back through his hair.

"All right, just who the hell is it? And what does he want?"

"The name is Tyson," Wyatt answered. "From Denver." Then he went to the door and opened it, calling through to the outside office.

"Come on in."

Jake downed his drink and started to turn around. Whoever Mr. Tyson was, whatever he was offering was preferable to hanging. There wasn't much to consider.

"Mr. Reno?"

Nothing Jake had expected had prepared him for this. Mr. Tyson was a woman!

She hesitated, standing in the muted light of the doorway, the brief assessment mutual. Then, as she stepped further into the marshal's office, the light from the windows chased shadows up the precise folds of her skirt to reveal a slender waist and the bodice of her traveling gown. It was worn over an immaculate lace shirtwaist that was visible at her wrists and throat.

"I was afraid I might be too late." The edge of uncertainty in her voice matched the soft whisper of the

32

fabric of her gown. From his few encounters with real ladies, Jake knew the gown was silk and very expensive. That only added to his confusion.

"You came damn close," he replied gruffly. Feeling the need for yet another drink, he reached for the bottle and splashed some of the whiskey into his glass.

"I think maybe we had better all sit down," Wyatt Earp suggested, seeing the dangerous look in Jake's eyes. "Miss Tyson is here to make you an offer, Jake."

Jake refused to sit. Instead he paced, an urgent restlessness driving him back and forth across the small office. When he finally stopped pacing, he stood before the window that looked out onto the small yard behind the jailhouse, onto the gleaming white timbers of the gallows.

"Just what the hell do you want from me?" he asked even though he'd already drawn his own conclusions.

"I need your help," she explained simply. "In exchange, I can save your life, Mr. Reno."

Oh God! Jake immediately thought, she must be one of those do-gooder church ladies, and because the hanging had been stopped—at least temporarily—probably one with influence. In exchange for the confession of his sins, along with his complete salvation, which she would undoubtedly initiate and take full credit for, she would promise to speak to the church elders or the priest, or whoever it was she knew who was connected to the Almighty.

Save him! From what? Eternal damnation? It wasn't the kind of saving he had in mind. Still, something wasn't right here. From experience he knew that ladies who belonged to church organizations were staunch, upright, God-fearing pillars of the community. He also recalled that they were never a day less than fifty years old, wore corsets that gave them a puffed-up appearance, and occasionally sported the beginnings of mustaches above their upper lips. They cloaked their righteous attitudes in pious dignity, guarding their young daughters from *men like him*, hinting in whispered conversations at what *men like him* were capable of doing to a woman.

He suspected more than one of those righteous old biddies would give anything to know firsthand exactly what it was a *man like him* did to young ladies.

His attention focused back to her. She wasn't fifty, he doubted she needed a corset, and the flawless softness of her skin . . . made him wonder what it looked like under the gray fabric of her gown.

Would it be that same soft color that reminded him of blushed satin? Or would it be softer still, like pale velvet; warm, supple, inviting a man's hand to touch and wander lower still where it would no longer be pale but filled with shadows and hidden secrets waiting to be discovered?

No, Jake concluded, she wasn't from the Ladies, Christian Aid Society. That brought him back to his first conclusion—she must be a reporter for one of those East Coast newspapers, looking for a sensational story about an outlaw about to be hanged. He'd heard the papers sometimes used women to get certain stories. Well, he wasn't providing her with one.

"I've got nothing to say to you, lady," Jake spat out.

"You do, unless you want to hang," she informed him bluntly. The silkiness he'd first noticed in her voice had gone to steel.

Silence was heavy in the hot, fetid air of the jailhouse. He looked first to Virgil, then Wyatt. Neither said a word.

"What the hell is going on here?" Jake asked warily, an uneasy feeling coming through his nerve endings, a faint warning.

Revel stood slowly. "A bargain, Mr. Reno," she announced, then hesitated as she came face-to-face with him. He was younger than she'd expected for someone of his reputation. She quickly composed herself. "Your help in exchange for your life. It's that simple."

Jake's instincts sharpened in spite of the substantial amount of whiskey he'd downed. Now, he noticed several things he'd missed due to his shock when Miss Tyson had stepped into the office.

In one sweeping glance he took in the dusty, but high quality, button-top boots that were just visible beneath the hem of her gown. The fabric swayed and rustled with faint agitation at each step she took. She wore finely made, black leather gloves, removed them in smooth, elegant gestures. And he discovered—the voice, the slender hands, the silk gown—were merely compliments to her striking features.

Her neck was long and graceful, encircled in a transparent lace collar that only heightened the texture of her skin—lace over satin. Her features were finely chiseled, with faint hollows beneath high cheekbones, and her finely boned nose was set over a softly sensuous mouth that curved faintly downward.

Shadows and soft angles—her face was shaped by them—revealing different facets with the play accompanying each change of expression. She was pretty, but he'd known prettier. Still, there was something about her that hinted at more; in the curve of her mouth, the slight parting of her lips. And her lashes, long and thick, were a shade deeper than the rich, auburn hair coiled neatly at the back of her neck. Then Jake discovered her eyes.

They were blue—an unusual blending of color somewhere between shades of midnight and morning— brilliant blue but haunted by dark shadows. Jake understood shadows and the darker emotions behind them.

It wasn't the unexpected elegance of her clothes, or her striking features, that stirred something inside Jake and pulled at him. It was that expression behind her eyes, a fleeting mixture of doubt, desperation, and hope. It made him think of Rachel.

He remembered that same expression of bravado and bluster. He also remembered that last time, how it dissolved into naked fear. He closed his mind to the memories. When he looked at Miss Tyson again, the shadows were gone, as if a curtain had been pulled across a window, blocking out all the emotions glimpsed within. And he reminded himself she was not Rachel.

Jake had known many women, even some refined, elegant women who called themselves ladies. But this one, with her carefully guarded emotions, touched something deep inside him that no one had reached for a very long time.

"Well, Mr. Reno?" Revel asked, trying to remain calm. "Are you at least willing to listen?"

The contact was brief, less than a heartbeat, and not even physical. Because of that it was all the more unsettling. If it had been physical, she would have simply pulled away. But it was on some emotional level that left Revel feeling exposed and vulnerable, as if all the layers of her careful façade were stripped away allowing him to see right through her. She reminded herself that was impossible and concentrated on what she knew about him.

She had read the wanted posters and reports countless times. He had no family, and as far as anyone knew no friends. He had a way with women, horses, and guns. He was considered an expert on all three.

Jake Reno had been described as being easy to anger, cunning at gambling and eluding the law. At one time or another, his name was connected with Quantrill, the James brothers, and the Daltons. He couldn't have been much more than a boy when he chose the life of an outlaw.

He had a reputation for a quick temper, and a draw that was quicker. If one wanted to believe the stories about him, he'd killed more than a dozen men. But he had been tried for the murder of three men, who incidentally happened to be outlaws.

Because of it, his trial had been controversial, his sentence even more controversial. There were some people who believed he did society a favor by gunning those three men down and should have been found innocent. He was found guilty, sentenced to hang; and she needed him.

His shaggy hair hung to his shoulders. It gave him a predatory look that not even a death sentence changed.

He wore buckskin pants that encased his lean hips and emphasized the heavy muscles in his long legs. The leather glowed with a deep rich patina that came only from wear. His double-breasted, black shirt was open at the throat. Soft-soled leather boots wrapped about his calves.

She had seen prisoners before. The dirty clothes, haggard features, and unshaven beard were no surprise. After all, jail cells weren't built for comfort or accommodation, and Jake Reno had come dangerously close to hanging.

What surprised her was the intensity that burned behind those crystal green eyes, like a raw hunger deep inside. There was a wariness and open mistrust in every movement, every glance, each word. But perhaps the most surprising thing about him was the complete lack of fear. He gave nothing away, not by a glance or a gesture. Even now, sentenced to hang, when most men would have begged for a last-minute reprieve, he begged for nothing. She was the one begging him to listen to her plan. Revel was quickly learning there *was* a great deal about Jake Reno that wasn't written in any report.

"Go ahead, talk." Jake glanced to Virgil and Wyatt. "It seems my time is yours."

There was something almost mocking in the way he said it. He might have been about to hang, but there was nothing at all defeated about Jake Reno. That cool gaze stared her down.

"I *can* help you," she repeated. "If you're prepared to listen. I think we can do business together."

Jake almost burst out laughing. Women like her didn't do business with men like him. She was far too elegant, too refined, and too damned beautiful. But something important had brought her here.

"Well, it's for certain you aren't a distraught lover," Jake remarked, with more than a little anger seeping through. Then his voice softened. "I'd sure as hell remember that."

He had to give her credit; she was cool. The faint rise of

37

color across her cheeks was the only outward reaction to his comment.

His head came up slowly, and he stared at her with narrowed eyes.

"All right." He slowly came toward her. "What the hell *do* you want?"

The animal fierceness in his voice jolted through her. She'd been prepared for crudeness, she'd experienced it too often before in situations like this not to expect it. But his response was different. There was fury in his stride, a restrained power with a subtle threat of danger.

Revel reminded herself danger was part of his nature. But she sensed it had nothing to do with Jake Reno, the outlaw, and everything to do with Jake Reno, the man. She resented it. He should be grateful.

She straightened her shoulders, fighting down an instinctive anger of her own. She reminded herself that he had come dangerously close to hanging. Perhaps he had a right to be a little upset. Her voice was once more calm, as she forced herself to remember precisely why she was here.

"I have a proposition for you, Mr. Reno. If you want to live, I suggest you shut up and listen."

Surprise. Anger. Control. Jake saw all those reactions in the widening of her eyes as emotion shifted them from that soft smoky color to brilliant blue. He'd expected the anger, but the firm hold on control, especially in a woman, surprised him.

Jake couldn't deny he was curious. "What sort of proposition?"

Revel repeated the speech she'd rehearsed countless times on the train out from Denver. She was prepared to make him an offer he couldn't refuse.

"It's really quite simple. I need your help to find someone."

Jake was stunned. Several questions came to mind, right behind the obvious ones of *who* and *why*.

She went on, concentrating on the speech she'd

prepared, and ignoring the nagging uncertainty that made panic taste like iron in her throat. He had to accept her offer. He had to.

"I also need someone who is good with a gun . . . and knows the man I'm looking for."

"And just *who* might that be?"

Revel took a deep breath, then said, "Sam Bass."

He looked at her for a long moment, his expression closed. Then he turned away. "Sam Bass is dead," he said bluntly. Then he reached for the bottle and poured himself another whiskey.

"He was gunned down three years ago by Texas Rangers."

"He's not dead," she informed him with equal bluntness. "He's alive and I intend to find him."

His gaze fastened on her as he tossed back the whiskey. He slowly set the glass on the marshal's desk. The whiskey burned through him, but it couldn't get rid of the cold knot that had settled in his stomach or the warning tremor across his nerve endings that had his fingers constricting around the imaginary comfort of the Colt revolver at the mention of Sam Bass.

Revel took advantage of his hesitation as she continued to explain, "You rode with him for over three years according to my information. Two men can become very close in that amount of time." He didn't bother to deny anything. She went on.

"You know him better than anyone. You know his hideouts, his friends, habits, and his weaknesses . . ."

"Sam Bass didn't have any weaknesses," Jake informed her gruffly as he stood and walked past her to the window.

As her courage gathered momentum, Revel followed him. "Every man has a weakness. It's just a matter of knowing what it is and using it."

Jake glanced sideways at her, trying to see beyond the silk and lace, the manners and elegant speech, past the careful control. "You forget, there were a half-dozen

39

Texas Rangers who swore they killed him three years ago." He saw the shadows in her haunted eyes expand until the blue color all but disappeared to slate.

"They followed him to Round Rock, where they gunned someone down at one of his hideouts. They brought back the body and swore it was Sam Bass. Except . . . there was very little of the body left to identify." She turned and paced across the small office, away from him, the edge of desperation in her voice. "Everyone was very eager to accept that it was Sam Bass."

She whirled around to him, calm once more.

"I have a witness who swears he saw him in the New Mexico Territory less than three months ago."

Jake leaned against the window frame and stared out at the gallows and the impatient crowd. His thoughts churned, trying to sort out everything she was telling him. Any second now he expected Virgil to jump up and throw her and her ridiculous scheme out. But he didn't.

"And just who might that be?" he asked, his thoughts already racing ahead as he tried to figure out what all this meant and how he could work it to his advantage?

"Ben Waters."

Jake's head came around at the sound of that name. His gaze fastened on Revel Tyson. She was full of surprises. At one time he, Ben, and Sam rode together. It was a part of the past he preferred to forget. But at the time it had been a means to an end.

Sam Bass robbed his first stagecoach when he was sixteen, killing the driver and three passengers. Then there were trains and a series of banks, most of them in Texas. Somewhere along the way his path crossed with Jake's because he knew a man Jake was looking for. Jake found his man—and a dangerous friendship with Sam.

From the beginning, Jake had no taste for outlaw life, but it had given him access to the men he was after. One way or the other he arranged to be someplace else when Sam pulled his jobs. It was only by sheer damn luck no one was ever able to prove he was part of Bass's gang. If that had happened, he'd have ended up just like Bass, gunned down in some hideout.

There was bad blood when Ben and Sam parted. He saw Ben sometime later when he heard about Sam getting himself killed, and knew Ben was glad. He didn't know of anyone who'd feel sad about Sam's death.

Jake frowned. He'd heard the rumors that Sam had somehow escaped that shootout with the Texas Rangers, but Ben Waters had no reason to lie about Sam. Waters had nothing to gain by it—and too many reasons to fear the man if, in fact, Bass was still alive.

"All right, suppose Ben is right and Sam is still alive. What does that have to do with me?"

Now that he was at least willing to listen, Revel was going to make certain he didn't refuse her offer. "As I explained, you know the man, perhaps better than anyone else alive."

Her choice of words had Jake snorting with bitter amusement. "I think a better choice of words is *temporarily alive.*"

She ignored his comment and continued. "Since you know him so well, I need you to find him. In exchange, the Territorial governor will commute your sentence and . . . set you free."

Jake looked at her sharply. This had to be some sort of joke. Then he looked to Virgil and Wyatt. They weren't laughing, they weren't even slightly amused. The expression on both their faces were dead serious.

One thing was perfectly clear by what was left *unsaid.* If he refused, she was prepared to turn around and walk right out of that office. In which case, he would hang. Already the crowd outside was restless. That brought him back to his original questions that needed some very real answers. Who was she? And what did she want with Sam Bass?

His eyes narrowed as he looked at the woman before him, "Can you really get my sentence commuted?" he

41

asked, with more than a little doubt.

Revel reached inside her reticule and produced a thick bundle of papers. "These have already been signed by the governor. All that is required is Marshal Earp's countersignature." She laid them on the desk.

Jake stared at the papers. With one look to Virgil for confirmation, he knew those papers meant his freedom. Still there was a great deal that bothered him about all this.

"What do you want with Sam Bass?"

His question surprised her, and it showed in the delicate arch of her auburn brows. Considering the trouble he was in, she was convinced he would jump at the chance to save his neck. She realized just how very little she did know about him.

She had stacked the deck in her favor. By allowing the hanging to proceed as far as it had, she was certain he would cooperate. Now she wasn't so sure of herself. She picked up the papers and put them back inside her reticule. She slowly drew the strings closed.

"As I said, Mr. Reno, it's business."

Jake studied her carefully. If she wrote for one of those East Coast newspapers, she was certainly going to a great deal of trouble for a good story. In this case trouble had a name—Sam Bass. Which raised another possibility . . . that maybe he had made the wrong assumption.

Something about all this nagged at him. He wanted to know more about what he was getting himself into, *if* he decided to take her offer.

"What kind of business?" he demanded.

Once again, Revel chose her answer very carefully. He was determined to have some answers. And she wanted him and Marshal Earp to know as little as possible.

"It's simple. Sam Bass is a wanted man."

Jake frowned. She hadn't yet told him anything he didn't already know. "He's dangerous, and if he's alive, he won't be easy to find. What do you want with him?"

"I'm well aware of the sort of man he is, Mr. Reno.

That is why I'm relying on you to find him." She carefully avoided a direct answer to his last question.

Jake came away from the window. He watched her, the subtle play of expressions across the soft angles of her face, the careful folding of her hands, the deliberately worded answers. There was a whole lot being said in what wasn't said. The problem was, he didn't yet know the language. Living by his wits as long as he had, Jake knew she wasn't telling him everything. He wanted to know what she was holding back and why she was being evasive.

"How many will be going after Bass?"

Revel had hoped to have this discussion at a later time—after they had left Tombstone. That would have been more appropriate. Then it would have been impossible for him to change his mind since he'd already accepted her offer. And there were certain details she didn't want revealed in front of the marshal. Once again she was careful, avoiding Jake's gaze as she answered.

"There will be three of us."

Wyatt Earp's sharp intake of breath whistled through his teeth. Virgil Earp shifted uncomfortably in his chair and coughed. Neither said anything but she felt the full weight of their disapproval.

She cast a quick glance at Jake Reno and wondered if he'd caught the subtle meaning of what she'd said. She decided by his expression that he undoubtedly had. It was time to end the conversation.

"Now if you will excuse me," she quickly announced, "there are arrangements to be made." She wasn't quite quick enough.

Jake saw the quick darting away of her eyes. He'd learned to read people—the silent messages to be found in a look or a subtle shift of the body. When a man lived by the gun as he had, he learned the unspoken language of the body. She wasn't telling them everything.

And then there was what she *had* said, that one little word—*us*.

"Hold on just a damn minute. I want some straight answers." Jake demanded. "Just *who* will be going after Bass?"

Her hand was already on the knob when the warning edge in his voice stopped her at the door. The words whipped at her through the hot, still air. She turned around slowly and met his gaze.

"There will be three of us—you, another agent, and myself."

"Now wait just a minute," Jake started to protest. "A ride like that is no place for a—"

She cut him off. "What, Mr. Reno? A woman?" she made a discovery and slowly walked back across the office.

"Is that what you were going to say?"

Revel had seen the objection in the hard green of his eyes and the tight set of his jaw. Before he could say a word, she went on.

"It's very simple. You're to take me to Sam Bass. In exchange, you will receive your freedom."

He cut her off. "If I live through it."

"Then I suggest you make certain we both live through it." She turned back to the door, ending the conversation. But Jake Reno followed her.

"Bass won't let you get anywhere near him."

She could feel the heat from his body; he was standing so close to her. She jerked back around, meeting his angry gaze.

"But he will let *you* near him. I'm counting on that, Mr. Reno. If that fails, if you fail, *then you hang*. It's that simple."

Jake came at her, not about to let the argument go. This whole scheme was dangerous.

"You'll need more than two men to go after Bass— you'll need a whole damn army!"

"Do you always curse, Mr. Reno?" she asked pointedly.

"When I feel like it," he flung back at her. "And right

44

now I feel like it."

"All right then," she went on. "There will be *three* of us," she stubbornly repeated. "The fewer there are, the faster we can ride, and the less risk we'll run of drawing attention to ourselves."

"There's no way in hell I'm riding after Sam Bass with a woman along," he informed her bluntly.

"There's no way in hell you're not," she informed him calmly.

"Do you always curse, Miss Tyson?"

"When I feel like it," Revel flung his own answer back at him. This conversation hadn't gone at all the way she'd intended. He should be grateful for the opportunity she was offering him. At that moment, grateful was the last word to describe Jake Reno.

"The decision is yours. I believe you know the alternative." So that there was no misunderstanding exactly what she meant, Revel glanced at the window where the gallows cast a skeleton shadow in the searing afternoon heat.

Jake knew all right—knew he was in an impossible situation. The trouble was, she knew it too. There was no bluffing his way out of this. He'd been dealt an impossible hand from the very beginning. Now, there was only one way to play it.

"It seems, I don't have a whole helluva lot of choice."

She met his gaze directly. "Not if you want to live."

Jake snorted. "The notion of going after Sam Bass gives that thought a whole new meaning."

Revel nodded. "Then we have an agreement?"

He slowly agreed, "All right."

She let out a sigh of relief. She had almost been too late. If Jake Reno had been hanged, all hope of finding Sam Bass would have died with him. But she had to admit her timing had worked to her advantage. His brush with death had obviously convinced him it would be wise to accept.

"Good. I'll be back in a couple of hours. There are

45

arrangements to be made. As I said, I would like to get started in the morning."

Jake nodded, his green eyes cold and calculating. "Anything you say." But one last question hadn't yet been answered.

"By the way, just who the hell are you?" he asked bluntly.

She knew he wasn't referring to her name. The introductions, brief as they were, had already been made. There wasn't any reason not to tell him, and it just might reinforce how serious she was about this.

"Revel Tyson," she said, then added, "Operative Tyson, of the Pinkerton National Detective Agency." She smiled.

"Good *afternoon*, gentlemen."

Jake turned and stared at Virgil and Wyatt as the door closed behind Miss Revel Tyson.

"Pinkerton?" he asked incredulously. "She's a damn Pinkerton agent?"

Jake couldn't believe it. For years he'd run from the law, including several Pinkerton agents. They had a reputation for being thorough and tenacious. No one ever escaped the Pinkerton's for long. He slowly shook his head.

"Of all the damned luck," he muttered disgustedly. As he recalled it was a Pinkerton agent who found Sam Bass's hideout in Texas.

Then, as he thought of Sam Bass, he realized that if he went along with this scheme, there was no doubt in the world that he was a damned fool. Jake Reno was a lot of things, but he'd never been called a fool.

"Well, maybe I'll just have to change my luck," he muttered.

Chapter Three

"You look bad, and you smell worse! And that, my friend, is a direct quote."

Jake glared from where he sat shoulder-deep in a huge vat filled with warm sudsy water. Miss Revel Tyson, Pinkerton agent, left him in jail for two hours, just so he wouldn't reconsider the merits of making the right decision about her offer. As the disgruntled crowd slowly dispersed outside the jailhouse, after the disappointing news there would be no more hangings, Jake had reason to believe he had made the right choice—at least temporarily.

Then, just a little over two hours ago, Miss Tyson returned to the marshal's office, left specific instructions "for the prisoner," and then left to send some telegrams. One of her specific instructions had landed Jake up to his neck in soapy water. It wasn't that he had any objections to baths, it's just that circumstances hadn't provided him with one lately. What he did object to was the high-handed way Miss Tyson had of ordering everyone about. Obviously Virgil and Wyatt Earp didn't have that same objection.

Now Jake sat back against the iron rim of the wood vat and blew out trailings of fragrant smoke while he contemplated his current situation—Miss Revel Tyson and Sam Bass. He had to come up with a plan.

He squinted as smoke curled lazily back around his head and stung at his eyes. After being up on those gallows, feeling anything at all was comforting. He contemplated Wyatt Earp sitting across from him on a long wooden bench. Earp appeared to be dozing, his large black hat pulled low over his eyes, but Jake knew better.

"What else did she say?" he asked bringing their line of conversation back around to it's original subject—in particular, Miss Revel Tyson, Pinkerton agent.

The black hat cocked back a notch as Wyatt's gaze met his. "As I recall, there was some mention about your attitude, lack of cooperation and general bad manners, not to mention your language."

Jake blew out a stream of smoke with extreme satisfaction. At least he and Miss Pinkerton understood each other. He had to admit, however, he didn't mind the bath at all, or the *cigarillo*, or the clean clothes that were obviously new—just so long as he got his clothes back once they were clean. He looked around the inside of the washhouse with lazy speculation and sank further into the sudsy water.

The washhouse was attached to the back of an establishment known as Purdy's Livery, Laundry, and Tonsorial Parlor. The laundry fronted onto the mainstreet of Tombstone with the tonsorial parlor immediately next door. The livery stables were two doors down at the end of the street, for obvious reasons that had everything to do with being downwind from the rest of town. Corrals expanded out back, butting up against sheds that housed the work area of the laundry. Chinese workers scurried like ants from the front of the laundry, where they sorted, mended, and ironed, to the back where a half-dozen vats churned with laundry. Another half-dozen were filled with steaming, clear rinse water.

Wing Poo worked for Clem Purdy. He came in every morning at four-thirty and started the fires to boil the water. By six the other Chinese workers had arrived. They poured boiling water into the vats, washed, rinsed, and hung laundry out to dry. By ten o'clock, the last of the day's work was either rinsing in clean water or hung out to dry. That was when Purdy doubled his profits by renting out the soap-filled vats for baths. Jake sat in one of those vats now, a curtain of dripping sheets, shirts, and other clothing forming a discreet barricade between him and the front of the laundry.

Clouds of steam rose from a dozen flat irons, clogging the late afternoon heat that poured in from the street and making the air inside the laundry humid. The Chinese workers babbled incessantly in a chicken-squawk banter that was unintelligible to anyone but themselves. One woman shooed a cranky child into a corner to play with handmade wood toys; two men held fingers aloft in a quick round of wagering over ivory tiles scattered across the wood-plank floor; Wing Poo scolded a young girl who was lazily ironing a client's shirt.

Jake slipped beneath the surface of the sudsy water as an old Chinese woman waddled back into the wash area with a large basket under her arm. She appeared to ignore his obvious nakedness as she removed dry laundry from the line. Then as she passed by him once more on her way back to the front of the store, filled basket balanced on a hip, she made some sort of comment that only she could understand. She then chuckled good-naturedly, gave him a wink, and patted him on a wet shoulder.

"You always did have a way with women, Reno," Wyatt Earp commented with a hint of grudging admiration. "You even got the old woman lookin' at you with that gleam in her eye." The famous gunfighter, who also happened to be brother to the marshal and occasional deputy, smirked as he sat on the long wood bench across from Jake.

Wyatt's legs were stretched out in front of him and crossed at the ankles, his arms folded across his chest. The black Stetson hat was cocked low across his eyes— obviously not so low that he missed anything that went on.

When the heat and humidity in the washhouse had got to be too much he had taken off his black coat. It lay draped across the bench beside him. On the other side of the coat was a Winchester rifle, a Colt .45 was strapped to his hip—reminders that there was nothing the least casual in Wyatt's presence. A faint smile quirked Wyatt's mouth beneath the curve of his dark mustache.

"She sure as hell is somethin', isn't she?"

Jake gave him a long look. "Yeah, she's at least sixty, squawks so you can't understand a word she's sayin', and I'll just bet she's meaner than a cat with it's tail under a rocking chair."

"I was talkin' about Miss Tyson."

Jake knew exactly who he was talking about, he simply didn't share that same appreciation. His mouth tightened as he frowned.

"Oh, she's somethin' all right, a real pain in the ass with her fancy talk, fancy clothes, and crazy ideas. How the hell she ever got to be a Pinkerton agent is beyond me." Jake lifted a foot out of the water and scrubbed it hard.

"We checked up on her," Wyatt informed him from behind the lowered brim of his hat, "Virg sent a wire off to Denver. It seems Miss Revel Tyson is very highly revered in the agency. William Pinkerton himself responded. He made it clear we were to give her our complete cooperation."

"Well, I'm not about to question her qualifications." Jake scrubbed his other foot, ankle, and leg, and then went on, "She could be a two-headed goat for all I care, just as long as she stopped that hanging."

"That was a mite close," Wyatt commiserated. "I don't recall a hanging ever comin' that close and bein' stopped. You sure disappointed ole Shorty."

Jake snorted with black humor as he recalled the hangman. "There is something seriously wrong with someone who takes that much pleasure from hanging people."

50

"It's a job." Wyatt shifted, trying to find a more comfortable position, "Jes' like any other."

Jake lathered the rest of his body and scrubbed hard, removing an accumulation of dirt and sweat. Going by the condition of his jail cell, he was certain a few bugs were included. He worked soap into his hair.

"Well, I got my own ideas about *pleasure.*" He grinned through a mask of soap. "Hey, Wyatt, do you remember that little gal up in Tucson at the Red Garter? I think Lilly was her name." At Wyatt's grinned response—all that was visible beneath the brim—Jake rinsed off the last of the soap, then eased back in the hot water to enjoy his bath a little longer, along with memories of Lilly.

"Now, there was a woman to make you forget your troubles. She was double-jointed, and she could do this trick with her hips . . ." His grin deepened as he saw Wyatt sit up straight and push back the Stetson to look at him. He had Earp's attention now.

"She could do things with those hips . . . that could make a blind man see." Jake shook his head with deep appreciation. Then he added, "I sure as hell couldn't see 'Miss Pinkerton' doing anything like that."

Wyatt's eyes narrowed, in them now an expression countless men had seen from twenty paces on deserted streets in countless towns. Few of them had lived to see it twice. Jake simply grinned.

"Lilly never did that trick with *nobody* else." Wyatt replied in a hard voice.

Jake shrugged. "Well, at least not more than a few of us. Not many men can afford a hundred dollars for two hours with Lilly."

"A hundred dollars?" Wyatt came abruptly to his feet. "She charged me two hundred!"

Jake gave him a long thoughtful look from over the rim of the vat. He frowned slightly, then shook his head.

"Well, actually she didn't charge me anything."

"Didn't charge you!" Wyatt spat out incredulously. His hand lowered instinctively to the Colt at his hip.

51

"I oughta shoot you for that."

"Yeah." Jake's grin deepened. "But you won't, because that little Pinkerton gal needs me and the governor wants her to find Sam Bass real bad. Besides"— the grin deepened into something very near a smirk— "I'm a friend. And you don't have too many of those, especially now that Ike Clanton and his brothers are after you and Virgil. You need all the friends you can get."

"Damn!" Wyatt muttered as he sat back down on the bench. But not before he had unholstered his gun. "You and Lilly," he muttered.

"And she didn't even charge you." Wyatt toyed with the gun. Then he slowly raised it and took aim at Jake. "I might just put a few holes in you—nothing serious."

Jake hooted with laughter. Then, before Wyatt could even think much less react in self-defense, Jake hit him with a soap-filled cloth square in the middle of his shirtfront. The gunfighter was immediately on his feet, gun drawn.

"The problem is, Wyatt," Jake pointed out, between gales of laughter at the sight of the notorious gunfighter soaked with suds, "you're not upset because I spent a few nights with Lilly—you're upset about the hundred dollars."

As Wyatt scooped the cloth from the floor where it had landed and plopped it back in Jake's bath he shook his head with rueful honesty.

"Damn if you ain't right," he admitted as he slowly raised the tip of his Colt and casually pointed it at Jake. "Now finish that bath. I got better things to do than baby-sit you for that Pinkerton gal.

"And I got orders to deliver you over to the hotel and put you in a room until she gets back. With a guard, of course," he added.

Jake took his time finishing his bath. The water had cooled by the time he was finally ready to step out. But he delayed, trying to recall exactly what Lilly Gentry looked like, aside from those outrageous, double-jointed hips of hers. Instead of blond hair and a pretty, painted face, however, he called up auburn hair, and deep blue eyes— Revel Tyson. He ran the sponge across his chest one last time, his mouth twisting down at the corners in a thoughtful frown.

"Did she really say I smelled that bad?"

Wyatt smirked as he pushed away from the rim of the vat and started to walk off now that Jake was obviously through with his bath.

"If I recollect, the comparison had something to do with an old dead billy goat." Then, just as Jake's head jerked around and he opened his mouth to make a comment about what he thought of Miss Tyson, Wyatt reached out and shoved him under the surface of the soapy water.

Jake came up sputtering and coughing. His long hair was plastered to his head, and water sheeted off his hard muscled body in rivulets.

"Damn you, Wyatt!" he cursed as his eyes burned from remnants of soap.

"Get a move on," Wyatt shouted back over his shoulder. He grabbed a thick muslin towel and tossed it at Jake, still too blind from the soap to see it coming. The towel plopped into the water around Jake's hips.

"That little gal is out making arrangements. I heard her tell Virgil she's plannin' on leavin' in the mornin'. You're to join up with someone else and then head out after Bass."

"Is that right?" Jake spat out as he wiped soap from his eyes. His thoughts were already racing far ahead. He had plans of his own, and considering the direction of his thoughts, he didn't bother explaining any of them to Wyatt Earp, even if Earp was a friend.

"Then, by all means let's get on over to the hotel." Jake deliberately changed the direction of the conversation. "I could sure use a good meal. Someone really should speak to Virgil about the food he serves in jail."

Wyatt tossed the second towel accurately, then stood in the doorway of the washhouse, one shoulder propped against the doorjamb. "I'll be sure to mention it to him," he said with a twisted smile. "So the next time you come our way, we'll have everything ready for you."

Jake looked up for a moment. His gaze met Wyatt's, something behind his eyes suddenly hard and cold.

"I don't plan on comin' back."

Revel slammed into Virgil Earp's office, capturing the collective gazes of a half-dozen surprised deputies and Marshal Earp. "Where is he?" she demanded.

Wyatt had just stepped back in from the back of the jailhouse, where the town drunk snored loudly in one of the cells. He and his brother exchanged blank looks.

"Just who are you talking about?" Virgil asked, looking up from the stack of papers spread before him on the desk.

"Who?" Revel descended on the desk, her voice shaking with barely suppressed fury. The silk of her gown snapped and crackled with every movement she made, charging the air with sparks of electricity. "Who the devil do you think I'm talking about? Jake Reno! Where is he?"

Virgil pushed back from the desk slowly, his posture relaxed in the chair. "He's over at the hotel. Room number twelve. Wyatt delivered him over there over two hours ago, just like you asked. My deputy is standing guard."

The fury bubbled up inside Revel. Her hands shook so badly she didn't dare loosen them from the folds of her skirt. Her body was absolutely rigid, and the color that heightened her striking features had nothing remotely to do with any sort of ladylike embarrassment. It was anger, pure and simple. She was waging a desperate battle to control it.

"Your deputy is lying on the bed in room number

twelve, roaring drunk," she informed them icily, "so drunk he can't even remember what happened. Needless to say he is alone, muttering some ridiculous story about someone named Lilly."

For some ridiculous reason, her last comment caused Wyatt Earp to choke. Revel had the nagging suspicion he might even have been laughing. She took a deep breath, not daring to risk her composure by explaining the remainder of the deputy's jumbled conversation—something to do with Lilly's hips.

She descended on Virgil Earp's broad oak desk, braced her hands far apart on the wood surface. "Gentlemen! Jake Reno is gone!" For several long moments the only sound that broke through the glaring silence that enveloped the marshal's office came from the street. Out there, creaking wagons churned up clouds of choking dust. A mule, hitched to a water wagon, balked and brayed noisily. Several children squealed excitedly as they chased a grunting, snorting piglet up onto the boardwalk. An irate old woman waggled her finger at an equally aged man, presumably her husband, all the while scolding him loudly about something he chose to ignore.

"Marshal?" Revel prompted, her anger rising several more degrees. "I demand to know where he is!"

Two of the deputies promptly mumbled vague excuses and disappeared out through the door at the back of the jailhouse. Another said something about checking up on something reported stolen over at the mercantile, while a fourth grabbed the coffee pot from the top of the pot-bellied stove.

"That reminds me, we need more coffee," he explained as he ducked out the front door, presumably in search of some fresh water even though a huge barrel stood at the back of the office. Sweltering heat smothered the office, making hot coffee the last thing anyone would want to drink.

Finding similar escape impossible, Wyatt Earp stayed where he was and silently stared down at the toes of his boots, as though he might learn Jake's whereabouts from the dull gleam of black leather. Virgil Earp shifted uncomfortably in his chair. He ordered the other two deputies to go over to the hotel and see about the deputy who'd been left to guard Jake.

His natural inclination was to ask if the Pinkerton agent was certain Jake was gone, however, considering her obvious displeasure at the situation, he decided it was safer just to take her word for that.

"There is the possibility he just stepped out for a drink," he suggested. It sounded like a lame excuse even to him. "We could check the saloons in town."

"I already did," Revel informed him tightly. "No one has seen him. And since most of the townspeople gathered to see him hang just this morning, I don't think they could have been mistaken."

She fought the churning of her stomach and the tightening of her throat. For the first time in a long time—longer than she could remember—she was dangerously close to tears. And she hated it. They didn't know—had absolutely no idea—what this meant. After all these years, Jake Reno was the only man who could help her. She'd followed him through countless backwater towns and cattle stops that crisscrossed the open territories and a dozen states. She'd waited a long time to find Jake Reno, and now he was gone. She swallowed back the anger that threatened to expose her plans. There was too much at stake for her to risk losing everything through stupidity.

"I've already checked every place in town. He's left Tombstone," she informed them tightly. "Now the only question is, where would he go?" She turned to Wyatt Earp.

"I'm aware the two of you are friends—you once rode together. Surely, you have some idea where he's gone."

Wyatt's gaze shifted up from the inspection of his boots. He cleared his throat uncomfortably. He hadn't liked any of this from the very beginning. She was right,

Jake was a friend. He'd hated the idea of being party to his hanging, and he hated the offer this little gal had made him. He knew Jake wanted no part of Sam Bass, and for all kinds of reasons any man alive would understand. Trouble was, this little lady held the power of life or death over Jake. Just one word from her could put Jake right back up on the gallows again. But going after Sam Bass wasn't a much better deal. No one ever went after Bass and came back alive. It was like trying to shoot a rattlesnake after it already bit you.

Virgil Earp spoke up. "Do you know where Jake might have gone?" The question was directed at his brother.

Wyatt had one last argument with himself. The problem was, when you argued with yourself, you lost no matter what. He looked up slowly.

"I might know."

"Where?" Revel demanded.

Wyatt's mouth thinned beneath his mustache. He hated doing this. But he knew there was no choice. If they didn't cooperate, Miss Tyson would undoubtedly contact the circuit judge. That would have serious consequences for Virgil, he could easily lose his marshal's badge. He let out a long, low sigh. He regretted telling her anything, no matter how dang pretty she was.

"He set great store by an Appaloosa stallion that was sold off when he was sentenced to hang. Knowin' Jake, I'd bet money he's gone after that horse."

"Are you certain?" Desperation edged Revel's voice.

"The only thing that's certain is the sun comin' up, Miss Tyson. But the fella that bought that Appaloosa stallion lives in Tucson. He has a big spread there. I'd say that's where Jake's headed."

Then he added, "And maybe the Red Garter Saloon." He cleared his throat. "Lilly Gentry owns the place. She and Jake are . . . old friends."

Revel could have sworn his coloring deepened several shades, which was surprising for a man of his reputation. There was no doubt that Lilly Gentry was the same Lilly the deputy had spoken of in his drunken stupor. Which led to the inevitable question about the vague description the deputy gave—and the extent of Jake Reno's *friendship* with the woman.

She couldn't care less about any of it except that it meant she might find Jake Reno.

"When does the next stage leave for Tucson?" she asked abruptly, her decision made. She had come too far and invested too much time to give up now simply because Jake Reno was gone. She'd learned through her training with the agency that anyone could be found.

"Not till mornin'," Virgil Earp informed her. "It connects with the railhead at Fort Buchanan. From there you can take the train on into Tucson."

Revel's fingers curled into the palm of her hand, the sharpness of her nails biting through the soft gloves.

Damn! she silently swore, frustration and helplessness washing over her. By her calculations, Jake Reno had been gone almost two hours. She knew from experience a man could cover a lot of distance in that amount of time. She bit at her lip, then looked up.

"How far is it to Tucson from here? Could a rider make it faster by himself?" She felt Wyatt Earp's gaze shift back to her. He knew exactly what she was thinking.

"Not at night, Miss Tyson," he said bluntly. "The trail isn't an easy one, and there are still areas out there that are Indian territory. It would be too dangerous."

Impotent rage curled deep inside her until it was a knot wound so tightly it constricted her breathing. Damn Jake Reno, anyway! Damn! Damn! Damn!

She came at it from all angles, but the result was always the same. There was nothing to do but wait for the morning stage to Fort Buchanan—and pray Jake Reno had stopped for the night somehwere along the way.

Virgil Earp sensed her anger and frustration. "I'm really sorry, Miss Tyson. I'll do all I can to help. I'll send a couple of my deputies along with you in the morning."

Revel shook her head. "That won't be necessary,

Marshal." At his surprised expression, she went on to explain, "Until I return with Sam Bass and you countersign that pardon, Jake Reno is a wanted man." She glanced to Wyatt and included him in her decision.

"If what you tell me is true and he has gone to Tucson, he'll be easy enough to find. At any rate I'm certain the authorities there will provide whatever assistance I need to convince Mr. Reno to fulfill his part of our agreement."

Tucson was almost seventy miles north of Tombstone. The quickest way to get there was an almost twenty-mile journey by stage coach to the railhead, then a transfer to the train.

Revel boarded the early morning stage in Tombstone, along with six other passengers. One was a lawyer who had concluded business in Tombstone, another was a middle-aged woman dressed in a black, stuff dress. Beside her sat her freckle-faced daughter, perhaps eleven or twelve years old. Her name was Tassie.

She was bright and energetic and kept up a constant chatter. Revel learned they had been to visit her aunt in Tombstone who was recently widowed. It explained the mother's heavy black dress, that obviously scratched uncomfortably, the sleeves and collar tightly buttoned.

The heat that built inside the lunging Butterfield coach throughout the long hours of the morning was worse than unbearable. Revel, who had no such problems with propriety as the matron, quickly rolled her own lace cuffs back to her elbows, and removed the white satin ribbon that tied the lace collar snugly about her neck. She received an inelegant sniff of disapproval from Tassie's mother. The woman reminded Revel of her aunt Adelaide—very proper, with a sense of decorum that in no way allowed for rolling back one's cuffs or opening one's collar.

The Reverend Mr. Weems sat across from Revel. He

was wiry with long bony hands, and thin hair atop his glistening head. He was deathly pale and each time the coach lurched over the badly rutted trail, his eyes closed and his lips moved, undoubtedly in some silent prayer for deliverance. Then, when he opened his eyes again, it seemed his color had gone to a rather sickly shade of green.

Tassie's eyes widened and she gently nudged Revel with her elbow. Within the first ten minutes of their journey, they had become fast friends.

"He's gonna be sick," she predicted, dire warning in her voice.

"Tassie!" her mother scolded, her lips thinning even further in disapproval.

"Well, he is," Tassie exclaimed, not about to be silenced. "He looks exactly like Toby before he upchucks."

"You mind your manners, Tassie Lee!" her mother warned.

"Well, he does." Tassie sniffed indignantly, but continued no further except to shift closer to Revel. She gave her a wink, and explained, "Just in case he does get sick." She glanced meaningfully at the empty space between her and her mother. Revel smothered a smile. She would have done precisely the same thing.

The sixth passenger was a dark-skinned old man. He sat completely silent in the far corner of the coach, long, black hair trailing past his shoulders. His face was as weathered as old leather and approximately the same color. His eyes were as dark as obsidian, his nose sharply angled as were the planes of his face. He wore demin pants, cambric shirt, and boots.

He ignored the occasional ebb and flow of conversation, remaining stoically silent. His gaze seemed permanently fixed on the far horizon that drifted beyond the coach, until Revel caught him staring intently at her. Tassie nudged her again, nothing missing the girl's inquisitive eyes.

60

"Is he a *real* Indian?" Tassie whispered discreetly.

"So it seems," Revel answered, watching as he turned back to stare out the window.

"Will he scalp us?" Tassie snuggled more tightly against her.

Before Revel had left Tombstone, Wyatt Earp had explained that the old man was called Broken Hand. He was a scout for the Army. She was just about to explain that to Tassie when the old Indian leaned forward. Before Tassie could even think to react, he gently seized the trailing ends of her light brown hair and held it aloft.

"Very soft, like rainwater," Broken Hand muttered, gently feeling the texture.

Beside them, Tassie's mother gasped. Her face drained to a color several shades paler than the Reverend Mr. Weems's. Tassie's eyes were as wide as saucers. She swallowed with a loud gulp that could be heard even over the noisy motion of the coach.

Revel said nothing as she watched the little scene play out. The reverend swallowed back his nausea long enough to spout righteously, "Now see here, my good man. Release that young girl. There is no room for your savagery here." For emphasis he thumped the Bible he clutched in one hand and then leaned forward.

She thought for moment he meant to physically assault Broken Hand. One quelling glance from the old Indian sent Mr. Weems back into the opposite corner of the coach, his handkerchief clutched against his mouth.

Revel found Broken Hand watching her again. She could have sworn he winked at her. Slowly, he released Tassie's hair and shrugged his thin shoulders as he sat back in the seat.

"You may keep your hair. You have more need of it than I do," he said.

For the first time in over an hour, Tassie was speechless. She wet her lips, glanced to her mother, then looked up at Revel.

"I think we're safe for now," Revel reassured the girl,

biting back a smile. She cut a quick glance to Broken Hand, who passed a gnarled hand over the smile that twitched at the corners of his mouth.

Tassie quickly bound her hair with a ribbon and pushed it back over her shoulder, sitting back against it. When her mother pulled her close, the child willingly complied, although that brought her back in front of the green-faced Mr. Weems.

For the next full hour, until they reached the railhead, Tassie said nothing, but stared warily at the equally silent Broken Hand.

The coach creaked and churned along the trail. The horses' hooves beat a staccato thunderous rhythm. Occasionally the driver shouted or whistled to them. Inside the coach, the heat became oppressive, lulling the other passengers into fitful sleep.

Revel was thankful she wasn't required to participate in any meaningless conversation. She needed time to think.

If he had stopped for the night, Jake Reno was only three or four hours ahead of her. If not, he was already in Tucson. He had taken a horse from the deputy found drunk in the hotel room, along with a gun and twenty dollars. None of that surprised her. What had surprised her was the fact that he had signed an I.O.U. and left it in the deputy's pocket.

It didn't make sense, at least not from what she knew about Jake Reno. But as she had already discovered, there was a great deal she didn't know about the man.

She would never have thought he would go to Tucson. It seemed logical that he would head south, perhaps over the border into Mexico where he would be safe. But both Wyatt and Virgil Earp were convinced he had gone north. She couldn't imagine a man risking his life for a horse. But then, she hadn't thought he would hesitate to accept her offer either.

It was early afternoon when they reached the railhead at Fort Buchanan. A small town extended beyond the military post. It included the train station, a mercantile, stables, one saloon, and a hotel.

They had left Tombstone so early that morning there hadn't been time to eat. Now, hunger gnawed at her, but they were late getting in and the train was about to leave. There wasn't time to go over to the hotel to eat.

Fort Buchanan was sparsely populated, so Revel was surprised at the number of passengers gathered on the wood platform waiting to board the train. They were an odd mixture of Mexicans, settlers, and Indians. Tassie and her mother boarded the train, along with the reverend.

Revel looked for Broken Hand, then realized that Fort Buchanan must have been his destination. As several soldiers also boarded the train, Revel glanced at the small pendant watch she wore about her neck. It was one-thirty in the afternoon.

She took the seat farthest from the windows left open to allow air into the stiflingly hot cars. From experience she knew the hazards of sitting next to an open window— wildly flying sparks and cinders blown from the locomotive.

She sank wearily back against the hard wood seat and tried to make herself comfortable. Her eyes closed against raw fatigue and the nagging pain between her shoulders due to bumping over a dirt trail in the stagecoach. In spite of the fatigue, hunger, and aching muscles, Revel knew it was worth it. She had come too far, waited too long, to simply let him slip through her fingers now.

"Damn you, Jake Reno!" she cursed softly to herself. "If I didn't need you so badly, I'd gladly see you hang for this!"

She opened her eyes at sensing the gentle pressure on her shoulder. A pretty, round-faced Mexican woman leaned across the aisle and held out the small wrapped object in her left hand.

"*Quiere comer algo?*"

"I beg your pardon?" She had no idea what the woman was saying, nor did she recognize the small object wrapped in what appeared to be a corn husk.

The woman smiled. *"Comida,"* she explained, and then unwrapped the husk to reveal something that looked very edible and smelled wonderful. She took a bite of the folded dough that contained a meat filling.

Revel hadn't eaten since supper the evening before. Fatigue and aching muscles were forgotten as her stomach grumbled loudly. Her Aunt Adelaide insisted a proper lady was known by the size of her appetite. She was expected to eat sparingly and with all the social graces that came from being raised in mainline Philadelphia society. How else was a man to judge a woman's true nature?

How indeed? Revel thought with a twinge of hungry indignation. Her mind filled with visions of dozens of women fainting at the feet of men—not from embarrassment over indelicate conversation but from starvation.

She realized the same profound honesty with which she confronted everything was just the sort of rebellious attitude that had caused Aunt Adelaide to have more than one case of the vapors.

Looking back on it all now, Revel knew it must have been very difficult for a wealthy spinster whose life was well ordered to have a high-spirited seven-year-old thrust upon her.

Revel remembered very little of her mother, who was actually Aunt Adelaide's neice, which made Aunt Addie her great-aunt. Lorena Davidson had died of child-bed fever shortly after the birth of Revel's brother. He had been terribly small, like one of Revel's pale, rag dolls, and he'd lived for only three days. Her father was devastated by the double loss. They lived in Denver then, because his work was there.

The care of a little girl was difficult for Adam Tyson. His work took him away for weeks at a time, and it quickly became apparent other arrangements had to be made. Those included a move to the Davidson family's home town in Philadelphia.

Revel had all the advantages the Davidson family name could provide—an excellent education at a private girl's school, music lessons, fine clothes. Her friends, if they could be called that, were chosen for her from the children of several old established Philadelphia families. She thought these girls shallow, insipid, and quite silly. Because of that, she spent a great deal of time alone. But she didn't really mind. It gave her time to dream and plan for the time when her father would return and take her away with him.

She was pretty, bright, and it didn't take very long to realize her mother had married against the rules of society and her family's wishes.

Aunt Adelaide referred to her parents' marriage as "that unfortunate lack of sound judgment" on her mother's part. It was considered something best forgotten, except when her father visited her.

His visits were few and far between; he moved about constantly in the course of his work. But Revel adored him. Everything about him was in complete contrast to the stuffy, restricted life she knew in Philadelphia. He laughed and told her jokes. He shared stories of his adventures. And he always remembered her on her birthday and at Christmas. His gifts were never lavish, but they were always meaningful. None meant more than the small, gold pendant watch he'd given her upon graduation from secondary school. It opened like a locket, to reveal the watch with it's soft rhythmic ticking on one side, a cameo portrait of her mother on the other.

They made after-graduation plans. She was to join him in Denver. He had made arrangements to take a different position within the company. That would allow him to remain in Denver instead of traveling so much.

On his last visit to Philadelphia, they were told that Aunt Adelaide had arranged for Revel to take the grand tour of Europe. Her father felt she should go, even though she saw his disappointment. She would be gone only a few months, and they agreed to meet in Denver in September.

She was in Rome with Aunt Adelaide, visiting friends, when the letter arrived informing her that her father was dead. Even though she left immediately, it was weeks before she was able to reach Denver. That happened three years ago, and she never went back to Philadelphia.

The hunger she tried to ignore all morning on that bone-jarring ride from Tombstone washed back through her in a wave of weakness. The tantalizing aroma of the food the woman offered broke through her reverie. Her stomach grumbled so loudly she was certain everyone in the passenger car must have heard it. Revel nodded and smiled as the woman took out another wrapped portion of her meal and held it out.

"Gracias." Revel could manage that, though her Spanish was limited. So much for all the French lessons Aunt Adelaide had insisted she pursue.

After many laughs over her awkward attempts to speak Spanish, Revel learned the woman's name was Consuelo and the food she offered was a tamale. It was spicy and delicious; Revel couldn't remember anything tasting so wonderful. Consuelo also shared the water she carried in a pottery flask tucked inside her neatly packed basket. She, too, was traveling to Tucson, although the reason for her journey didn't come through in the translation.

It was part of Revel's work to study people. She quickly assessed that while Consuelo's clothes were simple and a bit worn, they were clean and well cared for. The basket that sat on the seat beside her held not only food but an assortment of finely made items of clothing—several delicately stitched women's blouses called *camisas*, two finely woven shawls called *rebozos*, and several full skirts with brilliantly dyed threads woven through them. Consuelo showed her a piece of paper. Each article of clothing was carefully itemized with

66

numbers beside it. She was obviously taking the clothing to Tucson to sell.

From the clothes Consuelo wore, the simple sandals on her feet, the worn basket she carried, and the manner in which she carefully guarded her treasures, Revel knew life must be hard for the woman. Yet she also sensed from her immaculate appearance, the pride in her every gesture, that she would be offended if Revel offered to repay her for her kindness. Sharing her food had been an act of friendship. If Revel knew how to speak Consuelo's language, she would have told her so.

They sat across from each other in companionable silence as the miles slipped beneath the steel wheels of the iron horse. Revel forced back the wild restlessness that churned inside her. There was nothing she could do until she reached Tucson, except pray Marshal Earp was right about Jake Reno's destination.

The train bucked and squealed, lurching and jolting Revel from her exhausted dozing. She jerked upright in her seat, every bone, muscle, and sinew complaining about the position she'd slumped into. Across from her, Consuelo carefully gathered her possessions and neatly packed them away in the woven basket.

Pressing fatigue from her eyes, Revel glanced out the window. Buildings were just coming into view in the distance. The clack and clatter of the train's wheels slowed as the cars ground to a stop. She looked back at Consuelo, and the woman smiled. *"Este es Tucson,"* she announced, and Revel immediately understood. She gathered her own things, which consisted of a small carpetbag and her reticule.

The train lurched, bucked and rolled forward, then hissed like a warning snake before coming to a full stop. Revel turned to Consuelo and held out her hand.

"Muchas gracias," she struggled with a language she barely understood, "for . . . *la comida.*"

Consuelo nodded as she followed the broken trail of

Spanish mixed with English. She smiled softly.

"*De nada, mi amiga.*" She hesitantly translated, "You . . . are . . . welcome."

It wasn't necesary for her to translate the other words. Revel knew that *amiga* meant friend. Taking Consuelo's left hand in hers, she pressed a wrapped handkerchief into her palm and said, "*Gracias, mi amiga.*"

They both followed the other passengers to the end of the car. Revel stepped down and asked directions. A buckboard wagon was taking passengers into town. She climbed aboard and settled herself on yet another hard, wood seat.

As the wagon lurched toward the center of town, she glanced back and saw Consuelo unwrap the contents of the handkerchief. Several silver coins gleamed in the hot afternoon sunlight.

Consuelo looked up in stunned surprise. It was undoubtedly more money than she had ever seen.

Revel smiled and waved good-bye to her friend.

Chapter Four

The stranger's eyes narrowed beneath the brim of the leather slouch hat, and in spite of the heat that lingered into early evening a long overcoat was wrapped tightly over his faded cambric shirt and baggy denim pants. The pants were gathered and belted to half their width at the waist, their overlong legs stuffed into the tops of scuffed leather boots.

Light and laughter spilled out the front entrance of the Red Garter Saloon and Pleasure House, along with trailing wisps of cigarette smoke, the klink of whiskey bottles, and the gay tinkle of a tune from a piano.

The stranger casually leaned one shoulder against a wood post and watched the customers that began to trickle into the saloon.

This was Tucson. Until just a few years earlier it had been the Territorial capitol. Its population was a mixture of Anglos and Mexicans, living in a community that lay in a rich, heavily cultivated valley. They carried on a prosperous trade with Sonora across the border to the south.

There were many thriving businesses in town, including several general stores, milliners, flour mills, a bootery, and three barbers. In addition, lawyers and physicians practiced in Tucson, and the unmistakable odor of the town's four livery stables permeated the warm air.

The buildings that lined the streets were adobe structures interspersed with a few clapboards that looked oddly out of place.

The spires of the Catholic church under the charge of the Sisters of St. Joseph cast long pious shadows at one end of town, the ornate gilt facade of the Red Garter Saloon glowed like a flame at the other—like contestants for the souls of the townsfolks squaring off against each other.

A foul-smelling old man stumbled up onto the boardwalk. He was unsteady on his feet, and it was obvious that in spite of the early hour of the evening he had already spent several hours drinking.

"Outta my way!" he snarled in a slurred voice as he shoved past the stranger, throwing him back hard against some nameless drifter fresh off the trail.

"What the hell's goin' on?" the drifter grumbled as he shoved his grizzled face at the stranger.

"Sorry." The apology was muttered as the stranger jerked his hat lower over his face. He sidestepped both the drunk and the drifter as he walked into the Red Garter Saloon.

Standing just inside the front entrance, the stranger took in every detail of the establishment in one sweeping glance.

The floors were bare hardwood for ease of cleaning, but simplicity ended there. The Red Garter was appropriately named, and the stranger couldn't prevent a moment of wide-eyed wonder. At least two dozen tables filled the main part of the saloon. Their dark, gleaming wood surfaces were as out of place as the red velvet damask fabric in a floral design that covered the walls. Huge gilt lanterns hung suspended from the ceilings and were affixed to the walls, making the inside of the Red Garter as bright as day. It was a mixture of the plain and gaudy.

Even though it was early, over half the tables were already filled with customers who were drinking or playing cards. They were as colorful a mixture as the Red Garter itself. Some had obviously just arrived in town, the dust of the trail on their clothing leaving motes of soft silt on the floor and chairs they occupied. Other customers seemed almost elegant in black coats, vests, and string ties.

Conversing, giggling, flirting with them all were the girls who worked at the Red Garter. They were conspicuous in daringly cut satin gowns of every color of the rainbow, trimmed with sequins, black lace, or wispy feathers. Where there was no trim, a length of leg was exposed, a shoulder or swelling breasts. They seemed like brightly colored birds.

Hovering in the large room were the pervasive odors of dust and sweat mingled with cloying heat, the sharp tang of whiskey, and cheap, stale perfume.

The stranger was tired and hungry. He moved toward the mahogany bar that ran the length of one side of the saloon, framed by an equally long mirror that filled the wall behind it. Two men worked behind the bar, supplying a steady flow of expensive whiskey and cheap conversation.

"What'll it be, mister?" The barkeep asked, polishing a glass.

"I'm looking for a fella I was supposed to meet here."

The barkeep tilted his head slightly for a better look at the face of the man wearing the slouch hat, but the stranger simply adjusted the brim lower still.

"I thought you might have seen him," he went on in a casual tone. "He's tall, and wears a leather outfit. He has green eyes, and he's left-handed. He might be riding an Appaloosa, and he would have just gotten into town."

"You wanta buy a drink?" The barkeep asked bluntly, and by his tone the stranger knew he wasn't about to receive any information for free.

He swallowed, undecided, then made up his mind. If he tried to pay for information it would look suspicious, and the last thing he wanted was to draw attention to himself.

71

In a small betraying gesture, the stranger bit the edge of his lower lip and looked about uneasily. There really was no choice.

"Make it a whiskey," Revel Tyson said in her best imitation of a masculine voice. Then, to eliminate any suspicion on the barkeep's part, she added, "Give me a bottle . . . and some information."

She'd seen her partners do this countless times and knew buying a full bottle of whiskey might make the barkeep more cooperative. She certainly wasn't about to drink any of it. That is, until he poured a substantial amount into a glass tumbler, set the bottle beside it, and waited expectantly.

The train had arrived little more than an hour earlier. Revel had taken a room at the hotel, then had made several quick decisions.

First she'd checked with the U.S. Federal Marshal's office. Her inquiry about Jake Reno was met with a mixture of curiosity and amusement. No one had seen him—"You jes' let us know if you need any assistance . . . Miss Tyson."

She saw the quirked smiles hidden behind hands passed casually over mouths, heard the bark of a cough that covered laughter. Obviously they knew why she was there, Marshal Earp must have sent a telegram ahead. It was also obvious that they found the situation highly amusing.

Revel chose to ignore their amusement, but not the offer of assistance. She was certain she would need it, if only to prove a point to Jake Reno. But first she had to find him. There were two places where he might be at that moment.

The rancher who bought the Appaloosa lived several miles out of town to the north. He'd paid two hundred and fifty dollars for the stallion. With only the twenty dollars he'd taken from the deputy in Tombstone, Jake couldn't hope to buy back the horse. That meant he intended to steal it or somehow come up with the money to buy it back.

Stealing the horse would have been the obvious conclusion, but Jake was already sentenced to hang for one crime and he hadn't survived this long by being foolish. His only other hope was to increase his stake and buy the horse back. Revel thought that the more likely possibility.

That raised the question of where Jake was at the moment. Wyatt Earp had spoken of the Red Garter Saloon. It was a favorite of Jake's and, also according to Wyatt, the best high-stakes card games were played there. But a quick look around told her he wasn't in the place, which could only mean he hadn't arrived in Tucson.

You've done some pretty crazy things, Revel silently told herself, but this one takes the cake.

A half-hour earlier she had stood in front of the mercantile next to the hotel, swept by indecision. Over the past three years, since she'd become an operative with the Pinkerton Agency, she had donned many disguises in order to track down information or a criminal. It was part of the job.

She had once dressed as an old grandmother, with gray wig and floppy flowered hat. Then there was the time she'd disguised herself as a ragpicker and set up a post on a streetcorner in Chicago. She had played the part of an old-maid schoolmarm, and once, she and her partner, an operative by the name of Tom McDonald, had posed as husband and wife in order to trap another couple who were society thieves. The couple lived in Boston, belonged to the upper crust of society, secured invitations to all the affairs held by the wealthiest bankers and businessmen, and robbed them blind. They were caught. In each case Revel had worked with a partner and had played the role of a woman, even if her disguises had varied. This was different.

73

For the first time, she was on her own. There was no partner, no fellow agent to back her up if she got into a bad situation, no one to play the part of the hard-riding drifter fresh off the trail—except herself.

She'd bought secondhand clothes at the mercantile, picking through a box the storekeeper kept in his back room, but when she'd left the hotel, she had been confident of her disguise.

Now, she preferred not to think about possibilities, only the matter at hand. According to Wyatt Earp, Lilly Gentry owned the Red Garter. He was certain Jake would come here. She had to talk to Lilly Gentry.

Revel placed a twenty-dollar gold piece on the bar. The barkeep let it lie. He picked up his towel, and casually began drying whiskey glasses—standing directly in front of Revel. She swallowed uneasily.

Damn! she thought. So far, her disguise had worked. The problem was it had worked too well. He expected her to drink the whiskey! If she didn't he would know something was wrong.

She pondered the predicament she'd gotten herself into as she stared at the glass of whiskey. God's nightgown! What was she going to do?

Her thoughts flashed to the few, rare occasions in her life when she'd had anything stronger than milk to drink. The first time, she was fourteen. She and a friend sneaked her aunt's sipping sherry from the butler's pantry of the house in Philadelphia. It was a beautiful spring day, and they sat under the hedgerow behind the house in the dirt, their skirts up around their knees, and got quite pixilated. The worst of it was the dreadful headache she had afterward.

The other time, she was seventeen and graduating from secondary school. Aunt Addie gave her a party, and quite a lot of champagne was served to toast her graduation. She and Constance Appleton sneaked two bottles up to her room. The champagne was warm and explosive.

They crawled into bed with their clothes still on. Needless to say, the maid found them next morning in their rumpled clothing, saw the empty champagne bottles. Neither occasion had been memorable.

Revel wondered if whiskey was as intoxicating as sherry or champagne. It really didn't matter. Unless she wanted to draw attention to herself, she had to drink it.

Imitating a gesture she'd seen dozens of times while working on different cases, she picked up the tumbler and quickly tossed back the whiskey.

It burned! Her tongue burned, her throat burned, her eyes watered, the room tilted crazily.

She desperately needed air, but she knew if she dared take a breath, she would start choking. And all the while, the man behind the bar stood there casually drying another glass.

"What about that man yer lookin' for?" he asked.

Revel dug her fingers into the wood rail of the bar for support. The heat spread—to her arms, her hands, and down her legs—leaving behind a warm, liquid feeling.

If she tried to move, she was convinced she would fall flat on her face. That wasn't as surprising as the fact that she could think at all!

Her face felt hot, her ears were hot. She was certain if she could feel it, her hair would be hot.

The barkeep stared at her while she struggled to draw air into her lungs. It seeped in with a tiny, wheezing sound. She swallowed back the cough that spasmed in her throat, and closed her eyes. Tears squeezed from between her lashes.

"His name is . . ." Her voice came out a broken whisper. She tried again. "Jake . . . Reno." Revel took another breath, deeper this time.

"He's a friend of Lilly Gentry's," she said, barely above a whisper.

The barkeep's gaze slid away from hers. Had she seen a brief flash of recognition when she'd mentioned Jake Reno's name?

He leaned across the bar and shouted over the noise inside the saloon. "Hey, Sara! You seen Lilly tonight?"

A girl dressed in brilliant magenta slowly strode over to stand beside Revel and leaned against the bar. She gave Revel an appraising look from under pale blond lashes.

"She's showin' a customer upstairs." She smiled through vividly painted lips. "She was takin' him up to Maria. She'll be right back."

The barkeep motioned to Revel. "This here fella is lookin' for someone, a friend of Lilly's."

The girl looked Revel up and down, with an expression that could only be described as an open invitation.

"Lilly's got herself lotsa friends. But me, I just got here a few weeks ago. I'm lookin' to make me some *friends* of my own." She moved closer to Revel, brushing a well-curved hip up against her while she stroked the sleeve of the heavy overcoat.

Beneath the hat, Revel's eyes widened. They widened even further when Sara turned into her, pressing high breasts against her arm.

Revel swallowed hard. If she'd had any doubt as to exactly what Sara had in mind, it disappeared in the next moment as Sara slid her arm under Revel's, moving her breasts against it at the same time her right hand went to the inside of Revel's leg and began a slow, deliberate journey upward.

"I'm looking for Jake Reno!" Revel blurted out a little too loudly as she sidestepped away from Sara's inquisitive hand.

"Never heard of him," Sara purred, her lashes lowered as she snuggled up against Revel once more. "But, like I said, I am new in town."

"Was someone asking for me?"

Revel jerked around, grateful for the interruption— any interruption. Then her eyes widened once more at taking in the woman who slowly strode toward them.

She was dressed in purple satin adorned with sequins, and a black feather boa was draped about her pale-skinned neck and shoulders. Her hair, almost silver, was piled high atop her head and decorated with more black feathers.

Revel had never seen hair that color before. But then she'd never seen anyone like this woman before. Lilly Gentry was tall, taller still in the black satin, high-heeled boots she wore. Frills of black lace winked like rows of eyelashes from the center cut of her gown. The neckline plunged almost to her waist, exposing a great deal of her large, pale breasts.

She walked to the bar with a loose-jointed, flowing undulation that men undoubtedly found fascinating. As far as Revel was concerned it meant just one thing—this could be none other than Lilly Gentry of the famous hips.

Revel was careful to keep her voice low and even. The whiskey helped—her voice was husky from it.

"I'm looking for Jake Reno," she repeated.

Lilly stood with one hand planted on a loosely cocked hip. Thick lashes lowered over gray eyes that stared back at Revel without blinking. The only response was a subtle lifting of one artistically painted eyebrow.

"Is that right?"

"He's a friend of mine," Revel explained. "I heard he might be headed this way."

Lilly gave her a long, assessing look. "Jake's a friend of mine, too. But I haven't seen him."

She could be lying, but then again she might not be. There was the possibility that Jake hadn't gotten into Tucson yet. The other possibility was that Lilly had seen him but wasn't about to tell her anything. Jake, of course, would be suspicious of anyone asking for him and would have warned her to say nothing.

Revel told herself she had to be careful. She couldn't allow this opportunity to slip through her fingers. In a gesture, she'd seen duplicated several times since entering the Red Garter, she laid another twenty-dollar gold piece down on the bar, then shrugged.

"I think I'll wait around. He might show up." She kept

77

her voice low and casual, almost to the point of disinterest.

Her gaze met Lilly's briefly, then shifted to the gold piece on the bar beside the other money left from the purchase of the whiskey.

Revel caught sight of her own pale, slender fingers beside the coin, a dead giveaway if anyone thought to look. She jerked her hands back, curling her fingers inside the overlong sleeves of the coat.

When she looked back up, it was obvious Lilly hadn't noticed a thing. The woman had eyes only for the gold piece, and by the expression on her face she knew when there was money to be made. That was all that mattered. She smiled, bringing her gaze back to Revel's.

"If he comes in, I'll mention you been asking for him." She came closer as Sara had done earlier. Every muscle in Revel's body tensed. But instead of sidling intimately close as Sara had in ignorant invitation, Lilly simply looped her arm through Revel's.

"In the meantime, maybe there's something else to keep you occupied." She maneuvered Revel toward one of the poker tables. Revel hesitated. She would really be in over her head in a game of cards. Reaching out as she'd seen men do countless times, she patted Lilly's wrist.

"I'm not in the mood for cards tonight," she said in that low, gravelly voice, then remembered to pull her hand back as Lilly turned to her.

"No?" came the silken reply. A knowing smile spread across Lilly's face, revealing myriad tiny lines that thick makeup couldn't quite conceal. "Well, I think maybe we can find something else to keep you busy." Slender fingers clamped down over Revel's coat-sleeved arm and pulled her toward the stairs.

It took a full minute and several strides before Revel fully understood where they were going. By the time it did occur to her just what a trip up those stairs meant, it was too late. Lilly already had her halfway up, and the firm hold on her arm gave her little choice unless she wanted to make a scene.

At the landing, Lilly turned briefly. "I know just the girl for you." She smiled.

Revel practically choked, but still she followed as Lilly led her down a hallway covered with thick, red velvet carpet. It was her one hope of finding Jake. There was no other choice.

She tried to think clearly, but the effects of the whiskey slowed her reactions. Downstairs she would be out in the open, easily seen if Jake came into the Red Garter, and even though her disguise had fooled the barkeep and Lilly, it might not fool him.

It was better to be out of sight. From her brief experience with Jake Reno she knew that if he recognized her, he would try to get away again. She just couldn't let that happen. There would be no second chance at finding him, and another delay would make it impossible to find Sam Bass with or without Jake Reno. It was unfortunate that she hadn't considered this turn of events when she'd come into the Red Garter.

If she'd had any doubts about what the upstairs rooms in Lilly's place were used for, they vanished as they reached the next landing. The third-floor hallway was even more lavishly decorated than the one below.

The walls were covered in that same red damask, and the doorways lining both sides of the hall were draped with red velvet hangings. Several elaborately framed mirrors decorated the walls, along with paintings of women in various stages of undress. It was garish, gaudy and completely fascinating.

Lilly led her to the third door on the left. She knocked discreetly and, when there was no response, opened the door and pulled Revel inside. The entire room was decorated in white lace and pink satin. In the center was a huge canopied bed covered with a pink satin coverlet edged with pink braid tassels. It looked like a huge pink pillow.

"This should do very nicely," Lilly announced as she

turned to Revel. She looked her up and down, feeling her arms and shoulders through the heavy overcoat. Revel stepped back cautiously.

"There's no need to be skittish now," Lilly soothed as she slowly walked around her. "You're a bit on the lean side, aren't you?"

Lilly came back around to stand in front of Revel. They were very near the same height and were standing too close for the disguise not to be penetrated. Revel dipped the brim of her hat low so Lilly couldn't see her face.

"You're kinda young too, and maybe a bit shy, but that's all right." Lilly's voice was silky.

"I always did say there was somethin' real special about havin' 'em young."

She laughed, a deep-throated sound. "I can teach you young fellows a thing or two." She pouted, emphasizing the faint lines around her mouth. Lilly Gentry was no longer young.

"But I've got to get back downstairs, so I'll tell you what I'll do. I'm goin' to send up Rose. She's young too, with lotsa energy and . . . imagination, and she's real gentle. She really likes twenty-dollar gold pieces." Lilly winked at Revel. "You wait right here."

With that, she was gone in a cloud of smothering perfume, closing the door behind her.

Revel let out a deep sigh of relief as panic seeped out of her.

"I swear I am never going to do this again! I swear it!" she whispered, but all the swearing in the world wouldn't change the fact that her reprieve was brief. At any minute Rose would arrive. She had to think fast.

Wyatt Earp hadn't elaborated before she had left Tombstone, but it had been obvious that Lilly and Jake had shared some sort of relationship in the past. Revel was a complete stranger, albeit one in disguise. Lilly had every reason to protect Jake and absolutely no reason whatsoever to tell a stranger the truth. The woman had insisted she hadn't seen Jake Reno, but Revel knew from

80

experience that an agent could not rely on the word of a relative, a friend, or a lover.

Therefore it was safe to assume that Lilly might have lied, that she might even now be on her way to another room to warn Jake that someone was looking for him.

Revel had to search those other rooms. At the very least, she couldn't afford to be in this one when Lilly returned with Rose. Nothing in her past had prepared her to handle something like that.

Revel searched the room she was in thoroughly, then began a systematic search of the others off the long hallway.

That was easier said than done, considering at least half of them were currently occupied. She began with the room next to the one Lilly had put her in.

Her hand was on the doorknob when a pouty, childlike voice came from inside and stopped her cold.

"Ooooh, you're so big and strong. I love it when you spank me like that!"

This gushing declaration was followed by a loud, resounding whack vaguely reminiscent of the one time Revel's father had spanked her. She had been four years old, and he was punishing her for running into the path of a buggy. It had left a painful impression on her memory and her backside.

She shuddered. How could anyone *want* to be spanked? Was Jake Reno in there?

She had her answer in the next moment as a man's voice said, "Come on back to ole Pete, and we'll do it some more."

The words were thick in the man's throat, swallowed the next moment by a deep groan.

A feminine squeal, one of excitement rather than fear came next. Revel shuddered and moved on.

"Thank God," she whispered in the silent hallway, inexplicably grateful that Jake Reno wasn't behind that door.

She moved to the next one. There were no sounds this

time. Revel quietly pushed the door open and stepped inside. She was just about to close it and start her search for something that might indicate Jake Reno had been there when the light from the oil lanterns in the hallway fell across the bed and its two sleeping occupants.

At least she assumed there were two people despite her quick flash of panic. Arms and legs were intertwined. She saw the naked smoothness of a woman's thigh beneath the hair-roughened length of a man's leg. Then everything disappeared in a tangle of bed clothes, riotous henna-dyed hair, a woman's exposed breast, and the paunch of a gleaming white male belly.

The man stirred, covers falling away from his naked body.

"Come here, Clemmie," he muttered, rolling toward the woman and exposing a pale, fleshy backside.

Revel quickly ducked out of the room, closed the door. She collapsed against the wall in the hallway. She was absolutely certain *that* was not Jake Reno.

Her breath came in quick, hard gasps, her heart pounding in her ears.

Damn! She had almost been caught. She continued her search, more carefully now.

Three other rooms proved to be empty. A quick look in each revealed nothing to indicate Jake had been in any of them. Faint sounds of movement and muffled conversations came from the next two rooms, obviously occupied.

In the first a young woman called out, "Oh, Sam . . . oh, Sam . . . Ohhhhhh, Sam!" In the second, a man stuttered over every third word. He abruptly blurted out something, unclear to Revel because of his stuttering. Then there was silence. Revel quickly moved on. Jake Reno didn't stutter.

The next room was also occupied, Lilly Gentry certainly did a thriving business, Revel thought. She let out an unladylike snort, and was just about to move on when the voices on the other side of the door stopped her.

"Come on, Susie. Jes' lay yerself down over here." It

was quickly followed by, "Yeah, Susie. You know jes how we like it."

We? It?

Revel couldn't help herself. She knew it was eavesdropping of the worst kind, but she was fascinated. From the brief conversation, she could draw only one conclusion; Susie had two customers—at the same time!

That immediately ruled out Jake Reno. Everything she knew about him indicated he was a loner. She was convinced he wouldn't purchase the services of one of Lilly's girls and then share with another man.

There was soft laughter behind the door, presumably Susie's, followed by a squeal of delight, then the echoes of male laughter. Revel quietly tiptoed on, refusing to listen to any more.

The room at the end of the hallway was by far the largest, and it was empty. An oil lamp sat on a table, the wick turned down low. Soft light drifted over the surfaces of the elaborate decor—the carved mantel, thick carpeting, deep purple velvet portieres over sheer lace curtains, and the huge canopied, fourposter bed with its thick, purple velvet quilt.

Adjoining the room was a private dressing room with a brass bathtub sitting behind a screen of hand-stitched fabric. A tall gilt mirror stood in one corner of the dressing area, a large closet filled another.

Revel frowned. So far she'd found nothing to indicate that Jake Reno was at the Red Garter. Perhaps Lilly was telling the truth, after all. Her frown deepened at the thought that she might have guessed wrong. Perhaps Jake had decided to steal the horse, thinking to hell with the consequences. If so, he was already many miles from Tucson.

Frustration gnawed at her. She was always meticulous in her investigations, and it got her results. She knew just about everything there was to know about Jake Reno. It was logical that he would come here. But then, she had thought it logical that he would accept her offer in return for his freedom. He hadn't. Now what?

She returned to the main bedroom and was just opening the door to leave when she caught sight of a golden-haired young girl coming down the hallway. The girl stopped in front of the door to the room Lilly had originally chosen for Revel, and opened it. Then she stood on the threshold, a confused expression on her young face. This had to be Rose.

Revel quickly ducked back into the purple room. What was she going to do now? She couldn't go back down the hallway without being seen, but there was no other way out. And now that Rose had discovered she was gone, there would be all sorts of questions if she was seen downstairs.

Her gaze swept the shadows of the elegant room as she leaned back against the closed door. It was far more tastefully decorated than the others she'd seen, and larger. Then her glance settled on those deep purple velvet portieres and something clicked into place.

Purple!

Lilly was wearing purple, while all the other girls wore blues, reds, pinks, or greens. Her gaze swept to the large, purple covered bed. It was like a signature color.

"Of course!" she whispered. How could she have not noticed it before? It was so obvious.

"Lilly Gentry's room," she whispered aloud. It was quickly followed by another thought—there was still a chance that Jake Reno might come here.

She could go chasing all over the territory trying to find him or she could wait a little longer to see if he showed up. Revel quickly made her decision. She took off the heavy overcoat and tossed it into the closet, along with the slouch hat. Combing her fingers back through disheveled hair, she settled herself on the chair in the dressing room and sat down to wait. Whoever came in had to pass through the bedroom first. She would have plenty of time to hide.

She pulled a small revolver from the waist of her

84

thickly belted pants and rechecked the cartridges. That done, she flipped the chamber closed, laid the revolver on the table beside her, and waited.

Revel jerked awake, her senses clearing through the fog of exhaustion. She blinked back the bleariness in her eyes with a sharp twinge of anger at allowing herself to fall asleep.

It came again—the creak of a door opening, soft murmurs, a woman's light step on wood, then the muted, heavier tread of a man's foot on carpet. She was now fully awake.

The murmurs turned to faint laughter, then grew more distinct. Light suddenly glowed through the partially opened door that separated the dressing room from the bedroom. The glow became brighter, and with its flare came the remembered silkiness of Lilly Gentry's voice.

"You must be dead tired. I'll just slip into something more . . . comfortable and then we'll order up some supper." There was a faint whisper of satin as Lilly came to the door, then hesitated.

"Oh, and, darlin', don't forget to take off those boots."

There was a grumbled reply, then the door was pushed open.

"Who was it you said was looking for me?"

Revel immediately recognized Jake Reno's voice.

Lilly came into the dressing room, walking across in the half-light to the dressing table. Revel heard the faint clink of a glass chimney being removed from a lantern. Just as Lilly struck the wood match and lit the wick, Revel slipped noiselessly into the depths of the closet.

The flame sputtered, then caught. The chimney was replaced.

"It was some young fella," Lilly answered. "Looked like he was right off the trail." She began taking off her clothes.

There was a faint pause, then Jake's voice came from

the other room.

"What did he want?"

"Didn't say," Lilly answered as she moved about the dressing room, discarding first the black feather boa, then the daringly low-cut purple dress. It whooshed to her feet in a shimmering puddle.

"I put him in a room down the hall and sent Rose up, but he took off. Probably some green kid that hasn't had his first woman yet."

Revel rolled her eyes at hearing that description, then forced her concentration back to Lilly. Her eyes widened at the sight of the black lace undergarments Lilly wore—a camisole that barely covered her milk white breasts, lace-trimmed garters, inky black stockings. She had never seen such garments!

She held her breath and shrank back into the deepest corner of the closet as Lilly crossed the room. The door was pulled open and Lilly thrust a hand inside, sorting through several long, satin dressing gowns hanging on hooks at the side of the closet. Revel held her breath and tried to become as small as she could.

The door was slammed, and she was abruptly thrust into complete darkness except for the finger of light at floor level.

Through the wood door Revel could barely make out Lilly's soft dulcet tones and Jake's occasional responses. A second door closed and the voices were completely muffled. The light at the bottom of the closet door had disappeared. That could only mean that Lilly had rejoined Jake in the bedroom. Revel carefully turned the doorknob, wincing as it squeaked, and let herself out.

She walked lightly across the dressing room to the beckoning glow of light at the bottom of the door that led to the bedroom.

"It's been a while, Jake. You had me worried. I thought they had hung you." Lilly's muted words came through the wood door.

"Yeah, I can see how worried you were," Jake

answered. "You didn't even bother to come for the hangin'."

"You know how I feel about that sort of thing. Between crazy gunfighters shooting each other up and the gallows, I lose too many good customers." Then she purred huskily, "But you always were the best."

There was a brief silence then Lilly's soft laughter was followed by a muffled sound of delighted surprise.

"I always did say you had the best hands of any gunfighter I knew." Lilly sighed, then laughed. "You are impatient, aren't you?"

There was a deep masculine chuckle, followed by what could only be the thud of boots on soft carpet.

"I don't have a lot of time."

"You never did darlin', but you always made it worthwhile. By the way, how did you manage to save your neck?" Lilly asked.

There were the sounds of more clothing being removed, left to lie where it fell.

"I didn't. The damn Pinkertons stopped the hanging."

"The Pinkertons? What are they doin' in these parts? Who are they after?"

Now there was the whisper of a heavy coverlet being pulled back, the faint creak of wood and ropes under someone's weight.

"They're after me." There was an edge of anger and fatigue in Jake Reno's voice. "They wanted me to go after someone for them." He didn't bother to explain more, nor did Lilly ask. The choice he'd made was obvious by his unannounced presence in her bedroom.

"Can you rely on your girls to let me know if anyone else asks for me?"

"My girls know what to do, Jake. My business depends on it. Besides, you know the marshal and I have a special arrangement when it comes to my customers."

"Not this time."

Jake's remark was followed by the clink of a belt buckle hitting a hard surface, then the whispered sounds of more clothing being removed.

Revel slumped back against the wall that separated the two rooms, and tried to block out the other sounds of two people undressing with only one purpose in mind.

God's nightgown! Now what was she going to do?

This sort of situation was always left to her partner. For obvious reasons, the agency preferred to let male operatives take care of these sorts of things. But that was precisely the problem; there was no partner to take care of this.

Should she wait or go in now and confront Jake Reno?

If she went in both Lilly Gentry and Jake Reno would be undressed or very nearly undressed.

If she waited, how long was *long enough?*

She decided to wait and slowly began counting. There were sixty seconds in each minute. One . . . two . . . three . . . She heard a vaguely mumbled comment followed by soft, feminine laughter. She continued counting; seven minutes . . . eight minutes . . . ten minutes.

Was that enough? Not long enough?

Dear God, just how long did these *things* take?

Did two people continue talking when they went to bed, or did they stop. Revel realized she was at a definite disadvantage when it came to things like this.

Her thoughts flashed to her own brief experiences in such matters. Once, when she was little, she had come upon two cats in her aunt's yard.

They hissed and spit at each other, then began biting and clawing one another. She was certain they were trying to kill each other. Just as she turned to run into the house for help, the two cats suddenly came together.

She had been fascinated and a little confused. In a matter of seconds it was all over. The tomcat sauntered off with a pleased twitch to his tail. The female blinked, shook herself off, and went in the opposite direction. It completely changed Revel's naive and romantic notions about what went on between the male and female of the species.

And the spring she and Jenny Sullivan were sixteen, when Jenny's parents had taken an extended tour of Europe, Jenny stayed with Revel.

The spring cotillion was the social event of the year, a time when a young lady was supposed to make her debut in Philadelphia society and, hopefully, find a suitable husband. Jenny had been courted by John Holcroft of the Philadelphia banking Holcrofts. It was assumed the betrothal would be announced when Jenny's parents returned from Europe.

That evening Jenny and John disappeared at about nine o'clock. They were gone for hours, and Revel was beginning to worry. She had no idea how she would explain Jenny's absence to Aunt Adelaide.

Right after midnight Jenny and John reappeared. Jenny's dress was wrinkled, her hair was arranged differently, and she had a flushed look.

Later that night when both girls went to bed, she confessed that she and John had gone over to her parents' house. When Revel innocently asked why they would want to leave the cotillion and go to an empty house, Jenny shook her head in disbelief.

"Because we wanted to be *together*," she explained as they whispered to each other in Revel's darkened room.

"But you *were* together *here*," Revel protested.

"Not that way. We wanted to be *together*. You know." Then, to Revel's wide-eyed astonishment, Jenny clarified precisely what *together* meant.

It was the last time Revel ever had to have such things explained to her. She knew what Lilly Gentry and Jake Reno were doing *together*— or had done.

But there was one part she wasn't clear on—did it take the same amount of time for people as it did for cats? That was one point Jenny had never elaborated on.

Revel's neck muscles had cramped painfully from

leaning at an odd angle in order to keep her ear to the door. She wiggled her toes in the scuffed boots and felt only the pinpricks of numbness. Her feet had gone to sleep.

At least part of me is getting some rest, she thought with growing aggravation.

Once again she heard the murmur of voices and tried to make out what was being said.

She waited another few moments, then tightened her grip on the revolver in her right hand and reached for the doorknob with her left.

She pulled the door open just as Lilly Gentry was saying, "Relax, Jake darling. Can't you put that damn gun aside for just a little while?" Her voice was soft and petulant, with a slight purr.

Lilly was reclining on the bed, her long pale hair snaking across equally pale shoulders and purple satin sheets. She still wore the black lace camisole which barely covered her breasts, but the rest of her milk white body was concealed under the purple velvet coverlet on the bed. The room was bathed in shadows and sweet fragrance. Jake Reno was not in the bed.

"Yes, Mr. Reno," Revel called out in a clear voice as she stepped into the softly lit room, her gaze fastening on a sudden reflexive movement at the side of the bed. "Put down the gun."

The subtle glow from the lantern shimmered off the barrel of her small revolver. He was standing at the window, concealed in shadows. As Jake Reno whirled toward her, the light from the lantern fell across his naked body.

He was lean and tawny, muscles coiled with the instinctual awareness of an animal. His green eyes glittered above the curve of a dangerous half-smile.

"So, Miss Tyson, we meet again."

Chapter Five

"*Miss* Tyson!"

Lilly Gentry's astonished exclamation echoed in the ornate room. Neither Jake Reno nor Revel glanced her way. They concentrated on each other.

Lean. Wary. Handsome. Dangerous.

Revel had thought Jake Reno all of those things. Now she knew it was true. He was caught, trapped like an animal run to ground, and there wasn't an ounce of fear in him—or embarrassment—as he stood completely naked before her, except for the fingers of shadow that half concealed his lean body.

She was a professional, an operative for the Pinkerton National Detective Agency. She had been involved in dozens of cases, many of them dangerous. But this hinted at another more illusive danger than any she had encountered before.

She had confronted criminals—bankrobbers, thieves, even murderers.

All sorts. Lowlife scum who lived in the back alleys of cities; swindlers who robbed people of their dearest possessions; cold, emotionless scoundrels who easily cut a person's throat for a pouch of gold dust.

They were all bound together by the same cold indifference for their victims. She felt nothing for them—not anger, regret, or compassion. She couldn't even remember their faces.

Now, as she aimed the revolver at Jake Reno, she realized she remembered everything about him—the unwavering stare when any other man would have nervously looked away; the low, intense voice instead of angry abusive words; the relaxed stance when another would have made a desperate reach for a gun; and the carefully controlled power in his muscular body . . . the equally controlled emotions in his startlingly handsome face.

The beard was gone, along with the dirt, grime, and stench he'd had in the Tombstone jail. His long hair hung softly about his neck. The green eyes were watchful.

She had thought him much older than her information indicated, with a hardness accented by the rough clothes he'd worn and the chains that bound him. But that, too, had been deceiving. There was an angle to his chin that suggested strength, and his face was unlined except for a small scar at the corner of his left eye. Those eyes drew her attention.

Her first impression was that they were hard, like those of every criminal she'd ever met. They were a cold, green color and seemed to look straight through her. But she saw something behind the hardness, something faintly sad in the downward cast of his glance, an unreadable emotion that began in those eyes and ended in the curve of a frown.

Then Revel discovered his mouth. It was full, gently curved, the frown fading to an ironic smile. She had never noticed a man's mouth before, never thought of it. But Jake Reno's fascinated and frightened her. It should have been easy to look away . . . it should have been.

Some unfamiliar emotion uncurled deep inside Revel, like a slow-building heat. Her lips were suddenly dry— she wet them. Her grasp on the revolver faltered—she tightened her cold, suddenly numb fingers.

The uncertainty frightened her. She hid it behind anger.

"Get dressed, Mr. Reno." For emphasis she aimed the revolver right at his heart and warned, "Don't make any sudden movements."

"And you, Miss Gentry," Revel spoke without taking her concentration off Jake Reno, "get dressed, and then go get the marshal."

"Jake?" Bemusement had now gone to uncertainty, and there was an edge of alarm in Lilly Gentry's voice.

Jake met Revel Tyson's gaze evenly. Also, without breaking contact, he spoke softly to Lilly.

"You better do as she says, darlin'. I think she just might shoot me if you don't. And I'm not real crazy about where she's pointing that gun."

The tip of the revolver had lowered to a strategic position just a few inches below his waist.

At first Revel thought he was making fun of her, but the dark shadows behind the green of his eyes suggested he took her seriously.

"But Jake . . ." Lilly started to protest. Jake cut her off.

"Go on, get the marshal," he firmly instructed her once again, never taking his eyes off Revel. Then the deep frown lines about that softly curved mouth eased and the color in his eyes shifted.

"I'll just pull on my own clothes," he suggested, "that is, if you don't mind?"

Revel nodded. "By all means, Mr. Reno, make yourself presentable before the marshal gets here. And if she brings anyone else back other than the marshal, I swear I'll shoot you." The last was said loudly enough so that Lilly could hear every word and would have not the least doubt as to her intentions.

From the periphery of her vision, Revel saw Lilly hurriedly pull on stockings, shoes, and the satin dressing gown she'd pulled from the closet only a few moments before. She shoved her wild torrent of silver hair back over her shoulder. Revel saw her finish tying the sash to the dressing gown about her waist.

"And please be quick, Miss Gentry. It's been a long day. I'd just as soon shoot him as look at him."

It wasn't her threat but a reassuring nod from Jake that sent Lilly on her way. That incredibly handsome mouth quirked faintly at one corner as Jake Reno reached for the pants that lay across the foot of the bed. For the first time, Revel noticed that one side of the bed was still neatly made, the velvet bedcover and bedclothes tucked neatly under the edge of the feather mattress. She realized Jake hadn't yet gotten into bed with Lilly.

For some reason that completely eluded her, she felt an odd sense of relief. She should have been furious because she'd foolishly waited for them to finish whatever they were doing. Jake's voice jarred her from her thoughts.

"You won't shoot me, Miss Tyson," he said with calm certainty. "If you shoot me, who'll lead you to Sam Bass?"

"I didn't say I intended to kill you, Mr. Reno. There are a lot of places a man can be shot and still live. And you may turn around while you dress." She could have sworn what had begun as a smile turned to a smirk as he raised his hands in supplication and slowly turned around.

"Then you do know how to use that thing?"

He slipped one heavily muscled leg then another into the legs of the soft leather pants. The front closure was laced through with a strip of leather cord. He slowly tied it closed and then reached for his shirt. They were the same clothes he'd been wearing in the jail at Tombstone with one subtle difference—the shirt was freshly laundered and the leather had been carefully cleaned. Both garments clung to him like a second skin. She raised the tip of the revolver.

"Well enough to damage those clothes you're wearing beyond repair," she calmly assured him. He slowly turned around.

"Now what, Miss Tyson?"

There was no longer any trace of smile or smirk. There

94

was only that dangerous gaze that bored into hers with an unwavering calmness that, under the circumstances, seemed too serene, too certain, as if he knew something she didn't.

The sound came at her right, from the direction of the door to the dressing room. The light from the single lantern created shadows at the edges of the room, leaving the doorway in darkness. Then the door burst open, surprising them both. At least that is what Revel assumed in the fraction of a second before the room erupted into chaos.

The door to the dressing room crashed back on its hinges. She saw the gleam of steel—a gun—as she was knocked backward by someone who leaped at her from the shadows. Her reactions were completely instinctive—she couldn't let Jake Reno get away.

As her right arm came up, she fired the gun. It went off somewhere between Jake Reno's thigh and shoulder, and then she was on the floor, Lilly straddling her waist, pinning her down. The force of the blow knocked the revolver from her hand. It slid several feet beyond her reach.

Lilly had obviously doubled back and reentered the dressing room from some hidden door Revel hadn't discovered in her search.

Revel had been taught how to take care of herself. There were defensive moves she'd learned from other operatives with the agency. And she was wearing men's clothes, which allowed her more freedom of movement.

Lilly had had the advantage of slightly more weight— and of surprise. She had hold of her wrists and wasn't about to let go, but Revel had the advantage of leverage. She bent her legs and brought her knees up directly behind Lilly's back, pulling her feet in against her bottom. Even with her wrists pinned to the floor, she leveraged her hips upward with a quick thrust and dislodged Lilly in one agile movement.

Revel rolled to her side, twisted her wrists free with a

wrenching motion, and scrambled to retrieve her revolver.

She scooped back her disheveled hair as she slowly got to her feet. Her breath came in quick, hard gasps. There was a loud commotion out in the hallway as she looked around for Jake Reno.

He was sitting on the edge of the bed and looking up with an expression that was somewhere between tight-lipped fury and disbelief.

"You shot me!" He brought his hand away from his side, where his freshly laundered shirt was plastered against his skin by a dark spreading wetness.

Revel came a bit closer, holding the revolver in her right hand—away from Jake Reno—while she cautiously reached out to pull the shirt away from his side with her left. There was one neat, small hole in the fabric. She shook her head, frowning slightly.

"That's too bad."

"Too bad!" His echo was filled with incredulity. "Is that all you can say?"

She met his furious gaze with a calmness that would have mirrored his only moments before.

"Yes . . . too bad I missed."

At his furious expression, she went on to explain, "I aimed lower. But it looks as if you'll survive. It's only a flesh wound. I do wish I hadn't ruined that shirt, though. I suppose I'll have to replace it before we leave."

"Replace it!"

His tight-lipped responses never got beyond two words. He was angry, and she was pushing the matter a little far, but Revel couldn't resist. Especially after all the trouble he'd caused her.

"Yes, we have a long ride ahead of us, Mr. Reno. That is unless you'd like to go back to Tombstone."

Now another commotion found them as the marshal and three of his deputies burst into Lilly Gentry's bedroom.

"Lilly? What the devil is goin' on here?" the marshal

96

asked as he glanced from Lilly to Jake and then to Revel.

"Miss Tyson?" His expression was bewildered as he gave her a long look and finally recognized her. There hadn't been time for Lilly to summon him. He had obviously been close by when the single gunshot was fired. Revel remembered overhearing Lilly tell Jake that she and the marshal had a special arrangement.

"Yes, Marshal," she replied wearily, "And I'd appreciate your assistance with Mr. Reno. It seems he was accidentally injured. I doubt it's anything serious, and I would also appreciate the loan of one of your jail cells for him."

"What the . . . ?" Jake Reno came up off the end of the bed, but before he could say anything further, Revel cut him off. Fatigue pulled at her, making her voice edgy, drawing her patience thin.

"It's just until morning." And then, so the marshal would understand that she fully intended to find her prisoner in that cell in the morning, she added, "And I trust, Marshal, that you will cooperate fully. I will make a recommendation when I give my full report to the Territorial governor."

"Of course," the marshal stuttered. Then he cleared his throat, "Of course."

"Now wait just a minute." A deadly calm replaced Jake's anger. "I'm not going back to jail for any reason."

"Safekeeping," Revel explained, fighting for control over her own slow-rising anger, "just so you won't get any ideas about slipping out of town sometime during the night." When he started to argue further, the anger she'd tried to control bubbled to the surface, pushing her further than she liked to be pushed.

"Listen to me, Jake Reno. I traveled several hundred miles to find you, not to mention the trip from Tombstone. I'm tired, hungry, and these clothes are beginning to itch. I want a bath, some supper, and sleep."

The events of the last few days were beginning to wear on her. If he so much as made one little objection she silently swore she'd shoot him again.

"I'm certain you don't care at all about the first thing I want, considering the condition I found you in, but the marshal can provide you with the other two. I suggest you eat and get lots of sleep. We leave in the morning." With that she stuffed the revolver in the waistband of her pants and started for the door. She stopped briefly to speak with the marshal.

"Were you able to take care of that other little matter we discussed?"

"It's all taken care of," he muttered, then added, "I don't mind tellin' you I didn't think you'd find him." He inclined his head toward Jake.

Revel looked past the marshal to where Jake Reno stood, a deputy on either side of him to prevent him from slipping out of their custody. She didn't need to be told just how unhappy Jake Reno was at that moment.

"I'm certain you didn't, Marshal. Good night."

Back in her hotel room, Revel was too weary to eat. She soaked for over an hour in a warm bath, then crawled beneath the sheets on the feather mattress on her bed. She was exhausted, but one image seeped into her weary thoughts—Jake Reno.

The day dawned clear and bright, without a whisper of a breeze. The shadows were cool, but the choking dryness of dust kicked up by the hooves of an occasional horse gave a hint of the blistering heat that would soon follow. The sun broke over the spires of the Catholic church, then reached slowly down the street until it illuminated the red and gold facade of the Red Garter Saloon.

Just after seven o'clock, Revel roused the deputy at the marshal's office and asked that Jake Reno be released.

She had slept poorly the night before in spite of her exhaustion. Breakfast was a platter of biscuits floating in a mixture of greasy gravy and congealed egg yolks. She had shoved it aside and concentrated on the cup of steaming black coffee.

All arrangements had been made the evening before, so that when Jake Reno stepped out of the marshal's office, she was ready to leave Tucson. The last thing she wanted or needed was any criticism from him.

"He's all yours." The marshal stepped out onto the boardwalk in front of his office. And then he added, "Are you sure you don't want me to send along some of my deputies, Miss Tyson?"

"Thank you, Marshal, but I prefer to ride alone. We can move more quickly that way. I appreciate your offer, though."

The marshal nodded, his expression still skeptical. "All right, have it your way. I suppose you know what you're doin'. By the way, I sent that wire on to Marshal Earp in Tombstone."

"Thank you." Revel smiled faintly, then turned to Jake Reno. "I've arranged for supplies and horses. Everything is at the livery at the end of town." She immediately saw the hesitation, the flicker of speculation that passed across those green eyes.

"Don't even consider it, Mr. Reno. If you don't cooperate, the marshal has instructions to put you right back in that jail cell, in which case your previous sentence will be carried out. Whether it's here or in Tombstone doesn't really matter, they will hang you just the same."

"Just like that?"

The low timbre of his voice edged along her nerve endings, reminding her of one of the reasons she'd gotten so little sleep the night before.

"Just like that!" she snapped.

Jake shifted his weight as he stretched. He winced slightly against the pull of the small bandage at his side. The marshal had called one of the town physicians over to the jail last night. It was only a flesh wound and the doctor had cleaned it and pronounced that he would live. But it was a painful reminder of the fact that she had shot him without the least hesitation. He had little doubt she'd carry out this latest threat. For just a moment he seriously considered which was worse, hanging or going after Sam Bass. One was immediate, the other could buy him a little time.

"You don't leave me much choice, Miss Tyson."

"That was my intention, Mr. Reno." As she started down the boardwalk toward the livery stables, he reluctantly fell into step beside her.

"By the way," he added, as if they were carrying on a casual conversation any two people on the street would share, "you can call me Jake."

Revel gave him a sideways glance. He'd said it as if he were granting her permission. Considering the poor night's sleep she'd had and those damned nauseating eggs, it was the last thing she wanted to hear.

"You may call me, Miss Tyson," she informed him coolly, deliberately setting an emotional distance between them.

He readjusted his long-legged stride to keep pace with her shorter one. In spite of his height and broad-shouldered frame he moved noiselessly beside her.

"I'll call you Revel," he announced without breaking stride, setting an emotional pace of his own. "I prefer first names. It helps to know the person you have to rely on."

It was subtle, but it was a struggle for control . . . and an even more subtle warning—she could only push Jake Reno so far, and would have only so much say in future decisions.

Trying to control Jake Reno had had an inherent danger from the beginning. She'd known that from the information she had on him. He was a loner and liked doing things his way. But Revel had been on her own for a long time too, and was equally accustomed to making her own decisions.

She stopped, focusing in on something else he said. *"Rely on?* What are you talking about? You're the guide. I'm going to be relying on *you.* I'd say I'm the one who has something to worry about."

The knot of aggravation in her stomach tightened

100

another half-twist when he simply continued walking away from her. Revel quickly caught up with him.

"What did you mean by that?" she insisted as she jerked at his arm.

Jake stopped, turned, and looked down at Revel Tyson. He noticed a few things he'd been too angry to take in on the two previous occasions they met. At any rate, the occasions—his imminent hanging and recent shooting—had been anything but ideal. However, in both instances, he'd been confident of avoiding any further contact with Miss Tyson.

He'd been wrong. Like it or not, he was about to have a great deal of contact with Miss Tyson—until he could come up with a plan—and he wanted to know the person he was going to entrust with watching his back . . . at least for the next few days.

It was obvious that she could be stubborn as hell! She had a way of circling around something, coming in at it from different angles, not letting up until she got exactly what she wanted. And what she had wanted and been determined to have from the very beginning was him.

It occurred to him, she had more obstinacy, more stick-to-itiveness than any one he'd ever met . . . except perhaps himself. And the truth was he didn't know quite what he thought about that or what to do about it.

The only thing he was certain about was the fact that she was determined, come hell or high water, to go after Sam Bass.

Well, he was just as determined that he *wasn't* going after Bass. But until he knew exactly how he was going to accomplish *not* doing that, he had no choice. He couldn't outrun her, she'd proved that last night. And she was smart. She'd figured out exactly where he could be found. As it was, she had showed up at a pretty embarrassing moment. He didn't usually have an audience when he visited Lilly or one of her girls.

As he stared down at Revel, trying to figure out just how the hell to get himself out of this, he remembered the way she'd looked the night before, standing there in the middle of Lilly's fancy bedroom, all spit and fire, dressed like a man, with all that dark, shining hair waving down around her shoulders.

He knew she'd been just as embarrassed as he was. Even in the meager light he could see the stain of color that heated her cheeks. But she had remained cool and calm, just like ice on a frosty mornin'. Except for those blue eyes of hers. There was nothing frosty about those eyes.

They flashed hellfire at him, reminding him of brilliant blue stones he once saw in a jeweler's window in St. Louis.

Sapphires—rich, fiery, with deep-colored facets that kept changing when you looked at them. Her eyes had been like that last night, dark sapphire pools with glints of light from that lantern.

This morning, their fire was the morning sun reflecting through deep blue, and Jake felt a familiar warning. A man could get himself in lots of trouble over those eyes.

And there were other signs of the trouble that lay ahead. The angle of her small chin, notched higher as she met his gaze while standing toe-to-toe with him on the boardwalk. The delicate curve of her mouth, almost as interesting as those eyes, thinned with anger.

For the life of him, Jake couldn't figure out what she had to be angry about. *He* was the one about to get himself killed going after Sam Bass.

No, he decided as he stood there, trying to decide how to get himself out of this latest predicament, she wasn't pretty. Not in the sense that other women he knew were pretty. He conceded that most of the women he knew enhanced their features with paint, rouge, and powders. Revel Tyson's beauty was more natural. It was in the color of those eyes, the stain of embarrassment—or anger—that darkened her cheeks, the animation of her features, the elegant curve of her neck. And her skin was flawless.

When he first saw her back in Tombstone, her skin had

reminded him of fine satin. That hadn't changed, and he sincerely doubted she wore even a dusting of pale powder to enhance that translucent quality. He wondered if she had any idea what weeks on the trail, under a blazing sun, would do to skin like that. He doubted it. And then there were her clothes.

Two days ago she'd been dressed like any fashionable lady of quality. That was part of the reason he was so surprised when he learned she was a Pinkerton agent. All the agents he'd had any experience with were men. But it was nothing to compare with his surprise the night before in Lilly's room, when she stepped from the shadows calm as you please with a gun in her hand—and dressed like a man.

It was a disguise to get inside the Red Garter without arousing suspicion, but it proved she was clever and determined. This morning he had his doubts about that, though, along with everything else involved with this harebrained plan of hers.

She was waiting for an answer to her question, stubbornness strung taut in every angle of her slender body as she faced him with hands on her hips. Jake wasn't about to be cornered by someone who was almost half his size. And he wasn't going to give her the satisfaction of explaining himself—in any way. So, he simply changed the direction of their conversation as he tilted his head back and gave her a critical look from under the brim of his hat.

"Is that what you're goin' to wear?"

Keeping up with Jake Reno, figuratively and otherwise, was like trying to keep up with a whirlwind. His original comment and her anger over it evaporated like water in the hot desert sun. He had a way of sidestepping issues and conversations.

Now, he had done it again, making some innocuous comment that made her angry. She had a feeling it was precisely what he intended, and therefore she refused to be provoked.

103

"What is *wrong* with what I'm wearing?" she asked in a carefully modulated voice, as if they were simply standing there discussing the weather.

There was nothing simple or innocuous in the way Jake Reno slowly looked her up and down. Revel bit at the inside of her cheek with suppressed fury as she waited with outward calm for him to complete his inspection.

"I would have thought after the way you were dressed last night, that you had more sense about what to wear on a trip like this," he stated as if making a casual observation.

"The way I was dressed last night served a purpose, Mr. Reno," she calmly began to explain, only to be interrupted.

"Call me Jake."

Her fingers curled into tight-balled fists. She took a deep breath and let it out slowly.

"I chose to wear this"—she made a brief gesture down the length of her blouse and split, woolen skirt to the toes of her immaculately polished, and obviously new, black leather boots—"because it serves a purpose for the trip ahead." She went on to explain.

"It will be a long ride. I'm told the terrain will be rough, especially if we're forced to ride into Mexico."

"Uh-huh," Jake remarked, rolling his tongue into his cheek but saying nothing.

"I could hardly wear my regular clothing. A dress would hamper my ability to ride—"

"Then you *can* ride a horse?"

"Of course, I can. I've ridden a great deal," she snapped. "At any rate, a dress is hardly suitable for living out on the trail. I had this skirt made in Denver."

"Uh-huh."

"And my boots"—her voice rose a notch, for the simple reason that she couldn't possibly see why she had to explain any of this—"are sturdy and perfectly sufficient. They will keep my feet dry should we encounter any bad weather."

They were a typical man's boot; high heeled, stiff leather, but in a smaller size that might have been made for a boy.

"And of course, you have a poncho and a hat."

She blinked uncertainly. The only hats she had were coordinated to be worn with two of her finer gowns. She didn't really think either one would look appropriate with the outfit she had on, and she hadn't the slightest idea what a poncho was. What she did have was the vague feeling that Jake Reno was trying to make her feel ill prepared or inadequate. And she wasn't about to let him do that.

She settled the matter with an indignant toss of her long, bound hair over one shoulder. "I have everything I shall need for the trip, Mr. Reno."

"Good, glad to hear that. Now tell me, how do you feel about blisters," he gave her outfit another critical glance, "saddle sores, snakebites, and bein' scalped by Indians?"

He'd done it again. One minute they were discussing the merits of her clothing and the next he was off in another direction.

"You will find I can handle myself quite well, Mr. Reno."

He recalled how she'd aimed that gun straight at him the night before.

"Call me Jake, and we'll see about that," he said as he walked on ahead of her. He stepped down off the boardwalk and crossed the street toward the livery stable, not bothering to see if she was following or to wait for her to catch up. He stopped abruptly.

"All right, where is this fella who's goin' along with us?"

She was right behind him, but acted as if she hadn't heard his question as she sidestepped him and went to the stables in search of the owner.

"Mr. Adams, is everything that I requested ready?"

The burly owner came forward from the back of the huge barn. He was barechested and wore a leather apron over worn pants. Muscles bulged from his arms. In one hand he held a huge hammer, in the other was a large horseshoe clamped in huge pincers. The tip of the pincers and the horseshoe glowed deep, fiery red. Rivulets of sweat poured off him. He had obviously been working over the smithy's fire in back.

"Out back." He gestured with the hammer over his shoulder. "Corral on yer right. I got everythin' jes' like you asked, Miss Tyson."

"Thank you." She started to walk through the barn to the corrals in back when Jake caught up with her.

"About that other man—" he insisted, only to be cut off.

"I instructed Mr. Adams to outfit us with supplies for one month. I think you'll find everything we need. I also took the liberty of making a special purchase for you."

As they stepped out into the sunlit yard edged with paddocks and corrals, Jake had the nagging feeling that she was deliberately avoiding an answer. In the corral to the right he saw the two mules already packed with gear, along with a sorrel gelding that at a casual glance looked to be a sound animal. Then he saw the Appaloosa. He slowly walked over to the corral.

"Easy, boy," he said soothingly as he stepped through the gate and walked up to the stallion. He slowly reached out, running an appraising hand over the smoky blue hide that rippled over heavy muscles and taut tendons. There was no tension, no nervousness as the Appaloosa caught his scent, only a soft nicker of greeting as the stallion turned his finely angled head toward Jake and nudged him sharply in the shoulder.

"So, you haven't forgotten me, have you?" Jake combed his lean fingers through the coarse salt-and-pepper mane, scratched behind an ear that angled sharply forward, then stroked down that velvety, steel gray muzzle. The Appaloosa nibbled gently at Jake's hand, then tossed its head.

"No, you haven't forgotten. I didn't forget either." He

spoke softly. Then, ignoring the reins and grabbing a handful of thick mane, he swung atop the tall stallion. He leaned forward, untied the reins, and loosely draped them over the Appaloosa's neck. Then with only the subtle pressure of his knees he took the Appaloosa through his paces—walk, canter, trot, left turn, right turn, and then returned to the corner of the corral where Revel Tyson waited.

He knew what she'd done, bringing the Appaloosa here. And he knew exactly why she'd done it, extra enticement. She had also arranged for him to have his own saddle and bridle. His rifle with the distinctive carving on the wood handle was slipped inside the scabbard at the saddle, and unless he missed his guess, that was the belt of his holster protruding from the rolled blanket behind the saddle.

As much as he appreciated having all his things back, especially the Appaloosa, he knew he would pay fully for them if he went along on this trip. She must want Sam Bass awful bad.

He also knew something else now. "There isn't anybody else riding with us, is there?"

It was a question for which he already knew the answer. She had avoided an answer earlier. She didn't try to pretend any longer.

"No, there isn't." She met his gaze directly, then after several long moments looked away.

"I'd be willing to bet there never was."

Her gaze snapped back to his. She heard all the subtle, unsaid things behind the sarcastic reply.

"The fact is, *Mr. Reno*, the Pinkerton National Detective Agency is confident of my skills, and I have the authority to call in whatever assistance we may need."

"A woman."

It was a scathing comment that in two little words summed up Jake Reno's feelings about her.

"A woman," she clarified, "who managed to shoot you."

107

"You were so nervous, you almost missed," he pointed out.

Revel came at him. "I shot you exactly where I intended. Any other place and you wouldn't be of any use to me. Now"—she took a deep breath—"we're wasting time arguing. It doesn't matter what you think, Mr. Reno. The fact is we *are* going after Sam Bass. The only question is whether you want to go with one bullet hole in your worthless hide, or two."

Jake was no longer amused. Everything was all wrong, starting with the fact that there was no other Pinkerton agent, going right on down the line to the fact that Miss Revel Tyson was hardly prepared for the journey she was so damned determined to make. She was dressed wrong, she was ill equipped, and he had no idea how she would really react in a bad situation. And as far as he could see, nothing but bad situations waited for them.

He shifted in the saddle, the restrained power of the Appaloosa under him a subtle reminder that less than forty-eight hours ago he was seconds away from hanging. He'd been prepared to steal the Appaloosa back. It didn't much matter to him if he ended up stealing it from Revel Tyson.

"What's to keep me from just slipping out one night once we're out there on the trail and leaving you to fend for yourself?"

She squinted up into the morning sun that peaked over his shoulder. It narrowed the blue of her eyes, so that it was impossible to read the emotions there.

"I won't tie you up, Mr. Reno. And obviously I can't stay awake every minute of the day and night to make certain that you don't leave. But you're still a wanted man," she pointed out.

"What's to keep me from shooting you and simply riding on back to Tombstone and telling them you changed your mind? There would be nobody to dispute my word. Marshal Earp would sign those papers and I'd be a free man." The conversation had gone from simple antagonism to outright hostility.

"Except for one thing, *Mr. Reno*," she hissed with barely suppressed fury, "one small detail. *My* signature on those amnesty papers." She went on to explain exactly what she meant so there would be no doubt or confusion. It was the one precaution she'd taken against what he was suggesting.

"If anything happens to me, if for any reason I don't return to sign those papers, then you're still a wanted man and you're still sentenced to hang. It's that simple."

Jake didn't doubt she was telling the truth. Just by the little he'd learned about her over the past two days, he knew she was thorough. He was willing to bet that telegram she had sent to Tombstone gave Virgil Earp specific instructions in case he did show up without her. He had to hand it to her, she'd taken care of everything. At least she thought she had.

"All right," he slowly conceded, but in a way that made Revel wary. "It looks like I don't have much choice about that."

"No," she answered, "you don't have any choice at all." Then, taking the reins of her own horse, she put her foot in the stirrup and pulled herself into the saddle.

Just as she swung the sorrel about to lead the way out of the corral and begin their journey, Jake leaned over and grabbed the rope that secured the pack atop the closest mule.

He jerked the knot and the rope fell slack, immediately sending pots, pans, sacked flour and beans, along with numerous other items tumbling into a pile of manure under the mule's feet.

At the loud racket, the mule sidestepped and flattened back it's ears. Still tethered to the fence, it bucked and jumped, stiff-legged, dislodging everything else in the pack.

Revel stared, openmouthed, as Jake leaned over and grabbed the rope that secured the provisions atop the second mule. Before she could yell at him to stop, the second mule danced sideways, eyes rolling wildly.

She had her hands full as she tried to control the excited sorrel. When she finally calmed him and turned around to survey the damage, she could only stare with disbelief at Jake Reno.

In a matter of seconds, the packs atop both mules lay scattered in the dust across the corral or mired in manure.

Her furious gaze fastened on him with an expression that spoke volumes. He had no doubt she would just as soon shoot him again as look at him, and he didn't give a damn.

"I do have a choice about what I take with me. And *that*"—he pointed to the mules and their discarded packs—"will only slow us down and draw attention." He turned in the saddle and shouted over his shoulder to the stable owner.

"Stoney! Rig me two packs with supplies for a fast, hard ride."

The smithy had reappeared in the doorway. "The usual?"

"Yeah, the usual."

Revel was furious. She edged the sorrel over to Jake.

"Those supplies were expensive! We need everything."

"Most of them are completely useless on a hard ride," Jake flung back at her. Then he leaned across his saddle, and there was no doubt at all as to the emotion that glittered in his hard green eyes.

"If I'm gonna get myself killed, I'll do it my way," he spat out at her, "and I *do* have a choice about that, Miss Revel Tyson!"

He jerked the Appaloosa around and headed out of the corral as he shouted over his shoulder.

"I want those packs ready in an hour, Stoney!" he bellowed. Then he stopped the Appaloosa and looked back at Revel. "And I suggest you get yourself a poncho and some decent boots."

Chapter Six

If she didn't need him so badly, Revel would have joyfully shot Jake Reno, and this time it wouldn't be a simple flesh wound!

He set a murderous pace when they left Tucson, and she had no doubt it was to prove a very specific point. That point being that she had neither the sense nor the stamina to be making this trip.

After their confrontation at the livery stable, Jake had gone back to the Red Garter to pick up the belongings he'd brought with him from Tombstone. Revel had gone in search of a poncho. Once she discovered what one was—a tightly woven wool garment, sleeveless and with a hood, that was worn loosely draped about the body much like a tent—she saw that it did have merit. Although for the life of her, she couldn't figure out why he'd insisted she have one when the weather was blistering hot.

As for his suggestion about the boots, she was perfectly content with the boots she had. They were practical, fit well enough, and would no doubt hold up under rough conditions. If he dared make another comment about them, she would give him a suggestion about what he could do with his opinions in general.

Riding out across the small valley that surrounded Tucson, they struck a silent truce, which meant that as long as they didn't say anything to one another, they weren't quarreling.

111

She knew exactly what he thought about going after Sam Bass, and she didn't want to hear any more about it. If he so much as turned around in the saddle, she would tell him precisely that for no other reason than to emphasize the fact that she wasn't the least intimidated by him.

The problem was he didn't turn around, not even once throughout the long hours of the morning and afternoon when they didn't even stop long enough to stretch their legs.

So Revel continued to glare at his back as he led the way along some invisible path that at times looked vaguely familiar, at others seemed completely foreign.

She silently dared him to turn around so she could have the delicious satisfaction of proving to him that she could keep up and was indeed up to this trip.

But the truth was, the pace was beginning to wear on her. All the bragging and confidence in the world couldn't disguise the fact that it had been years since she'd ridden a horse for any length of time, and then not astride as she rode now. If Jake Reno knew her most recent experience was riding sidesaddle he would laugh himself to death.

"I won't give you that satisfaction," she whispered angrily at his back through dried lips, "and I won't go back."

For all her bravado and determination, Revel faced the facts. Not only were her lips and throat dry, but her face burned, her back ached, and her leg muscles were cramped. And those were the parts of her body she could still feel.

By late afternoon, when he pushed them onward through a pass in the hills, they had already spent almost eight hours in the saddle. And her bottom was numb.

Revel's only consolation was that what she couldn't feel obviously couldn't hurt.

Jake gave her two days—three tops—before she begged him to stop and turn around, and finally admitted all this was a lousy idea. Because he preferred two days instead of three, which would put them at the edge of Indian territory, he set a grueling pace that would have been hard for a man, much less a fancy-dressed, fancy-talking, high-minded, East Coast female.

They rode long past dusk as Jake picked his way past landmarks that were familiar even in the ghostly gray moonlight as night descended.

He'd had plenty of experience traveling at night. Like other night predators, a man with a price on his head could move about then in the open.

It must have been after midnight when they finally made a cold camp beneath a stand of trees. Further south there would be no trees to speak of, only wide-open flatness occasionally broken by the upward thrust of pinnacled rock formations. But here, Jake intended to make good use of the tree cover while they could.

They were up before first light, and not once did Revel Tyson complain. In fact, they hadn't exchanged more than two words, which suited Jake just fine. The only thing that wasn't fine was the fact that she obviously hadn't changed her mind about going after Sam Bass. He could tell that by the defiant angle of her chin.

If she isn't careful, he thought as he glanced around once, she'll get the damned thing sunburned, she has it jerked so high.

The second day, Jake called a halt just as it was getting dark. The horses were tired, and he found a suitable place to make camp at the edge of a small wash. This time of year, the water was reduced to nothing more than a trickle.

Jake tethered and unsaddled the Appaloosa. Then, without so much as a passing word, he walked away with his saddle, saddlebags, and blanket roll.

Still astride the sorrel, Revel stared after him. She blinked several times and only then realized she must have dozed in the saddle. The lack of motion had awakened her.

"Where are we?"

"South of Tucson," came the terse reply.

Revel glared at the spot where he'd disappeared in the gathering inky darkness of night. She knew directions very well, and was prefectly aware they had been traveling south and southeast much of the time.

She swallowed back the dryness in her throat and groaned through parched lips. That was another thing, he had insisted they ration their water. He hadn't allowed her to drink more than three times yesterday or today, and only one swallow each time. He insisted they had to conserve water, just in case.

In case of what, for heaven's sake? She tried again, smothering back her aggravation.

"What is this place?" she croaked dryly.

Jake reappeared briefly to remove the Appaloosa's bridle. He looked around as if taking survey of the land, which was for the most part impossible considering the growing darkness.

He shrugged. "That's a rise, that's a wash, and that is water."

Jake Reno was being deliberately sarcastic, and for the second time in as many days, Revel considered shooting him right where he stood.

Let the buzzards have his damned hide!

At that moment she didn't care one whit that she'd promised she wouldn't let him intimidate her, which was precisely what he was trying to do. But if the buzzards did get his miserable hide, she wouldn't get Sam Bass.

She came back to the safe territory of trying to extract simple information, which in itself was anything but simple. "How far did we ride today?" There that was easy enough and not controversial. He should have no problem answering something like that.

"I'd say twenty, maybe twenty-five miles." He neatly wrapped the reins of the bridle about his arm, patted the Appaloosa, and then turned to leave.

"Well, which is it, twenty or twenty-five miles?"

114

He shrugged as he walked away. "We'll know tomorrow."

Revel's eyes narrowed. "Why don't we know tonight?" She persisted, wanting to be certain of exactly where they were. She heard a deep sigh that could have been fatigue, but she suspected it meant his patience was wearing thin. His tone of voice was one he might have used with a child.

"Because we're not there yet."

"Where?"

She could just make out the outline of his tall, lean body in the fading twilight. For a moment there was no answer, then he said, "You'd better get down off that horse. You might not need the rest, but your horse does."

Revel shifted uncomfortably in the saddle. She would have liked nothing better than to get down, but this was one of those situations where the mind was willing but the body wasn't. And he still hadn't answered her question. Why the devil did he have to be so damned difficult?

"I'll be down in a minute," she mumbled, and then continued conversationally since he was at least speaking to her again. "Where, specifically, are we going?"

There were faint sounds of movement, the unpacking of a saddlebag, something heavy being dropped into place—probably his saddle. Then she heard the familiar klink of metal as he unscrewed the cap from his water canteen. She tried to lift her right knee. Nothing.

She tried again, but she simply could not lift her knee to dismount.

Oh, God! What was she going to do? The numbness had spread to her legs. She couldn't get down off that horse!

The reality of that predicament wasn't nearly so humiliating as the idea of what her only solution was— Jake Reno would have to lift her down.

She groaned. That is, if he would lift her down, which

115

she was quite certain he would contemplate long and hard before lifting a hand to help her. It had been that way last night and she had every confidence nothing was changed tonight.

"Be sure to tether the gelding after you unsaddle him," he called back to her. "You don't want him to run off in the middle of the night. It's a long walk."

Tether? Unsaddle? Walk?

It was clear, Jake Reno had absolutely no intention of helping her. But at that precise moment, that was the least of her troubles. She would have gladly walked anywhere, just to have feeling back in her legs. The problem was, she wasn't certain she could stand, much less take a step.

Jake untied the cotton sacks inside his leather saddlebags and found dinner, which consisted of hardtack and corn tortillas. Then he made a small fire. Here there were downed limbs and rotted-out tree stumps. Once they reached the desert there would be no trees and no wood.

In spite of the way he felt about Revel Tyson, he grinned when he heard that groan. If he calculated right, she should hurt in just about every part of her body. That would give her something to think about.

He heard another groan, and then looked up with faint surprise as a muffled curse came to him.

He grinned again. "My, my, Miss Tyson, what a temper you have."

He'd been hard on her, deliberately hard. By late morning tomorrow, they would reach Fort Buchanan and he would hire a guide under the pretense of being taken into the Indian territory. If he found the man he was looking for, he gave her one more day to change her mind about this damned trip. Then he would be on his way to Wyoming.

Revel slid down the side of the sorrel, holding onto the saddle for support. Her legs buckled under her.

"Damn!" she hissed as she pulled herself upright, clinging to the saddle.

Miraculously, in the next few moments feeling tingled back into her legs. She soon regretted it. Her muscles spasmed, her bones ached, and she felt as if liquid fire burned through her skin. What was worse, her limbs wouldn't respond to even the simplest command.

Her hands limply grasped the saddle cinch. She tried to move one foot and both feet went out from under her. She landed on her bottom in the dirt. Instead of crying out, she simply slumped forward, too weary to know or care what happened next.

That was precisely where Jake found her, and silently cursed, knowing how lucky she was that the sorrel was an even-tempered animal. Any other horse would have trampled her to death.

At first he thought she was just sitting there, head slumped forward, stubbornly gathering her strength to get up. He knew the ride had been grueling. Then, as he came closer and gently prodded her shoulder, he realized she was sound asleep! He bent down and scooped her up.

"Damn little fool!"

Several more curses were on the tip of his tongue.

"I should leave you here; you deserve it," he muttered.

But he didn't. Maybe some small twinge of conscience needled him for the way he'd pushed her the past two days. Maybe it was insanity, the same insanity that had crossed his path with hers in the first place. Or maybe it was because all her anger and muleheadedness was temporarily silenced so that he could really get a good look at her.

Miss Revel Tyson, Pinkerton Agent, and the world's most incredibly foolish and stubborn female, was also the most aggravating woman he had ever met.

She was also much smaller than he'd first thought, and incredibly soft snuggled against him. She should have

117

smelled of sweat and leather and dirt, but she smelled faintly of lilacs and sun and wind. The combination made other old memories rush through him.

Jake wanted to push her away and hold her close at the same time. For a brief moment he gave in, feeling her softness mold against the roughness of his jacket and the hardened planes of his body beneath it.

That brief contact awakened more memories, and emotions he'd thought long dead. Relaxed against him, her cool reserve stripped away, Revel seemed younger somehow.

Her lashes brushed against her sunburned cheeks like dark half-moons. Her long hair had come undone from the twist of ribbon and lay tousled and tangled about her shoulders. Her lips were softly parted as she breathed in exhausted slumber.

She was suddenly so small in his arms, the fight and stubbornness worn out of her, that for an instant she seemed like a child. And, like a child, there was something achingly vulnerable about her.

The vulnerability cut right through him.

Jake swallowed hard and pulled himself together. He stood in one quick movement and carried her to the small fire he'd built. For a moment he stood in indecision. Then he set her down on the blanket he'd already spread beside the blaze. She murmured something unintelligible as he worked at removing her boots, but never opened her eyes.

Her boots finally came off, but not without a struggle. He threw them aside disgustedly; she was going to have blisters.

"Go back to sleep," he whispered gruffly, as he squatted down beside her and wrapped the blanket about her. He snugged in the edges much as he would if she were a child that needed protecting.

As he tucked the blanket around her neck, his callused fingers brushed against her skin. Her pulse beat like the brush of a bird's wing.

118

He should have stood and simply walked away. Jake knew that. He also knew he shouldn't touch her again, but he did. Memories whispered to him as he gently stroked her cheek with the backs of his fingers. Her skin was like satin, incredibly soft . . . and warm . . . incredibly alive. Not cold, pale, and lifeless . . .

Jake jerked his hand back as if he'd been burned. He angrily stode over to the horses and unsaddled the gelding. But still he wasn't able to shake the feelings she'd unexpectedly roused in him.

He jerked the saddle off, startling the gelding and causing him to sidestep nervously.

"Sorry, boy." He reached out and stroked the soft muzzle.

Bringing his emotions under control, Jake loosened the tether for each horse, allowing them enough lead to graze. Finally he was able to retreat once more behind the wall of cool indifference that always kept everyone at a distance. He hoisted Revel's saddle onto his shoulder and returned to camp.

"Tomorrow this is your responsibility," he said over his shoulder, as if she could hear him.

"I'm not going to wet-nurse you. If you can't hack it, then you'll just have to go back to Denver or wherever it is you came from and forget this damned idea."

The only answer was the faint hiss of wood on the fire.

He carried her saddle and saddlebags closer to their campsite, then settled himself in her blanket. But long after the night air had turned cold, and the fire had died down, the memory of soft skin against his hand burned in his memory.

Revel didn't remember anything of the night before. Everything was a blur the next morning, except for her pain. She hurt everywhere. She hurt in places too delicate to mention, not that she would have discussed them with Jake Reno anyway. And she hurt in places she didn't know existed.

He sat across the fire from her, casually sipping a cup

119

of that strong black mud he dared to call coffee. He looked disgustingly well rested, but worse, as if the ride hadn't had any effect on him.

So much for the thoroughness of my training as a Pinkerton agent, Revel thought. Nothing in her experience had prepared her for the grueling pace he'd set the last two days.

Her eyes narrowed as she stared at him. He was trying to break her. As if he sensed that she was staring at him, he looked up.

"Coffee?" He gestured with the tin cup. "It's good for what ails you first thing in the morning."

Revel was certain she saw a trace of a smirk on his lips. *You're what ails me!* she wanted to scream at him, but didn't dare let him know that anything he was doing had the least little effect on her. She wouldn't give him that satisfaction, and simply said with a shudder, "No, thank you." She began picking at the tangles in her hair. She would try standing in a few minutes.

Jake nodded thoughtfully as he cradled the cup in his long fingers.

"I guess you're one of those who likes tea instead of coffee."

Her gaze snapped up to meet his. From anyone else a statement like that could have been considered polite conversation. Jake Reno was anything *but* polite. Revel was convinced everything he said and did had a very specific purpose. And by his tone of voice, she knew she'd been right about the smirk.

She tossed her hair back over her shoulder and reached for a cup.

"I think I will have some coffee," she said, a thinly disguised challenge in her voice. Jake poured from the tin pot that simmered over the open fire.

Revel reached for the cup, then jerked her hand back.

Jake smiled, making a halfhearted attempt to smother his smugness. "I can see you don't have much experience in the kitchen. Did you bring gloves?"

120

Revel's fingers curled protectively over the blistered palms of her hands. He knew perfectly well she hadn't thought about gloves. She pulled a handkerchief from the cuff of her sleeve and used it for protection as she reached for the cup.

"Sip it slow. It's real hot."

She gave him a withering glare. "Thanks for that advice."

"I'll give you some more." He seized the opportunity since it had presented itself.

"No, thank you," she replied coolly.

"I beg your pardon?"

"You don't need to beg anything, Mr. Reno. The point is I don't need or want any advice from you."

Jake breathed in slowly as he finished his coffee. "Fine by me." He decided to change tactics. He was going to tell her she was a fool to continue this trip, but he could see that would only lead to another argument. He stood and tossed the remnants of his coffee into the grass. Then he kicked sand over the fire.

"I was simply going to point out, you should wrap something around your hands. I've seen men die of blood poisoning when blisters like that open up."

Revel frowned as she looked down at the palms of her hands. Overnight, angry red welts had been transformed to white, water-filled ridges on one hand. Yesterday, two blisters had opened on the other. When she flexed her fingers, it was obvious, the skin was badly inflamed and burned. He was right. It was just common sense. And she'd always prided herself on being practical.

"Thank you. I'll put something over them."

If she were anyone else, her agreeable answer would have surprised him, but as she'd already demonstrated by the mere fact that she was able to track him down—twice—she had more than average intelligence, and at times something that came close to common sense. That is, when she didn't let her stubbornness get in the way of it.

He shoved his hat down over his head and reached for his saddle and bridle.

"Be sure and drink all that coffee," he quipped as he went to saddle his horse. "It'll put hair on your chest."

Revel practically choked on the strong brew. Of all the insufferably rude things to say!

She glared at Jake Reno's back—the continuing target for her fury the last two days—and tossed the rest of the coffee out. She didn't need his coffee or his advice!

"Sun's up. Get your gear together, Revel."

The sun was just peeking over the eastern horizon. Revel hardly called that being up. The birds weren't even up yet; maybe they had better sense. Certainly no other creatures were up, and Revel definitely wasn't either. Not in the most literal sense.

Every muscle, sinew, and bone complained loud and clear as she tried to get to her feet. And he persisted in calling her by her first name, which moved her from aggravation to fury.

"Put your boots on. You never can tell what you might step on," Jake called casually over his shoulder.

"Thank you." Revel bit the words off sarcastically. Did he actually believe she didn't have enough sense to put her boots on?

"You might want to shake them out first," he suggested.

Revel closed her eyes. "Dear God, give me strength!" she whispered. Strength not to kill Jake Reno before he led her to Sam Bass, that is.

Jake glanced back over his shoulder, his mouth twisting into a pleased grin. He'd learned in four short days to judge the level of silence between them. At the moment she was silent, but she was fuming, and he couldn't resist a small feeling of satisfaction.

"Did you shake them out?"

Revel didn't need a gun!

At that moment anything that vaguely resembled a weapon would have done nicely. As a matter of fact, she

122

could have strangled him until he choked on that smug tone of voice. She didn't really want to know why she should shake her boots out. But if she didn't ask, he would simply keep at her with that damn superior attitude of his.

"All right, why should I shake out the boots?" She knew perfectly well they couldn't possibly have any dirt in them.

"Scorpions."

Revel blinked. "I beg your pardon?"

Jake tightened the cinch strap on the Appaloosa, then flipped down the stirrup. It seemed conversation this morning, if it could be called that, had gone from a word here, a word there to stiffly polite exchanges. He didn't know if that was an improvement or if he wanted it to be.

He gave her a quick glance. She'd combed her hair and straightened her clothes. Once again, she was the prim and proper East Coast lady, hellbent on finding an outlaw who had probably been dead the last three years. He preferred the winsome, vulnerable creature who'd snuggled against him last night.

With perverse humor he wondered just what she'd say if he mentioned that to her.

"Probably deny the whole damn thing," he muttered under his breath, without the slightest notion why that should irritate him. He shoved the memories of last night back, just as he shoved all the feelings they roused back into the safe oblivion of indifference. He slowly walked toward her.

"Scorpions," he repeated, since she seemed to have a difficult time grasping something the first time it was mentioned. And then he explained further. "They like to crawl into little nooks and crannies and hide. Boots, blanket rolls"—he paused for effect—"sometimes clothes. You just never know where the little devils are going to show up." He shook his head.

"Their sting can kill a person. It can be real painful too. You just swell all up, your skin gets real tight, and

123

you get a fever. It's the fever that gets you—causes huge blisters all over a person's insides. Then your throat swells shut and you can't drink any water. The fever just slowly burns you up. And all the time those blisters inside are breaking open and you swell up more and more, until . . . Pop!" he shook his head, his expression somber. He shuddered.

"It's not a pretty sight."

Revel stared at him wide-eyed. She'd never heard of such a thing!

Surely he was joking! Or . . . trying to scare her.

She wouldn't put anything past him. Still as she picked up one boot, she peeked inside.

"Well, I suppose it doesn't hurt to be careful."

She upended the boot and shook it, then shook the other boot. Nothing fell out, which raised the interesting question as to whether or not a scorpion was stuck in one of those nooks and crannies. He seemed to read her thoughts.

"That should do it, but you never know. One of them could be stuck up inside."

He gathered the rest of his things.

"I'll tell you what. If there is one still inside and he stings you, I'll try to get your body back to your family."

With that, he sauntered off toward the horses, whistling some disgusting tune that made Revel certain he was playing a joke on her. Well, almost certain.

She shook the boots out again, banging each one against a tree stump to dislodge any unwanted visitors. When she glanced back at Jake Reno she could have sworn his shoulders shook. He swung onto the back of the Appaloosa.

"Come along, Revel," he said as she pulled on her boots. "It takes a few hours for the swelling to begin. We can reach Fort Buchanan before that."

She had to scramble to keep up with him, which caused her to discover another source of pain—her backside.

Revel groaned inwardly. Just like the first night they

made camp, he had no intention of helping her saddle the gelding or pack her things.

She glanced down at the blanket she'd been sleeping on. It wasn't *her* blanket. Then she looked up at Jake Reno's departing back and frowned. That was all she had time for if she didn't want to be left behind.

Over the next couple of hours, Revel discovered why the terrain had seemed vaguely familiar over the past two days. Just over the rise of the wash lay the very same railroad tracks she'd traveled on her trip to Tucson.

It raised some very interesting questions, not the least of which was, why had Jake Reno felt it necessary to travel by horse when they could have traveled by train and reached Fort Buchanan in half the time?

She had the sneaking suspicion it was all part of his scheme to convince her against continuing this trip. Well, he certainly had another thought coming on that subject.

The long hours spent in the saddle the two previous days, plus little sleep throughout the night made Revel weary after only two hours of riding. She was grateful when the outbuildings at Fort Buchanan appeared in the distance. She was bruised, every part of her ached, and the sun was blistering hot. Revel silently hoped they would have time to rest, but she would die before she would ask him if that was the case.

They passed the small train depot and reined the horses in at the mercantile, which along with several small business establishments formed a small annex to the fort. Revel didn't dare try to dismount for fear she would embarrass herself and fall into the dirt, so weak were her legs.

Jake gave her a brief look as he dismounted and tied the Appaloosa to the hitching post before the mercantile.

"This shouldn't take too long, if I can find the man I'm looking for." He squinted against the sun as he looked up at her. Before she could pull back or protest, he seized one of her hands and turned it over in his.

125

She winced at the pressure of his grasp, blisters forming liquid arcs across the soft pads of her palm. In spite of the handkerchief she'd wrapped around her hand, several of the blisters had popped, the handkerchief sticking to the raw skin now exposed.

"I've seen people die from blood poisoning before." Jake glanced down at the hand he held captive.

Revel tried to pull back, but he wouldn't release her hand. The harder she tried to free it, the more pain that caused. She finally gave in.

"I suppose it's very much like your experience with scorpions," she snapped waspishly.

"Something like that." Jake grinned up at her in spite of himself. He knew she was hurting—and from more than just the blisters. He could see it in the way she held herself rigid against even the slightest jarring in the saddle, the strained look about her eyes, the constant shift of her body as she tried to find a comfortable position. He inclined his head toward the mercantile.

"C'mon. We need supplies." Without waiting for a comment much less her agreement, he reached up and unceremoniously hauled her down out of the saddle. Revel gasped at the pain that assaulted every part of her body.

"Damn you!" she gasped as she collapsed against him and was forced to hang on for support.

Jake supported her slender form with ease. He knew exactly what she was feeling, although it had been some time since he'd been that sore from riding a horse. It served her right, he told himself, at the same time his eyes darkened with a far different emotion than anger at the feel of her slender body against his.

"I'm already damned, Revel," he said softly, causing her to look up. "It happened the day you walked into that jailhouse in Tombstone."

Need.

It was subtle, riding along every nerve ending in little frissions of restless energy—a raw physical ache that

126

clamored with a deeper emotional need. She was soft beneath his hands, her hair like sweet sunshine.

He took a deep breath to get back the control that meant safety, and felt it skitter beyond his grasp at just the touch of her.

Smell. Touch. Taste.

The sun drove relentless heat through him. She *was* beautiful. It was impossible not to see it. The sweet-sunshine smell, the feel of her, was all woman. It hinted at other women he'd known.

She would be different, and he found himself wanting to taste the difference. Right here, right now.

He could pull her closer and kiss her.

She would taste of sun and wind, dry desert and cool nights.

And there would be heat. She was capable of it in a way he was certain she hadn't even discovered yet.

Even as he cursed himself for it, he gently shoved her away, holding on just enough to make certain she was steady on her feet.

As she slid against the length of his body, trapped by the gelding at her back, he shifted his hands higher to steady her.

It was a simple gesture. Revel had been lifted down from atop a horse before, but nothing prepared her for the brush of his bare, rough hands against the sides of her breasts.

The contact was brief, over almost before either realized it had happened, but Revel's skin tingled beneath the fabric of her shirtwaist. Something deep inside her curled into a knot of tight-wound heat, and her breath caught in her throat. Even as she recoiled away from him in the small space allowed between man and horse, some small part of her wondered what it might feel like to turn into those hands and feel them close completely over her. She should have been embarrassed at the very least, but instead felt only an unreasonable anger. If she had to say where the anger came from, she couldn't have. It was

127

simply there—a self-protective reaction. But against what? Her voice was a shaky whisper.

"Don't touch me like that."

There was an amused expression on Jake's face. He threw his hands up in mock surrender.

"It was a simple mistake."

"See that it doesn't happen again."

His expression shifted to curiosity tinged with anger as she tried to sidestep and escape around him.

"Why?"

Her head snapped up. She wasn't used to accounting to anyone, least of all an outlaw—someone who less than four days ago was sentenced to hang and could be again with just a word from her. Her anger shifted to controlled coolness.

"We don't know each other, Mr. Reno, and beyond what I need of you, I have no intention of associating with you."

"What do you need from me, Revel?"

Those penetrating green eyes pinned her back, making it impossible to escape even if she could step past him.

Everything she'd ever thought about him came winging back to her in a rush of fear. This man was dangerous, more dangerous as he took a half-step closer, shutting out the safe distance between them.

He brought both arms up, reaching around her to brace his weight against the gelding, creating a prison of muscle, sinew, and masculine heat.

"I . . . I need you as a guide . . ." She stumbled over the words, and tried again. "I need you to take me to Sam—"

He silenced her with fingers gently pressed against her lips.

"What do you need, Revel?"

Then he took his fingers away, aware of the look of confusion that darkened her blue eyes. She drew in an uncertain breath.

128

"I need you . . ." She got no further in this confusing game of words.

"Yes, you do," he answered simply, as he dropped his hands to his sides.

Then his expression changed. That and the unexpected softness in his voice made Revel think she had been mistaken in what she'd heard.

"Let's get those supplies." His voice was once more indifferent. "We'll need more than just hardtack and coffee after we leave here."

Revel stared after him as he disappeared inside the mercantile. For that one moment when he'd held her, he hadn't been the outlaw described in those handbills and Pinkerton case files—the cold, hardened gunfighter she'd saved from the gallows in Tombstone. For just a moment, she had seen a side of him she knew nothing about, and she wondered about all the things that never appeared in a file—about Jake Reno . . . the man.

He was already standing before the long wood counter, when she walked inside the mercantile. He gave the owner a list of the supplies they needed. That revealed something else she hadn't known about him—he could read and write. Once again, she was surprised.

He nodded to the owner of the store and then turned around. "You might be able to find some gloves here. I suggest you buy yourself a pair. It'll help with those hands." Then he moved past her to the door.

"And a hat," he added, giving her a thorough inspection.

"Oh, and some pants. It'll make it easier to ride."

"I'm doing very well, thank you. I'm quite comfortable the way I am." She bit off the growing anger that always seemed to be there between them.

"Yeah." Jake rolled his tongue in his cheek. "And I'll just bet you've got blisters on your backside to match the ones on your hands."

Of all the insufferable, rude, overbearing, thought-

129

less things to say!

Her sunburned cheeks flamed a few shades deeper in embarrassment. But before she recovered enough to tell Jake exactly what she thought of his suggestion or to remind him of his still very precarious position with the law, he was on his way out the door.

"If I find who I'm looking for, we can still ride several more hours before sundown," he called back over his shoulder.

Revel tried not to show her disappointment. She had hoped they might be stopping here for the night. Just a few hours of sleep on anything that wasn't the ground, or the constantly moving backside of a horse, would do wonders. But she realized Jake Reno wasn't the least concerned with her need for sleep or comfort. The only thing he was concerned with was that she not die of blood poisoning before she signed the authorization for his amnesty papers.

Well, she could keep up with him any day of the week. She would be ready to leave when he was.

Jake had obviously forgotten something on the list. He poked his head back inside the store and smiled at the owner of the shop.

"Just total everything up. The lady will pay for it." With that, he was gone, the door snapping loudly behind him.

Revel added a few purchases of her own, including the gloves he'd suggested.

It's only practical, she told herself. But she refused to buy a pair of men's pants when the split skirt she wore suited her just fine.

The storekeeper totaled the bill and she paid it. Ten minutes later she stepped out onto the boardwalk, pulling on the buttery soft, leather gloves. The pressure over her blistered palms was excruciating, but she knew the gloves would prevent further damage.

She refused to acknowledge, much less consider, that

he might also have been right about her backside.

Revel ordered a glass of lemonade over at the boardinghouse. By the time she finished it and returned to the horses tied in front of the mercantile, Jake was waiting for her.

His gaze immediately fastened on the leather gloves that covered her hands.

"Where's the hat?"

Her jaw muscles went rigid. "There wasn't one that fit. I can do very nicely without one."

She cried out as he tweaked her sunburned nose.

"Uh-huh. I'll remind you of that in a few days, when your nose peels raw."

Before she could say anything, he introduced her to the man standing beside him.

"This is Broken Hand. He'll be taking us into Indian territory."

Beside him stood a bent, gnarled old Indian. She immediately recognized those mahogany eyes and the faint hidden smile that worked behind a crooked, misshapen hand. It was the Indian guide she had met on the stage from Tombstone.

Jake saw the look of recognition. "You two know one another?"

"We met briefly, on the trip from Tombstone," Revel answered simply. In their brief contact, she suspected she had found a friend in the old Indian. She strongly suspected she would need a friend on the journey that lay ahead. And she knew it wouldn't be Jake Reno.

"He knows the way across the high desert," Jake explained. "That is, unless you've changed your mind about all this."

In answer, Revel seized the gelding's reins and carefully pulled herself into the saddle. She swung the gelding around, her mouth thinned into a determined line.

"I haven't changed my mind." Then she added, "I

131

thought you knew the way across the desert."

"I do," Jake said as he grabbed the Appaloosa's reins and swung effortlessly into the saddle. The saddlebags were filled with supplies and secured behind his and Revel's saddles.

"Broken Hand is our insurance."

She frowned. "Insurance for what?"

Jake gave her a steady, penetrating look. "Insurance against getting scalped."

Chapter Seven

"The Valley of the Blood Moon," Broken Hand was saying as they stopped to water the horses at the fork of the river they had been following since leaving Fort Buchanan the day before. They were traveling steadily eastward, toward the New Mexico Territory.

Broken Hand gestured to the cut in the canyon walls and the valley beyond.

Revel shaded her eyes as she gazed in the direction he was pointing.

"Why do they call it that?"

The old Indian guide grunted, "Many blue-coats die there, trapped between the canyon walls."

As she had learned was his way, he said nothing more, leaving it to her imagination to guess about the *blue-coats* and the *Blood Moon*.

"The Blood Moon is an old Apache legend," Jake explained as he joined them in the sparse shade of a tree at the water's edge. "Supposedly the Blood Moon appears when some tragic event is about to take place. The Apache believe in it's magic."

Revel was fascinated. "When did it last appear?"

Jake had doused himself in the river and now shook droplets of water from his long hair. "It has appeared twice in recent years," he said. "Once when the Indians made the journey over the Trail of Death and so many died on the way. The last time was when the Apache renegades followed the soldiers into that canyon and killed them all in revenge."

"Revenge?"

Broken Hand nodded as he stood. "They were warned about the Blood Moon, but chose not to believe. They all died." He made a slicing motion with his right hand. And then added, "Scalped!"

With that he left their circle to refill the water skins he carried instead of the metal canteens.

"Broken Hand is a full-blood Apache. His wife, two daughters, and three grandchildren died on the Trail of Death."

Revel's gaze came back to Jake Reno. "What is the Trail of Death?"

He refilled his canteens with fresh water and carefully screwed the cap down tight on each. He thought he heard a trace of apprehension in her voice and bowed his head to hide his smile.

Good, his little plan was working. With Broken Hand's cooperation and his colorful imagination, he might convince Miss Pinkerton of the foolishness of all this yet. Not that what Broken Hand had said wasn't true. It was true, all of it. And Jake intended to use it to his full advantage. He thought he just might add a little color of his own to the story.

"Over the last several years in the Territory, since the settlers came, the Indians have been pushed farther and farther off their land. There were Indian wars, a lot of people were killed." He paused for full effect before continuing his story.

"The Indians simply wanted their land back. In their eyes it was the land of their ancestors, and theirs by right of ancient territorial domain. The settlers didn't quite see it that way."

Revel knew something about the recent history of the Territory. "And then the soldiers came," she added solemnly.

"Soldiers to enforce the white man's laws," Jake clarified, "along with politicians from the East who had no idea what to do with the Indians and couldn't have cared less about their welfare."

There was a bitterness in his voice that surprised her. It made her wonder about Jake Reno. She wouldn't have thought a man who chose to be an outlaw would have cared about anyone else, much less the plight of many.

"And the Indians chose to fight for their land," she concluded. He shrugged and at first she thought it was indifference, but his tone of voice suggested something much more, a sense of hopelessness.

"For a while. But it's hard to fight when there isn't enough to eat. They were driven off their hunting grounds and the land they farmed. If a man can't eat, he can't fight. If he can't fight, he can't be free."

She watched him with growing fascination. He had revealed something very personal, very private . . . his feelings—something she was certain few ever saw. She listened as he explained further.

"Eventually the Army rounded up most of the Indians and placed them on reservations. It was a poor compromise at best. But they did make promises to the Indians." Once again, bitterness edged his voice.

Revel had read a great deal about the Indian problems in the Territories. "And they failed to keep those promises."

Jake looked up at her in surprise. "They moved them off prime land because the settlers wanted it. They barred them from ancient hunting grounds because settlers wanted them. They promised to provide food, shelter, land for farming and hunting."

"Then when the Indians were established on reservations the government officials decided to move them. They sent several hundred of the Apaches from the Verde River reservation to the reservation at San Carlos in the dead of winter.

"It was on the night of the Blood Moon, when the full

moon has a red cast to it.

"The trip was brutal, over two hundred miles. The only food the Indians had was what they could carry. Many of the children and old people weren't strong enough for such a trip in the winter. Over half of those who started died along the way."

"And that's why they called it the Trail of Death," Revel concluded sadly.

"It has many names. It's happened before, it will happen again in other places. The federal government promises land to the Indians and then takes it away because of special interest groups, like the railroad. That's why the Indians don't trust the white man. The Army calls them renegades. And there's a bounty on them."

Just as there had been a bounty on Jake Reno. She wasn't blind to the similarity. "And you agree with the Indians."

"I think the government should keep it's promises, no matter whose pockets it robs."

"What happened to the renegade Indians?"

He poked at the dirt with a stick, making half-moon arcs in the silty dust.

"Some of them were hunted down and taken back. Others were killed. The rest, are still out there. They take their revenge where they can."

"The Battle of the Blood Moon, in that canyon," she surmised.

"It happened not long after the Trail of Death. It was revenge for their wives and children who died. The Apache renegades led the soldiers into that canyon and then boxed them in. It was slaughter, but to the Indian it was only a small payment." Then his mood shifted, and he became thoughtful.

"Are you afraid?" He didn't actually expect her to give him an honest answer.

Her head came up, her gaze meeting his. "No, Mr. Reno, I'm not afraid. I've seen death before, and I do know how to use a gun," she reminded him.

136

"Yeah, I remember," he said wryly, then he added, "You should be afraid. Guns didn't do those soldiers any good."

He watched her thoughtfully. "You seem to know a great deal about all this. I wouldn't think those Eastern papers would tell the truth about it."

"They don't," she admitted, "but I've traveled around a great deal and I've heard a lot of things the newspapers don't print."

"An enlightened female?" He smiled as he said it. He found it humorous that politicians and newspaper reporters were so certain they controlled what people thought. It was clear, in her case they had failed.

That smile caught Revel completely off guard. It was devastating, his white teeth flashing against bronzed skin, his almost boyish expression of delight completely taking her breath away. The outlaw had vanished, along with the wall of cynicism and anger between them.

It was as if a heavy, dark drape drawn over windows was suddenly pulled back, revealing something unexpected beyond the glass.

"Enlightened?" She repeated the word as she struggled with her composure. Then she shook her head. "My father taught me to think for myself. He said God gave me a brain, and I should use it. Not let other people use it for me."

His smile shifted subtly to that thoughtful expression of a few moments earlier, as if he might have seen something he too hadn't expected. "You father was a brave man."

"He was the wisest man I ever knew." Her voice had become wistful, and for a moment Jake glimpsed something behind her eyes that he'd seen only fleetingly before—a certain sadness and . . . vulnerability.

"He was a good man . . . a strong man. And he was kind." Her voice faded to hardly more than a whisper.

The silence that surrounded them for those few moments as Jake considered what he had seen was

137

interrupted only by the soft whisper of the water that bubbled over the rocks in the river and the rhythmic chomping as the horses nibbled at the sparse grass that grew on the banks.

Then as her thoughts snapped back to the present and the reason she was here, Revel abruptly came to her feet.

"Hadn't we better get going?" she said with sudden coolness.

The change was abrupt, like the chill of a wind that sometimes comes up unexpectedly on the desert. It could ache a man clean through to the bone. With the words as well as the way she'd stood, distance had been firmly reestablished between them.

"I want to cover as many miles as possible," she reminded him stiffly. "After all, that is why we are here."

"Anything you say, Miss Tyson!" Jake snapped, the change in her rubbing him raw just below the surface. "We don't want to lose any precious time getting ourselves killed now, do we!"

Revel was immediately aware that she'd succeeded in bringing back the anger between them. She heard it first in the hiss of fury in his voice, and then in his use of her last name. Before, he had stubbornly insisted on calling her Revel.

Without another word, he turned and walked back to the horses. He jerked the Appaloosa's reins hard, the stallion's eyes rolling at the rough treatment. As he swung up into the saddle and turned his mount about, Jake gestured across the river to the far bank.

"That's where the renegade Apaches staked out the cavalry captain and slowly stripped away his skin." He added, "They still haven't caught most of them." Then he whirled the Appaloosa around and set off at a steady pace along the river.

Revel didn't know whether to believe him or not. He was probably just trying to scare her. She didn't doubt in the least that he would be more than pleased to turn

138

around and forget this trip.

She looked to Broken Hand who sat stoically astride his paint pony. At her questioning glance, he nodded.

"They roam the land. For them there is no life, their families are dead. There is only revenge."

He turned his horse and rode ahead, leaving Revel to catch up on her own. A frisson of fear tingled across her skin, leaving her cold beneath the afternoon sun.

Damn Jake Reno! She had come too far, waited too long to turn back now. And in some remote sense, she felt a kinship to the Apaches of the Blood Moon. She understood revenge.

By riding late into the night, they had traveled almost eighty miles in two days between Tucson and Fort Buchanan.

If her aches and stiffness were indications of distance, Revel was convinced they had traveled eighty miles on that first day after leaving Fort Buchanan.

Of course, she had only herself to blame for the numbing pace Jake set. By the time he found a place to make camp, she was about to fall out of the saddle. Still she wouldn't give him the satisfaction of knowing the pace was killing her.

It will get better, she told herself. It has to.

As she slipped to the ground beside the gelding the first sensation that registered was a pressing need for privacy. Obviously Broken Hand felt that same need, for he quickly tethered his pony and then disappeared down the embankment toward the river.

That was fine for him, but Revel required some sort of cover—rocks, a tree, bushes, anything would do. Except this particular location was abundantly lacking in any sort of vegetation. The closest thing to a tree was a tall, skinny cactus that would offer little cover.

"Are we stopping here?"

"That's right." By his sharp reply, Revel knew Jake Reno's mood hadn't improved. If anything it had worsened.

Dear God, how could she put this delicately?

"There aren't any trees."

"Nope."

"Or bushes either," she added tentatively.

"You're real observant," he bit off sarcastically as he tethered the Appaloosa. He hoisted the saddle off the tall stallion. "It must be all that training as a Pinkerton agent."

Revel bit back several scathing replies, all of which would have been appropriate but would hardly solve her problem.

She had a growing suspicion Jake Reno knew precisely what she was hinting at and was taking a great deal of pleasure in pretending innocence. Very well, under her dire circumstances, she saw no reason to beat around the bush.

"I realize it's hardly your problem, but I do need a little privacy to take care of certain matters," she snapped.

As he dropped the saddle to the ground in the small clearing, he turned briefly. Hands planted on his lean hips, he gave her a long appraising look.

"I suppose that does present a problem under the circumstances. But then you like to be considered just one of the men, don't you, *Miss Tyson*? You can handle a gun, you can ride a horse . . ."—he hesitated ever so briefly on that one, as if there was still a great deal of doubt about it—"and you like taking care of business like a man." His tone was scathing.

"In which case, *Miss Tyson, ma'am,* I suggest you solve the problem like a man." Without a backward glance, he turned and stalked back to the Appaloosa, then tied a burlap nosebag filled with grain over the stallion's muzzle.

"Of all the . . ." she muttered to his back. But precise

140

words failed her. She'd already called him every colorful name she could think of and had also invented a few.

All right then, she would solve the problem herself. It was practically dark. Night soon should provide enough privacy, and there was no one around for miles.

As she stepped from the small clearing into the low brush, she hesitated. At least she hoped there was no one around.

She immediately recalled Broken Hand's story about the Apache renegades and made a quick side trip back to the gelding. She removed the small revolver from her saddlebag and snugged it in the waistband of her skirt, just as a precaution.

Revel walked several paces out into the flat darkness that surrounded their camp. Low scrub brush scratched her legs, the tops of her boots. She was hesitant at first, uncertain of the terrain. But she remembered how flat everything was since they'd left the rolling foothills the day before. The only exception had been the unexpectedly majestic rock formations they saw occasionally and the wide gully of the river; but that was at her back.

She walked a little farther to insure privacy. In the distance she could hear faint sounds—Jake and Broken Hand talking, the snapping of wood being broken up for their evening fire, the lively snorts of the Appaloosa stallion, which cared little for the company of the gelding or Broken Hand's paint pony. They were familiar sounds.

Then there was the sudden burst of golden light as the fire was lit. The flames wavered, sputtered, and eventually took, sending spiraling fingers up through the scrub brush, then lapping tentatively at the denser wood. The fire hissed as heat met wetness, the wood evidently came from down by the river.

Revel made certain she was beyond the reach of the spreading arc of light about the campfire. Jake Reno's scathing remarks cut at her. She didn't consider herself the same as a man, it's just that she had learned to be self-sufficient. She had to be, or she would have been dead

141

long ago. That was the risk in what she did.

Dammit! she thought. It wasn't to prove she was as good as any man. That thought had never occurred to her. It had simply been the easiest means to find the man she wanted. She angrily adjusted her skirts.

"Damn, Jake Reno, anyway!" she fumed. As quickly as she had prepared to take care of her delicate problem—for which Jake Reno had no concern and even less sympathy—she bolted upright.

"Ouch!"

Revel whirled around, tears filling her eyes. Anger and pain tightened her throat.

"Damn! Of all the . . ." She choked up with frustration. Several choice words came to mind. Stupid. Inexperienced. Naive.

The self-deprecating list grew as she realized with growing mortification that she'd just sat on a cactus.

"Are you all right, *Miss Tyson?*"

Jake Reno's jeering concern grated against her wounded pride.

"Yes, of course!" she called back to him, as she tenderly rubbed her wounded bottom. It was adding insult to injury, she was already so sore from all the riding she'd done over the past three days.

"Do you need any assistance?" he offered, making a suspicious sound that sounded very much like laughter.

"No!" she blurted out, the forced herself to sound politely calm. "I'm quite all right," she replied coolly. "Thank you."

I'm not all right, Revel thought, and she wondered if anyone had ever died from being wounded by a cactus.

"Oh, God, I don't dare tell him."

At that moment she had never felt so inadequate, so ill prepared to handle a situation. All her experience as an agent had done little to fortify her for the last few days or the journey ahead. She knew that.

In her training, in every case she'd worked on previously, she had always been assisted by another agent, and extensive as her experience was, it didn't prepare her for survival out in the wilderness.

Not that there hadn't been unexpected situations before. When they'd arisen she had simply improvised, relied on those around her, and kept her wits about her. The problem was she refused to rely on Jake Reno.

He would just as soon leave her as look at her, Revel was convinced of it. That was precisely the reason she slept so poorly at night, constantly waking up to see if he was still there. She had no doubt that at some point he would try to leave.

I will simply have to rely on myself as I have always done, Revel concluded as she carefully smoothed her clothes back down over her bottom. *Dear God, I'll be lucky if I ever sit down again.*

Jake Reno greeted her with a bemused smile as she stepped back into the perimeter of light from the campfire.

"Are you all right?"

She looked at him coolly. "Yes, of course. I just took a misstep out there in the dark."

"Next time stay closer to camp," he suggested as he turned back to the fire. She could have sworn he was smirking again.

"That way you can see where you're going."

The way he said it made her wonder if he knew exactly what had happened out there, but she decided he couldn't. He was just playing his little games.

Broken Hand provided dinner that night, a rabbit he'd killed down by the river. It was a welcome change from hardtack and tortillas, just so long as Revel didn't have to look in that cute, fuzzy creature's little eyes beforehand.

Most of her experience with food had been in the kitchen at her aunt's house in Philadelphia where meat, fresh produce, milk, and butter were delivered daily. They certainly never went out and killed the food they ate.

After leaving Philadelphia, she'd spent the next two

years in Denver. It was modern, bustling, and in some ways quite cosmopolitan for an overgrown cattletown.

Once again her experience with food was limited to fine restaurants or the meals cooked by Mrs. Ferguson at the women's boardinghouse where she lived.

Her various cases had taken her to cities, frontier towns, and railroad camps, but in all these there was a cook tent, a restaurant, or a boardinghouse where she could find a good meal. She'd never provided food for herself and therefore had never given much thought to where it came from. That is, until that night.

She was starving, and the aroma of rabbit roasting over the open fire almost made her forget the throbbing pain in her backside. Almost.

She sat on her knees while she ate. The rabbit was slightly chewy but tasted wonderful, a lot like roast chicken. There were tortillas again, but tonight they had cooked beans to roll inside them and hot coffee to drink. It *all* tasted wonderful to Revel.

Jake and Broken Hand sat across the fire from each other. Jake lit a cigarette, took several puffs, then passed it to the Indian. Broken Hand inhaled deeply, nodding his appreciation.

"There is a ring around the moon tonight," he announced with a grunt of thoughtfulness.

Revel looked up at the night sky. It was true. The moon hung in a midnight black sky, that iridescent ring radiating out from it like a halo.

Jake put more of the damp wood on the fire. It hissed, then caught, spreading warmth to the edge of the camp. Revel had noticed that the days could be blazing hot, but nights out on the desert were cold.

"We'd better turn in," he suggested. She was certain he spoke to Broken Hand, since he hadn't said more than two words to her since their exchange earlier.

Broken Hand nodded as he grabbed his rifle and noiselessly disappeared beyond the ring of light that surrounded their small camp.

144

"Where is he going?" Revel asked.

"For a walk."

"In the dark?"

"He can see where he's going."

It was obvious Jake wasn't going to discuss it further, for he spread his blankets beside the fire and then lay down. He wrapped one blanket around his shoulders, adjusted the brim of his hat low over his eyes, and laid his gun across his chest. It was a very reassuring gesture. She glared at him.

"Is it because of the Apaches?"

"He has trouble sleeping at night. But I don't. You'd better get some sleep too," he suggested, as if he knew she watched him. "It's going to get real miserable when it starts to rain."

Rain? She looked up at the brilliant night sky. Stars twinkled overhead, and the moon was just starting its night journey on the far horizon. So much for Jake Reno's ability to predict the weather.

She tried to make herself comfortable. But no matter which way she twisted or turned, her backside throbbed. She shifted again, lying as far over on her side as possible, but just the added weight of the blanket made her miserable. She turned over on her stomach and groaned as a sharp rock cut into her side. She dug it out from under the blanket and tossed it aside.

"Will you quit thrashing around?" Jake grumbled.

Revel rolled over, careful not to further abuse her left side. It hurt no matter which position she got into. After several more minutes of misery, she finally gave up and gathered her blankets.

She looked down at Jake Reno. He lay in that same position, his eyes shielded by his hat, looking very comfortable.

Well, good riddance! she thought as she picked up her poncho and tucked everything under her arm.

She'd just sleep someplace else so that she wouldn't bother him. As she fought with her anger, she silently hoped a dozen scorpions found their way inside his boots.

"I hope he swells up and bursts," she mumbled miserably as she recalled his horrible story about the dangers of being stung. She tucked her blankets under her arm and headed for the edge of the river.

"That's not the best place to sleep."

She stopped and slowly turned around. She hadn't made a sound, and she'd been certain he was already asleep. How did he do that? How did he hear things she couldn't hear? In this case, her leaving camp.

"Why not?" she asked, because she knew whether she wanted to hear it or not, he would tell her.

"If any of those renegades are around they'll need water," came the mumbled reply.

"I'll rely on Broken Hand to warn me if they should come around." She turned and started back toward the river.

"Then, of course, there are other things."

Teeth clenched, Revel stopped. "What other things?"

"Wild animals, especially the ones that come out at night. And, of course, there is that storm."

"There isn't going to be any storm," she ground out angrily. "The sky is completely clear. Good night, Mr. Reno." With that, she turned and without another word stalked off toward the river. She vaguely heard his parting comment.

"You'll be back."

Don't bet on it! Revel fumed as she laid out her blankets in a niche tucked under the high, dry embankment. She was still within sight of the camp up on the bank, but far enough away from Jake Reno.

Sometime during that long, miserable night it began to rain.

Revel cursed herself for not being better prepared, the weather for being uncooperative, and Jake for being right. Her only answer was the loud spattering on the hard, dry earth. She snuggled deeper into her niche, pulling the sodden blankets and woolen poncho more

146

tightly about her. Morning couldn't come quickly enough.

Jake wasn't certain whether he heard it first or felt it—a distant rumbling that seemed to seep up through the wet ground beneath him and churn through the cold air above him. Having lived by instinct so long, he was immediately on his feet and shedding the oilcloth slicker he'd wrapped about him when it first began to rain.

It was a typical desert storm. It came on quick, with a force that drenched everything that wasn't protected. He'd grown accustomed to such deluges. It was as if nature chose to make up for the lack of water in one fell swoop. The earth was hard and flat, the driving rain forming small rivers that ran through the low spots that surrounded the encampment.

He and Broken Hand had deliberately chosen this location because of the slight rise that would protect them when the storm came. A cave or outcropping of rocks would have been preferable, but they were rare in this part of the territory.

In the gathering gloom he vaguely made out the forms of the horses at the edge of camp. They were huddled together, their heads bowed against the driving storm.

Across what was left of the drowned fire, Broken Hand slept in a sitting position. His slicker, one of his few concessions to the trappings of the white man's world, formed a tent over his bowed head and shoulders. He had obviously returned to camp when the storm began. It was pointless to stay out in a storm like this. No one was going to attack in a downpour.

He found the mound of Revel's saddle, but her blankets, saddlebags, and poncho were gone. The little fool hadn't returned to camp.

Anger at her stupidity hit him first. He'd warned her not to go down to the river. Then the unexpected, sharp tang of fear backed up into his throat.

The indistinct rumbling that he'd first sensed had

147

grown to a dull roar. Broken Hand heard it too, upon stirring from his dry cocoon.

"The river," the old Indian said with certainty.

Jake nodded, "I heard it too."

Broken Hand glanced across the camp. "Where is the woman?"

Jake ran to the embankment, cursing. "The damn river."

The night sky had gone from moonlit black to gray as torrents of rain exploded against the dry ground, blending everything into a wall of driving water and making it impossible to see anything clearly. He shouted her name over and over as he reached the top of the embankment.

The first thing Revel was aware of was the loud hiss that filled her ears. The next thing was that in spite of the overhanging protection of the niche and the tightly wrapped poncho and slicker, she was soaking wet.

That wasn't so surprising when she came fully awake and realized the intensity of the sudden storm. What *was* surprising was that it wasn't the rain that had soaked through her blankets, but the rim of water lapping around her legs and hips.

The river had swollen beyond the cut of the shallow gully. In a little more than a few hours, perhaps less, it had risen over the shallow embankment and reached all the way to where she had laid out her blanket roll.

Revel pulled at the dragging weight of the wet blankets, but she was already partially submerged and the water was tugging the blankets from her grasp. It was then she became fully aware of the strength of the current.

"Oh, my god," she whispered, swallowing down her instinctual fear. She sat up and made a desperate grab for her saddlebags. The leather, slick from the rain, was slipping through her fingers. She scrambled to her knees, oblivious to the water that rose steadily and soaked her to the skin.

It was then she saw the small carpetbag bob precariously as it was lifted by the water. She lunged at it, was able to grab hold of the coarse-grained fabric. When she turned back to her blankets she realized with sickening reality that they'd been sucked away by the rising swell.

Her split skirt and shirtwaist were plastered to her skin, the sodden skirt weighted her down. And her boots were gone, also washed away. She wanted to curse, but there wasn't time. She had to get farther up that embankment or be washed away, just like those boots.

Revel thought she heard someone shouting, but couldn't be certain, not with the persistent spattering of rain and the ominous hissing of the rising water. She stubbornly clung to the saddlebags and the carpetbag, refusing to let either go.

A tangle of roots protruded from the eroded riverbank. Scrabbling for a toehold, she lunged at them. As she grabbed hold of one, its decaying spine snapped. She grabbed another—a thick, gnarled root. But it was slippery, and she was now up to her shoulders in the swirling muddy river.

The precarious lifeline held, and she slowly pulled herself up the embankment.

"Revel!"

The call came from somewhere along the crest of the riverbank above her. Or perhaps she'd only thought she heard it.

The niche where she'd made her bed earlier was three to four feet under the cut of the embankment. The shriveled riverbed had been at least another twelve to fifteen feet below that.

Now as she clawed for a handhold in the crumbling mud embankment above her, she realized the water had risen over fifteen feet! It had been transformed from a slow-dying trickle to a raging river.

"Revel!"

She heard it again, this time closer. Straining to see through the pouring rain, she vaguely made out a shape

149

that seemed to move along the embankment above her.

"Here!" she cried, spitting out mud and water. Please, dear God, let it be Jake Reno and not my imagination, she thought desperately, as she felt strength seep out of her cold body.

She was submerged in water, the weight of her skirt pulling her down every time she tried to inch her way up. And she was constantly buffeted by the rising current, floating debris cutting and scratching her bare legs and feet.

"Revel!"

This time it was more distinct—and only a few feet above her. She shouted back. Through the hair plastered against her head and face she could barely make out the shape of a man.

"Jake!"

"Give me your hand!"

He shouted something else, but it was lost to the deafening roar that built behind her.

Revel's muscles and bones ached; still she held on. Finally, she saw the dark shape of a long arm and hand extended above her.

Dear God! What was she to do? She held onto the tangle of roots with one hand, the saddlebags and carpetbag with the other. She wasn't about to lose them. But if she let go to take his hand, she'd be swept away before he had a chance to grab her.

Jake shouted down to her. "Dammit! Take my hand!"

Revel quickly made her decision. With the meager strength she had left, she swung the saddlebags and carpetbag over her head as far up the embankment as she could. Even through the driving rain she heard the string of curses.

"What the hell do you think you're doing?"

The last curse died on the wind as saddlebags and valise were jerked out of her fingers. The water pulled at her, sucking her down as she held on with only one hand. She

150

screamed. The sound was immediately drowned out by water and mud.

Revel twisted and jerked around blindly now as she fought to grab hold of the tree roots with her free hand. The water had risen even farther. She could not keep her head above it, and wondered what it was like to drown.

Her lungs ached. She clung to the tree root with one hand and fought her way back to the river's surface. She gulped cold air as she clawed her way above the water.

Everything about her was cold—the water, that brief blessed gasp of air, the mud that oozed about her legs.

She was slipping, being pulled and dragged down. The flesh on the palms of her hands was torn by the splintered and gnarled roots. Even her blood was cold.

Chapter Eight

Jake grabbed her hand, lost his grip, and grabbed again. This time he had hold of her wrist.

"Hold on!" he shouted above the hiss and gurgle of water. Then it abruptly changed. Somewhere through the veil of water that fell in torrents around them, he heard the engulfing roar of water on the move—a massive amount of it.

It sounded as if the earth were splitting open, being physically wrenched apart. Beneath him the muddied embankment shuddered as it eroded into rivulets and gave way.

Flash flood!

They happened in the desert. The terrain was so flat that low spots quickly filled, ran, and became rivers of dangerous mud. Then they ran together, pushing shoving, all the water tumbling into one narrow groove worn in the earth.

Now it churned toward them. Without seeing it, Jake knew it swept everything in its path before it. He thrust himself farther over the embankment, tightening his grasp on her wrist as he struggled to grab her other hand. It was useless. She had slipped too far down the embankment.

There was little time. Yet, Jake knew his only chance was to go down that embankment after her.

He'd be a liar if anyone asked and he said he never considered simply leaving her where she was. He considered it, rejected the idea for reasons even he couldn't begin to understand, and then scrambled down the embankment.

She was submerged in water almost to her shoulders when he reached her, the swirling current of the swollen river tearing at her precarious hold on the snarled tree roots. Mud ran in streamers through her hair. As he slipped down beside her, he was surprised at how small she was.

Her hands were twisted about the spine of the roots. Her arms were no bigger around than his wrists. Yet he recalled how efficiently she had held that pistol on him, and the surprising strength she'd shown when she'd easily escaped from Lilly.

He shielded her as best he could with his own body from the bruising rush of water. His arms were wrapped around her, as he grabbed hold of the roots. He shouted instructions, but they were drowned in the rush of water and wind that engulfed them. Still, she nodded that she understood, and tried to pull herself up the embankment. They might have made it if they had had a few more precious seconds.

The roar behind them intensified, until it seemed that wind and water became one. When it hit, the wall of water slammed against them, tore at them, and then yanked them from their tenuous hold as if they were no more than rag dolls.

Instead of wasting precious strength fighting the swirling torrent, Jake let go and grabbed hold of Revel. Even as they were helplessly swept along, he shouted at her.

"Swim!"

In her fragmented thoughts, Revel was certain she was either delirious or someone had made a ridiculous joke. Trying to swim in that huge swell was impossible, and something was pulling at her.

After several seconds in that bone-chilling sweep of water, she realized the *something* was Jake Reno.

She was exhausted, her efforts to swim nothing more than feeble flailing attempts. But he had hold of her and actually seemed to be moving them in a specific direction.

They bobbed to the surface, were just as quickly sucked down, and again surfaced. More than once, she was certain they'd been swept apart, but Jake's hand grabbed her wrist, her arm, or the back of her shirt.

She was bruised by debris, blinded by gritty mud, choked by water. She gave up trying to see where they were going, kept stroking with her arms, and alternately coughed up water and gasped for air.

When she was certain neither of them had the strength to fight the flood any longer, she felt the persistent tug of Jake's grasp. He refused to let her go.

It occurred to her that it would be easy for him to simply open his hand and let her be swept away. Then, when her body was found somewhere downriver, he would be a free man. Just as quickly the thought was gone. All that was left was her instinct for survival.

She was cold as death, covered with mud and matted clumps of weeds. Her clothes were torn, exposing more than they covered.

They washed up in a swirling eddy of water as the flood churned against a sheltered curve of the river, both more dead than alive.

Revel crawled farther up the embankment. Her arms and legs shook. Her hair blinded her, a wet heavy blanket. She collapsed, dragging the sodden mass of hair back from her face as she sucked huge gulps of air into her stinging lungs. She coughed and choked, bringing up river water. As the coughing finally subsided, she looked around.

Rain still pummeled the ground. The thunderous pounding of the river had lessened to a dull roar. She

155

vaguely made out a huddled shape several feet closer to the water.

"Jake! Oh, my God!" She scrambled to him. He lay half in, half out of the water, and he wasn't moving.

His shirt was torn open. She felt for the rise and fall of his chest, but there was no movement. Panic hit her. She sought a pulse at his neck. If there was any at all it was so faint she couldn't feel it.

"No! No!" she screamed in growing desperation. He couldn't be dead. He was too strong, far stronger than she. Somehow he'd managed to get them partway up the embankment, or he must have, for she remembered nothing of it.

Dear God! How long had they lain in the mud?

"Jake!" she slapped him in an effort to rouse him, but still there was no response. She felt his face, his chest, his arms and hands. He was cold but no colder than she was. Still there was no telltale rise and fall of his chest.

Panic was there, right at the edge of superimposed composure. She looked around wildly. She had to think. Time was precious.

How far had the river carried them from camp? Where was Broken Hand? Was he looking for them? Did he even know they were gone? Or had he been caught by the river too and swept away?

Countless accusations splintered through her fragmented thoughts in fractions of seconds. Among them was the reality that she was a fool to think she could go after Sam Bass . . . all her experience hadn't prepared her for this . . . everything she'd lived for in the last five years was slipping away . . . she'd been a fool and now Jake might be dead . . .

She was certain she hated him and everything he stood for. She had cursed him, belittled him, and shot him. She had convinced herself it meant nothing to her if he hanged just as long as she got what she wanted. But at the moment she wanted nothing so much as she wanted him to live.

156

"Damn you!" She grabbed his shirtfront, twisting the fabric in both hands. "Don't you dare die on me!" She shook him hard. Still there was no response.

"No! I won't let you die! Do you hear me?" she screamed at him. Her panic grew as his head rolled to the side. She shoved her fingers through her hair, as if she could physically drive back fear and confusion. *I must think!* She stared down at him.

She had no experience of flash floods, but maybe she could save Jake Reno.

She quickly rolled him over onto his side, her mind scrambling to remember precisely how this procedure had been explained to her. Her father had once described seeing a small boy revived after almost drowning.

As she rolled Jake onto his side, a small trickle of water slipped from his mouth and down his chin. She rolled him onto his back once more. There was still no visible sign of breathing.

How much time had passed? Seconds? Minutes? How long could a person go without breathing?

She brushed his long hair back from his face. This was the part she wasn't certain about. But the way her father described it made sense to her. If Jake couldn't breathe, she had to breathe for him. She simply wasn't certain of the technique.

She tentatively placed her mouth over his and blew. The immediate problem was apparent as air escaped. She tried again, repositioning her lips over his so that no air escaped.

Once again, she blew into his mouth. His cheeks puffed slightly, but again it seemed wrong. Air was still escaping. She took another deep breath and was about to try again when she released air through her nose.

Of course! That was it. Air was escaping through his nose. Quickly taking another deep breath, Revel clamped his nose shut with her fingers and placed her mouth over his.

She blew firmly. This time there was a faint rise of his

chest. She took another breath and blew again—another quick rise of his chest. Encouraged, she repeated the steps several more times.

She wasn't at all certain this was how it was supposed to be done, and Jake still didn't seem to be responding on his own. With every gulp of air she inhaled and breathed into him she knew deadly fear. But she was more afraid to stop.

"Don't die!" she breathed for them both, then inhaled again.

"Dammit, don't die!"

It was tiring, but she persisted. How long had it been now? Too long for him to survive? Was this doing any good?

She was very near breaking down, but there wasn't even time for that. She mentally went through the steps, changed the position of her mouth on his slightly and took another breath, willing him to live.

Rain continued to pour down on them. The cold night air made her bones ache. She refused to give up.

At first there was only the shallow rise and fall of his chest each time she breathed into him. Then there was a subtle change. His mouth moved beneath hers.

But when she pulled back and felt his chest there was still no movement. She resumed the breathing steps. Perhaps she had been mistaken about the movement, but she had to keep trying.

She leaned over him, gently closing his nose as she angled her lips over his. She breathed.

His mouth moved, shifted, and opened. Before she realized what was happening, in an unexpected invasion his tongue slipped between her lips. It was quick, hot, and devastating to her already shattered senses.

Revel jerked back. But when she looked down at Jake Reno, he still lay motionless, his eyes closed.

She prodded his shoulder. "Jake?" She gently shook him, but still there was no response.

Had she only imagined that momentary flash of

contact with her lips?

She leaned over him and began again, this time more determinedly. Her parted lips fit over his perfectly. As she breathed into his mouth, once more there was that thrusting pressure of sweetness as his tongue slipped into her mouth. It was like a caress, hot, wet, and arousing.

Revel was startled. A small warning signal went off in the back of her brain. Something was very wrong. She pulled away from him in alarm.

"I wouldn't have guessed that you were such a good kisser, Revel."

She sat back on bent legs, completely dumbfounded. And stared at Jake Reno through the driving rain as he struggled to sit up.

"You!" she choked out. Then she stopped, unable to put two words together. As she gaped at him openmouthed, surprise slowly gave way to anger. She came up on her knees, hands doubled into fists.

"You aren't drowned!" she accused.

Jake shrugged weakly, a devilish grin slowly spreading across his handsome face as he propped himself up on bent elbows.

"Apparently not."

"You aren't even close to being drowned!" It all slowly began to dawn on her. He had never been close to drowned.

"I will be forever thankful to you for your"—he hesitated as he searched for the right words, then continued with something very near that familiar smirk—"your skills in saving my life." There was a rakish quirk to his mouth now.

"My skills!" she exploded. "I should have let you drown . . . I should have left you in that river. I should take you back down there and finish what the river started!" She was so furious, nothing made sense.

"You tricked me!" She flung the accusation at the same time she flung a fistful of mud at him, striking him in the middle of his torn shirt.

159

"You seemed to know what you were doing," he pointed out, a devilish gleam in his green eyes. "I didn't want to interrupt anyone as determined as you were."

"I thought you were dead!"

"If I was, what was the point in trying to save me?"

"Damn you! I don't need you dead, I need you alive!"

He came up on his knees. They were now facing one another, their words whipping at each other through the driving wind and rain.

"That's right!" Jake hurled back at her as strength and anger seeped back into his battered body. *"You need me!"*

He grabbed her, one arm snaking around her waist as he hauled her up against him. Her head jerked back, her eyes widening in stunned surprise as her hands flattened to push him away. The contact was complete, their bodies molded together as the rain slashed at them.

The softness of her breasts pressed into the hard wall of muscle at his chest. She felt the cut of metal against her stomach—his heavy belt buckle. His hips drove against hers, forcing a more intimate contact.

"And you need a helluva lot more than that, Revel Tyson!"

It was a threat and a promise all wrapped up in anger, resentment, frustration, and a desire to wound her and prove something to her.

Stupid little fool! He wanted to scream that and more at her, as if he could force her to understand what she was up against.

His fingers bit into the soft flesh of her arms. There would be bruises, but at that moment all he could think of was the stark contrast of the softness and the tough resilience of the woman who'd survived that river.

Woman.

All his anger, resentment, and desire came back to that one word, and there was no more reasoning, or logic, only the need to prove something she would never be willing to admit to herself.

He wrapped his free hand in the wet tangle of her hair

160

and jerked her head back. Lightning shattered the night sky above them, illuminating everything in a stark, blue-white light that stripped away all shadow for a few brief seconds.

The woman he held trapped in his arms was no longer the proper, well-bred, Eastern lady with elegant clothes and equally elegant manners. Her clothes were torn and stained, clinging to her in a transparent exposure that no refined, proper woman would ever allow.

Her shirtwaist lay plastered to her skin, which was visible beneath it. The top buttons had been torn away. The cloth gaped open over the mound of one pale breast. It concealed just enough to tease.

The cold night air had tautened the dark tips of her breasts into hard nubs that seemed darker still against the wet fabric.

The breath that had filled him hot and sweet now came out in hard sharp gasps as she stared back at him.

Raindrops beaded on her pale face, tipped her dark lashes, and ran into tiny rivulets that dripped from her small nose, caught at the corners of her mouth, and trickled off her defiant chin.

Her eyes were wide and luminous, reminding him of flash fires and the night sky all at once. Her dark hair was like heavy velvet at her shoulders and back.

Of all the countless emotions she'd provoked in him, none was stronger at that moment than the desire that seared his nerve endings.

He wanted to shout at her; at the same time he wanted to whisper her name.

He wanted to strike her, to pull her close and caress her.

He wanted to throw her right back in the damn river and be rid of her . . . and he wanted to push her to the ground and feel her woman's flesh beneath him, surrounding him, closing over him.

Everything he felt was pure instinct and had nothing to do with right or wrong, good or bad, or anything that had brought them there. He knew only the heat of desire that had lain just beneath the surface ever since they'd met.

It was primal. If he chose, he could have willed it away. He didn't choose.

One hand tightened its grip on her hair; the other moved down from her waist, across the curve of her bottom, kneading soft flesh as he rhythmically rocked her hips against his.

"Don't touch me," she gasped between hard breaths. He answered by lowering his head toward hers. Held by that long twist of hair and by the arm he had about her, there was no escape.

"You need to be touched." His mouth ravaged hers.

There was no sweetness, no tenderness in him, only the oblivion of plunder, and God help her, she welcomed it.

His mouth alternately bruised and caressed. He pulled away. Her gasp for air came out a soft moan of loss, only to be answered by the sweet thrust of his tongue between her lips.

Revel had never felt anything like this. Before, kisses had been brief, subdued experiences. But there was nothing brief or subdued about Jake Reno. He was hot, wet, and hard in her mouth. He tasted of something wild, untamed, primitive, and he fed something equally untamed within her.

Her fingers curled into fists, her nails biting into the palms of her hands as she mentally fought him and what he was doing to her.

She should push him away. She should be angry, humiliated; she even thought of shooting him.

Then as his body shifted against hers, his thigh riding hard between hers, her fingers uncurled and dug into the skin at his chest.

As he pulled her hard into his body and lowered her to the wet earth, there was no longer any thought of what they had just survived. There was only his body and the sharp pain of need he slowly built with his hands and mouth.

"I hate you." The weakened protest shuddered out of her as his lips moved against her throat.

"You *need* me." He tasted rain and flesh at the hollow of her throat, her collarbone, the indentation just below. He gently sucked at the tiny rivulets of water that coursed down over her breasts, tearing the fabric when it hindered him.

"I don't need . . . anyone. I loathe you." It came out in a startled gasp as his mouth found and closed over her breast.

"You *want* me."

"No!" The denial was sharp and painful, hurled into the churning storm. But there was no way of knowing whether it was a denial of him or the feelings he aroused within her—feelings she had never allowed herself, feelings she was certain she neither possessed or needed.

It came back to the one small word—need. Without being spoken, it was there deep inside her.

She had never confronted this kind of need before. Always it was the old need that drove her—the desperate desire for revenge. But this was far different. It was an emotion that unleashed a torrent of uncertainty, one in which the only certainty was her response to this man.

It began as a dull ache somewhere below her stomach, hunger that wasn't hunger, pain that wasn't pain.

Every time he touched her with his hands, every time he tasted her with his mouth, the dull ache twisted and tightened, until it became a knot of liquid heat that seemed to feed on itself and grow.

Her body strained against his, every muscle taut with a raw, expectant energy she could neither control or ignore.

"Revel."

He whispered her name over and over, saying it in ways she'd never heard it spoken, against her mouth, her throat, her breast; the roughened texture of his skin, making her raw with apprehension.

Instead of pushing him away, she pulled him closer, tearing at the remnants of his shirt until his shoulders and back lay bare to her exploring hands.

Reason surrendered to the wind. Rain drenched them as he pushed away her shirtwaist and then pulled at the fastening of her skirt.

All the hard and well-muscled surfaces beneath the soft buckskin were exposed by her insistent fingers. She wanted to feel the heavily corded sinews, the sharp angle of muscles, the smoothness of skin drawn taut over his lean body.

Power. It was something sensed and felt rather than seen in Jake Reno. It fascinated her.

Danger. Half-clothed, his body entwined with hers, the danger was like a second skin, inherently a part of him. It lured her.

Fire. It ignited beneath his fingers everywhere he touched, and was longed for in places he hadn't yet touched. It made her ache.

Wildness. It was there in the stroke of the hands that threatened pain but brought only pleasure. It trapped her.

Like pieces of skin, their clothes were stripped away leaving them naked to the rain and wind . . . and fire.

Where there should have been caution, there was only abandon as their hands feverishly explored.

The savage storm and flood were forgotten. Hand touching hand, lips that stroked and caressed, skin against skin—these were all.

The soaked earth was at her back, the turbulent night sky slashed by rain and wind and lightning was above. And there was the man.

His calloused hands kneaded her pliant flesh. His hairroughened thighs twined with hers. The sharp angle of his hip crushed against her curved softness.

His lips caressed where his teeth raked her skin, making her writhe beneath him with some emotion she only now explored and which he had experienced countless times, but never like this.

Her slender hands braced his shoulders, her fingers digging into straining muscles. Where he led, she followed. As his hand slipped beneath her at the small of her back, curving her upward toward him, her hands sleeked down his back in imitation, until they clasped his hard muscled buttocks.

Every touch, every breath, every movement was guided by that primitive instinct.

Taste, feel, sight, sound . . . became the storm.

Every part of Revel cried out that this was wrong for countless reasons she could have once named, but now they were scattered on the wind.

His callus-roughened hand caressed her belly, and her skin leaped beneath his fingers. No man had ever touched her this way, this intimately.

She gasped as his fingers traced lower, stroking over the indentation at her hip, then slipping lower still to that most intimate place.

She should have pushed him away, but it was too late to run away, too late to hide. Her skin ached to be touched again and again. And he touched her, filling all the sweet secret places of her until she ached in places she hadn't known existed.

If he had allowed that there was any reason to go slowly with her, he would have thought twice about what he was about to do. But reason had long since abandoned them both. Instead he plunged into a storm more dangerous than the one that raged about them.

Jake had known countless women in his life; young women, older women, pretty women, bawdy women, even a lady or two—or at least they put on the airs of ladies. But there had never been any woman like the one who'd bedeviled his mind and soul these last few days.

She'd entered his life when it was about to end. The offer she made was a devil's bargain. She was a lady on the outside. On the inside . . . she was molten fire.

Jake knew the dangers of playing with fire. He'd learned them long ago. But like a child, he found it inherently fascinating.

He'd never thought of anyone's pleasure but his own. It was the selfishness, the loner in him, that made him set the limits, leave at the end of an hour or with the rising sun, his physical needs satisfied.

That was one side of the desire that rode him like the devil. But there was a need that lay deep inside him, undefined, frightening in the quiet moments when he was alone, hidden away when he wasn't.

Unexpectedly, that deeper need surfaced, overriding all other needs except one, to be inside her, to lose himself in her woman's softness until there was only the oblivion of passion; and in that passion perhaps he could purge the demons that were always there just below the surface, perhaps he could ease the pain he'd carried for so long.

If she was a virgin there was no easing into what they were about to share. If she wasn't it wouldn't matter.

He hadn't expected her to be, and therefore he was stunned as she shuddered in pain beneath him when he entered her.

Passion. Heat. Pain. And again . . . the passion.

He gave them all to her. The passion built the heat. The heat consumed the pain. Then the pain once more became passion.

As rain coursed over her body and Jake Reno filled her, Revel surrendered to the storm.

Chapter Nine

The rain stopped as suddenly as it had begun. The clouds broke apart as if giant hands had scooped them aside. A brilliant three-quarter moon illuminated the rain-soaked landscape.

Jake had no idea where they were, except the obvious changes in terrain indicated they must be several miles south of their original camp. He found shelter under an outcropping of rock and pulled Revel inside with him.

They were too exhausted to speak, even if they knew what to say to each other. He was certain she was asleep even before he pulled her, half-clothed into his arms.

As the whispers and sighs of water receded about them, he simply held her. Anger, bitterness, and mistrust had been lost somewhere out there in the swollen river. Something far different had replaced them in those frantic, desperate moments when they'd made love.

He didn't honestly know what that left them, but right now she was small, warm, and soft in his arms, and he just wanted to hold her without asking why.

The sun broke through the churning clouds on the far horizon, spilling purple, fiery red, and blazing orange into the morning sky. All the questions that had no easy answers were waiting there in the piercing cold, morning air.

Jake sat crouched before the struggling fire, coaxing

meager flames from damp matches and the wet wood he'd found down at the river by adding dried twigs he'd taken from an abandoned animal burrow in the rocks.

The tentative flames sputtered, found the spindly dry twigs, then caught and sent spiraling yellow fingers up through the damp wood.

The fire puffed tendrils of heavy smoke into the crystal air. There wasn't much heat yet from the wet wood, but at least the fire would take now.

He stared at the flames as they wove upward, veiled by transparent streamers of smoke, seeking, searching, like hot golden tongues driven by consuming hunger.

He poked carefully with a short stick and felt the intense, radiating heat build. He sat, mesmerized by the flames. In their golden, fiery depths he thought of another fire, the intense heat, the choking smoke, and the unforgettable gagging stench of burned hides and . . . death.

Rachel's image drifted to him from within the flames, as surely as if she were sitting across from him: the sweetness of her face, the innocent trust in her eyes, the vulnerability of the tentative smile on her lips.

As quickly as it came, it was gone, chased by other memories: the rough-timbered house in the clearing, the corrals in the shadow of the barn, the wide-open meadow beyond filled with spotted-rump mares and colts that lazily grazed in the warm spring sunshine. All of it sheltered by the towering Wind River mountains.

Then it was gone, along with his own youth, innocence, and dreams. The shimmering images of the land and the ranch disappeared through the veil of smoke.

Only the images of Rachel remained as they always did, etched into every waking thought, stealing into his dreams. His throat tightened and something deep inside him burned, bringing the old familiar pain.

Then the images changed, were brutally altered, the features disfigured, just as Rachel's had been . . . before she was raped and killed.

The piece of wet wood Jake clasped in white-knuckled hands snapped like a dry twig. His hands shook, not from fear but from impotent fury.

He flung the pieces on the consuming fire.

Too late.

The words haunted him. He'd been too late to protect Rachel or save her from Charlie Trask and his men.

As he confronted the ghosts of his past, Jake felt a deep twinge of guilt about Revel Tyson.

He'd never in his life raped a woman, they'd always come to him willingly enough. But with growing anger and self-loathing, he realized there wasn't any other name for what had happened the past night.

He could blame it on a lot of things: the way she got under his skin by arguing with him, the way she kept pushing at him since they first met, the fact that she shot him.

But no matter how he looked at it, he'd been angry enough to hurt her. From the past he understood that rape came from an anger deep inside a man.

It was a brutal, violent act that had nothing to do with making love with a woman and everything to do with power.

During the storm, what happened between them began in anger. But somewhere between the anger and the fight to survive the flood, there had been something more that Jake wasn't ready to accept. Whatever it was, it should never have happened.

He jerked his hands back from the searing heat, curling them into tight fists. He hadn't meant for any of it to happen, but maybe now Miss Revel Tyson would realize how dangerous this trip was—how dangerous he was— and go back where she belonged.

Jake Reno was crouched before the fire when Revel finally awakened. He was lean and golden in the glowing light, wearing only buckskin pants. His long dark hair hung to his shoulders. The leaping flames were reflected in muted shades against the hard chiseled muscles of his shoulders and back. Another ridge of muscles swelled over his ribs, marred by the pale slash of new skin at his left side where her bullet creased him.

His back was toward her, his face visible only from an angle. She cradled her head on her bent arm and stared in fascination as the emotions played across his finely chiseled features.

She already knew he wasn't the kind of man who revealed much about himself. He closed himself off emotionally. Perhaps that came from the years he'd been an outlaw. She wondered what his life had been like before that, and if his past had anything to do with the emotions that alternately played across his lean, handsome features.

If he knew she watched, those features would change, all emotion carefully hidden behind a façade of cool indifference. But he didn't know, and she saw a deeper side of Jake Reno and realized he was capable of feeling pain and sadness. It was the momentary flash of vulnerability that surprised her most, however, before it too, was gone.

She curled within herself. Only now did she realize she wore his shirt and nothing else. She pulled it more tightly about her. His expression hardened to one she remembered from the day they had first met in the marshal's office in Tombstone. It was the look of death.

Revel shuddered, against the early morning chill and a different coldness that seeped deep inside her.

Dear God! How could she have let Jake Reno make love to her?

She almost laughed out loud. What had happened between them could hardly be called an act of love. They had done what barnyard animals do, without the slightest bit of emotion, least of all regret.

It had happened. It was over. Best get on with the business at hand. With quick, efficient movements to hide the shaking of her hands, she buttoned the shirt.

She pulled her tangled hair back over her shoulder and tried to smooth the shirttails about her thighs for the sake of modesty, then simply gave up. She joined him, saying nothing as she knelt and spread her hands before the inviting warmth of the fire. In a reflexive gesture, she tugged at the shirttail as it crept up her bare thigh. If he noticed, he gave no indication, but simply continued staring into the fire.

God help her, as much as she tried to ignore him, it was impossible not to be aware of Jake Reno—acutely, intimately, completely aware of him.

With his clothes on he radiated an aura of power and strength. Without them—as she'd been so well aware that night at Lilly's—he was dangerous, in ways she'd learned last night. He was lean and hard, every muscle, each sinew and tendon tautly drawn beneath the sheen of smooth, glistening skin. His hands were rough, callused. And God help her, she remembered the feel of them against her skin.

His waist narrowed from wide shoulders, his hips even leaner. His buckskin pants rode low at his waist, revealing a hard, flat stomach that last night had pressed so intimately against her. Her gaze beckoned lower still by the ribbon of dark hair that disappeared below.

A dull ache began low in the pit of her stomach and grew at the memory of their bodies together, that dark silken hair blending with her own, and Jake Reno touching her . . . everywhere.

"About last night . . ." His voice was gruff and trailed off uncertainly. He thrust another piece of wood into the fire with an almost angry gesture, and frowned, the expression on his face hard, the emotions hidden away.

"It should never have happened," he said with a deepening frown. As if it were something he felt compelled to say, a weak apology he didn't really believe.

Revel swallowed uncomfortably. Oh, God, she thought. I don't want to talk about this. I can't. She took a deep breath, as he continued.

171

"It wouldn't have happened . . . if I'd known."

Known? Revel thought with weary confusion. Known what?

Almost as if he read her thoughts, he went on to explain, his gaze meeting hers briefly with an odd, unreadable expression, then darting back to the fire as if he were escaping.

"I didn't expect you to be a virgin," he said simply, tossing more wood onto the fire, sparks bursting angrily into the chill air.

Didn't expect it? Revel struggled with that simple admission. It took her completely off balance. Of all the things she might have expected—an apology, or maybe some vague excuse—this wasn't one of them.

But even as she considered those two possibilities, she realized neither was typical of the Jake Reno she was slowly coming to know.

He dealt with things head-on, no matter what the consequences. Good or bad, win or lose, live or die, Jake Reno didn't back away from anything or anyone.

His openness about what had happened shouldn't have made her angry, but it did. It wasn't the brute honesty, it was the meaning behind it.

For some inexplicable reason it bothered her— bothered her a great deal—that his regret apparently had nothing to do with anything that had passed between them, but obviously had everything to do with the fact that she wasn't his usual, experienced whore. Well, at least he is honest, she thought painfully.

"I see." Her tone was deliberately cool. "Well, I hope you weren't too disappointed."

The minute she said it, Revel could have bitten her tongue. She sounded waspish, as if her feelings were hurt or she was disappointed. She detested that in anyone else, refused to accept it in herself. She had always taken pride in her calm judgment and her ability to handle matters when under pressure. Well, she wasn't calm, and she certainly wasn't handling this situation very well.

Jake thoughtfully chewed on the end of a twig as he looked at her across the fire. She was disheveled, her long, dark hair, hanging in wild torrents about her shoulders. Traces of mud were smudged across her face and neck, reminders of the night before. She was dressed in his shirt, her long, slender legs bare below it, another reminder of the night before.

She was the last woman in the world he should want, but God help him he'd wanted her last night and he wanted her now. But it was wrong, all wrong, and could only mean more trouble, for both of them.

He continued chewing on the end of the twig and wished like hell he had a cigarette.

"It has nothing to do with disappointment, Revel."

His unexpected gruffness surprised her. She looked up as he went on to explain.

"It's just that I didn't figure a woman out on her own, and in your line of work, would still be a virgin."

"I didn't realize losing one's virginity was a requirement."

"It's not. But the fact is you're not exactly the type of person who becomes a Pinkerton."

"Oh? And just what is the type of person who becomes an agent?"

"Well, it's the first time, I ever heard of a *woman* being a Pinkerton agent," he remarked casually, without the least trace of condemnation or ridicule.

Revel rubbed her hands together to warm them. His comment grated against her nerves, as if a woman weren't capable of doing as good a job as a man.

"There are several women agents. In certain situations it can be an advantage for a man and woman to work together on an investigation. It's less conspicuous, especially in a social situation."

"But you aren't working with another agent," he pointed out.

He'd never believed for a minute that another agent was to join them. It had simply been a convenient lie for

173

her to tell Virgil Earp so as not to rouse his suspicions. But suspicions about what? He wanted some answers.

"I explained that to you," Revel said carefully.

"Yeah, right. Your partner couldn't get to Tucson and your superior decided to let you go after Sam Bass alone."

By his tone, she knew he didn't believe that for a minute. She fully expected him to question her further about it, and when he didn't she became uneasy. Everything Jake Reno did was done for a reason.

"So, why aren't you married with a passel of kids?" He asked, taking the conversation in a completely different direction.

"At your age, most women are settled down—married, with a home, a husband—and living a very proper life."

"At my age?" She gave him a sharp look. What was he up to?

He shrugged. "You must be at least twenty."

"Actually, I'm twenty-three. I'll be twenty-four on my next birthday," she informed him, watching for his reaction.

"So, why aren't you married?"

His bluntness surprised her once again. He certainly had a way of slicing through all pretenses.

She kept her voice even, determined not to betray any emotion. "The opportunity simply never presented itself."

"Unh-unh." Jake wasn't buying any of it. She was well spoken, articulate, and beautiful in a compelling sort of way. He already knew, whatever the circumstances, she wasn't the sort of woman a man easily walked away from or forgot. And he didn't buy the fact that there had never been a man in her life.

"I beg your pardon?"

"You don't have to beg anything from me, Revel," he said with a thoughtful smile. Then the smile vanished, and his voice had a hard edge as he turned on her. "The fact is, you're a liar."

She blinked at him. "Of all the . . ."

He shrugged and cut her off. "You're beautiful, enticing as hell, talented in ways I'm only just beginning to appreciate, but still a liar." He went on without allowing her the chance to argue, interrupt, or deny anything he was saying as he slowly stood and walked around the fire toward her.

He moved like a stalking animal, wary, dangerous, and unpredictable.

"My guess is, you're well educated. You probably went to one of those fancy finishing schools." He held up a hand when she started to protest, and went on.

"You've got breeding and brains, and undoubtedly a great deal of money. You walk, talk, and dress like a lady. And believe me, I've had enough experience to tell the real ones from the ones that wanna be."

"Like I said, a woman like you should be married to some well-dressed gentleman, with a fine house, servants, and some kids. But you aren't, and it isn't because no one ever asked. Besides, your family would arrange that sort of thing."

He went on, taking his time. "In which case, I'd say you don't have any immediate family."

"Is that right?"

"Yeah, that's right," he explained precisely how he had arrived at that conclusion. "You only spoke once about your father, and the way you said it, it's my guess he's dead." He noticed the momentary flash of pain in her eyes.

Just as he'd thought, the subject of her father was a very emotional one. He continued.

"It's hard to say about your mother; you've never mentioned her. Either she died when you were very young, or maybe there was a big disagreement about your chosen profession. Truth is, no proper Eastern lady would allow her daughter to set out alone, much less take on such dangerous work." He paused.

"Is that all, Mr. Reno?" Revel asked coolly, which

175

only convinced him he'd struck closer to the truth than she liked.

"Almost. Now this is the part that doesn't make any sense. Just *why* are you doing all this?"

"I'm certain you have your thoughts on that matter too," she answered brittlely, hating with every passing second that he had guessed so well.

"Yeah, I do. At first I thought it was a joke. I thought maybe you were one of those Eastern newspaper people always looking for an exciting story about the West. Then I overheard Wyatt and Virgil Earp say they checked on you. And you're a fairly good shot with a gun." He paused, then qualified that last statement, "At least at close range."

"So precisely what conclusion have you made from all of this very interesting information, providing you're right, of course."

He gave her a long speculative look. "I'd say that I'm right about most of it. I've made it a habit to know people, Revel. You're a Pinkerton, all right. The question is, why?"

She stood, wrapping the shirt more tightly about her body as if it were a protective shield. She didn't care for people prying into her private life. "Are you quite through?"

"No," he said with dangerous softness, and then mimicked her, "I'm not *quite* through. I want some answers. Just who the hell are you? And what do you want with Sam Bass?"

She lifted her head slightly. The expression on her face was cool, completely unemotional, and very unreadable. He understood that expression. More, he understood the emotions that lay behind it. He'd had a lot of practice at hiding his own emotions.

"I've explained all of that to you before, *Mr. Reno.*"

Once again he wasn't swallowing any of it. When she retreated a few steps toward the shelter in the rocks, where they'd passed the night and where her skirt lay drying in the early morning sunlight, he followed like a stalking animal.

"Unh-unh," he said again. "You explained what you wanted everyone to believe. But it wasn't the truth."

When she whirled around he was so close she had to look up to see into his arrogant green eyes.

"I don't owe you any explanations."

"You do, if I'm going to risk my neck helping you find Sam Bass."

Her voice shook with suppressed fury and something else that was unexpected . . . tears. If he wasn't mistaken she was very close to breaking down.

"You'll help me find him, or I'll see you hang," she spat out.

"I don't buy that either, Revel. The truth is, you can't find him without me, or you would have done it already. If you have me arrested and hanged, you lose Sam Bass." He stepped closer, roughly took hold of her upper arms, and shook her.

"Dammit, why are you after Bass? What could he possibly mean to you?"

"Sam Bass is a wanted man, and he's alive. That's reason enough."

"Not for me." His words whipped at her. He shook her again, hard. "As difficult as it may be, I want the truth."

She winced. "You're hurting me."

"I'll do more than that. I'll leave you out here for the renegades. Now, tell me!"

Her eyes were like blue fire tipped with gold flame, and dangerous. She clawed at his fingers to try to break his hold. She might as well have tried to break a steel chain.

"Answer me!"

Her eyes were bright, vivid, haunted with pain.

"He killed my father!"

As she said it, she wrenched out of his grasp, the shirt fabric tearing beneath his white-knuckled fingers.

Her shoulders trembled with every painful breath. She wrapped her arms around her as if she could physically

177

hold on to the slender thread of control. Deep, hard gasps choked her. She tried to swallow the knot of anger and pain.

"Who was your father?" he quietly asked.

She closed her eyes against the mental images that filled her thoughts, trying desperately not to give in to the tears. Dear God, she didn't want to cry in front of him. She took a deep breath and it caught in her throat as a dry sob.

"Matthew Gibson," she whispered.

Jake's eyes narrowed. The name was familiar.

"Matt Gibson, with the Pinkerton National Detective Agency."

Revel nodded. "He met Mr. Pinkerton during the war. Afterward, he went to work for him in Chicago. Later he moved to Denver."

Jake didn't know all the details, but he did know what had happened to Matt Gibson.

"Your father tracked Sam Bass and his men to Round Rock in Texas." When she said nothing in reply, he went on with what he remembered.

"He was the one who took the Rangers to Sam's hideout."

She nodded slowly. "They never would have found him without my father."

"But your father died at Round Rock and Sam Bass and his men escaped," Jake concluded.

Revel sniffled softly. "The official report said that he got caught in a crossfire, the same crossfire that supposedly killed Sam Bass."

"It does happen," Jake offered sympathetically, aware more than she could ever know of how much pain she felt. She had obviously loved her father very much.

"I don't believe it." Revel turned back around. Having fought her way past the pain, she was once more cool, calm, and perfectly controlled.

"My father survived the war and almost twenty years with the Pinkerton Agency. He wasn't careless and he wasn't stupid. He'd been on Sam Bass's trail for months and had never made a mistake. He didn't make a mistake that day."

"How can you be certain?"

Her voice became very small. "I insisted on seeing him before he was buried. There was only one wound, in the heart."

Jake frowned. "It's not the first time a man died from a single shot."

Revel shook her head adamantly. "One bullet in the back." Her voice caught with emotion. When she was once more in control, she went on. "It was the kind of wound made by a rifle shot from a great distance."

"Sam Bass?" Jake suggested what he knew she already believed.

"I'm convinced it was Bass. My father had been after him for months. Mr. Pinkerton gave him the case. The last time I saw him was just before he left for Texas. I'd never seen him like that before. He was determined to find Bass. Bass knew it and hated him. He even sent letters to the agency, bragging about how he was going to kill my father."

"That doesn't mean Bass shot him. It could have been one of his men. Supposedly three of them were with him at Round Rock when the Rangers found him."

"There were four besides Sam Bass." She said it quietly, matter-of-factly. The haunting image of the hangman's gallows flashed briefly through her thoughts. Then it was gone, carefully tucked away with other ghosts.

"I heard there were three." Jake's gaze narrowed as he studied her. "I also heard they're all dead now. The last was Pete Dawson. He drew on a deputy who was taking him to jail."

Revel met his gaze evenly, the memory of those gallows like shadows behind her eyes. "There were four," she repeated without hesitation. "Quint Burdett was hanged in El Paso three months ago."

179

It wasn't what she said, but what she left unsaid. Jake realized that without a doubt Revel Tyson was responsible for finding Sam Bass's men. He knew some of them, had ridden with them—briefly. Two of the men joined up after he left. He knew them only by reputation, and it was all bad.

"How can you be so certain Bass didn't die at Round Rock and one of his men shot your father?"

"When I went to Texas to take my father home to be buried, one of the Rangers who was at Round Rock was there to meet me. He tried to make me feel better by explaining how Sam Bass died. Then he showed me Bass's revolver, a memento that he was allowed to keep."

She took a deep breath as she worked her way through the emotion brought to the surface by painful memories. "It didn't mean anything to me until I was going through my father's things. He was a very thorough man and an excellent agent. He kept very accurate notes about the cases he worked on. Because he traveled so much when he was on a case, he turned the information over to the agency when he finished." Her gaze was very somber.

"He kept meticulous notes on Sam Bass—where he was seen, who he knew, relatives, friends, conversations people remembered. He even made notes about what Bass liked to eat, and how he dressed. An agent can learn a great deal about a man's habits from information like that."

Jake wondered just how much she'd learned about *him*, since she'd gone to so much trouble to find him. She'd obviously studied her father's files on Sam Bass.

"What else did you learn?"

She looked down at her hands, clasped before her. "As I said, my father was meticulous. He made a specific note about how Sam Bass wore his gun. It seemed particularly important to him, because the way a man wears his gun tells how he shoots." At Jake's thoughtful silence, she went on.

"The revolver the Rangers claim belonged to Sam Bass

180

was set up for right-handed draw."

Because Jake once rode with Bass, he knew exactly what she was going to say. "And you discovered that Sam is left-handed." When she simply nodded, he filled in the rest.

"That's when you knew the man the Rangers killed wasn't Sam Bass."

"That's right. And that's when I joined the Pinkerton Agency."

"I'm surprised they let you, knowing you were Matt Gibson's daughter."

"They didn't know. I only met William Pinkerton once when I was very young, on a visit with my father in Denver. Tyson is my mother's family name."

Jake was silently impressed. He knew from the beginning she was intelligent, but his admiration increased another notch. She was not only intelligent, she was very clever. Even if she was a fool.

"And once you became a Pinkerton agent, you began tracking down Sam's men, one by one."

"They were all wanted by the law. I had access to records, files, and reports. Once I was given field assignments outside the Agency offices, it was easy enough to make inquiries on my own."

"And you found them," he concluded with a mixture of quiet contemplation and growing respect.

"The agency was very appreciative. Sooner or later, I knew one of them might lead me to Bass. That's when I found Ben Waters. He signed an affidavit that he saw Sam Bass alive no more than six months ago."

"Did you take this to the Rangers?"

"No. I want Bass first."

"Revenge. That's what it's all about, isn't it?"

That one, hard word took her aback. She'd confronted the truth of it often enough over the last few years, especially in the darkness of some strange hotel room in a strange town, while on the trail of a deadly outlaw. And long ago, somewhere along the way, she'd given up the

181

illusion and the lie that what she did was out of some inherent sense of justice. She swallowed tightly.

"Yes, I did it for revenge." When she said it, the expression in his green eyes changed. It was that same expression she first saw that day in Marshal Earp's office at the jail in Tombstone. It was the hard, cold look of death.

"Revenge can destroy you, Revel." There was a hard edge to his voice that made her think he knew precisely what he was talking about, and he understood only too well the high cost of revenge to one's soul. But it changed nothing.

"It's all I have, Mr. Reno," she said softly.

"Are you willing to kill for it?" he asked with brutal honesty.

After only a moment's hesitation, she met his gaze directly. "Yes," she answered solemnly.

"Are you willing to die for it?"

He saw her confidence waver momentarily. The night before they had both come close to being killed in that flash flood. It was fresh in her mind as it was his. But that was only the beginning. Ahead of them lay the wide-open New Mexico Territory and beyond, the Sonoran mountains, renegade Indian tribes, and Sam Bass if they lived long enough to find him. In a flash the uncertainty disappeared, replaced by that cool defiance.

"I want Sam Bass," she said determinedly.

Jake frowned. If she was determined to go on, he would be forced to go with her. Somehow, he had to find a way to stop her. It was clear no amount of argument would change her mind.

"Then you'd better get dressed." His voice was hard as he gestured to her split, fabric skirt, laid out on the rocks.

She was grateful their discussion of Sam Bass was over, at least temporarily, even though she had no doubt there would be future discussions. He hadn't given up trying to dissuade her from going on, but she wouldn't give in. If necessary, she was prepared to exert her full authority. Nothing was changed between them.

He returned to the fire and placed more wood on it as she retrieved her damp skirt from the rock. There was no private place where she could dress. She winced painfully as she sat back against the rock and started to pull the skirt on.

Jake turned back at her painful gasp. "What is it?"

"Nothing," she quickly reassured him, now standing to pull the skirt on.

He walked over to her. "Sit down before you fall down with that thing around your ankles." He pushed her back down on the rock. She cried out painfully as she tried to twist away from him.

"I don't need your help," she spat at him angrily.

"You do!" Jake's first thought was that she might have been hurt during their dangerous trip down the river. His next thought was that he was responsible. Whatever it was, was painful enough to bring tears to her eyes in spite of her anger. He grabbed her by the shoulders.

"Are you hurt?"

"No! I mean, not exactly." She closed her eyes as the expression in them shifted to something very near embarrassment. "It's nothing," she repeated firmly.

He rested one hand on her shoulder while the other came up under her chin. He tilted her face up so that she was forced to look at him.

"Are you going to tell me, or do I have to find out for myself?"

It wasn't a question but a subtle threat that she knew he would carry out. She swallowed hard.

"I . . . it's nothing really," she protested.

"Revel." It was said low, ending in quiet warning.

"It's just that I . . . last night . . ."

"What about last night?" he demanded, then thought, Oh God, did *I* hurt her?

Something deep inside him twisted at the thought, a feeling that was anger and something he hadn't felt in a very long time . . . caring.

183

"It happened before the storm . . ."—her gaze darted away from his—"when we first made camp."

Jake didn't have any idea what she was getting at. "What happened before the storm?"

"When I left camp for those few minutes . . . you said to be careful in the dark . . . I guess I wasn't careful enough."

He vaguely remembered that she had hurt herself. "You twisted your ankle?"

"No," she replied with growing humiliation and exasperation. "It was the damn cactus!"

"Cactus?" Now it was his turn to be surprised. Again she bit at her lip.

"Well, it's a little embarrassing." She went on hesitantly. "I must have . . . sat on it in the dark."

"You sat on a cactus?"

She looked up, catching the suddenly incredulous tone in his voice.

"Yes," she said testily. "After all, it *was* dark. How was I supposed to know there would be a cactus right *there!*" At a faintly strangled sound, her head snapped up.

The sound wasn't a snicker, or even a chuckle. It was an outright roar of laughter.

"A cactus?" he asked with disbelief.

"Damn you! That's what I said. Now, if you will excuse me, I would like some privacy while I finish getting dressed."

"You sat on a cactus!"

She gave him a murderous look, then turned her back on him. "Don't push your luck, Reno."

In between coughing fits of laughter and attempts to draw a deep breath, he said, "Something will have to be done, you know."

"What are you talking about?" She pulled on what remained of her shirtwaist. It was torn in several places, but covered the important areas.

"Come here, Revel."

184

She still had his shirt draped around her waist. She looked up suspiciously at the sudden change in his tone of voice. He was slowly walking toward her.

"What are you going to do?"

He was making a monumental effort not to laugh and not succeeding very well.

"I'll have to take a look at your . . . er . . . your wound."

Her mouth dropped open. "I beg your pardon?"

He liked the way she said that, all proper and elegant and innocent. He swallowed back all traces of laughter.

"Some cactuses in the desert have poisonous spines. It can be dangerous if that poison gets into your blood."

"Like scorpions," she asked with growing suspicion.

"It's a little more serious than that. Some cactuses can kill you."

"I see."

"I'll have to take a look at it. I can tell by the look of the . . . wound. If it's poisonous there are remedies that can be taken. Broken Hand will know which one to use."

"He's not here," she pointed out.

"He will be."

"How can you be so certain? We must be miles from our original campsite."

Jake was confident. "He'll find us. Until he does, I need to know how bad that wound is."

"Couldn't this wait until we get to a farm or settlement?" she asked with growing uneasiness. Somehow the thought of baring her backside to Jake Reno, in spite of what had happened the night before, or maybe because of it, seemed the ultimate humiliation.

"It'll be days before we reach the first settlement once we cross into the New Mexico territory. You may not live that long."

She was certain he was deliberately trying to scare her, his way of proving a point—that she had no right to be out there in the first place. After all, he'd made his

185

feelings about going after Sam Bass clear from the very beginning. Still, there was the possibility he was telling the truth.

"Revel?"

"All right!" she finally agreed. "But it's on the left side. You have to promise not to look anywhere else."

"Come here." He sat down on the rock and held out his hand to her.

"Promise?"

He bit back another smile. "I promise I will only look at what's necessary."

Revel groaned as she walked toward him. She wished she could fall into a hole in the earth. She stopped just in front of him. He took her by the hand.

"You'll have to lie across my lap."

"Oh, God," she whispered.

"God has nothing to do with the thorn in your backside, Revel. Come on, now. There's a good girl." With a gentle but insistent tug, he pulled her across his lap. Just as gently he lifted the tail of his shirt that hung to her knees. Revel clamped her eyes firmly shut in complete mortification.

They immediately flew open again as his fingers carefully probed her tender bottom.

"Ouch!"

"Um-hmmmm."

"What does that mean?" His fingers gently caressed the left side of her bottom.

"Um-hmmmm."

"Jake!"

As efficiently as he'd pulled her across his lap, he turned her over, and even though she winced painfully, he held her pinned in his lap.

"Well?" she demanded, squirming to get up. He refused to let her go.

"Just as I thought."

In spite of the fact that she would rather have died

186

than discuss such a matter as her injured bottom with Jake Reno, she had to know.

"What is it?"

One strong arm pinned her around the waist, the other cradled her against his chest, her face only inches from his.

"It's just as I thought." His gaze fastened on the full curve of her lower lip, and he remembered the taste of it.

"What does *that* mean?"

He looked up, losing himself once more in the deep blue of her eyes.

"Jake?"

Unexpectedly and suspiciously, he smiled. "Sooner or later I knew I'd get you to call me by my first name."

Her eyes narrowed with the nagging thought that she'd been had. "And what about my injury?"

"Oh, that."

"Yes, that! Is it poisonous?"

"I don't think so."

"You don't think so! Don't you know for certain?"

"Nope."

"Then, what was all that . . ."—she gestured furiously as she searched for the right words—"what was that examination all about?"

He shrugged. "I heard once that's what you're supposed to do."

"I see." She tried to scramble off his lap, but he refused to let her go.

"Take it easy, Revel. Actually, I do know what I'm talking about and you're perfectly safe. Your . . . wound will be a little tender for a few days, but you'll live."

"That is so reassuring." She gave him a scathing look. "Now, please release me. After all, Broken Hand will be here soon."

"He already is here," Jake informed her as he looked over her shoulder.

Revel turned. Broken Hand sat astride his black and

187

white pony at the edge of their small camp. He led the sorrel and Jake's Appaloosa. Dear God, how much had he seen?

She was completely mortified. She twisted out of Jake's grasp and darted behind a rock to finish dressing. She tossed his shirt aside, not caring where it landed. When she stepped from behind the rock a few minutes later, she was fully dressed, except for boots.

The conversation between Broken Hand and Jake immediately ceased. The old Indian guide gave her a long look.

"You ride on ahead," Jake told him. "I'll tell her."

She looked at him suspiciously. What was he up to now?

"Tell me what?"

He'd wanted some way to convince her of how dangerous this trip was. Now he had it.

"Get on your horse," he gruffly ordered.

"What is it?"

He said nothing as he mounted the Appaloosa and turned southward. Revel had to scramble to keep up with him. She winced as she sat in the saddle and slipped her bare feet into the stirrups, noting that her saddlebags and carpetbag had been returned by Broken Hand.

They rode hard along the winding course of the river. It amazed her that the roaring wall of water that had practically drowned them both last night had receded to nothing more than a shallow stream this morning.

She nudged the gelding to keep up with Jake's Appaloosa. On the distant rise she made out the form of a single rider. As they came closer, she recognized Broken Hand. A faint curl of smoke rose behind him.

Thank God, she thought. There must be a farm or ranch on the other side, although the surrounding land didn't look as if it would support livestock or crops.

Broken Hand turned his pony and headed down the other side of the rise. Revel followed Jake. As they gained the crest she looked down the opposite side, where the

Indian guide had ridden. The smoke was more distinct now, and her eyes widened at the sight before her.

It wasn't a settlement. It was burned-out wagons, carcasses of dead horses and mules. Over all of it was the pervasive stench of bloated and mutilated bodies.

In the middle of the massacred encampment a single Apache war lance was spiked into the hard ground. It was decorated with stark white feathers that were in startling contrast to the bloodied bodies.

The wind caught at the streamer of feathers. They fluttered, an ominous warning of death.

Chapter Ten

There was no need for Jake to tell her anything.

The ghastly sight spread out on the hill below them spoke for itself.

Revel had seen death before: when she was seven and her mother died; when she went to Texas to take her father home; several times in her work as an agent, the most recent being Quint Burdett's hanging. Even his death, despite her cold detachment from knowing he deserved to die, had affected her profoundly, because in a very real way she had been the cause of it.

When her mother died, she'd accepted it with a child's innocent lack of any understanding of death. When her father died, that was the first time she had confronted the senseless tragedy of a life taken, brutally ended before its time. But even through her grief, she had understood, as she always had, that her father's *choice* was to be a Pinkerton agent. He'd willingly put his life on the line, taken risks.

This senseless carnage had nothing to do with choice. These people had died violently, horribly, fighting with their last breaths to survive. And she suspected even after they were all dead, the carnage had continued, just as Broken Hand had described in the massacre of the soldiers not far away.

The bodies were stripped, flies swarming on bloodied

191

limbs and torsos. In one horrified, sweeping glance, Revel counted at least eight bodies. They had been carved up, horribly disfigured in a brutal, savage manner. Even the mules that drew the wagons and horses had been slaughtered.

She swallowed down the bile that clogged her throat as she covered her mouth and nose aginst the stench of flesh already decomposing in the desert sun. Jake dismounted and went to speak with Broken Hand. She couldn't look at any of it any longer and turned the gelding about before she was ill.

When she was several yards away, she stopped and waited, closed her eyes. But the horrible images followed her, and she knew as long as she lived she would never forget that ghastly scene.

She inhaled deep gulps of fresh air, upwind from the wagons, and finally overcame the dizziness and cold clamminess she'd first felt. She was a strong person and had always considered fainting a ridiculous affectation, but back there she had come very close to being ill, fainting, or both.

She heard the distinctive crunch of bootheels and looked up as Jake Reno strode toward her. His face was hard, his expression set into harsh lines and angles. He had obviously been affected by the sight of the mutilated bodies. But his reaction was far different from hers. His eyes were cold, his words angry; every gesture, each movement of his body emanated danger.

"Get down off that horse!" he ordered, grabbing her by the wrist and pulling her out of the saddle before she even had a chance to react.

"What is it?"

"You're coming with me," he said determinedly as he dragged her along behind him. "There's something I want you to see!"

She half fell, half ran behind him. Stumbling barefoot over rocks and uneven ground, she cried out as a sharp stone cut into her foot, but he was relentless as he pulled

192

her down the hill toward the burned-out encampment.

As soon as she saw where he was dragging her, Revel tried to pull free of his grasp. She had seen enough, there was no point in going through that again. But he had other ideas, and ruthlessly pulled her along, not even looking back when she stumbled, fell, clung to him for balance, then scrambled to keep from falling again. He never broke stride, never stopped.

When they reached the edge of the encampment, a charred wagon on their right, he stopped and flung her to the ground before him.

"Take a look!" he shouted at her.

When she fell, her long hair tumbled over her eyes. She scooped it back, staring at him wildly. But before she could say anything, he grabbed her painfully by the shoulders and forced her to turn around.

"Look at them!" Even then he wasn't satisfied. He took hold of her jaw with bruising fingers and forced her to take a long hard look.

She didn't dare close her eyes for fear he'd tear them open. He was like a mad animal.

"That," he emphasized with cold fury, "is what is waiting for us out there! Do you understand? Do you?"

Her heart raced wildly, partly from fear, partly from horror and a growing rage. She tried to jerk free of his grasp, wincing as his fingers bruised her neck and jaw.

"Take a good, long look, Revel. And believe that if the Apache get hold of you, it will be *worse.*" He jerked her around to face him.

"Now do you understand? These were miners, but as far as the Apache are concerned they are trespassers. Is it worth it, Revel?" Fury hissed through his voice, slicing brutally at her. He had no mercy, no compassion. He was relentless. He shook her hard.

"Do you understand?"

"Yes! I understand!" she screamed at him, twisting painfully out of his grasp. *"I understand!"* she repeated in a shaky voice edged with fragile control.

"It doesn't change anything. I intend to find Sam Bass, and I don't care how long it takes." Anger bubbled up in her.

He still had hold of her wrist, his grasp so strong it felt as if he would crush her bones.

"I asked you before if you were willing to die to find him. Take a good look at those men, and then tell me again." He shoved her around to face the mutilated bodies.

"Yes," she said softly so softly that he almost didn't hear it. He jerked her back around. Before he asked again, she repeated it.

"Yes! I'm willing to die to find him."

"Even if it means riding through hell?" His voice was hard; the words were flung at her.

Again she answered, *"Yes."*

He threw her to the ground. His voice was cold as death. "And you're determined to take me with you."

"Yes."

He stalked angrily past her. Revel shoved her tangled hair back from her face with a shaking hand. She hurt. She would have bruises in all the places where he'd touched her, and her hand was badly scraped from trying to break her fall when he'd shoved her to the ground.

She felt miserable and for a moment she thought of being clean, safe, and a thousand miles away. Then it passed, and not even the horrors around her could make her change her mind. She wouldn't give in, and she wouldn't turn back.

Before she got up, she heard Jake's angry stride behind her. She scrambled to her feet and turned on him as he approached, determined that he wasn't going to touch her like that again. But he never even looked at her. He simply threw a wrapped bundle at her and stalked past to his horse.

"Put those on," he ordered through tight lips. "If it doesn't bother you to see them dead like that, then I don't suppose it'll bother you to wear their clothes."

194

He didn't wait, but jerked the Appaloosa around and signaled to Broken Hand. Revel stared at him, horrified. As he started to ride off, she ran up to the Appaloosa and grabbed at his leg.

"Aren't you going to bury them?"

He looked down at her with an expression unlike any she had seen before. It was cold, remote, devoid of any emotion.

"You can stay to bury them if you've a mind to, but that raiding party is probably not far away. I don't intend to wait around for them to come back."

With that, he dug his heels into the Appaloosa's flanks and headed to the top of the ridge. Revel ran to the gelding. Her carpetbag was tied to the side of her saddle. She jerked it open and pulled out her small revolver.

"Stop!" she yelled the warning after him. Her hand shook, from fear or anger or possibly a mixture of both. He didn't slow his pace, didn't even so much as look back.

"Damn you, Jake Reno!" she shouted after him as he rode out of range of her voice and her gun. She jammed the revolver back into the carpetbag. Her head jerked up as Broken Hand stopped beside her.

"It would do no good to bury them," he explained in that quiet way of his. "The Apache intend them as a warning to others, like the blue-coats."

His meaning slowly dawned on her. "You mean they would dig them *up?*" Revel was horrified.

Broken Hand nodded stoically. "The ways of the Apache are not your way. You must think as they think to understand them. It is meant as a warning to others." Then he added in that quiet way of his, "We must go. They will be back." He lifted his gaze and scanned the high, flat terrain.

"Even now, they watch."

"What do they do to white women?" She had to know if Jake was lying to her about that as well.

Broken Hand studied her with dark contemplative eyes as if penetrating deep into her soul to know her character

195

for himself. Evidently satisfied, he decided to tell her the truth.

"Among the Apache, each brave would have his time to do what he chose with a woman taken as a slave. Then he would pass her on to the next brave."

She swallowed back her revulsion. His meaning was all too clear.

"And then what?"

The old Indian's gaze never wavered. He understood her unspoken fears. "Keep a knife with you at all times."

She naturally assumed he meant as a weapon to be used against the Apache if they should attack.

"Do not hesitate to use it on yourself. It would be far more merciful."

She was stunned, and swallowed with great difficulty. "I see." Then she looked up at him. "What would they do to you for helping us?"

"The punishment would be *worse* than death."

He said nothing more, but urged his pony to the top of the hill over which Jake had disappeared. Revel quickly mounted the gelding. She wanted to throw the bundle of clothes to the ground and simply ride away, but Jake's words still stung her. And the truth was, her own clothes were ruined. Her boots had been lost in the flash flood along with her coat, hat, and poncho.

She swallowed hard and forced herself to take one last look at the massacre. Then she stuffed the clothes into her cloth valise, and urged the gelding to the crest of the hill.

The last person to see Sam Bass alive was Ben Waters. She had found him in Las Cruces, in the New Mexico Territory. Jake led them steadily eastward through the high, flat desert.

The land changed as they steadily climbed shale-covered hills and wound their way through barren canyons. They stopped at midday to rest the horses. They ate strips of beef jerky and stale bread in silence. A rifle lay across a lap, the horses were loosely tethered within easy reach, eyes scanned the rising peaks about them. They were being watched, they could feel it.

The rest was brief. They watered the horses from their canteens and prepared to go on. Broken Hand rode on ahead, disappearing through a gap in the canyon wall just ahead.

Revel had put on the boots Jake confiscated for her. They were far too big, and she practically walked out of them each time she took a step. To make matters worse, which she hadn't thought they could be, their rubbing brought new blisters to her already tender feet.

When she had trouble getting her loosely booted foot into the stirrup to mount, she finally pulled herself up into the saddle. Looking up, she found Jake sitting astride the Appaloosa calmly watching her.

"Where is your revolver?"

If she'd expected an apology for what had happened earlier, none was forthcoming.

"It's in my valise."

He gave her a long, steady glare. "It'll do you a lot of good in there," he remarked sarcastically, "especially when the Apache decide to attack."

Her throat went try. "Do you think they will attack?"

"Oh, yeah," he answered almost indifferently. "It's just a matter of when."

"*When* would you say?" she shot back at him irritably, completely fed up with his arrogance. His reply made her blood run cold.

"Probably tonight. And this isn't where I'd like it to happen. It's too open, there's no place for us to protect ourselves."

"I see," she replied coolly.

"Are you really any good with that revolver? Or do you just use it for comin' up on a man without his clothes."

He was deliberately being peevish, but she wasn't

197

having any of it.

"I'm good enough, Mr. Reno." then she added, "But if we are attacked by the Apache it might be better if you were careful. My aim might be off just a little, and I would hate to shoot you instead of an Apache." For a moment she thought she saw the beginning of a grin play at the corners of his mouth. Then it was gone.

"Like I said, Revel, that gun isn't any good to you inside that valise. Put it in the waist of your skirt. That way you can get to it real easy if there should be trouble." He whirled the Appaloosa around and turned to follow Broken Hand through the gap in the hillside, calling back over his shoulder, "If you have to use it, be careful. Don't shoot your horse."

Once again, she found herself briefly considering shooting *him* as he rode away from her, tall in the saddle, shoulders straight, hat jerked low over his eyes.

Damn Jake Reno and his cursed arrogance. If she didn't need him so badly . . .

Then her gaze swept along the mountain rim above them, watching for any telltale movement. The breeze stirred, lifting a red-tailed hawk higher above them and reminding her of that war lance embedded in the ground. She shivered in spite of the afternoon heat that beat down on them.

It was an eerie feeling, knowing they were being watched by someone they couldn't see. Every mile took them closer to Sam Bass—and closer to nightfall.

She hadn't been afraid of the night since she was a child. Then monsters lurked under her huge, fourposter in Aunt Addie's elegant Philadelphia house. When she had to get up at night she always jumped from the middle of her bed out into the room where the light from the gaslamp in the hallway kept the demons at bay.

But now monsters stalked even in the daytime. They lurked behind trees and rocks, waiting . . . waiting . . .

Revel was getting used to cold camps, dry food choked

198

down with meager swallows of water, hurried trips behind a rock to solve more intimate needs, finding some small comfort in a single blanket tightly wrapped for warmth. She had even become quite good at hobbling the gelding to keep him from wandering off.

On this night, Jake chose not to hobble the horses, but left them saddled and tied to a nearby scraggly pine tree.

As they had climbed throughout the long afternoon, the flat, rock-strewn, high desert had given way to mountains with sparse vegetation, a gray shale instead of dirt, an occasional scrawny pine tree instead of saguaro cactus.

The sun had beat down on them relentlessly. When it went down behind the rim of mountains that surrounded them, it was cold. They made their camp in a shelter cut into a cluster of huge boulders.

Revel thought of snakes, spiders, and scorpions as she carefully placed her bedroll in a niche in the rocks.

Jake treated her no differently than Broken Hand, sparing her none of the work or responsibilities. She wouldn't have had it any other way.

It established the fact that he thought no differently of her now than before last night. Except for his resentment at being on this trip, it was an invisible boundary of indifference that she desperately needed in order to sort through her own confused emotions.

When Jake asked Broken Hand to take the first watch, she spoke up, "I'll take it, if that's all right."

Both men turned and looked at her with unspoken but obvious doubt.

"I won't nod off, I have excellent hearing, and I've done this before."

"This is a little different than hiding out in someone's closet, Revel."

"I'm aware of the difference," she informed him quietly. "I can handle my part of the watch."

She knew by the look on his face, the way his mouth

199

thinned, that he didn't share her confidence. He looked past her to Broken Hand. Whatever passed silently between them, he simply shrugged his shoulders.

"All right. The first watch, till midnight. I'll relieve you."

That was it. No instructions, no warnings, no vivid reminders of what would happen to them if she failed to stay alert. He stalked off in the direction of the horses. She stared after him, not wanting to follow, but not having much choice since the carpetbag with her blanket and clothes was still hooked over her saddle.

She glanced briefly back over her shoulder. Broken Hand was no longer standing behind her. As was his habit, he had probably gone up into the rocks to take a careful look around their location.

It was almost dark. She had no choice but to follow Jake. He certainly wasn't about to bring her carpetbag to her. She squared her shoulders and walked to the edge of camp.

Jake stood quietly stroking the Appaloosa's satiny neck, talking softly into dark, smoke-colored ears that flicked back and forth as if the stallion listened intently.

The words were unintelligible, made up of muted sounds, soft clicking, and deeper almost guttural phrases, all spoken in a soothing rhythm that was almost a song or quiet chant.

"What is that language?" she asked, forgetting how dangerous conversations with him could be. Without looking around, he combed his long fingers through the stallion's coarse black mane and stroked the smoky neck.

"It's the language of the Nez Percé Indians."

"Does he understand it?" she asked with a mixture of disbelief and awe.

"He was born and raised as a colt among the Nez Percé."

"And you talk to him."

He looked at her briefly, then went on smoothing his

200

hands over every inch of hard muscle and tightly drawn sinew.

"I find animals preferable to most people I know."

Revel's gaze snapped to his. There was no mistaking his meaning. She stepped stiffly to the gelding, retrieved her carpetbag, and turned to leave when his voice stopped her.

"Yes, he understands. He's also very sensitive to the night sounds out here," he went on to explain, which he wouldn't have done had he wanted her to leave. "He'll know before the other horses, if the Apache come near the camp tonight."

It was a tentative gesture at a truce, and considering how angry he had been with her earlier, it surprised her. In all those months, trying to find Jake Reno, she had learned a great deal about him. He didn't forget and he rarely forgave. Whatever it was in his past that had made him the man he was, he seemed to have no regrets. He hadn't even revealed any as he was about to hang. That could be said about few men.

She stepped quietly toward the Appaloosa. As he caught her scent, he jerked his head around and fixed her with wide, dark eyes as if he, too, were making some sort of assessment. She reached out slowly, having learned long ago that one had to be careful, calm, and assertive with animals. Just as a dog could smell fear, a horse could sense it also. She patted him firmly.

When he swung his muzzle up and tried to nip her arm, she caught him with her hand and firmly shoved his head away. She didn't believe in striking an animal, but they had to know who was boss.

He turned back again, but only to look at her with a new curiosity. Jake chuckled softly.

"He likes you."

Revel smiled. "That's why he tried to take a bite out of me."

"If he'd wanted to bite you, he would have." He

watched her keenly. "You understand animals."

"My father taught me about horses. We spent a lot of time around them when I visited him."

"Then you didn't live with him?"

She met his gaze briefly. "No, I didn't live with him. He traveled a great deal in his work for the agency. He didn't think it was the way to bring up a little girl. I lived with my aunt in Philadelphia, but I saw him frequently. He would stop in for a few days when a case brought him East, and I spent several weeks with him each summer. He always remembered my birthdays and sent me presents at Christmas. He brought me a puppy once, but my aunt didn't let me keep it. Next time, he brought me a kitten."

Jake had heard of Matt Gibson. There wasn't an outlaw alive that hadn't. Gibson had a reputation for being tough and relentless. When he went after a man, he didn't quit until he had him, dead or alive. Jake had had a brief encounter with him years earlier, and knew enough to realize he didn't want anything to do with him. There had obviously been two distinctly different sides to Matt Gibson.

"Philadelphia, huh?"

By the way he said it, she knew exactly what he was thinking—that he'd been right in his earlier assessment of her background.

"*Yes, Philadelphia.*"

"Why didn't you stay there?"

"I never intended to stay there. I had planned to move to Denver to be with my father. He was going to leave the agency, he had some money set aside. But then . . ."— she hesitated, finding her way through the painful memories—"things changed."

From what she had told him earlier, he knew she referred to Sam Bass and the shootout at Round Rock. The thickness in her voice, the sudden catch in her throat, pulled at him. Her vulnerability was exposed, briefly, and he was reminded of someone else.

It will be all right, won't it Jake? You'll make it all right, you have to. Jake? Please, don't let them hurt me! Jake!

The desperate screams echoed through his mind. When they had finally disappeared again, safely hidden away in memory, he looked back at her.

He understood. Her memories of her father were of brief visits, special occasions, tiny moments found along the way, that, when added up, didn't fill an empty childhood. And then her father was dead, killed by Sam Bass. At least he'd known both his parents. Still, he understood her pain.

"My folks were killed when I was fourteen," he said softly, trying somehow to offer comfort, at the same time not at all certain why he wanted to. "They were good people. My pa had plans for the ranch he was building up. But sometimes things don't turn out the way you plan."

There was such sadness and pain in his voice. Revel couldn't imagine what it must have been like to be without a family at such a young age. At least she'd had Aunt Addie, and she'd been older when her father was killed. From what she knew about Jake that must have been just about the time he started riding with different outlaw gangs. Because she somehow sensed his need to talk about it, she asked, "How did it happen?"

His expression changed, hardened into the likeness from hundreds of wanted posters.

"Five men rode in, asking for water for their horses." Something in his voice changed, requiring effort to keep it even and devoid of the emotions that still cut through him after all these years.

"They didn't want water."

"What did they want?" Revel asked.

"Blood and death." His voice was stark, his face suddenly emotionless, except for his eyes. If death had a look, it was in those eyes. "They shot my father when he came out to give them water. Then they killed my mother, but only after they all took turns raping her."

"Dear God," Revel whispered softly. She could see the

203

pain the memories caused and didn't want him to go on. But this was something that, once begun, seemed to tumble out in a torrent of long-stored rage.

"I followed them for days—I just left the ranch and started riding." He was staring off, looking at nothing, seeing all those vivid images that had changed his life. He chose not to speak about his sister. That memory was so much more painful—she had been so young and innocent.

His voice was hard, emotionless, as cold as death itself. "Then I went after them. And I found them one by one— and made them pay for what they did to my family."

And you paid an even greater price, Revel thought to herself. Now she understood. "You were just a child," she whispered incredulously, filled with pain for what he'd endured at such a young age.

"Sometimes you grow up fast and hard, Revel. After that, I wasn't a child anymore." Then he shrugged, as if mentally shrugging off the memories. "Sometimes life does that to you. You take what's handed you, and you have to choose. You either live or you die."

"And you decided to live," she concluded.

"In a manner of speaking. If you can call running from the law any kind of life, never having a home or anything to call your own."

Once again, his voice betrayed him. It was wistful, filled with pain and such a profound sense of loss that she knew he had hated the life he'd lived but had nonetheless followed that chosen path. She didn't know how to respond to what he had just revealed about himself.

"But you have the Appaloosa," she said softly, stroking the velvety gray muzzle.

"Yes, I have the Appaloosa. And I suppose I should thank you for that. But I think I'll wait to see if we live through this."

"He is magnificent," she went on, wanting to know more. "How did you come by him?"

"He was born to one of the mares given to my father by the Nez Percé."

Her gaze met his briefly. She'd just learned more about him with a few simple questions than she'd been able to find out in the last six mnths.

"I've heard of these horses, but I've never seen one before. I heard the Nez Percé didn't part with their prize spotted horses."

"They usually didn't. It was an agreement of honor between the old chief and my father, made a long time ago, before the Nez Percé were forced to leave their land. He wanted the Appaloosa to survive, and my father promised him he would keep the bloodline true." His voice grew quiet.

"But he died and wasn't able to keep his promise."

"Are there other Appaloosa?"

"There's a small herd of a dozen or so mares and their foals. Friends take care of them." He was deliberately evasive and obviously didn't care to discuss it further. But Revel wanted to know more.

"Entrusted to another white man?"

Jake's gaze met hers. "Friends," he repeated.

Once again, the door that had opened briefly was carefully closed. She decided to try another direction.

"Your father must have been very special to be entrusted with the Appaloosa horses."

"He was honest, not afraid of any man, and he once returned something of great value to the old chief."

She probed a little deeper. "The chief repaid his debt with the horses?"

He stooped down beside the stallion, gently running his hands down slender legs, separately lifting each hoof, inspecting it carefully, then setting it back down. He looked up at her briefly.

"It was a blood bond between them. The chief simply entrusted the horses to my father." He slowly stood.

"Where are the horses now?"

"A long way from here, but then I suppose you already know that from the information the agency gave you."

She took a wild guess. "Your home?" In one of the agency files she'd studied there was an old notation that he supposedly had come from somewhere in the Wyoming Territory.

The expression on his face startled her. It was so filled with pain, and then it was gone.

"There's nothing there anymore, just the land."

"But you intend to go back."

He shrugged. "Maybe."

"That's why this stallion is so important to you."

He pulled his saddlebags from behind his saddle and turned to her briefly.

"Most likely none of us will make it back to anywhere, Miss Tyson. Now you'd better find yourself a comfortable spot, and don't forget to take your revolver. If you hear anything, wake me." Then he walked back to their camp in the rocks.

The evening was long. Broken Hand pointed out a place high in the rocks which gave her full view in the moonlight of the camp just below and the perimeter of rocks above. Then he dropped down to the campsite. She could see Jake, curled beneath his blanket, but the old Indian guide had obviously chosen another location. He simply disappeared into the shadows.

She was scared and would have been a liar if she'd told anyone she wasn't. She had done this before on a few occasions, but would go to her grave before she would admit that Jake was right about the circumstances.

Still, she had excellent eyesight and hearing. She quickly became accustomed to the usual night sounds, the occasional nickering of a horse, the distant howl of a coyote. She knew the Indians mimicked those same animal sounds, and each time one echoed through the chill night air and off mountain walls around them, she wondered if it was really made by an Apache.

But the sounds came no closer. There was no break in

the rhythm of night movement about them. Her only unsettling moment was when an owl whoosed past, only inches from her head. It swooped close to the ground, the night air churned by its wings.

There was a startled squeal, immediately silenced as huge talons found their prey. Then the owl disappeared over the top of the rocks. Below, Jake appeared to be asleep, although if she knew him at all, he was sleeping with one eye open, not about to trust in her abilities completely.

More than once her eyes played tricks on her, shadows shifting, changing, transforming as the moon climbed the sky. But it was nothing. She stretched her legs and arms, arching her back against the stiffness that came from sitting too long in one position, and kept her fingers loosely wapped about the revolver. She could endure it, all of it, if the reward was Sam Bass.

Somewhere near midnight, she gently nudged Jake. He was immediately, alertly awake, the steel of his Colt revolver gleaming just inches from her face. As he recognized her, he visibly relaxed.

"What is it?"

"It's late. I want some sleep," she answered a little tightly, amazed that he'd actually been able to sleep under the circumstances—both eyes closed. She knew she wouldn't have slept as soundly.

"I haven't seen Broken Hand since early evening," she added.

"Don't worry, he's around. He prefers doing things his own way."

"I just wish I knew where he was. I was afraid I might shoot him." She could have sworn he grinned at her.

"He'd never let you do that," Jake assured her.

"Are those blankets still warm?" she asked wearily.

"Sure. Help yourself."

"Thank you, I will." Revel immediately scooted past him, snuggled into his blankets and curled into the niche of the rocks.

"Pleasant dreams," he said with faint sarcasm, and then moved off silently.

She placed the revolver beside her head, her fingers resting on it.

"Uh-huh," she said wearily, but when she looked for him, he was already gone. "I hope you have sore muscles and freeze your backside up in those rocks, Jake Reno."

As she snuggled farther under the blanket, she was again reminded of the childish notion that blankets are protective coverings that keep all monsters at bay. It was foolish, of course, but she found herself snuggling in even deeper.

It was impossible to get comfortable. The hard rock made her restless, the cold made her restless, Jake Reno made her restless.

Without intending to do so, he'd revealed little bits and pieces of himself, making what she knew of him from the agency files—and rumors and speculation—take on a new perspective. There were reasons a man turned against the law. Usually it was greed, sometimes craziness, oftentimes pure meanness that came from something hidden deep inside him.

Jake Reno might be cunning, but he wasn't crazy. And as for greed, it was obvious the only thing that mattered to him was the Appaloosa. His records showed he'd never actually participated in any robberies, he'd simply associated with different outlaw gangs, never staying with one long enough to get caught. Oddly enough, the men he'd killed were all outlaws, and it wasn't in him to be mean or cruel without extreme justification. God knows he'd had plenty of opportunity to reveal a cruel streak while with her.

Oh, he'd been angry with her, infuriated to be more honest about it, and he could be hard and cold and, she was certain, utterly ruthless at times.

There was a survivor's instinct about him that made her believe he would never play the hero at the cost of his own life. It simply wasn't important to him. But something had once been important to him, something or . . . someone. That was the other side of the hardness, the anger, and the danger that seemed like second nature to him.

He *was* capable of gentleness, even tenderness. She saw it every time he handled the Appaloosa, and God knows she'd experienced it the night before.

He could have hurt her, humiliated her, brutalized her. She had been vulnerable enough because she'd feared they were both going to die. But he hadn't hurt her, except for those moments when they first came together. Even then he had been gentle with her.

Afterward, even though it had been obvious he regretted what had happened, he hadn't embarrassed or humiliated her.

As she became drowsy, Revel realized the Jake Reno was a mass of contradictions. Nothing of what she had learned about him the last few days had anything to do with the man she thought she knew from the agency files.

"Not that it matters," she murmured sleepily to herself as her eyes became heavy. All that mattered was that he find Sam Bass.

She was convinced she'd never be able to get to sleep. But eventually the cold no longer mattered, nor did the hardness of the rock. Numbing exhaustion shut out everything else.

Five minutes, an hour, longer?

Revel had no idea how long she'd slept. It seemed she had only dozed for a few seconds, but something made her sense it was longer. The night air that invaded her blankets had a different damp chill to it. The moon was no longer high overhead, but was slipping down the western horizon.

Groggy, her senses numb and slow to respond, she moved stiffly, groaned, then tried to sit up. Something wasn't right.

She listened for the familiar night sounds; the distant call of a coyote, the click and chirp of insects in the brush, the hoot of the owl. It was quiet, too quiet.

Beyond the rocks, the pale light of the moon illuminated where the horses should have been. They were gone.

She tried to spot Jake wrapped in the bundle of blankets several yards to her right where she remembered dropping them. Surely it was past the time when Broken Hand would have relieved him for the next watch. And where were the horses?

The blankets were gone, and there was no sign of Jake.

The subtle shift of a shadow drew her attention back to the center of the small clearing. In the moonlight, there were other shadows that she was certain hadn't been there before.

She rolled onto her stomach, a cold tingle spreading across her skin as her fingers tightened over the revolver.

Then she saw it again, movement like a careful stalking. First one shadow, then another, and another . . . the Apache!

Where was Jake? Broken Hand? What had happened to the horses?

Even as panic became a steely taste in her mouth, she fought it back. If she gave in to it she was as good as dead.

Think! She had to think!

Logic told her the Apache knew exactly what they were looking for; two men and a woman, three horses, possibly rifles. But the horses and the two men were gone.

In fact every trace of their camp in the rocks was gone, except for her.

She was hidden in the niche of the rocks. As the shadows increased in number, converged and surrounded what had once been the camp, she knew there was no chance for escape unless she could make it through the rocks above without being seen.

That could only be done by crawling out, exposing herself for however long it took to scramble to a higher level, and pray she wasn't seen.

Then what? Could she even do it?

Her imagination ran wild with visions of what the Apache would do to her if they found her.

A cold nausea churned in her stomach. Even if she were the best shot in the world, there were only six shots in the gun. She thought fleetingly of the knife Broken Hand had suggested. No, her only chance was escape.

But Revel had absolutely no idea what she would do if she did manage to sneak away. As far as she could tell she was alone and without a horse.

Damn Jake Reno anyway! She had known he might try something like this. Now he'd taken off and left her to be killed.

Her death would certainly solve all his problems. He would undoubtedly tell Marshal Earp they had found Bass, she'd been killed when they were attacked by Indians on the way back, and he'd demand that the marshal sign over his clemency papers.

Because of the past friendship of Jake and Earp, Revel was certain the marshal would do just that.

Her hand shook as it tightened on the revolver. Well, that was not going to happen!

She scooted as far out of the niche as she possibly could and still remain in shadow. A few feet below she could see the Apache as they searched the camp and then spread out to search farther. The longer she waited the greater the chance she would be found.

She glanced briefly down at her white shirtwaist. It would be a glaring beacon in the moonlight. She wrapped the blanket about her shoulders and crept farther out along the edge of the rocks. If she could only make it to the cut in them to her right, she might have a chance.

Just as she crept out onto the ledge, a hand clamped tightly over her mouth. A strong arm encircled her waist, and she was yanked back into the darkness of the niche.

Revel clawed at the pressure of that strong hand, she tried to scream. She fought, trying to kick out but her legs tangled in her skirt and the blankets.

A leg was thrown over her, pinning her helplessly onto

211

her stomach, her arms pinioned at her sides. She was caught, trapped like some helpless animal. And all the while she could see shadows move along the rocks below, swarming up the surrounding slope, seeming to come from every direction.

Panic choked her, and she shuddered at the close physical contact of a hard, male body. The distinctive scent of man filled her nostrils; the smell of dirt, sweat, and . . . something very dangerous.

Chapter Eleven

"Revel!" Her name was hissed in her ear.

"Be quiet! Quit struggling!"

The understandable words, the familiar voice, sliced through the cold grip of fear. She quit her frantic struggling, loosened her clawlike grasp on the hand clamped over her mouth. As she did so, those fingers slowly relaxed. With his other arm about her waist, Jake pulled her back hard against him and into the protective dark shelter of the rocks.

"Lie perfectly still," he whispered against her ear, his breath warm against her neck.

She nodded her understanding and his hand came away from her mouth. She let out a slow, shaky breath. Then fear returned—the Apache were scrambling through the rocks below them.

Revel strained to see through the early morning light. At one moment the unusual silence was broken by an occasional sound that might have been the wind in the rocks or a faint rustling in the brush. In the next moment, she couldn't be certain that she'd heard anything at all.

All the while her heart beat furiously, a loud, frantic sound that pounded through the blood in her veins. The Apache would surely hear it and find them.

Then it came to her ears—a light scraping sound, very

close and to the right of where they lay hidden. Jake heard it too. His body tensed, his left hand jerking up so that the tip of the Colt it held was very near her face and was pointed in the direction of the noise.

She heard it again and gasped. Jake's other hand immediately covered her mouth. As her eyes strained through the darkness she thought she saw a shadow shift on the exposed ledge of the niche. She jerked back, turning her head in mute warning, afraid, Jake might not have seen it. But his face was completely obscured by shadow. There was only his heat and the reassuring hardness of his lean body.

Still, she felt the wary shift of muscles and knew he had picked up the movement as well. She closed her eyes briefly, fighting back fear, offering up a small prayer.

Then she forced her eyes open. She hadn't come this far to die like a cornered animal up in these rocks. Carefully, silently, she shifted her right hand and brought her own revolver up. She had no idea how many Apache were out there, but she wasn't about to give up easily.

The skin Revel had exposed by pushing sleeves up her arms and opening the neck of her shirtwast was cool. This close, their bodies intimately entwined, Jake felt the faint dampness that broke out, smelled the unmistakable tang of fear edged with the equally unmistakable essence of woman.

Without words, he knew what she felt: fear, panic, desperation. Then he sensed the subtle shift in her body, and the cold brush of steel against his hand told him she had brought her revolver up.

He closed his free hand over hers. Her fingers were ice-cold, but her grasp was rock-steady. He didn't much care for the fact that she'd gotten them into this mess, but he had to admit to a grudging admiration for her. Any other woman he knew would have been screaming her fool head off, bringing every Apache within ten miles down on their necks. But Revel Tyson was cool, calm, in

214

control. They just might get out of this.

He gently squeezed her hand, giving her the encouragement he knew she so badly needed. It was a small gesture, but he immediately felt some of the tension ease out of her.

The shadow changed, edged past the ledge and then disappeared. Jake watched and listened. He slowly began counting off seconds, until several minutes had passed.

Then he heard the soft warble of a morning dove. It was clear, distinct, and came only once—a signal.

He waited several more minutes, then gently nudged Revel.

"Come on, we're getting out of here."

Her head jerked around in startled surprise.

"But—" As she started to protest, he pressed a finger against her lips.

"Quietly," he said. "They're still out there, somewhere." Without another word, he crawled over her, slithered out onto the exposed ledge and silently pulled himself to his feet.

She vaguely made out the shadow of the hand he extended to her. Revel hesitated. Dear God, she hoped he was right about this.

While on watch earlier, she had quietly changed into the trousers Jake had salvaged for her. The idea of wearing a dead man's clothing was repulsive, but practicality had won out over sensitivity.

Now Jake looked at her curiously as she emerged from their hiding place. She could see his bemused expression in the soft moonlight. But he said nothing about the pants.

"C'mon."

She stuffed the revolver in the waistband of the pants.

"Wait, my carpetbag," she whispered frantically.

"Leave it. It'll only slow us down."

She hesitated a moment, then took his hand and scrambled out behind him.

Instead of climbing down to the camp and the horses,

215

Jake led them up, crawling over rocks, silently grabbing for a secure handhold, inching through narrow cracks and crevices, hiding in the shadows as much as possible.

It was treacherous in the dark with only the shifting moonlight to guide them. Revel quickly discovered the best technique was to put her hand precisely where Jake put his, step where he stepped, crawl where he crawled.

Forget about trying to find a better way on my own, she told herself, I don't know these mountains.

It seemed they climbed for an eternity. Her hands and elbows were scraped, and she'd left her boots behind. Once more she was in stockinged feet. But that was the least of her problems.

They stopped to rest for a few minutes, hiding in a shadowy notch eroded into the adobe face of the mountain.

Revel collapsed wearily, brushing stray tendrils of hair out of her eyes.

"Where is Broken Hand?" she asked in a muted whisper. She saw Jake gesture vaguely overhead.

"Hopefully somewhere out there."

"Don't you know what happened to him?"

Jake heard the edge of anger, the accusation in the hissed question.

"He's all right."

"How do you know that?"

"Because Broken Hand is Apache too. He knows the price if he gets caught." He hesitated, giving emphasis to what he left unsaid, then he added, "He won't get caught. He'll try to meet up with us."

"What about the horses?" Revel was no fool. They were several days' travel from the last settlement. God only knew how much farther ahead the next one lay. They would have little chance of making it on foot.

"I turned them loose," he stated flatly.

"You did what!"

Revel was on her feet, no longer bothering to keep her voice to a whisper.

216

"Be quiet, and sit down!" Jake ordered, jerking her back down into the shadows.

"Your voice can carry for miles in these mountains, and the Apache will know just where to find you. If you want to keep your hair on your head I suggest you speak as quietly as you can."

She swallowed hard, wanting to say more, too frightened to risk it.

He knew what she was thinking. "If I'd left the horses the Apache would have them now, and that wouldn't do us any good at all. I'm hoping they'll find their way through these mountains. There's only one way in and one way out, and the last time I checked, horses didn't climb up rock cliffs."

"Then what you're saying is we have a fifty-fifty chance the horses will go in the right direction," she concluded angrily.

"Not bad odds," he said evenly.

She could have sworn he was grinning at her again. She groaned.

"Actually, I hedged that bet just a little."

He was still grinning at her. How could he do that at a time like this?

"And just how did you manage that?"

"I sent them in the direction that will lead them out."

"Unless, of course, they get spooked, turn around, and double back," she pointed out.

"Not likely."

Now he was being smug. She could almost see that devilish grin widen.

"And why is that?"

"Because there isn't any water back where we came from, and there is water on the other side, an underground spring. The horses will be drawn to the water."

"I see. And of course, the Apache don't know about this spring," she shot back.

"Oh, they know about it. That's why we have to get

217

there first. Off your butt, Miss Tyson. Time to get moving." He was on his feet, already slipping through a narrow opening between the rocks and grabbing for an overhead handhold for the upward climb.

Revel groaned. Between the Apache and the climb, there wasn't much choice. She could either go back and get scalped and be tortured or she could climb. There was one other choice too. She could stay right where she was and wait for help.

But that meant trusting Jake Reno to come back for her if he found the horses and the water, and she knew precisely what he thought of her. He'd just as soon be rid of her. There really was no decision to make. She squeezed through the opening after him. Watching as his shadow moved just above her, she reached for a handhold.

"Do you know where you're going?" she groaned as her ribs scraped against the rocks.

"Yeah," he quietly called back to her, "up."

They climbed *up* for hours, until the sun was poking through the jagged peaks, threatening to expose them. Their clothes were torn, their hands scraped, they had little water left in the canteens Jake had brought with him. But as far as they could tell the Apache hadn't followed them up the mountain. That left only the uncertainty of what they would find when they reached the other side and started down, hoping to find that spring.

By midmorning they inched their way over a narrow cornice and reached the other side. The descent was almost as treacherous as the climb.

Jake told her these were the Dragoon Mountains, and at one time they had been the stronghold of a notorious Apache chief, Cochise. The renegades they'd seen last night were remnants of his warriors, Apaches who stubbornly resisted life on the reservations.

218

The sun was high up when they made the final descent to the place where Jake hoped the spring was located. As he'd explained, it could be anywhere in the maze of rocky clearings at the foot of the mountains. But he was fairly certain of its location, having followed the course of the sun pinpointed through an unusual rock formation at the summit of the mountain. Revel fervently prayed he was on target.

They had stopped to rest at the base, too exhausted to speak of their fears that they might be completely off course and might never find the spring.

Revel's skin was covered with a fine, powdery dust from scrabbling through the rocks, her lips were dry and cracked, her hair was a mass of tangles. She sat on a rock, trying to escape the sun in the shadows cast by the rocks at her back.

She drank sparingly from her canteen, slowly lowering it as she watched Jake unscrew the lid from his, start to drink, then close it once again without taking any water. She had seen him do that several times during the morning and knew he was conserving water.

"You don't think we'll find it, do you?"

He looked up, those green eyes fixing on her in a contemplative gaze. They crinkled slightly at the corners, revealing pale fingers of tiny lines in the dust and grime that covered his lean, handsome face.

"We escaped the Apache," he reminded her, then added confidently, "We'll find it."

"Do you think we'll find the horses?" She knew their chances without them weren't good.

He gave her another long look. "If we don't, it's one helluva long walk to the nearest town. But then, Miss Tyson, *you were willing* to take the risk of this trip." With an efficient gesture he slung the canteen over his shoulder.

Then, for the hundredth time that morning, he checked his revolver, flipping open the chamber, slowly spinning it while he checked the bullets, and snapping it

219

closed again in a not-too-subtle reminder that they still couldn't be certain they were completely out of danger from the Apache.

"We'd better look for that spring. It's our only hope for water out here." He turned and started around the cluster of rocks that sheltered them.

Revel didn't immediately follow. Instead, she took a careful bearing on their location based on the rock formation Jake had used to get them down the mountain. Her father had once taught her how to plot a course, using the sun by day and the stars at night.

They were just east of a direct line with that rock formation. Jake had started off in the opposite direction—due west.

A small shadow passed over her. Revel shielded her gaze as she looked toward the sky. A single hawk soared low over the mountain, so low she could see it angle its head back and forth as it scanned the landscape below. It abruptly altered it's course, caught a downdraft off the mountain and swooped low with blinding speed.

It disappeared briefly. When it reappeared, stroking the air with strong, powerful wing sweeps, effortlessly climbing the sky, a rabbit was clutched in its powerful talons. It had found its prey farther east of their location. Revel decided it was time to split up and double their efforts.

"Where the hell are you going?" Jake had doubled back.

"East," she said simply, pulling the strap of the canteen over her shoulder.

"We need to find that spring."

"I'm aware of that."

"Then let's get going. It's not going to get any cooler out here."

"I'm aware of that too. I'm also aware we can cover twice the area if we split up. You go that way, I'll go this way."

"That's ridiculous. You'll only get yourself lost."

220

"That shouldn't matter much to you, should it?" she asked, then added, "If we haven't found anything in an hour, we'll meet back here in two hours."

"What if you don't make it back?"

She could hear the irritation edging into his voice.

"I'm not coming after you," he threatened.

"I know that," she answered quietly, "so I guess I'd better not get lost."

"Those Apache could still be out there. They know these mountains inside out. They could have come through another way."

She turned on him in a brief flash of anger. "We have just one chance at this. We should make the most of it." She turned to leave.

"And what if I find the water first and decide to just leave you here?"

She answered him with a question of her own. "Why did you pull me out of that river? Why did you come after me last night?"

"I was trying to keep you alive. You're my ticket to freedom."

"Are you trying to tell me you haven't thought of walking out before? You could simply slip away and take your chances."

"Oh, I thought of it, all right. I'm thinking about it right now. The problem is I want a clean slate. I don't want any bounty hunters dogging my trail, no sheriffs looking for justice, no fast gun trying to make a name for himself."

"Then the choice is up to you," she said with more confidence. "I'll see you in two hours, with or without water." She turned and started off around the eastern base of the mountain.

"Damn fool woman . . . stupid little . . ." It ended there. Jake wasn't willing to waste any more precious time or energy worrying about her.

He retraced his original course around the western base of the mountain, vaguely wondering how lost she

221

could get in two hours.

Revel knew where she was going. She simply didn't know if the spring lay in that direction. She had misgivings about striking out on her own, but as she saw it, that gave them a fifty-fifty chance that one of them would find it. What was the point in both of them going in the wrong direction?

Jake Reno should have appreciated that logic. He obviously hadn't.

She didn't believe in blind luck, fate, chance, or any superstitious notions. She believed people made their own luck, and she believed in herself. That was why she walked steadily toward the location where that hawk had scooped up the rabbit—or she tried to walk steadily. It was a bit difficult, her feet were painfully raw.

But she was convinced that where there was life, there had to be water. And it was a plausible theory. After all, creatures needed water. Not only rabbits, but rodents, prairie dogs, and . . . rattle snakes.

By her best calculations, she'd been heading east for almost an hour. If she didn't find the spring soon, she would have to go back.

She rounded a cluster of rocks, then reached up to steady herself as she climbed over another, almost grabbing the damn thing by the tail. She had once seen a harmless garter snake, but never a rattlesnake. There was no mistaking that immediate rattle of alarm. She froze, her hand poised in midair.

It was ugly, that was the only way to describe it, half-coiled, half-reclined, not fully round like the other snake she remembered, but flattened on the warm rock, like a half-empty waterskin. Its head was sharply angled, with black beads for eyes. As she tried to slowly withdraw her hand, that head reared up and the coil tightened, gathered to strike. The warning rattle sharpened.

It was answered by the loud crack of gunfire, a bullet passing not even an inch from her shoulder.

Revel screamed. The snake recoiled as if it were jerked back by some invisible wire. It twisted and spasmed, the head completely severed from the body. She spun around and stared at Jake Reno.

Then fear was smothered by a stronger emotion—anger. "Damn you!" she flung at him. "You almost shot me!"

Jake stared at her with a mixture of bemusement and annoyance.

"If I'd wanted to shoot you, I would have." He said calmly as he pushed past her to inspect the snake. He nudged it with a stick and shook his head. "Damn, I hate these things."

"I had everything under control," she informed him shakily. "I was simply going to back away."

He looked up at her with faint disgust. He lifted the snake's limp body with the stick. It stretched out a full five feet.

"Snakes have been known to strike the distance of their body," he mentioned casually as he glanced from where the snake originally lay coiled to where she still stood, a distance of no more than eighteen inches.

She ignored the obvious, hating it when he was right. "I don't suppose it occurred to you that the Apache might still be around and that they might have heard that gunshot."

"Oh, it occurred to me," he admitted. "But the snake was here and the Apache aren't . . . yet. And as I said, I don't like snakes."

"I don't suppose you found that spring," she immediately shot back at him, wanting desperately to be angry. Anger would keep her from breaking down and admitting she was more scared of the snake than she had been of the Apaches.

"Nope. It's not in that direction."

"And what made you arrive at that conclusion?"

"Broken Hand."

223

She blinked. "What?"

He looked up with that faintly smug, almost amused expression of his.

"Broken Hand said it was this way."

"When did he tell you that?"

He shrugged in that maddening offhand way of his. "Oh, about an hour ago."

"An hour ago?" None of this made sense. Then she heard a noise behind her.

Broken Hand carefully wound his way through the boulders and rocks at the base of the mountain, astride his paint pony. He led Jake's Appaloosa and her gelding.

Jake grinned at her. "I told you he knew his way through these mountains. He came riding up right after you started off in this direction. The horses found the spring."

Broken Hand came up beside her, dismounted, and walked over to Jake. He prodded the snake with the barrel tip of his rifle.

"I hate these damn things," he muttered, then grunted and looked up, a sly grin on his face. "But they make good eating."

With that he returned to his pony and removed an empty flour sack from one of his saddlebags. He picked up the snake's body, dropped it in, tied off the end of the sack, and then secured it to his saddle.

"Good eating, when we make camp," he said to Jake as he mounted his pony. "Fill canteens and then we must ride. If the Apache are near, they heard the gunshot."

Jake nodded as he strode past Revel and mounted the Appaloosa.

"That is unless you want to wait around for them, Miss Tyson. By the way," he asked, "what made you think the spring was in this direction?"

She mounted the gelding.

"Animals," she said simply.

"Animals?"

"They all need water, even snakes. They're attracted to it. I saw a hawk catch a rabbit. Rabbits wouldn't be out in this heat, unless water was very near."

"Very good, Miss Tyson. You're observant."

"That, and the fact it was the opposite direction from where you were headed."

"In that case, maybe you can't trust in my ability to find Sam Bass," he said calmly, but his eyes glittered like green ice.

"Oh, you'll find him, all right. As you said yourself, it means a clean slate." She whirled the gelding about and headed after Broken Hand who was already winding his way through the rocks to a spot just east of her encounter with the rattlesnake.

They quickly watered the horses and filled their canteens, then moved out. In the distance lay a flat plain, occasionally broken by numerous sugar-loaf mountains, which rose abruptly. Jake explained they were called *picachos*. Some rose thousands of feet. They were strung along the high plain at odd intervals, disconnected from each other, as if a gigantic hand had simply scattered them about.

The sun was steadily at their backs, as they constantly searched the horizon for any sign of Apache.

Jake pushed hard along the course Broken Hand set for them. No one complained, not even when he pressed on long after dark. A full moon illuminated the countryside, and he was determined to reach the small town of Las Cruces just over the border of the New Mexico Territory. It was after midnight when they arrived.

Jake roused the owner of the livery stable, asking for clean stalls and fresh hay for the horses. The wizened little man, dressed in long johns and overalls, gave them a wary stare.

Revel didn't blame him. She could imagine how they looked. But the old man's wariness turned to outright surprise when she took off her hat.

"Well, I suppose I got room fer the horses," he

225

conceded, looking appreciatively at Revel.

Jake glanced over to Broken Hand.

"I'll stay with the horses," the Indian said with a nod. "I don't much care for hotels. I can't sleep on those damn soft beds."

In spite of the fatigue that made her ache, Revel smiled. She liked Broken Hand, and she had come to appreciate his honest observations about everything, even if most of those observations included the word '*damn.*'

"Sleep with one eye open, my friend," Jake advised him.

Broken Hand nodded, "Always do, that's why I've kept my hair as long as I have. I'll bed down with the Appaloosa. He doesn't snore. That damn paint pony snores somethin' fierce."

Jake grabbed his saddlebags and headed out of the stable. Revel was so weary, her muscles no longer complained as she grabbed her own saddlebags and followed him. The owner of the stable stopped them at the door.

"Hey, that'll be three dollars for the horses, and an extra dollar for the Indian—in advance."

Jake looked back at Revel with a sly grin.

"The lady will pay you," he stated. Then he simply walked out of the stable.

Revel slapped four dollars into the stablekeeper's hand. They'd been hunted by Indians, barely escaping with their lives, and had ridden almost fifty miles that day. She was so tired she couldn't see straight. If she'd had the strength she would have told Jake Reno exactly what he could do with that grin.

"Where could we get a couple of rooms for the night?" she asked the stablekeeper. He rubbed a whiskered chin thoughtfully.

"Madge Perkins runs the boardin'house. Got the best rates in town and the best food, but she's full up on

226

accounta the cattle drive bein' in town. Yer best bet is probably over at the hotel. The owner's name is Hoskins. He'll fix you and yer husband right up."

He had obviously missed the part where she'd asked for *rooms*. She wasn't about to share a room, or anything else with Jake Reno. She wanted a bath, hot if possible, but at this point almost anything wet would do. She was too tired to think about food. All she wanted was a bed— one that was soft and gave just a little, unlike hard ground or rocks. She thanked him.

Across the street, and about halfway down, she found the one hotel in Las Cruces—and Jake Reno. He casually leaned against the front desk. He had obviously already met Mr. Hoskins. The owner looked up with heavy-lidded eyes as she came in.

"I signed us in, darlin'," Jake gave her that sly grin again. "Just go ahead and pay the man, since you have all the money."

It was one thing for him to take such arrogant pleasure in her paying for everything. It was something completely different for him to call her *'darlin.'*

"I can sign for my own room," she bit off testily, dropping the heavy saddlebags right where she stood. And if he made just one more remark of any kind to her, she silently vowed she'd slug his arrogant grin.

"That's the problem, darlin'." He'd done it again. "There is only one room. It seems the town is full up with wranglers fresh off a cattle drive up from Mexico."

In her weary condition it took a moment for all this to sink in. When it did, there was just one solution.

"Well then, I guess you'll just have to sleep in the stable with your horse!"

If she hadn't been so tired, had been more alert and on her usual guard when it came to Jake Reno, she would have seen that subtle shift of light in those green eyes— the change from playful to predatory in a single blink.

"Aw, now darlin'"—he moved before she even looked

227

up, scooping her and her saddlebags up into his arms—
"you wouldn't want us to be apart on our wedding night, would ya?"

She was so stunned, she couldn't believe what was happening. One moment she was standing wearily against the front desk, and the next she was on her way upstairs with barely time for a glance back at the startled hotel owner who simply shook his head, closed his registry book, and muttered something about "bein' woke up at this late hour."

Jake stopped before room number six and unceremoniously dropped Revel to her feet.

"Darlin'? Wedding night?" she asked incredulously, "Jake Reno . . ."

He'd opened the door to the room, and in one fluid motion whirled back around. The expression on his face was one of mock contrition.

"I know it isn't the Palace in Denver, darlin', like I promised yer daddy, but it's clean and Mr. Hoskins promised the bed is soft." Those green eyes sparked mischief at her.

"Jake . . ." she warned.

"Besides, when did we ever need a bed, the way you carry on when we make love? We always end up on the floor anyway. And it isn't exactly as if we haven't already been in the saddle together."

"Damn you, Jake Reno!" she whispered furiously, surprised that she had the strength to be embarrassed. She tried to shove past him.

"I hope you like the hard ground, because that is where you're going to sleep!" She reached inside her pocket and flung a twenty-five cent piece at him.

"Here, buy yourself some hay!"

She pushed inside the room and turned to close the door behind her. Jake blocked her move, forcing the door back open.

"Tonight I'm sleeping in that bed." His tone of voice held a subtle warning.

Revel was in no mood for his warnings or him. "You're forgetting who paid for this."

"And you're forgetting our arrangement," he quietly reminded her.

She was caught in a dilemma of her own making, and she knew it. After several moments she finally stepped aside and let him into the room.

"Very well, you may sleep here. Over there." She gestured to a narrow-backed, overstuffed chair. "You can pull up the other chair and, with a few blankets, make yourself quite comfortable. That is my final say in the matter."

He dropped his saddlebags on the floor beside the bed and slowly turned around, those eyes now holding a different expression.

"Unh-unh. Not tonight, Revel."

Chapter Twelve

"It's after midnight!" Jake growled at her. "Are you going to stand in the middle of the floor all night?"

Revel frowned at his back—his very comfortable back. He was already reclining on the one, narrow, feather-ticked bed in the last available room in the only hotel in town.

She chewed her lip, indecision on her face. After all, *she* had paid for the room, and she looked upon it as *her* bed.

"If you were a gentleman you would have offered me the bed," she reminded him. There was only a slight shrug of his right shoulder as he lay turned toward the far wall.

"I think we're a little beyond any false notions about my being a gentlemen," he pointed out as he fluffed a pillow—*her* pillow—and settled himself more comfortably.

She stood rooted to the center of the room, tired, hot, and out of sorts, hands on her hips, a dull ache beginning at the base of her skull. Jake Reno had that effect on her. He caused fatigue, headaches, exasperation. She was deep in thought about just how aggravating he could be when he turned over and snapped so loud at her that she jumped.

"Sleep on the damn floor for all I care! But if you stand

there one more minute, tapping your foot you'll sleep in the hallway."

"Is that right?" she fumed.

"Yes, that's right! Christ! I never saw anybody so mixed up. You didn't mind snuggling into those rocks with me last night when the Apache were after us, but now you act like your virtue's in danger."

"My virtue—such as it is—has nothing to do with it." Revel quit tapping her foot as she stood firmly planted, her temper rising. "It's just that the bed is very small. A bed, which I might add, I paid for."

His green eyes narrowed at her. "The crack in those rocks was even smaller, as I recall. And you forget, I already know you quite intimately. Besides," he pointed out, "we've already slept together several nights on the trail. Or have you forgotten?"

She had a feeling she was losing this argument. "I don't consider sleeping around a campfire quite the same as this."

He came up on his elbows and looked at her, a weary sigh escaping him. "What is it that bothers you so much about this?"

She shifted uneasily from one badly bruised foot to the other. "Well, it just doesn't seem very proper."

"Proper?" Damn, he thought. She can aggravate a man more than anyone I've ever known. "Do you mean to tell me this situation never came up before in your work?"

"Well, of course it did. Once or twice," she admitted without the least bit of chagrin.

"How did you handle it those other times?"

"Other arrangements were made."

"What sort of arrangements?"

She rocked onto the other foot, not at all certain she wanted to discuss this.

"In one instance my partner and I took turns sleeping."

232

"Uh-huh." He just listened.

"It worked out quite well."

"What about the other time?"

"The agent was a gentleman and offered me the use of the bed."

"Of course," Jake said.

"Well?"

"Well, what?"

She took a deep breath. This was getting them nowhere. "What are we going to do about this?"

Jake sat up and swung his legs over the bed. He rose and came toward her. Revel watched him warily.

"Let's get a few things straight right now, so there's no misunderstanding."

As he advanced, she took careful steps backward. She didn't like the look in his eyes or the sudden edge in his voice. She stopped when she came up against the small chest of drawers. He took another step forward, trapping her.

"It's late, we only have a few hours till sunrise, and I'm not taking turns in that bed with anyone. And as for me being a gentleman, we both know different. Now, that leaves you just three choices: the floor, the chair, or that bed with me in it. And if you're afraid of what might happen in that bed, you've got nothing to worry about."

"Is that right?"

"That's right. Because all I want is some sleep. Besides"—he hesitated, looking her up and down from head to toe as if he were making an inspection—"you're too much damn trouble already. I don't need more of it.

"I meant it when I said what happened that night shouldn't have happened. You can damn well rest assured it won't happen again." He leaned over her, his face only inches from hers. "You can also be assured, that if you don't quit fidgeting around and get in that bed, I'll throw you into it! Do I make myself clear?"

Revel was faced with a dilemma; her revolver, which

might have been of use, was in her saddlebags across the room, and Jake did look as if he was considering strangling her.

"You do," she whispered angrily as she scooted away from him and headed for the bed. "But stay on *your* side of the bed."

"That is my intention," Jake informed her as he followed her across the room.

She slipped under the coverlet, fully clothed, and lay on her side, as close to the far edge of the bed as she could manage without falling off. She was turned away from him, and waited expectantly for the bed to sag. After several seconds she turned over.

"What are you doing?"

The lamp had already been extinguished. Moonlight pooled softly through the open window, bathing the room in shadows. Jake was very clearly illuminated as he unbuttoned his shirt and pulled it off. His green eyes glittered at her through the gray moonlight.

"I want you to restrain yourself, Revel," he said in mock warming. "It's hot, in case you hadn't noticed. Just because I took my shirt off, I don't want you to lose control. Stay on *your* side of the bed."

Evidently he thought the sight of his chest and shoulders might be too much of a temptation for her. Her mouth fell open. "You really are the most conceited ass I ever met!"

"Nope," he said with conviction as he crawled into the bed beside her. "I'm just honest. The truth is, Revel, you may have lived on your own and had a lot of experience in some ways, but before the other night you'd never been with a man and we both know it."

"And just what is that supposed to mean?"

"It means you have some cock-eyed notion about what takes place between a man and woman in bed. Sometimes it's for money, sometimes it's like what happened the other night, and sometimes it's a whole helluva lot better. And you haven't gotten to that part yet."

"I see," she said tightly.

"No, you don't. The truth is if I wanted to make love to you, Revel, I wouldn't ask for permission and I wouldn't start out in bed."

Revel was completely mortified. How the devil had they gotten into this conversation? She thanked God for the darkness, for without it, he would have been able to see just exactly how embarrassed she really was. Mercifully, it hid her mortification and her profound curiosity about precisely how he would start out.

"Then we don't have to worry about that at all, do we?" she said between clenched teeth.

"Not at all," he assured her.

"Good!" Her irritation was growing.

"Fine!" he flung back at her.

"Good night!"

"Good night!"

It should have been easy to go to sleep, knowing that she had absolutely nothing to worry about as far as Jake Reno was concerned.

It should have been, but it wasn't.

She would never admit it to anyone, but his words had hurt. Revel was acutely aware that while she was well educated in a book sense, and very experienced as an agent, the more personal side of her life—the intimate side—that included relationships with men, or more particularly one man—was sorely lacking.

Like all young women of her position in society, she had been raised with the notion that she would one day marry and have a family. God knows, all her friends and acquaintances in Philadelphia had dedicated all their energies to that precise end. But her father's death had changed all that for Revel.

She could have remained in Philadelphia with her aunt, made her official society debut, and ended up married and, by now, the mother of several children. It was the singular pursuit of all the young ladies she had known. But she had been compelled to leave Philadelphia, compelled to become a Pinkerton agent, compelled to find her father's killer; and she had neglected that other aspect of her life.

She had had no regrets, no desire to alter her plans. She had had one purpose, and she had never thought beyond the day she would find Sam Bass. Until now, when Jake's words had cut deeply.

She knew men were attracted to her; she had learned to understand and handle the appreciative glances and attentions of young beaus and, later, the men she worked with. But until the other night, she had had absolutely no idea of what happened beyond that. Especially if what Jake had said was true, that making love didn't start in bed. If it didn't start there, then where the devil did it start?

She tossed and turned. She was exhausted, perhaps too tired. Jake's words kept churning through her mind, making her restless.

Several times her hip brushed his thigh, separated by clothes and bedcovers. Whenever either of them moved on the small bed, they inevitably rolled to the center of the feather mattress. Her foot nudged his leg. His outstretched hand brushed her breast. She turned into his bare shoulder, her cheek cushioned by hard muscle.

It was unsettling, but not nearly so unsettling as Jake's dreams.

On the trail she'd been too worn out to heed the vague, disjointed words he spoke as he relived, in dreams, his past. And he'd been so wary, rarely sleeping, that there had been almost no time for dreams. But here, off the trail, away from constant danger, it was different.

Whatever the reason, she was consciously, vividly aware that Jake was haunted by demons from the past.

He thrashed on the bed and muttered fragmented words, lashing out at something dangerous. Nothing much of what he said made any sense. Something about

236

being hanged, something else about a man named Trask, and something about a fire. He'd been desperate to save the horses.

Then his wild mutterings changed. A sheen broke out over his body and dampened his shoulder-length hair. The muscles in his arms and across his chest twitched, then contorted. His fingers spasmed into hard fists. He seemed to reach out at one moment and then try to protect himself the next. And over and over, he kept calling out a name . . . Rachel, Rachel, Rachel.

Revel understood dreams. She had one that constantly came to her. It was about her father. In this dream she was a child, no more than ten or eleven years old, and her father was coming to visit her in Philadelphia.

She and her aunt waited at the station. The train arrived. Passengers disembarked. Everyone about her embraced loved ones and friends. She searched all the faces, looking for her father's tall, wide-shouldered stance in the crowd. Then she saw him, shouldering his way through, pushing people aside to get to her. And she ran.

In her dream she always ran; she was so excited to see him at last. But just as she reached him, the crowd on the platform surged between them. She cried out, calling to him, but he was gone. And no matter how she searched or how long she called, she couldn't find him.

Over the years she had come to understand that the dream would probably always come to her. She also instinctively understood that the dream had to do with the loss of her father and with her unresolved feelings about his death. Perhaps when she found Sam Bass . . .

Beside her, Jake flung an outstretched arm across the bed, pinning her down. Whatever demons haunted his dreams, they seemed to have left him alone for now. But the woman's name he'd called out haunted Revel.

They had been such anguished cries, filled with pain and a profound sense of loss, and they had touched something deep inside her. She understood loss.

Whoever Rachel was, whatever she had meant to him, he still carried her inside him.

Revel was restless too. Her thoughts churned over what she'd just learned about Jake. She slid from under the weight of his arm and carefully slipped from the bed.

There had been no opportunity for a bath, and considering their circumstances, she was still fully clothed. She'd lived in her clothing for days except for the salvaged pants. They were overlong and hobbled her as she made her way to the overstuffed chair she'd so sweetly suggested he make into a bed for himself.

She pulled the only other chair—a straightbacked wood one—up against the padded chair and tried to make herself comfortable. It was easier said than done. As she drew the light quilt she'd pulled from the bed over her shoulders, her bent legs slipped, and her bottom fell through the gap between the two chairs. She ended up on the floor. Rubbing her bruised bottom, she pushed back her disheveled hair, grabbed the quilt, and curled up in the overstuffed chair once more.

Her chin propped on her hand, she contemplated Jake Reno in the soft light that poured in through the window.

There was so much about him that wasn't written in any official agency report or on any wanted poster. He was a mass of contradictions, an enigma, a puzzle with pieces that refused to come together and make a clear picture.

He was a cold-blooded killer—something he'd never denied. He was dangerous, deceptive, unpredictable. He was more comfortable around animals than he was with people. And yet people—or at least one person, Rachel—had meant a great deal to him.

She grew drowsy contemplating Jake Reno, finally concluding that it didn't matter how much she knew about him. She suspected there would always be secrets he kept.

"I don't care what they are"—she yawned sleepily—

"just as long as we find Sam Bass. Then you can go back to your Rachel," she whispered to the dark shadows in the room, but deep inside her some emotion twisted into a tight little knot. When she slept, she dreamed.

Again she searched the crowded train station for that tall, wide-shouldered man. But this time when he turned to her, it was Jake Reno's eyes that looked back at her.

Jake found her there in the morning, huddled in a tight cramped position in the chair, her head nodding forward onto bent knees. The quilt had slipped to the floor, and she had curled up to keep warm.

He guessed that she had found their sleeping arrangement unsatisfactory and had chosen to try the uncomfortable chair.

"Stubborn." He shook his head. "Too stubborn. It'll get you in trouble one of these days, Miss Tyson."

Swinging his long, fully clothed legs over the edge of the bed, he found his boots and pulled them on. He holstered the revolver he'd kept under his left hand all night. It was barely light outside, time to get moving.

He crossed the small room, poured water from the pitcher into the tin basin, and washed. He would have liked a bath and a shave, but he wanted to get out of town as soon as possible. Las Cruces wasn't a place a man wanted to stay in very long.

Jake pulled his shirt on over his damp shoulders and then reached for his guns. Once again, his gaze fell on Revel and he hesitated, hands on his hips. She looked so young. Curled up like that, she reminded him of someone else. Her dark lashes were like silky halfmoons against her cheek, her lips were slightly parted as she drew in the faint, shallow breaths of sleep. She looked so damned innocent.

Then he smiled faintly. He wouldn't be at all surprised if she slept with her revolver.

It would serve her right if she woke up with a kink in her back. He was tempted to leave her right where she was.

He should have, but he didn't.

With a snort of disgust, Jake slipped one arm under her knees and the other around her waist. He gently lifted her.

"You, lady, are more trouble than you're worth and you'll end up getting us both killed." Something thumped to the floor at his feet. Jake looked down at the silvery gleam of a small pistol and smiled softly as he shook his head.

"It figures. You're plain dangerous with that thing, Miss Pinkerton."

She murmured something as he turned with her toward the bed. In his arms, she seemed somehow smaller, softer . . . vulnerable.

It was the vulnerability that cut right through him and made him instinctively hold her closer. It brought back memories of another time and place, and someone else.

Jake carefully laid her on the bed. She turned toward him, curling up once more in that little-girl way, snuggling into the soft mattress without ever opening her eyes.

He pulled the blanket up over her shoulders. There was no point in waking her right now. They needed supplies, and he wanted to make some inquiries.

It was light outside, and the townsfolk were already starting to stir. Voices came from the street below and a wagon rattled through town. He looked back at her and suddenly stopped.

Maybe it was the curve of her hand on the pillow beside her head, maybe it was the silken blanket of dark hair cascading across the bed. Maybe it was the angle of her face or the way the early morning light shifted across her cheeks and touched the tips of her lashes. Or maybe it was something far different and less easily explained that compelled him to touch her.

240

He gently caressed her cheek with the backs of his fingers. He'd once imagined her skin to be like satin. It was. Like warm satin, with a feeling of softness and heat a man would ache to touch over and over again. He ran his finger along her bottom lip, remembering how she had tasted the night of the storm—of wind and rain, and desire.

Need curled tight and painful inside him, but it was tempered by another more remote craving that he'd kept buried for a long time.

Impulses were dangerous. No one knew that better than Jake Reno.

Impulse was a bank robbery. It was a train blown apart for a measly payroll shipment. It was the power to snap a man's neck with one's bare hands.

And it was the sudden need to taste her, as he'd tasted her that night.

Jake bent over the bed, driven by needs and impulses and emotions less easily understood. When he first kissed her, it was just a brush of his lips, lest he wake her. But he knew even that was dangerous and not nearly enough.

His mouth moved over hers, tasting, gently probing, exploring the sweet softness; his tongue tenderly running along the curve of that full bottom lip until he slowly slipped inside.

And then it was all the more dangerous when he felt her respond through the languorous haze of sleep, her lips parting softly, her small tongue wrapping around his, a moan escaping her throat. Jake jerked away from her.

Control. It was something he demanded and lived by. It had kept him alive this long. But he was rapidly learning that with Revel Tyson he had very little control.

Fear. Anger. Desire. With each there was that inherent loss of control that brought with it danger and risk. Most of his life he'd known danger and risk. He'd lived by it, been willing to die for it. But this wasn't the same. It was different, and for the first time in a long time . . . frightening.

It made Jake look deep inside himself and see something he thought no longer existed, something buried so deeply he'd almost forgotten what it was. There was just a glimmer of it now, and before he was forced to confront it, it was carefully hidden away again as he broke that vulnerable contact.

He left the room and closed the door behind him, telling himself it didn't matter. But something deep inside made him ache in a way he hadn't ached in a very long time.

When Revel woke, he was already gone. Her first thought was that he'd finally managed to run out on her. Then she saw the gleaming barrel of the rifle he carried. Jake Reno wouldn't leave without that gun.

She hastily dressed and went downstairs to inquire about the possibility of a bath. As long as she was in town she intended to make the most of it. Mrs. Hoskins, wife of the hotel owner, informed her there was a bathing room at the end of the hall upstairs.

For a dollar, hot water would be brought up. It was outlandish to pay that much extra for a bath on top of what she had already paid for the room. But considering the way Revel felt, she thought it was worth it.

She had never been in a situation where she suspected there might be other inhabitants in her clothes beside herself, not until now. After days on the trail, under horrible conditions, crawling around in the rocks, wearing some poor dead stranger's clothing, she had reason to believe her clothes had tenants.

An hour later, her hair was washed and rinsed, and she was soaking up to her neck, in warm soapy water. The bath was wonderful. It even helped unknot some of the kinks in her back, which of course raised the very interesting question of how she had come to wake up in the bed.

She had complete privacy to enjoy her bath. Mrs.

Hoskins had assured her everyone else in the hotel was already gone, so she had left a message for Jake to join her over at the boardinghouse for breakfast. Then she had latched the door and prepared to enjoy a bath.

Sometime later, Revel sank back against the rim of the metal tub and closed her eyes. They flew open as the door was thrown back and Jake Reno strode into the room. Revel sat up in alarm.

"That door was locked!"

"Well, it isn't now," he informed her.

"If you don't mind!" She made a desperate grab for the bath sheet on the chair beside the tub to shield herself.

"I don't mind at all," Jake said, his expression unreadable as he turned around and slowly came toward her. He grabbed the sheet before she could retrieve it and then sat down on the chair. He dropped a bundle on the floor.

Since escape was impossible, Revel sank low in the tub, trying to hide in soapy water.

"Please remove yourself," she firmly ordered. "I don't especially care for an audience when I bathe."

He looked at her somberly. "I've got news about Ben Waters."

She immediately forgot about modesty and soap bubbles as her head jerked up, giving Jake a very enticing view of a long neck, exquisite shoulders, and the deep shadow between her breasts.

"What about Ben? Did you find him? Did you talk to him about Sam Bass?"

Jake gave her a long thoughtful look that had nothing to do with Ben Waters or Sam Bass and everything to do with the sight she made in that slightly rusty tin tub.

Her skin was wet, recalling to him the night of the storm, as did her wet hair, which was cascading in dark ribbons over her shoulders. A faint, rosy glow spread across her arms and what was visible of her breasts.

She should have smelled of lye soap like every other woman he ever knew except Lilly. But unlike even Lilly, she smelled of spring flowers. That same scent was thick in the moist air of the room.

He frowned at the scent as much as at his reaction. "It's a damn good thing you didn't take a bath before we got here. The Apache could have smelled you from miles away."

She gave him a murderous look. "The way I smelled it's a wonder I didn't start to draw buzzards." Then she quickly changed the subject. "You know, you could use a bath and maybe a shave." She sat up in the tub, arms wrapped around her bent knees for modesty's sake. "I'm not the only one who was beginning to smell. Now, what about Ben Waters! We should both talk to him," she insisted.

"You didn't seem to mind the way I smelled last night." His voice had deepened.

Her gaze snapped to his. "Nothing happened last night," she reminded him.

A thoughtful expression crossed his face, handsome in spite of the heavy growth of beard.

"You mean you don't remember?"

She gave him a narrow look. "I don't remember because *nothing happened.*" She maneuvered the conversation back to safer ground. "Now, about Ben. What did you find out?" Her voice had risen a notch as her patience slipped.

His expression sobered, the playful mood broken. "We can talk about it downstairs."

Her head thudded against the back of the tub as she collapsed in frustration.

"Tell me what you found out. If you don't, I'll question Ben, myself." She quickly rinsed her hair one last time. Jake crossed the room, his back toward her. He said nothing for several minutes.

"If you don't mind," she spoke up. "I'd like to get dried off and dressed." Jake had turned around, his expression unreadable.

"You know something, you have a very pretty neck."

Then quite unexpectedly he added, "You can still forget about all this, Revel."

She frowned. "I can't forget it. You know that. Now, if you won't leave, will you at least have the courtesy to turn around so that I can get dressed?"

When he did so, she stepped out of the tub and quickly dried off. She had no wrapper, so she merely wrapped the bath sheet about her. Jake stood between her and her clothes. When he turned back around without warning, all she could do was hold the bath sheet closer about her body.

Beads of water shone on her shoulders, so did the gleam of dampness across the rise of her breasts above the bath sheet. Her hair hung in long dark ribbons.

Conflicting emotions twisted inside Jake. He'd never liked a woman less or wanted one more than he wanted her at that precise moment. Because of it, and what he'd learned about Ben, his voice was harsh.

"Ben Waters is dead."

The strength seemed to seep out of her all at once. Whatever she'd expected, this wasn't it.

"What are you talking about? He can't be!"

"The stable owner told me about it."

Revel tried to get her stunned thoughts under control. Her voice was hollow.

"When?"

"About six weeks ago."

She tried to swallow past the tightness in her throat. Ben Waters had been her one link to Sam Bass.

"How did it happen?"

"He worked a small farm outside of town. It was raided and burned to the ground."

She slowly pushed her wet hair back, her thoughts slow to come together.

"What kind of raid? Indians?"

Jake shook his head. "Comancheros."

Revel frowned. She'd heard of the Comancheros. They were a mixed band—Indians, Mexicans, and any kind of

245

renegade on the run. In the past few years they'd taken to striking at small settlements along the border between Mexico and Texas and the territories.

They were ruthless killers and gunrunners, supplying rifles and ammunition to outlaw bands of Indians who in turn attacked farms, ranches, and remote mining communities. The Comancheros took no prisoners and never left anyone alive. And they seemed to take particular delight in torturing their victims.

Everything she'd heard of the Apache paled in comparison to what she knew of the Comancheros.

"I didn't know they rode this far north. I thought most of their raids were down along the border."

"They usually don't. It seems they were after something in particular this time."

She immediately thought of gold, guns, possibly horses. But Las Cruces was a poor town. It was a long, dangerous way to ride for so little.

"What could they possibly want here?"

Jake gave her a long, steady look. "Ben Waters."

"What are you talking about? Ben wasn't involved with Comancheros. They would have no reason to go after him."

Jake's expression was grim. "Not the Comancheros, but someone who rides with them."

Even before he said it, she knew what he was going to add.

"Sam Bass," she whispered.

"He's been seen with them, Revel. When they hit Ben's place they didn't take anything. They killed him and burned everything to the ground. Retribution."

Her fingers tightened into fists as she clutched the edges of the bath sheet.

"You're saying Ben Waters died because he talked to me about Bass."

"Sam always paid back anyone who betrayed him. By his way of lookin' at it, Ben betrayed him."

246

Fury bubbled up inside her. "Is that some sort of outlaw code?"

Jake was grim. "Call it whatever you like. Sometimes it's the only way to stay alive."

"And you should know all about that shouldn't you, Jake Reno," she spat out at him, angry because of Ben, angry because Jake believed in that damned code, angry because now Bass knew someone was after him.

She knew it was dangerous to push Jake, but she didn't care. Ben had been important to her. Now he was dead.

"Yeah, I know all about it." His voice now held a subtle warning. "Because I lived with it the last fifteen years. That was a choice I made. This isn't."

When he turned and walked away to retrieve his hat, she followed. "What is that supposed to mean?"

"It means the trail ends here, Revel." Jake turned. "I was against going after Bass from the beginning. You have no idea the kind of man he is. Ruthless. He doesn't feel anything at all when he kills a man." He pushed past her to the door.

She refused to back down. "Like you?" She plunged recklessly ahead. "Did you feel anything when you killed those men?"

That stopped him. He slowly turned around, his face hard, his eyes like green ice.

"Yeah, I felt something." His voice tightened to a harsh whisper. "I was glad."

She shivered even though the room was already quite warm, then wrapped her arms tightly about herself, but refused to look away from him.

"Good! Because you'll need that feeling when we go after Bass." Before he could argue or curse at her, she went on.

"It doesn't end until I find him."

Jake stared at her a long time.

"You'll get yourself killed."

"That's always been a possibility."

"Is it worth it?" he flung back at her.

Revel took a deep breath and a big chance. "Was it worth it for Rachel?"

The expression on his face was stark, unlike any she had seen before, and frightening. One moment it was filled with pain and wrenching sadness, the next it was devoid of emotion. But if she thought his expression was frightening, what he did next was terrifying.

He grabbed her, his fingers wrapped around her wrist so tightly she thought her bones would be crushed. And he pulled her violently against him, the force of the move driving the air from her lungs.

"There were six men, Revel. They raped her and then beat her. Then they raped her again. But she was still alive so they took her with them. She wasn't alive when I found her."

"There were six of them, and I hunted them all down and killed them. And yes, I was glad." Then he added, "They were no different than the Comancheros."

"I'm not Rachel," she whispered furiously as she tried to free her bruised wrist.

He seized her wet hair with one hand and jerked her head back, so that she was forced to look up at him. "You can't even imagine what they'll do to you if they get hold of you."

"I don't care," she breathed from between teeth clenched against the pain. "I want Sam Bass."

He shoved her away from him so hard she stumbled and fell to the floor. The bath sheet came undone, and she scrambled to pull it closed over her body. But even then she felt Jake's gaze burning her as if she were completely naked.

He flung open the door and strode furiously out into the hall. Without looking back, he said, "Be downstairs in a half-hour, or I ride out alone and to hell with you and Sam Bass."

She was ready and waiting in the hotel lobby in twenty

minutes, absolutely convinced he would ride out if she wasn't there.

Whoever Rachel was, Revel realized she had crossed some invisible line with him. Rachel had been important to him, someone he cared a great deal for.

His sweetheart? His wife? She had no idea, but whoever Rachel had been, her death tormented him.

The wrapped bundle Jake had dropped on the floor contained soft leather boots, exactly like those he wore only in a smaller size. Only then did she realize he had bought them for her.

Revel was confused, baffled, and thoroughly angry. She didn't know whether to thank him or yell at him.

A few minutes later he met her in the small lobby of the hotel. She breathed a sigh of relief.

He was clean-shaven and had obviously bathed. He'd also obviously had a drink—or several drinks.

"Come on, Miss Tyson," he bit off angrily. "If you're so hellbent on getting yourself killed, let's at least get some breakfast first."

He walked ahead of her without looking back, without waiting. As they left the hotel a man quickly stepped between them.

He was heavyset, wearing a black coat, hat, and pants. A full beard darkened his face. His eyes seemed sunk in heavy folds of skin. A tarnished star was pinned to the stained fabric of his vest, and thick hands clutched the rifle pointed straight at Jake's back.

"Hold it right there, Reno! I'm takin' you in."

Chapter Thirteen

Jake had learned to live by his instincts. Now, he stood completely still, left hand poised over his holstered Colt and mentally cursed himself for letting someone come up behind him.

"Easy, Reno," the man in black warned. "I know all about your reputation. But even *you* can't outdraw a gun at your back."

Revel was just coming out the door of the hotel when the heavyset man stepped between her and Jake. She didn't hear precisely what was said, but by the subtle tensing of Jake's shoulders and the shift of his weight onto the balls of his feet, like a cat ready to pounce, she knew what came next.

For a man who lived by the gun, there was only one way this could end unless she did something quick.

"Jake, don't!" she called out as she stepped around the stranger and wedged herself between the two men. Then she saw the dull gleam of the badge on the stained vest. She immediately looked up into the sheriff's heavily bearded face.

"Is there a problem?"

"Not anymore," he growled. "Now you jes' step aside and let me go about my business here." He reached out to shove her out of the way.

Revel carefully sidestepped his grasp. "I'm certain this

is all a simple mistake," she said, careful to keep her voice calm, authoritative. She'd met countless men like the sheriff. Their bluster was usually exceeded only by their ignorance.

Those small, beady eyes glistened from the heavy folds of his face. "And yer makin' it, *boy*, interferin' with the law," he hissed low. "Now, stand aside, before I have one of my men move you aside."

Because of the clothes she wore, the sheriff had assumed she was a boy. If she wasn't careful, Revel knew she'd get herself and Jake shot. Men like the sheriff shot first and asked questions later.

"I appreciate your help, Sheriff," she said politely, then swept the hat off her head, releasing a torrent of very long, very feminine dark, satin hair. "But I'm on official business and this man is in my custody."

She heard Jake's distinct groan of displeasure from behind her and chose to ignore it. She was well aware this wasn't how he would handle a situation like this.

"Yer what?" The sheriff looked dumbfounded.

"On official business," she repeated, then went on to explain. "I'm with the Pinkerton National Detective agency. This man has been released to my custody. You can verify everything with Marshal Earp in Tombstone. Now, if you will please put away that gun, we can all go about our business."

Revel turned to leave, careful to keep herself between Jake and the sheriff as they stepped down off the boardwalk in front of the hotel. She didn't get far before she heard the distinct sound of rifles being cocked from more than one direction.

"I said hold on!" the sheriff bellowed behind them.

"Nice try," Jake muttered under his breath. "Now we do it my way."

His hand started to drop to his pistol. Hers stopped it.

"No! We'll never make it. He's not alone. And I don't know about you, but this isn't quite what I had in mind for a way to die," she whispered furiously.

252

"I didn't think dyin' concerned you, Miss Tyson," he spat back at her.

"It concerns me at the moment. Now please, shut up and keep your hand away from that gun!"

"What the hell are you going to do?" His tone suggested he considered her crazy or incompetent—or possibly both.

"I'm going to try to keep us both alive," she hissed back at him.

"Well, good luck! Because that ass of a sheriff has other plans for me!"

"I have plans for you too," she reminded him in a furious whisper.

"My, my," Jake murmured sarcastically, "and I thought you didn't care."

She glared at him. "Let me handle this."

Before he could make some other comment, she turned around, a devastating smile on her face.

"Is there something else, Sheriff?"

"There's a great deal more, Miss Whoever-the-hell-you-are. You take just one more step and my men will shoot. Don't make no never mind to me whether Reno hangs or we settle it all here. Either way I get that reward money.

"And as for you, little lady, I might just find some reason to take you in and lock you up too." Then he cautioned her. "Before you try anything, you just have yerself a look around."

Her gaze followed his outstretched hand to a man with a wide-brimmed hat who stepped away from the side of the hotel. A rifle was cradled in his arms.

She had been certain she heard the distinct sound of more than one gun. Now she realized how right she was. As the sheriff gestured in the opposite direction, Revel saw a second gunman leaning against a post, his hand resting warily on a holstered Colt.

He squirted a brownish yellow stream of tobacco spittle into the dirt. Then he looked up to the rooftop of

253

the building directly across the street from the hotel.

A third gunman leaned out the second-story window over the adobe cantina. His rifle was aimed straight at them.

"My men," the sheriff said with a smile, and then added so there could be no mistake, "My deputies."

The smile deepened into a dangerous grin. "Now I don't really give a hoot in hell who you are little missy. Jake Reno's a wanted man, and I'm takin' him in for safekeeping until the federal marshal gets here."

He leaned closer. His breath was foul and hot. It was all she could do to keep from gagging as bile rose in her throat.

"I don't know nothing about no *official business,*" he was saying. "But just in case you are who you say you are, you bring me an authorization of some kind and we'll talk about it. Otherwise, don't go interferin', or I'll have your little butt thrown in jail too."

He pushed past her and shoved the tip of his rifle into Jake's back.

"Now you move real nice and easy, Reno. Remember, my men are pointin' their rifles right at you. Just step down real slow and we'll head on over to the jail." Then he added, "You make just one wrong move and it all ends real quick, right here."

As they started across the street, Revel went after them only to be stopped by one of the deputies.

"Jake Reno's dangerous, not the kind for a pretty little thing like you. Now me, on the other hand, I know how to treat the ladies." He reached out and took hold of a tendril of her hair.

She slapped his hand away. "Keep your hands off me!"

From the corner of her eye, she was aware Jake and the sheriff had stopped in the middle of the street. They were several feet away, but she heard their exchange clearly.

254

"Easy now, Reno. I wouldn't want to have to shoot you in the back on account of a woman," the sheriff was saying. "I never knew you to give a hoot in hell about one before."

The deputy glared at her but slowly backed down. Revel knew it wasn't finished and didn't dare take her eyes off him. She couldn't see Jake's expression, but she heard his response.

"I don't give a damn, Sheriff," he said with brutal indifference.

The sheriff grunted. "Then you won't mind if I decide to pay the little lady a visit later on over at the hotel."

"You're welcome to her with my deepest condolences. She's more trouble than she's worth."

It was then she looked at him.

What he said shouldn't have mattered to her in the least. She had no illusions about how he felt about her. The pardon from the territorial governor was all that mattered.

But she felt an unfamiliar and unwanted tightness in the pit of her stomach, like the time she'd taken a fall from a horse and had the air knocked out of her. It was almost painful, and for a brief moment she couldn't breathe.

She wished she could just walk away and let them hang him, or turn him over to the federal marshal or send him back to Tombstone. But she needed him too badly. He was the key to Sam Bass.

The deputy blocked her from following, and the sheriff shoved Jake down the street toward the jailhouse. When they stepped inside the deputy finally turned and followed, glancing back over his shoulder as he reached the jail. Then he, too, disappeared inside.

In a nervous gesture, Revel rubbed damp palms on her pantlegs. She casually looked up at the second-story window in the cantina across the street. But even before she looked, she knew a rifle was still aimed at her.

Dear God, what was she to do?

The papers that guaranteed Jake's release were in her valise somewhere in the Dragoon mountains. Other than that, she had absolutely no way to prove who she was, and she dare not contact William Pinkerton in Denver.

He knew nothing of this case or of her whereabouts. At the very least she had lied about the case she was working on. In the extreme, she had overstepped her authority, had persuaded a federal marshal to release a prisoner with false documentation, and had risked countless lives, not to mention the reputation and integrity of the agency.

If Allan Pinkerton had any idea where she really was or what she was up to, the very least she could expect was that he would have her immediately released from the agency. Beyond that, there was every possibility he would have her arrested. But that was if she failed to find Sam Bass.

It would be an entirely different matter if she succeeded. He might be willing to overlook certain indiscretions and policy violations in consideration of the substantial benefit to the agency of tracking down such a notorious outlaw.

Revel tried to appear casual as she returned to the hotel. Once inside, she ducked out the back and slipped down the alley. She had to find Broken Hand.

She came up behind the stables and was about to round the corner, when a hand clamped down hard over her mouth and she was pulled back out of sight of the main street.

"Do not cry out," Broken Hand warned as he cautiously pulled his hand away.

Revel whirled around. "The sheriff has Jake."

He nodded. "The stable owner recognized him and told the sheriff." He gestured silently around the corner of the stables. The stable owner stood in the doorway to the barn, watching as the two other deputies disappeared inside the sheriff's office.

Revel stared at the stable into which the owner had just gone.

"I've got to figure out a way to get him released."

"Then it must be done quickly. The sheriff does not intend to turn Jake over to the federal marshal. He intends to kill him."

"What are you talking about?"

"The sheriff wants the reward money. He discussed it with the owner of the stable."

Revel jerked around. "How do you know that?"

He shrugged. "I have my ways."

"Apache ways?" she asked, fascinated that he could know so much.

"Nah!" he scoffed. "I overheard the sheriff tell his deputies."

She gave him an astounded look. "You eavesdropped!" He shrugged, as if he considered it unimportant. "It's easy with *your* people. They talk too much, give everything away." He grunted.

"No Apache would let himself be caught that way, but the sheriff doesn't care who knows it. He wants the reward money for Jake Reno."

He made a series of gestures with his gnarled old hands. The last was a slice through the air that ended as he drove one knuckled fist into the palm of his other hand.

"The sheriff is *sha-ka-te!* And not to be trusted."

"I agree with you. I've met men like him before. Even if I had the papers that could get Jake released, he would simply refuse to let him go. We have to find another way to get Jake out of there."

Broken Hand agreed. "It's necessary to have a good plan." Then he looked at her. "Do you have such a plan?"

"I've got one," she admitted. "But I don't know how

good it is. We could get caught . . . or killed."

Broken Hand looked up at the brilliant blue sky overhead. His eyes narrowed as if he searched the cloudless expanse. Then he ran his hands down along the rifle he carried. He nodded.

"It is a good day to die. What is your plan?"

Jake leaned back against the adobe wall at the back of the cell. Heat simmered beyond it, the sun creating long shadows as it slipped down the western horizon.

He heard some muttered comment in the outer office, the scraping back of a chair and the splash of coffee in a tin cup.

"Do you think the sheriff will keep 'im til the territorial marshal gets here with that reward money?" one deputy asked.

The reply was the unmistakable sound of someone spitting tobacco juice into a spitoon.

"Too much trouble," the other deputy grunted. "My guess is the prisoner will be shot while *trying to escape*. Don't make no difference if'n he's dead or alive. Long as there's a body, the sheriff'll get that reward money."

"You think the sheriff'll kill him?" the first deputy asked incredulously.

"He'll do whatever's necessary for that reward," the other man explained.

There was the sound of someone moving uneasily in his chair. "That's Jake Reno in there. They say he's got more lives than a cat. Ain't no one been able to kill him, and some of the best have gone up against him."

"Don't make no difference who the hell it is. He ain't got a gun now."

"I still don't like it. He's got a reputation for not leavin' nobody alive that he goes up against," the first man replied uneasily.

"Without a gun, he ain't goin' up against nobody," the other deputy pointed out. "Now, deal them cards so's I

258

can beat the pants off you again. By the time we're finished, you'll owe me your portion of that reward money to cover yer gamblin debts."

Like a caged animal, Jake paced the small cell. It was long past sundown but the heat was oppressive, still and smothering inside the jailhouse. His shirt was plastered to his back and shoulders. The night wore on.

A lantern hung on the wall opposite his cell. In the meager light, he loosened the leather ties about his wrap boots. He carefully twined them together, making a strong, lethal thong. Wrapping the ends about his hands, he jerked the leather taut. In a single stroke he could break a man's neck.

He rolled the thong into a tight ball and slipped it inside his shirt sleeve.

Then he worked at the inside seam of his left boot. A gleaming, sharp tip protruded through a narrow slit. He pulled the long blade from the seam. With another piece of leather he wrapped one end and made a handle. In one stroke, he could cut a man's throat.

These were just two of the tricks he'd learned to stay alive. In Tombstone, Virgil Earp was cautious, and Jake had been carefully searched for any concealed weapons. But here the sheriff was as lax as he was stupid. He'd taken Jake's guns and then simply thrown him into a cell, locking the door.

There was the slightest chance that Revel might be able to get him out, but he'd learned a long time ago not to rely on anyone else but himself. A man lived a helluva lot longer that way.

Besides, as confident as Revel Tyson was of her abilities, he didn't share that confidence.

The truth was, if he hadn't come into town asking about Sam Bass, he wouldn't have ended up with a gun in his back. In that regard he blamed her for this mess.

He tried the bars at the window. They held fast. He concentrated on the movements and conversations of the deputies, trying to find a pattern that might provide him

259

an opportunity for escape.

The three deputies alternated at standing watch. But as the night grew long, they all dozed. The sheriff came in sometime after midnight, kicking them all awake. Then he sauntered back through the heavy wood doors to the cells. He smelled of sweat, smoke, cheap whiskey, and even cheaper whores.

"I sent word about that reward money," he informed Jake through the barred gate.

"I'm goin' to have me a fine piece of change for turnin' in your hide. Imagine, me gettin' the drop on Jake Reno." He started to laugh.

"Yessir, five thousand dollars." Then he sauntered back out into the outer office and collapsed across a bed in the corner.

It was then Jake knew the sheriff had no intention of turning him over to anyone alive.

Shadows fell across the empty streets of Las Cruces as the dawn broke through the eastern horizon. Revel gazed to the far end of town, in the opposite direction from the jail, and saw the telltale curl of smoke thread its way out the doors of the livery stable.

Broken Hand had said it was fitting justice. When she'd asked if he meant Apache justice, he'd simply looked at her in that way of his, then winked. *Whiteman's* justice, he'd said, an eye for an eye.

He'd assured her he would create the diversion she needed. She hadn't questioned his reasons or his method. Now she understood what he meant by an eye for an eye.

She stopped a small Mexican boy who struggled under the weight of a basket laden with fresh vegetables.

"The stable's on fire," she called out anxiously as she pointed down the street.

He glanced down toward the stable, his mahogany eyes widening as he saw the first flames lick at the frame of the open door.

"Get the sheriff!" she quickly urged.

He dropped the basket, scattering ears of corn, carrots, and potatoes. Then his wide-brimmed sombrero clasped to his head, he ran for the sheriff's office.

His voice rang out through the town, in a mixture of English and Spanish. Slowly, one person after another emerged from a home and a business.

The sheriff and his deputies staggered from the jailhouse. They pulled on shirts and pants, buckled on holsters. Revel smiled as she ducked down an alley and mounted the gelding.

Jake heard the commotion in the sheriff's office. There was a wild scrambling as booted feet thumped across hard wood, followed by a mixture of cursing and confusion.

The front door was thrown open. The slam echoed all the way back to the cells. There was a great deal of shouting and commotion, and one word he recognized—*fire!*

Through the small barred opening in the door that separated the cells from the rest of the jailhouse, Jake saw the deputies run into the street. Then there was silence.

A frantic scratching noise at the barred window of the cell brought Jake around abruptly.

He crouched low and reached inside his left boot. His fingers closed around the leather handle of the crude knife. It was a comforting feeling.

There was more scratching, and Jake thought of the rats he'd seen scurrying about last night. Jails were full of them, both the animal and human kind. The four-footed kind came around looking for food left in bowls or a scrap of bread that fell to the floor. It was the two-footed variety a man had to look out for.

The shadows in his cell lightened to pale blue as the first streaks of light filled the sky beyond the window. He watched and waited, the knife clutched in his left hand.

A long, sinuous form slipped through the window then slowly snaked down the wall. He was immediately on his feet. If that was the tail of a rat, it was one helluva rat.

261

"Jake!"

His eyes narrowed. Rats suddenly had voices—very feminine, very familiar voice.

"Are you going to help me with this, or do you want to stay in that cell?"

He shoved the narrow cot over to the window and climbed atop it.

Revel grinned up at him from astride her horse. "I thought you could use some assistance."

"You sure took your sweet time about it."

The grin immediately disappeared. "There were a few details to work out."

A slow smile began at the corners of his mouth. "He didn't buy it, did he?"

She knotted the other end of the rope around the pommel of the saddle.

"Who?"

"The sheriff. He didn't swallow for a minute that you're a Pinkerton Agent."

She looked up briefly as she cinched the knot of the rope around the saddlehorn. "The sheriff has other plans. Nothing I could have told him would have made any difference."

"Yeah, I kinda figured that out for myself. He's a greedy bastard."

"Besides," she went on to explain as she dismounted and slowly walked to the back wall of the jailhouse, "all my papers, along with the signed release from Marshal Earp are in my valise." She paused, then went on.

"The same valise you wouldn't let me go back for."

Jake leaned comfortably against the barred window. "In other words, it's my fault I'm in here."

"In a manner of speaking. Your reputation did most of it though. You just seem to bring the killing instinct out in people. You really should try to do something about that."

She looked up at him, making a very fetching sight with the first light of day at her back, sunlight burning her hair to a dark henna color.

She wore the pants he'd taken from the massacred miners along with a clean shirt. The pants molded her in all the right places, accenting the slight roundness of her bottom, her long, curved thighs and incredibly small waist.

The shirt was sizes too big across her shoulders, its sleeves rolled back several times, but it was nicely filled out in front. She'd left several buttons undone at the neck, and it gaped open enough to tease. A man would want to see more.

The boots, like his own—he'd purchased them from a young Indian woman the morning before—were snugged about her long calves, their soft leather molding small feet. Having already gained an appreciable respect for how stubborn she was, he wouldn't have taken any bets she'd wear them. But she had. And damned if she wasn't the most incredibly desirable woman he'd ever laid eyes on.

That realization immediately brought back the memory of that night in the storm, when there were no boots, no pants, no shirt. Only her slender body, naked and wet, clinging to his as they came together.

"Are you going to get me outta here, or are you going to stand there talking about it 'til the sheriff gets back."

She finished tying off the rope and took up the slack. Her head snapped up at the unexpected edge in his voice. She hadn't slept, hadn't been able to eat a thing the day before or last night.

Too much depended on getting him out of jail. She was out of patience, and the last thing she wanted was to fight with Jake Reno.

Still, leaving him in the cell was tempting. It would serve the arrogant bastard right.

"You could leave and not bother with all this," he conceded in that slow, smug way of his as if he'd read her thoughts. He watched guilty emotions play across her face.

263

She stubbornly shook her head. "And let you hang? We settled that before."

"I have no intention of hanging, Revel, or of letting that fat stupid sheriff collect that reward money. One way or the other, I'll get outta here."

"If you could, you would have already," she pointed out as she returned to her horse and pulled herself up into the saddle. She refused to discuss it with him any further.

"You could help with this," she reminded him. "Tie your end of the rope around those bars. The sheriff and his deputies will be back any minute. We don't have much time. Unless, of course," she added with a wicked smile, "you'd rather come up with some other idea."

He frowned. "We'll give it a try. Who knows? You might get lucky and this might work."

"Lucky!" Revel fumed under her breath. She would just love to wipe that smug expression off his face. She whirled the gelding about.

"You'd better stand back."

As he tied off the rope at the window, Jake asked skeptically, "Are you sure this will work? Do you know what you're doing?"

She gave him a long look over her shoulder. "In theory it should work. God knows, others have tried it countless times."

His eyes narrowed. "What is that supposed to mean?"

"It means this is a new experience for me. I'm used to working *with* the law. I've never broken anyone out of jail before."

"Then what convinced you to do this?"

"The sheriff was less than cooperative. I misjudged him. He's more stupid than I thought. This seemed to be the next best solution."

"Besides, theoretically it should be simple—a rope, a horse, and the window pops out. But there are a lot of variable factors."

Christ! He'd never known someone to have so much

trouble breaking the law. It must be that stubborn streak of hers.

"What variable factors?"

She began to list the possibilities of what might go wrong. "The strength of the rope, the strength of those bars, how well the jail was constructed, and the horse."

Jake stared out through the bars. They had just one chance at this. At any moment the deputies would be back. If this didn't work, he'd be forced to take matters into his own hands. It would have been better if they'd had help.

"Where's Broken Hand?"

"He'll meet us outside of town," she assured him. "He had a few things to take care of."

Jake had checked the bars at the window for any telltale signs of looseness when he'd been brought in. Now he checked them again. They held tight. He checked the rope one last time. The knot was secure. He gave her a signal that all was ready, then jumped away from the window.

The rope tautened around the iron bars. Beyond, he heard scuffling and scraping sounds as the gelding strained against the pull of the rope.

The bars held, then groaned. Then all hell broke loose.

The window jerked loose as the dry adobe wall crumbled. Then the entire back wall of the jailhouse collapsed.

From the front of the jail there was a commotion as one of the deputies came running back in.

Revel saw him and turned the gelding and quickly rode back toward the jailhouse.

"Come on!" she shouted at Jake.

There was a sudden gunshot, and he abruptly turned to the jail.

"What are you doing?"

"Get out of here."

"I'm not leaving you," she shouted at him. "Jake?"

"Get my horse!" he shouted over his shoulder at her as

he doubled back into the jailhouse.

Seconds seemed like hours. From the street she heard shouts and then voices very close by. She had only her small revolver. It wouldn't be much use against the sheriff and his deputies.

She silently cursed. Where was Jake?

Revel whirled the gelding about. The Appaloosa was in the alley, precisely where she had left him tethered.

She tied the reins to her saddle and quickly returned to the back of the jailhouse with both horses. There was still no sign of Jake. Another gunshot came from inside the jail.

Panic began to spread through her. Then she saw him crawl over the pile of adobe bricks that had once been the back wall of the jailhouse and run to the horses.

He wiped his left hand on his pants. Blood smeared the leather that encased his lean thigh. His face was set in hard lines. His gaze darted away from hers as he grabbed the Appaloosa's reins.

"My God! You're hurt!"

He quickly swung into the saddle and whirled the Appaloosa about. She caught his arm.

"Jake?"

He didn't look at her, but said, "Unless you want to meet up with that sheriff and his deputies, I suggest we ride out of here now. Where are we supposed to meet Broken Hand?"

"Just over that rise."

Without a word he turned and spurred the Appaloosa hard toward the distant rise at the edge of town. Revel quickly urged the gelding into a run to catch up with him.

They pulled the horses to a stop at the top of the rise, then jerked around at the sound of an approaching rider.

Relief poured through her. It was Broken Hand.

He pulled up beside them and handed Jake's guns to him. "When the deputies ran out to see about the fire, I slipped in and got these for you."

Jake nodded his appreciation as he buckled on his gun.

He slipped the rifle into the scabbard at his saddle.

Broken Hand shook his head as he stared back at the town of Las Cruces and the crumbled wall of the jailhouse. He nodded. "That sure is one damn big mess." Then he turned his paint pony around.

"We must go. The sheriff and his men will come after us." He sent the pony at a full run down the back of the rise, heading south toward Mexico.

Jake turned the Appaloosa to follow. Revel stopped him.

"Are you all right?"

He twisted back around in the saddle, for the first time meeting her gaze. His eyes were cold, ruthless, filled with an expression unlike any she'd ever seen before.

"Don't worry about me," he replied gruffly and tried to pull away.

"But you're bleeding. If it's serious—" she started to object, only to be interrupted.

"I'm not hurt." His voice cut like shards of ice.

She reached out to touch his arm. "But the blood . . ."

"It's not my blood."

"But I heard gunshots. You didn't have a gun."

Jake kept tight control on the Appaloosa, nervous as it smelled the fresh blood.

For the first time, Revel saw the crude knife in Jake's left hand. He shoved it down inside his left boot. Her startled gaze met his cold one.

"It's not *my* blood," he repeated slowly.

The words froze her as they rode hard, south to Mexico.

Chapter Fourteen

"Damn you! You killed that deputy!" Revel furiously accused.

They had ridden hard for over three hours. The horses were exhausted, she was exhausted.

Anger, confusion, and fatigue had pushed her past the point of caution. She threw herself out of the saddle and confronted Jake.

He ignored her as he led the Appaloosa to the edge of the stream that was little more than a trickle this late in the season, before the winter rains set in.

For just a moment Revel stood there, hands planted on hips, feet set apart in a furious stance. Her muscles ached. If she had thought the ride from Tucson was hard, the hours since they'd left Las Cruces had been grueling, pushing both man and beast past the point of endurance.

Broken Hand was stonily silent as he led his paint pony to the stream and let him drink. The horses' sides heaved and they made loud, greedy sounds as they took in water. Jake insistently pulled the Appaloosa back, refusing to let him drink too much. Horses had a tendency to bloat themselves when they were thirsty.

He tied the stallion to the thick branch of a tree, giving him just enough lead to crop dry grass.

Revel followed Jake, intent on having this out. The sight of dried blood on his pants sharpened her anger.

She jerked at his arm.

"Aren't you going to say anything?"

He whirled around so fast that she jerked back and almost lost her footing. She'd forgotten how quick he was—and how dangerous he could be. She quickly recovered, anger and loathing eating away at her.

"Well?" she demanded.

His eyes held that hard, cold look, but weariness was reflected back from those green depths—and something more. It was a dark shadow of warning that she was too reckless to heed.

He took hold of her hand, his fingers crushing hers as he physically disengaged her grasp of his sleeve.

The expression in his eyes changed to a look she'd seen only twice before—when he'd stepped down from the gallows in Tombstone, and again when he'd escaped the jail at Las Cruces.

The muscles at his jaw tightened, his lips thinned to a hard line. It was the expression of Jake Reno, the killer.

Conflicting emotions twisted his face—a face she had once considered handsome—as if he struggled with a violent desire to strangle her. Then, as if he'd lost that struggle and was disgusted with himself, he shoved her away from him.

"See to your horse," he said gruffly. "He'll drink himself to death if you let him." He turned back to loosen his saddle cinch.

"You're concerned about a horse?" Revel spat back at him, incredulous. "My God! You care more about a horse than a man's life!"

Without turning around, he simply said, "Out here, I know the value of a horse. The value of a man is questionable."

"Like that deputy you murdered?"

The Appaloosa snorted and jerked its head, wide-eyed, as Jake turned on her. He came after her in long, angry strides. He reached out, and his fingers banded both her wrists.

270

Anger, like a red-hot iron that burns and scars, drove them at each other.

"I did what was necessary." His tone was low and dangerous. "And I'll do it again if necessary. You'd better get use to it, Miss Tyson. After all, it's the reason you wanted me, isn't it? A cold-blooded killer to hunt down a cold-blooded killer?"

"No!" she cried out as she tried to pull away. His grasp tightened, bruising bone, muscle, flesh.

"Not innocent people! There wasn't any reason to kill that deputy!"

"He had a gun," Jake explained tightly.

"You could have disarmed him. It wasn't necessary to kill him. But you did. Just like you killed those other men! I think you enjoyed it!"

"Yeah, I killed those men. I don't regret it. I'd do it again just the same. They weren't men, Revel. They were animals. They deserved to die."

Loathing tightened her throat. "That deputy didn't do anything to you."

Jake's fingers tightened around her wrists as he recalled the two deputies discussing how the sheriff would kill him and collect the reward money.

He knew by the wild-eyed expression on Revel's face she'd never believe him if he tried to explain it. She was too refined, too civilized, to understand how easily a man's life was bartered.

It was a glaring reminder of how different they were, how naive she was, how foolish they both were—she for going after Sam Bass, he for allowing himself to be pulled into it all.

There was no turning back for either of them. Trouble was following them. The sheriff from Las Cruces would soon set out with a posse—if he hadn't already. The sheriff wasn't the sort to let five thousand dollars reward money slip through his greedy fingers.

At best they had a few hours' lead on the posse. The only way out of this now for either of them was to get Sam

Bass. Then he would have his amnesty. And like it or not he couldn't get it without her.

"I did what was necessary, Revel," he flung at her angrily. "Remember that, *it was necessary*. Sometimes you have to do what's *necessary*." Then he shouted at Broken Hand.

"Did you get those things I wanted?"

The old Indian guide nodded. "In my saddlebags."

He rose from beside the stream and tied off his pony. then he pulled a wrapped bundle from his saddlebags. He tossed it to Jake. It was a Colt revolver—heavy, gleaming, and deadly.

Jake reached around and encased her slender hips with the belted holster. As he jerked the belt tight, she winced. But she said nothing.

His hands were on her hips. He was close, too close, extremely angry and dangerous.

"Stop this, at once!" she spat out, trying to twist free. He seized her arm. With his other hand, he reached down and pulled her small revolver from the waistband of her pants.

"If I'm going to risk my neck, you're going to learn how to shoot a real gun. Not that damn peashooter!" He tossed the small pistol into the dirt at their feet.

Cold fury ran through her like ice. Revel screamed in anger and frustration as she swung at him. He caught her wrist, then the other, pulled them both behind her back. He jerked her hard against him.

"This is what you wanted, Revel! It's called revenge. It's not chasing some jewel thief. It's not tracking down a bank robber. It's not exposing some society matron who's stolen charity funds."

He bent over her. His face was so close she could feel the sweet heat of his breath, the rough scrape of the day's growth of beard on his chin, the bruising strength of the hard muscles across his chest. But there was nothing sensual or intimate about the contact.

It was brutal and cruel, the side of Jake Reno she had

read about in those agency files and reports.

His mouth was so close to hers, she had only to turn her face and her mouth would have found his. But this wasn't desire. It was truth, a truth she hadn't wanted to face, a truth he was determined she confront now.

"When someone dies, revenge becomes murder. Only the reason behind it is different. Can you live with being a murderer?"

"I just want Sam Bass. He's committed enough crimes to hang six times over."

"He'll never allow himself to be taken alive. You know that."

"Then that's the way it'll have to be," she answered.

For several long moments, they simply stood there looking at each other as if they might see something else behind the anger they found in one another.

Revel refused to back down, she'd come too far, risked too much, waited too long to let Jake see even the smallest trace of fear or uncertainty, though both churned inside her.

She'd fought those emotions often enough over the past two years since she'd set her plan to go after Sam Bass in motion. The doubt always waited for her in every lonely hotel room hundreds of miles from home, around every darkened corner in every nameless city, cattle town, or outpost.

Was it wrong to want Sam Bass dead?

Was it wrong to deceive William Pinkerton with half-truths about the other cases she'd worked on that always brought her back to Sam Bass?

Had she gone too far by intervening in Jake Reno's hanging?

Was she wrong to take the law into her own hands?

All the questions were there, along with the fear and uncertainty. They waited for her like faceless voices whispering in her dreams, following her everywhere she went.

Did Jake Reno ever have those same fears and doubts?

Looking at him now, anger etched in every hardened line of his handsome face, she doubted it.

She was convinced he never knew fear or doubt. He wasn't capable of feeling it.

"If you say so," Jake was saying, his voice low and edged with anger. "But you're going to learn how to use that gun. Because where we're going you'll need it."

His fingers tightened, biting into her arms as if he seriously considered shaking her until her teeth rattled. Then he abruptly released her.

"Use that as a target." He gestured to a tall saguaro cactus approximately fifty feet away from where they stood. "Take your stance and squeeze off several shots for aim and distance."

She felt ridiculous with the holster strapped around her hips and was certain she looked it. But she suspected what the consequences would be if she took the gun off.

Jake didn't look as if he was in the mood to argue. And that was all they seemed capable of doing lately.

Revel widened her stance a few inches, unholstered the revolver and took careful aim.

For just a split second she actually considered putting a bullet in Jake Reno. Then the urge was gone, quickly smothered by the cool rationale that she needed him far too badly to indulge in the gratification putting a bullet in him might offer.

He was standing about six feet off to her right, halfway between her and the cactus.

"Aren't you afraid I might miss and shoot you instead?" she couldn't resist asking.

"I'll take my chances," he said in that aggravatingly calm way of his. Then he asked, "Do you always fire a gun without checking to see if it's loaded?"

She knew better, she had simply assumed since he'd offered the gun it was undoubtedly loaded. It was a subtle lesson—*assume nothing*. She clamped her jaw tight as she lowered the gun, flipped the chamber open, and checked to see that it was indeed loaded.

"An *unloaded* gun can kill a man, Revel. Never forget that."

She understood the point he was making. In a situation where she needed to protect herself, she'd better know whether the gun was loaded or not. In a tight situation, there would be no second chance.

"Now, take aim. Sight along the barrel, using your arm as an extension of it. Squeeze off the round slowly."

As she did so, the kick from the revolver jerked her arm up abruptly.

"Something else," he added, his cold eyes narrowed as he watched her, "you might want to use two hands. A gun that size and caliber has a lot of recoil."

"Thank you for that bit of timely advice," she bit off angrily as she prepared to take another shot. This time both hands were wrapped around the handle. Like the first time, the shot went high off the intended target.

"With an aim like that you might just manage to hit an elephant at ten feet." He strode back to her.

The Colt lowered to her side, Revel stepped back and glared at him.

"I'll get used to the feel of it."

"We don't have time for you to get used to it. Come here and let me show you."

When she hesitated, he went on to explain, "At this moment the sheriff and his deputies from Las Cruces are probably on our trail. Ahead of us, somewhere across the border, are the Comancheros. Take your pick."

There really was no choice. He was right. Whether they went on or turned back made no difference. either way trouble waited for them. The sheriff wasn't the most ethical man she'd ever met. He was the kind who shot first and asked questions later. If he even bothered to check on whether or not she was a Pinkerton agent, it would be too late. She would be dead.

According to Jake and Broken Hand, the Comancheros were far more dangerous than the Apache.

Back in Las Cruces she'd unwittingly taken a final,

275

irrevocable step when she'd broken Jake out of jail.

There was no going back. There was only what lay ahead, and she best be prepared for it.

"All right." She raised her chin slightly, refusing to allow him to see even a shadow of uncertainty. "Tell me what to do."

"It's not something I can tell you." He walked over to her. "I'll have to show you."

Jake handed her more bullets. She reloaded the revolver and stood patiently, waiting. Jake demonstrated.

"Don't worry about speed. It's not important at this point. Accuracy is the most important thing. Make every shot count. Pick your target, sight in along the barrel. Breathe in slowly, relax your grip. A person always has a tendency to hold a gun like they want to strangle it. It creates too much tension and ruins your aim."

He raised his own gun and carefully sighted. Then he slowly squeezed back on the trigger. The shot rang out. The bullet easily finding its target, a notch blown away from one outstretched limb of the cactus.

"The most important thing is concentration." Jake continued to explain, in between squeezing off several more shots, each systematically enlarging the notch until a plate-sized half-moon was cut out of the cactus.

"Anyone can shoot a gun. But it takes concentration and coolness to aim correctly and hit the target."

"Is that also true when the target is a man?" Revel bit off sarcastically.

He turned, momentarily breaking his concentration on the cactus which had now become his target. The expression in his eyes was cold, completely devoid of feeling or emotion.

"It's especially true when the target is a man. Because a man is likely to move, your concentration has to be stronger. You have to be prepared for any movement, any change, any surprise."

It seemed it all happened in the blink of an eye. He fired six shots, readjusting his aim, his concentration, his intensity as he whirled in a circle and found a half-dozen different targets. Each bullet found its mark. One was a lizard that tried to slither over a rock. Another was a stalk of dry brush that waved in the hot afternoon breeze.

He was good with a gun, but Revel refused to be outwardly impressed. "I'll try to remember." She resumed her stance.

"Concentrate," Jake said as he came to stand beside her.

She raised the gun, making a continuous sight line down the length of her arm to the barrel.

He moved to stand behind her, so close that the front of his shoulder brushed the back of hers as he wrapped his arms around her, his hands closing over hers as they clasped the revolver.

"Relax your wrists. Drop them down just a bit," he instructed her as he brought his right hand down. His fingers brushed her waist, then closed gently over her hip.

"Turn your body just a little this way, always face your target straight on."

Revel breathed in slowly as his hand slipped down her denim-clad thigh.

"Keep your stance on both feet," he instructed. "You'll be better balanced that way, less likely to be thrown off balance by the kick of the gun."

She clenched her teeth together, telling herself she was concentrating on her aim and not the sensations his hands roused. He bent his head low next to hers, his cheek brushing her cheek.

She could feel the heat of his body wrapping around hers, smell the disturbing essence of sun, leather, and man.

As they stood there together, taking aim at the cactus that had become their target, their bodies touched, brushed together, then moved apart as she changed her stance.

Each contact—every touch of hard muscle against soft

277

curve, the brush of his thigh at the back of hers, the brief touch of his hip against her bottom, her back pressed into the hard wall of muscles at his chest—was illusive, teasing, more maddening than if he suddenly turned and took her in his arms.

Memories of that stormy night on the high desert came to her, reminding her of all the times they had accidentally touched since, of the looks, the glances, the emotions that raged between them.

And it made her ache for something she'd discovered briefly that night and been afraid to confront ever since.

The confusion and uncertainty she felt had nothing to do with firing the gun. She slowly squeezed back the trigger. The bullet easily found it's target only slightly off Jake's mark on the cactus.

But her emotional state remained the same even as the loud roar from the pistol spread to silence across the vast wide terrain that surrounded them.

"Again," Jake whispered gruffly against her cheek as if he, too, felt the physical undercurrent that pulsed between them.

She fired a second, third, and fourth time. Each mark was more precise. Then his hands came away from hers. She no longer felt the rock-solid strength of his shoulder molding hers or the heat of his body at her back.

"Empty the chamber," he instructed her once again, his voice calm, controlled. Once more he was the cold, ruthless gunfighter.

When the revolver was empty, she turned around.

"Is that good enough?"

He pulled on his gloves. "It'll do for now. Hopefully it's good enough to keep you from getting your head blown off."

"Thank you for the vote of confidence in my ability." She bit the words off angrily, her pride more than a little wounded as she watched him walk over to his horse.

Broken Hand silently watched their little exchange. Now he mounted his horse.

278

"Sound travels a long way. We must go. The sheriff may be near."

Jake swung astride the Appaloosa and joined Broken Hand. He turned about and looked down at her from the shadow under his hat brim, making it impossible to see his face or any emotions that might be revealed.

"It'll take more than being able to aim and shoot a gun to kill a man."

Revel walked stiffly past them to her own horse and swung herself up into the saddle. She jerked the gelding about.

Her emotions were too fragile, her control was too tenuous. She dared not look at Jake. She took refuge in the familiar territory of anger.

"I'm certain you can teach me that too." She cut past him and turned the gelding south.

In the days after they left Las Cruces, Jake barely spoke to her. It wasn't necessary. She knew precisely how he felt.

It was abundantly clear in the way he looked past her as if she weren't there, in each terse word he spoke when forced to break the rigid silence between them, in the way he coldly walked away after their hands accidentally brushed.

But he didn't turn back. They rode steadily south and followed the bloody trail of the Comancheros toward the Mexican border.

La Mesa. San Jacinto. Piedras Blancas. Estancia. Tres Pinos.

Small towns. Farms. Ranchos. Stage outposts. Stops along a cattle trail.

They were small and remote, days apart from each other. They offered food and water for a price, the sanctity of the Catholic church for the soul.

They were dusty, hot, barren little places, similar to one another in their smallness and the mixture of Mexicans, Anglos, and Indians found in each one. And they all shared the common bond of death and

279

destruction at the hands of the Comancheros.

An old Mexican man had been ridden down and trampled to death in the middle of the street at La Mesa, because he wouldn't give the Comancheros the few meager coins he carried to buy a candle for the altar at the church.

The town store in San Jacinto was burned to the ground, the owner and his wife shot to death, when they no longer had for sale a particular lady's shawl one of the outlaws had fancied for his woman on an earlier raid.

At Piedras Blancas, a poor farmer barely able to provide food for his family, lamented the senseless slaughter of two mules and the burning of a field of corn ready for harvest. He and his family were fortunate to have survived the raid, but the winter would be long with no corn to grind for their meals.

It was difficult to appreciate their good fortune at being left alive when they faced starvation in the months ahead.

At Estancia, the Comancheros raided and looted the town, taking whatever struck their fancy. They gunned down anyone who stood in their way.

They rode off with the small amount of gold from the church offering box, an abundance of whiskey, and weapons taken from the town people.

In their path they left a continuous message for any who followed after—death and destruction awaited.

As long as she lived, Revel knew she would never forget the misery and suffering on the faces of the men, women, and children. She found some of her own anger and sense of loss reflected in both young and old. She was particularly struck by the vacant stare of an old woman, the fear of a child. She wanted to do something for these people, give something back to them, ease the pain and suffering of those who had survived.

But Jake truly understood the devastation the survivors had experienced, and his small gestures of kindness stunned Revel.

In La Mesa, he made certain the widow of the man who was ridden down had sufficient money for candles at the church, and food, which her husband no longer would provide.

The store owner and his wife in San Jacinto had no family. Jake made certain they had a decent marker for their graves.

The farmer in Piedras Blancas arose the morning Jake and Revel left to find several large sacks of corn at his front door. His family wouldn't starve through the winter ahead.

In Estancia, Jake gave money to the church to provide for three children orphaned by the Comancheros raid.

Over the past weeks Revel had seen another side of Jake Reno, the part of him that, in an unguarded moment, was capable of kindness and gentleness. But the last thing she'd expected him to be capable of was compassion.

Outlaws, killers, gunfighters didn't gain their reputations by showing compassion. They earned them by demonstrating ruthlessness—as had the men who had killed the relatives and friends of those who'd survived.

This was another piece to the puzzle of Jake Reno. At some time in his life, there had been people who'd given him a sense of compassion, kindness, and decency. Somewhere along the way, he'd lost it or it had been destroyed.

The key to the abrupt change in him apparently was the fate of the woman named Rachel. After that horror, there had been no going back for him.

She felt envious of Rachel—whoever she was. Jake had loved her.

But he refused to discuss Rachel, just as Revel was certain he would refuse to discuss the source of the money he'd left with the people who hadn't died in the Comancheros' raids. Although she was fairly certain of how he had come by it.

He'd had no money when they'd left Tucson. In fact,

281

he'd taken a perverse pleasure in having her pay for everything. She suspected he'd taken the money from the miners they'd found massacred. But it would do no good to confront him with that; he would simply tell her it was none of her business.

As they left Estancia, Jake tried to get her to turn back. But she refused. It was likely that Sam Bass was with the Comancheros, and she was determined to find him. He had to be stopped.

Revel was certain nothing could affect her more deeply than what she had already seen, but by far the most wrenching, heartbreaking encounter was with the Mexican girl they found in Tres Pinos, just across the border from Mexico.

Her name was Teresa. She lived at the far end of town in a small, adobe hut. Most of the residents had fled to the nearby hills when they heard the Comancheros were coming. Teresa had doubled back for something left behind. Then it was too late for her to escape.

The Comancheros raided and looted the town as they had all the others. The few townspeople who tried to defend their homes were killed. When the rest returned, Teresa was the only one left alive after the Comancheros rode out.

Revel knelt beside the girl in the small house. Teresa sat on the dirt floor in the corner, knees drawn tight to her chest. The clean skirt she wore was pulled tentlike over her legs. Her arms wrapped about her.

She was freshly bathed. Her long, glossy black hair hung over her shoulders. At first glance everything seemed normal, nothing amiss as her mother stood before a brick stove, stirring a pot of beans.

Then Revel saw the swollen eyes, the battered face, the purple bruises darkening Teresa's olive skin though she hid in the shadows.

The girl's lower lip was split, and beneath the fall of raven bangs a small bandage could be seen on her forehead. But it was her eyes that haunted Revel. They

282

were dull, lifeless; shadow drowning in shadow.

She'd hoped the girl might be able to give her information about the Comancheros. Now she smoothed back a long tendril of glossy black hair and inwardly wept for Teresa.

Her heart ached as it hadn't since she'd lost her father. It was all so cruel and senseless. Looking around, she knew Teresa's parents had nothing of value. The Comancheros hadn't come here to steal, they had come to destroy.

"Teresa, my name is Revel Tyson, I would like to help. I would like to be your friend." She began softly, hating to intrude when the girl had already suffered so much. But there were questions she must ask. She had to know whether Sam Bass was with the Comancheros.

"Can you remember anything about the men who came here? How many were there? Was there an anglo with them?" There was no response.

Revel reached out tentatively and touched the girl's arm trying to offer some small comfort.

"I'm looking for a man," she went on to explain. Somehow she had to break through the wall of silence, but she wasn't even certain the girl understood English.

"Un anglo," she explained in Spanish.

"He has light hair—*pelo de oro.* And blue eyes—*ojos azules.*" She gestured to her hair, then her eyes.

"And he has a scar." Revel hesitated. Dear God, she had no idea what the Spanish word was for that. "A scar. On his left cheek."

Revel made a long gesture with her finger down the side of her face. When there was no response, she took Teresa's hand and with *her* finger traced the motion of a scar down her own cheek.

"A scar. Did you see an anglo with a scar?"

Nothing. Not a blink, not a frown, not even a twinge of emotion. No reaction.

She held onto Teresa's hand and gently stroked it. There had to be some way to reach the girl, something she

283

could say that might make her understand. She tried again.

"The man I'm looking for has killed many people." She hesitated, then went on, pulling her own fragile emotions up from deep inside herself.

"He killed my father," she said quietly, her eyes filling with tears.

"I want to find him and make him pay for what he's done. I've been looking for him for a very long time, Teresa. You're the only one who can help me find him."

She wanted to take away the girl's pain, to put her arms around the child and hold her, to somehow make Teresa understand that she was safe now. Revel wanted to deny Sam Bass yet one more victim.

In the end all she could do was place Teresa's hand back atop her bent knees. She got up to leave.

"Un hombre tiene la cicatriz." A small voice called out to her.

Revel whirled back around and went down on her knees before the girl. A somber light wavered in the girl's uncertain eyes. Revel took hold of her hands.

"Cicatriz?" Revel looked quickly to Teresa's mother for an explanation of what the girl had said. The woman came to stand beside them, hope banishing the sadness in her eyes as she knelt beside her daughter.

"What does she mean? *Qué es una cicatriz?"*

Teresa's mother held up her hand. Across the golden bronze skin was a small white scar.

"Cicatriz," she explained, pointing to the scar.

"A scar?" Revel asked in disbelief, then made the gesture of a scar on her own cheek once more for Teresa.

"Did the anglo have a scar? *Un anglo tiene una cicatriz?"*

It was like holding onto a lifeline that was no more than a single, fragile thread, and yet Teresa held on, fighting her way back as she nodded slowly.

Her eyes cleared, filled with pain and fear, and then pooled with tears. She nodded again vigorously.

284

"Sí! Una cicatriz." Again she made a gesture of her own, indicating a scar.

Revel held tight to Teresa's hands, afraid that if she let go physically the girl might slip back into that black void.

"How many man? *Cuántos hombres?*" She held up her own hands and slowly counted. *"Uno, dos, tres?"*

"Quince," Teresa whispered vaguely, then her voice became stronger. *"Quince hombres."*

Quince. Fifteen. Revel nodded that she understood. But she desperately needed to know more. She needed to know which direction they'd taken when they'd left.

"Dónde iban los hombres?"

It was frustrating and frightening. She was terribly afraid she might push Teresa too far, force her to remember too much that was better left forgotten.

"Allá," Teresa gestured out the door. Her voice was tremulous, *"A las montañas."*

Revel understood. *A las montañas.* They'd ridden into the mountains.

She knew from the trail they followed into Tres Pinos, that the nearest mountains lay south, across the border in Mexico. But could she rely on what Teresa had told her?

Teresa curled into her mother's arms and whispered something, then she was fast asleep. The woman looked up and conveyed the message.

"Un anglo es el jefe. Ellos iban a las montañas," she said softly and then turned to her daughter, cradling her in her arms as she softly sang to her.

El jefe. Sam Bass was the leader. He had ridden into the mountains with the Comancheros.

Then the woman explained in Spanish how she'd found Teresa after the Comancheros had finished with her, leaving her more dead than alive. Teresa had been raped many times as well as beaten, she said softly.

Revel fought back the tightness in her throat that choked her, and tears welled in her eyes. Trying to clear her vision, she quietly thanked Teresa's mother. She was

285

just standing up when a shadow fell across the doorway. She looked up.

Jake stood on the threshold. How long had he been standing there?

By the expression on his face, she knew he'd heard at least the last of the terrible tale.

Chapter Fifteen

Revel ran after Jake. She caught up with him as he reached his horse.

"She'd be better off dead!"

"You're wrong!" she shouted at him. "She wouldn't. And her family certainly wouldn't be better off." The reins were tightly wound around his hand as he started to mount the Appaloosa. Certain he would leave, she had to stop him.

"Is that what you thought about Rachel? If you'd found her alive, would you have have wished her dead?"

She grabbed his arm and pulled him around. There were a dozen accusations she wanted to scream at him, but they all evaporated in the smothering arid heat that shimmered across the small yard in front of the adobe hut. The expression on Jake's face was unlike any she'd seen there before.

She'd thought she had finally seen every side to him: the outlaw who'd been condemned to hang; the man who could gentle animals with a mere touch or a soothing word; the ruthless gunfighter who was capable of taking a man's life without a second thought or a regret.

But nothing she'd learned about him had prepared her for what she now saw.

The implacable, perfect control over every emotion— every glance, every gesture, each spoken word—was gone.

His expression was stark, filled with anguish and pain. His mouth worked as he fought to bring those emotions back under control, as if a crack had opened in the careful façade he kept firmly in place and, once opened up, it could never be closed again.

Instinctively, she realized he was revealing more than anyone had ever seen of him. Moisture glistened in his eyes.

All the anger seeped out of her. Even as her hand dropped away from his sleeve, he jerked away from her and pulled himself into the saddle. When he looked down at her again, his control regained, his expression was closed.

"You saw what happened to that girl. Maybe now you understand why we have to turn back."

She knew what he meant. If they went on there was every danger that what had happened to Teresa could happen to her.

Revel laid a hand on his booted leg as she looked up at him, squinting against the sun at his back.

"She'll recover," she said gently. "She has her family. In time, she'll be fine." And then she added in a quiet, adamant tone, "She *wouldn't* be better off dead, Jake."

He stared silently out over the expanse of flat terrain that spread before them to the base of the distant mountains. He swallowed, his mouth twisting into a frown, then looked down at the reins laced through his fingers.

"You can't be certain Bass is with them. All we have are rumors. We might be chasing trouble right to its doorstep and for no reason."

"Teresa saw him. She identified Bass as one of the men with the Comancheros."

Jake's gaze fastened on her.

"There must be at least a dozen of them."

"There are fifteen," she admitted, "including Bass."

For a moment his expression changed, she would have sworn to one of almost grudging admiration.

288

"You learned all that from the girl?"

"Part of it. Her mother told me the rest. I know a little Spanish."

He shook his head. "Fifteen men. And no telling how many more they'll meet up with at their camp. Did she also tell you which way they were headed?"

He was being sarcastic, but she refused to be baited into another argument with him. There had been too many of these.

"They're headed for those mountains."

Jake's mouth pulled into a frown. "The Sierra Madre Mountains, Bass's old hideout. You realize that, if we go after them, the odds we'll come out alive are—"

". . . Terrible at best. I know. I also know the sheriff from Las Cruces is somewhere behind us."

Jake let out a disgusted snort. "And just itching to put the reward money for me in his fat pocket. I should have put a bullet in him when I had the chance."

"The reward for Sam Bass is even higher," she pointed out, then added with a small smile, "I hate to say it but he's worth more than you are."

He gave a long sigh. Of frustration, anger, resignation? She couldn't be certain.

"So what ridiculous, foolish, poorly-thought-out plan do you have now, Miss Pinkerton Agent?"

"We should make the best use we possibly can of that sheriff. I suggest we lead him to the Comancheros and Bass."

"There have been others who went after them and got themselves killed," Jake pointed out, just in case she had forgotten.

"I know that too. But according to Teresa's mother, Bass is the leader. If we get him, we get the Comancheros."

"Just the two of us, and a sheriff with a posse that would just as soon shoot me as look at me?"

"There are three of us," she reminded him.

Jake shook his head. "Broken Hand will turn back

289

when we cross into Mexico. I only intended for him to bring us this far. Apache renegades ride with Comancheros. It would be too dangerous for him to go any farther. They take their revenge very seriously."

"So do I," Revel said quietly.

"A lady Pinkerton agent isn't exactly going to have them quaking in their boots," he pointed out. "You need more men. You have to contact William Pinkerton and wait until he can send more men down here."

"I can't do that." She didn't quite meet his gaze.

"You can't or *won't?*"

"I can't," she repeated.

"What is that supposed to mean?"

"It means I showed Mr. Pinkerton the information I had proving that Bass was still alive months ago. He refused to believe it. He cited 'lack of sufficient proof.' He didn't consider Ben Waters a credible witness."

"What exactly does he think you're doing down here?"

Revel shifted uneasily. This was the part where Jake Reno told her to go to hell with her idea. But there was no turning back now. He deserved the truth.

"He thinks I'm investigating a series of stolen Wells Fargo gold shipments. We didn't specifically discuss Sam Bass."

"In other words you lied."

She looked down at the toes of her boots. "Not exactly."

Jake sat back in the saddle and stared out across the expanse of arid land that shimmered in the midday sun.

"Go on. I want to hear this." He was getting angry again. It was there in the edge to his voice.

"I have the authority to investigate anyone I think may be involved in a crime, following the usual agency procedures."

"And what are those procedures?"

"I'm supposed to contact my superior at regular intervals for appropriate authorizations where a crime may be involved."

"I see. And you haven't bothered to contact anyone."

"Well, I did try—several times. But you know how it is. There was some trouble with the telegraph lines at Tombstone. And since then there hasn't been an opportunity. You know as well as I do there are no telegraph lines running to any of these small villages we've passed through." She could tell by the slightly bemused expression on his face that Jake Reno wasn't swallowing any of this.

"Under *those* circumstances what are you supposed to do?"

Her eyes narrowed. Now she could swear he was doing his darnedest to keep from laughing at her. "Under these circumstances, I'm supposed to contact the Denver office as soon as I possibly can."

"And, of course, you're assuming there isn't a telegraph line anywhere near where Bass has gone," he surmised.

She gave him a wide-eyed innocent look. "I'm certain of that. It's far too remote an area. We probably won't be able to contact anyone until after we find him."

Jake stared down at his hands, which were resting atop the saddle pommel. "And by then William Pinkerton won't be about to turn Bass loose simply because one of his agents overstepped her authority just a little bit."

"That's right." She gave him a straight-faced look.

"What about those papers you gave Virgil Earp? Were they fake?"

"No, the release papers were real." She felt those green eyes on her.

"Just how did you manage that?"

Revel met his gaze evenly. "I made a deal with the Territorial governor."

Jake looked heavenward as he shook his head. "You lied to him, too?"

"I didn't lie. Not exactly. I told him I was a Pinkerton agent on special assignment. I had papers to prove who I was."

"Go on; this is getting good. I haven't heard a yarn like

this in a long time."

She gave him a narrow look. He was taking too much pleasure in all this, but there was no point in holding anything back.

"I told him I had proof Sam Bass was alive, but I needed someone to take me to him. It was really very simple. He immediately saw the merits of exchanging you, if he could have Sam Bass."

"And I suppose you allowed the governor to *assume* that you had the full backing of the Pinkerton Agency to go after Bass."

"We didn't precisely discuss that part of it."

"Uh-huh. I thought you probably didn't. You just didn't bother to fill in all the holes in your little scheme."

"I couldn't. If I told the governor the truth, he would have shown me the door and I wouldn't have gotten that release warrant. Your release was necessary. It was the only way I had to find Bass."

"What about the pardon?"

She'd been afraid he would get around to asking about that. "The governor and I discussed it."

"What does that mean?"

She'd been truthful up to now. Revel suspected it was in her best interest *not* to be too truthful now.

"The governor is in a position to offer a full pardon in exchange for Sam Bass."

Jake began to chuckle. "I see."

"I don't see anything funny about any of this."

"No, I suppose you don't, Revel. The point is, you're completely serious about all of this. And considering what sent you here, I suppose I can't blame you. But I'd be willing to bet the governor didn't specifically promise a pardon."

She squirmed. He was absolutely right, and they both knew it. She should have known she couldn't lie to a liar and pull it off. Still, she had to know where he stood.

"I *can* get that pardon for you."

"You seem pretty damn sure about that."

"I am."

"That is, *if* we make it back alive," he reminded her.

Revel looked down at the toes of her boots as she gathered her thoughts. Then she looked up. "As you've told me a hundred times, if we don't make it back it won't matter."

He sat, silent and thoughtful, a long time. The Appaloosa shifted restlessly under him. The sun poured down from a cloudless blue sky so intense it made her eyes ache to look at it. The longer the silence, the more convinced she was that he was going to tell her exactly what she could do with her scheme, now that he knew the truth.

"Jake? I have to know whether you're in on this or not."

"And if I'm not?"

"I'll go after him anyway."

"I don't suppose there's anything I can say to talk you out of it."

She smiled up at him. "Nope."

Again there was that unbearable silence. Only this time he stared past her to the small adobe house where Teresa's mother comforted her daughter. Something he saw in the shadows of that doorway, or perhaps beyond it, seemed to make his mind up for him.

"The weather changes quickly this time of year up in those mountains," he said thoughtfully.

She grabbed hold of his hand. "Then you'll go?"

He looked down at the slender fingers wrapped around his scarred hand—at the contrast of light and dark, smooth and callused. Her touch was cool against his thick-veined skin. As long as he lived he knew he would remember it—light, fragile yet with an unbreakable hold on him. Just like her.

He looked once more to the small adobe house. Then his gaze met hers.

"We can still cover a few more miles in the daylight that's left."

* * *

They traveled twenty miles the remainder of that first day. The next day they rode over forty. At dusk they gazed across the border into Mexico. There was no official line, no marker, no sign, nothing Revel might have expected to indicate they were leaving one country and entering another.

Jake simply declared they were at the border. He knew this part of the territory having ridden here with Sam Bass.

"We'll stay on this side tonight and cross over in the morning."

"Why don't we cross over tonight?" Revel asked. "There's still plenty of daylight. We might as well cover as much distance as possible."

Jake gave her a long, contemplative look. "Once we cross over, we leave law and order behind, such as it is."

She gave him a bemused smile. It seemed ironic for someone like Jake Reno to say that. "Except, of course, for that sheriff from Las Cruces."

"It depends on whether or not he's greedy and stupid or just plain greedy."

"I think we can count on greedy," Revel assured him.

"What makes you so certain about that?" Jake asked with mild curiosity.

"The letter I left for him back at Tres Pinos."

"What letter?" His curiosity went to mild suspicion.

"The one I left with Teresa's mother. It explains that we're after Sam Bass, that Teresa verified Bass is with the Comancheros. And the last part . . ." Her voice trailed off.

Broken Hand spoke up. "What last part?"

She squirmed just a little. Jake wasn't going to like this part. "I mentioned in the letter that Sam Bass is worth ten thousand dollars, dead or alive."

Both men exchanged a long look, then Jake spoke up. "Do you really expect the sheriff to believe all that?"

"As I said, I trust his greediness. And he's not *that* stupid. After all, he did arrest you and try to collect the reward money for you."

"He might still try that," Jake pointed out.

"Except he needs you to lead him to Sam Bass. So you see, we really should stay as far ahead of him as we can, at least until we need him."

Jake sat back in the saddle. "Great. I was hoping we'd lose him once we crossed the border." He was no longer amused. He gave her a long, steady look and then said, "From here on out, I make the decisions. And that includes decisions about the sheriff. Is that understood?"

She frowned. "Now wait just a minute. I thought we could use the extra help—"

"All the decisions," Jake stated flatly, and his tone suggested he would accept no argument. "If we have one chance in hell of surviving this it's going to depend on outsmarting Sam Bass and those Comancheros. I don't want that sheriff complicating things. At least not until I want him to.

"Besides, I know this territory. You don't. When we cross the border, we do things my way. Is that clear?"

When she started to object again, he cut her off. "*I* make the decisions. Is that understood?"

She knew he was right. "It is," she said.

Jake nodded. "We'll cross the border at first light. Then we'll have plenty of time to get to the base of the mountains, where there's a small valley—and some people I know. We can rest the horses there before starting up into the mountains." He dismounted and started to make camp for the night.

Revel looked to Broken Hand. "Will you be going back in the morning?"

The old Indian shrugged. "I might go with you into Mexico." Jake looked up at hearing this unexpected comment.

"It's too dangerous for you," he reminded Broken Hand. Again there was an unconcerned shrug.

"Can't be worse than those renegades who shot at us,

295

or that stupid sheriff who arrested you. You will need another gun." He gestured to Revel. "She has a way of finding trouble."

Jake grinned. "I'm inclined to agree with you."

Revel gave them both a withering glare. "Present company included, of course," she said, referring to Jake.

Broken Hand agreed. "That is true," he grunted. Then he looked at Revel. "With a little more practice you might become a pretty good shot with that revolver. I'll be along to help. Besides, where you are going you will need two sets of eyes to see the Comancheros, so I think I will ride with you."

"That's not necessary," Jake reassured him. "You've done enough bringing us this far. You know what they'll do to you if they catch you."

The old Indian's face creased into a mass of lines accented by the deep-set rut of his frown. "That is true. But it is necessary, my friend. Besides," his face crinkled into one of his rare smiles, "*first* they have to catch me."

"Suit yourself," Jake answered solemnly as he jerked the saddle from the back of the Appaloosa.

Revel tethered the gelding, then loosened the saddle cinch. She looked up as Broken Hand reined his pony in beside her.

"You should go back," he said simply.

"Did Jake tell you to say that?"

He frowned. "I don't understand."

"You understand, all right," she shot back at him with a knowing smile, then added, "I won't go back."

"I told him that's what you'd say."

She looked up at the old Indian across the back of the gelding. "It's more dangerous for you. Why are you going on?"

"I, too, have an old score to settle." When Revel looked up at him with a puzzled expression, he simply said, "There is an Apache warrior who rides with the Comancheros. He betrayed his people."

"But how can you be certain he's with this band of Comancheros?"

Broken Hand's dark eyes bore into hers for a long time as if he considered something of great importance. Then he reached inside a large pouch tied to his saddle. He took out a leather thong. Several feathers were tied together and attached to the thong, along with a strip of intricately woven beads.

"What is that?"

"It is the mark of an Apache warrior. He was called Toscaneh. Many believe he died at the massacre of the cavalry blue-coats."

She remembered the story he had told her. "But you don't believe it?"

He held up the leather thong, elaborately decorated with the white feathers and beads. "I found this at the place called Tres Pinos. Before he died, one of the townspeople took this from an Apache warrior who rides with the Comancheros. The pattern woven in the beads is his."

"Why do you want this Apache warrior?"

Broken Hand answered simply, "He betrayed his people."

Then he turned his pony away from camp as was his habit each evening. He rode until after dark, moving noiselessly on ahead, scouting the countryside. When he returned he always brought a rabbit or quail or wild turkey that he had caught.

He stopped briefly before disappearing into the night darkness.

"He did not kill the deputy at Las Cruces."

She looked up, startled. "What did you say?"

Broken Hand turned back around in the saddle and guided his pony away from the camp. He called over his shoulder, "He did not kill the deputy."

Revel frowned as she slowly walked toward the crude camp that was like so many others they'd made over the past weeks. Jake had gathered what meager scrub wood

297

and dry, dense brush could be found nearby. Fuel was scarce in this area, and it was cold at night.

She unsaddled the gelding and carried the saddlebags that contained food and the few personal belongings she had left. Additional food, blankets, and heavy coats were packed on the mule they'd bought from Teresa's family in Tres Pinos.

They'd paid twice what it was worth, but Revel had said nothing. Once again, Jake had paid for all their supplies and the mule out of his own pocket. At Tres Pinos something had unalterably changed between them.

Or had it begun before that?

She slowly walked toward the encampment, sheltered on three sides by an unusual cluster of mammoth rocks. There was only one way anyone could approach, should someone decide to pay a visit during the night. She knew Jake had chosen this place for precisely that reason.

The fire sputtered feebly on the meager wood, a cloud of heavy smoke hanging in the quickly cooling night air. Then the fire caught with a small burst of flame, yellow fingers creeping tentatively through brush that was snapping and crackling.

It was dusk now, the last golden light of the sun clinging to the blue-gray twilight that was chased by early stars. The sunset was bloodred on the distant horizon, dripping to deep purple then midnight blue.

No matter how many times she saw the sky at this time of the evening, it was a constant wonder to Revel. Everything out here seemed bigger, grander, more breathtaking . . . more dangerous.

As dangerous as the man who sat crouched before the fire.

Firelight played across the planes and angles of Jake Reno's face.

It was a face she had seen many times, and with many different expressions. She'd learned them all, had often thought she'd seen them all, but he was constantly surprising her.

298

At that very moment, lost in his own thoughts, his face was relaxed. There were faint lines of fatigue at his eyes. Others pulled at the slight downturn of his lips.

They reminded her that the pace he set was just as grueling for him as it was for them. But there was a softness about his eyes now, and something almost vulnerable about his mouth . . . something that hinted at regret.

It was the one thing she would never have thought him capable of.

Nor would she have thought him capable of compassion. But in the past few days she'd learned a great deal about Jake Reno, the man. It had made her rethink what she knew about Jake Reno, the outlaw. *He did not kill the deputy.* . . .

He didn't seem to hear as she quietly approached the fire. She reached out and laid a hand on his shoulder.

Quick, catlike, and completely without warning he sprung about from his crouched position. His right hand shot out and grabbed her wrist at the same time he drew his revolver with his left.

In less than a heartbeat, before she could even react, Revel was staring down the barrel of that deadly Colt .45.

She had never seen Jake draw on anyone, but she knew his reputation. Some said the speed with which he could draw a gun was like the wind—you never saw it, you simply felt it.

Another description she'd once read called Jake Reno in motion the sting *after* a rattlesnake has struck.

Still another description compared his speed with a gun to lightning striking—even when you thought you saw it, it had already happened.

Revel experienced all those sensations as she saw the gleam of golden firelight skitter along that gleaming barrel.

Her breath wedged in her throat. She was certain her heart ceased beating.

Time hung suspended on an icy shaft of fear.

Then that steely, cold taste of fear was backing up into her throat. She stared wide-eyed at death, frozen, unable to move.

For long moments they both stared—Jake at her colorless expression, Revel at that deadly gun. And each struggled with the horrifying realization of how close she had come to dying in that split second that required no thought, no emotion, only instinctive reaction.

Revel had seen guns before. Her father had always carried one. On occasion, she'd used one herself.

She knew the damage they could cause. That was partly why she still wasn't comfortable with the revolver Jake had given her, and why it was safely stashed in one of her saddlebags. But she understood that there were places, like this, where a gun was often the only justice there was.

Still, nothing in her experience had prepared her for that moment when she'd looked at death.

"Damn!" The curse hissed out of him. "Don't you know better than to sneak up on someone?" Slowly, he eased the hammer back. But even as he holstered the Colt, she backed away from him.

"Revel?"

She held out a hand as she took another step back. "No. Please." She turned hesitantly, looking for escape. Her mouth was dry, her throat ached, blood pumped violently through her veins. Nonetheless, she was cold, absolutely frozen through.

As he came toward her, she backed up even farther and shook her head. Reason failing before instinct.

"Revel." Jake frowned as he took another step forward.

"No!" She bolted like a frightened animal. Jake caught her before she reached the edge of the clearing. She turned on him.

"Let me go!"

"Revel, it's all right." His voice was low, slicing away at her fear. But she still struggled.

Even as she whirled back around and fought his grasp, his arms closed around her and he pulled her back against him.

"Revel."

He refused to let her go, talking to her, stripping away the layers of fear and panic.

"It's over. I'm sorry. I never meant for that to happen."

"I know," she answered, for lack of anything more coherent to say.

It was an automatic response. She didn't even know precisely what she'd said. She only knew she had to get away from him, from that gun and the look of death she'd seen on his face.

She had no idea why she was so scared, why his reaction had affected her so profoundly, only that it had. She couldn't think, couldn't reason it out.

She felt trapped, cornered by other, undefined fears that were hidden deep inside her. All she wanted was to get away from there—from him.

He wouldn't let her.

For almost as long as he could remember, Jake had lived without the need for kindness, gentleness, tenderness.

There had been no room for them in his life after Rachel. When she'd died, it was as if his ability to feel any emotion had died with her.

But now, from somewhere deep inside, had come the need to comfort and protect Revel, to take away her fear, to give her some small amount of gentleness and tenderness. And from somewhere deeper still he found those qualities.

She struggled, but Jake held her tight against him until her resistance stopped. He could feel the frantic racing of her heart beneath his arm, the desperate fear that made every muscle go rigid in her slender body. She was like a wounded, frightened animal, ready to leap at the first opportunity.

He turned her in his arms so that she was facing him, his right arm firmly anchored around her waist, preventing escape. She refused to meet his gaze, her blue eyes averted, downcast. Her chin trembled.

Her hands were firmly wedged between them, flattened against his chest. She thrust herself as far away from him as possible while still firmly held within the circle of his arm.

He brushed a disheveled tendril of dark silken hair back from her cheek, a gentle, soothing gesture. The fear was still there in her eyes as she gave him a wary glance. He slipped his fingers behind her neck and insistently pulled her head to his shoulder.

"I'm sorry," he whispered against her hair, as his fingers stroked the back of her neck, the corded tendons, then spread through her long hair to cradle the back of her head.

He stroked her, easing her fear and tension with soothing, circular motions of his long fingers.

"I never meant for that to happen." He pulled her closer, feeling some of the resistance and wariness ease out of her.

"It's all right now. It's over. I promise it will never happen again." A sigh shuddered out of her and she began to relax against him. But the cold trembling of fear remained. He recognized it from living with it himself.

She raised her head to look at him warily, her brilliant blue eyes deep, dark pools. A faint frown creased her delicate brows. She didn't trust. Not yet.

"I promise," Jake repeated softly as he gently took hold of her chin. He lowered his head and brushed his lips against hers.

"I promise."

What began as a need to comfort and be comforted, quickly burned to a much deeper, more primal need.

Chapter Sixteen

Fear and desire knotted deep inside Revel—reminding her of how truly dangerous Jake Reno was.

There had been so much anger between them, she'd almost convinced herself that night on the desert never happened.

Now all the feelings and emotions she'd discovered that night came flooding back to her in an aching wave of longing so intense it overwhelmed every other sensation.

He was brutally tender as he brought both hands up to cradle her face, brushing his lips across hers with a soft stroking that continued the rhythm his fingers had begun on her skin.

His hands were callused, scarred. They were accustomed to hard leather or the cold caress of a gun. Nothing prepared her for the gentleness of his touch. She might have been made of the most fragile glass, might easily break, so gentle was he.

That made her feel delicate, treasured, and more vulnerable than she could ever have imagined.

Jake Reno was a man of power, violence, danger. There had been nothing gentle or tender in him the night they'd made love. The violence, power, and danger in him had been mirror images of the storm that had surrounded them and built within them, driving them at one another.

Because she thought she knew him, Revel had

expected all of those things. The surprise came from her equally violent and dangerous response to him.

The tenderness and gentleness he showed her now were contrary to every other aspect of Jake Reno. That made them even more dangerous.

His mouth was soft and warm, almost a whisper against hers, lingering only long enough to make her want more. Then it was gone, only to return again.

He was like the brush of the wind, the caress of the sun, filling her senses, taking away the horror and fear.

They were soft, sweet kisses at one corner of her mouth, then the other. They required nothing of her, simply gave strength and weakness all at the same time.

They were quick, light kisses and yet they robbed her of breath.

She had no time to recover before he began a more devastating assault, gently nibbling at her bottom lip. Each soft bite set off shock waves that raced through her and settled somewhere below her stomach.

Her eyes flew open at the strange and wondrous feelings he was creating in her.

His green eyes were filled with strange, dark shadows. His fingers stroked along her jaw.

"Revel."

Her name was like a caress. And then his eyes shut as his mouth closed once more over hers.

Revel gave herself completely over to sensation. Then the knot inside her tightened and she shivered as she felt the warm, velvet caress of Jake's tongue at the vulnerable nub of her upper lip.

She made a small sound as her lips parted. He lightly stroked her lips with his tongue, as if he were caressing, tasting. Then there was only the warm, roughened sensation of his tongue wrapping around hers, like hot, wet velvet. Her fingers curled into the soft fabric of his shirt.

Jake . . . His name tumbled through her thoughts.

The outlaw was forgotten. Fear was forgotten. This

was Jake Reno—the man.

From somewhere behind them came the faint sound of movement through the brush and the hoofbeats of a horse.

"Damn!" Jake whispered against her mouth as he slowly broke contact.

Broken Hand had returned to camp. He called out something to them both as he crossed to the fire.

Revel drew away from Jake as if she'd been burned. She was too stunned, too uncertain of what had just happened, to meet his gaze.

"Revel?"

"I'm all right," she answered shakily, as she backed away from him.

His hand caught at hers. "Are you sure?"

Her gaze met his briefly. She saw something behind his eyes, some emotion she'd never seen before.

"Yes, I'll be fine." Her voice sounded strange to her. "Please . . ."

She didn't know what she was asking of him. Please go away? Please stay? Please, kiss me again?

She turned and headed for the far edge of camp. To any casual observer, it undoubtedly seemed that she merely went in search of privacy for more intimate needs. What she needed desperately was to be alone, to sort through her jumbled thoughts and emotions.

"Stay within sight of camp," Jake called after her, an odd, concerned edge to his voice.

When she returned several minutes later, he looked up at her from across the fire. The light danced in the golden depths of his green eyes, and one corner of his mouth was pulled down a bit.

What did she see? Regret? Disappointment?

He had offered her comfort when she was frightened. But it had quickly changed to something more.

Was he disappointed because she wasn't Rachel? Or did he regret what had happened *because* of Rachel?

It shouldn't matter, but it did. It mattered so much

that it hurt, deep inside where he had caused a much different ache only minutes earlier.

Revel busied herself adding another stick of wood to the fire, pouring some of the dried beans into a shallow pan of water that already simmered, unwrapping the last of the Mexican corn bread they'd brought from Tres Pinos—anything to keep from thinking about Jake Reno.

It worked. At least that's what she told herself while she was busy helping with the supper, cleaning the metal plates afterward, checking the horses, trying to make her bedroll more comfortable.

But they were alone again when Broken Hand left camp to scout the countryside on foot. There was only the occasional hiss or snap from the fire.

She tossed and turned in her blankets, unable to get comfortable.

"Revel! Lie completely still! Don't move!"

"What's wrong?" Her gaze snapped up as Jake whispered the warning to her.

"Dammit! I said don't move!"

She lay still, frozen in one position as her pulse began to hammer wildly.

What was it? A wild animal? Indians? The Comancheros?

She started to ask, then screamed as he swatted at something beside her head.

"What are you doing?" she screamed at him as she came up from the blankets and scooted away from him as fast as she could.

"You had a visitor." He gestured to where she'd lain only seconds before. Something small, light brown, and indiscernible was smashed into the blanket.

"What is it?" Revel asked warily.

"Scorpion."

Her eyes narrowed as she looked at his bare hand. "I thought you said they were poisonous."

"They are. The sting can be real painful."

"But not deadly?" she asked, recalling the story he'd told her when they'd first started out.

He gave her one of those long looks that said she'd been had.

"Not usually, although I hear there are some in Mexico that can be very deadly."

"But not this one?"

Jake gave the squashed scorpion careful inspection. "Nah, not this one."

She brushed the dead scorpion from her blanket.

"I'm so very glad," she commented sarcastically; then she tried to make herself comfortable once more, turning on to her side, her back to him.

After several long moments there was still no sound of his moving away. He was crouched beside her, and she could feel those green eyes watching her.

"Is there a snake in my hair?" she asked, less unsettled by that possibility than Jake's eyes.

"I don't think so," he said with a soft chuckle. "I could check for you."

She vividly remembered the feel of his hands in her hair and the devastating results. If Broken Hand hadn't come back . . .

And then there had been the look on Jake's face afterward, an expression that was almost painful.

"No!" she said a little too quickly, a little too urgently, then added, "I'm certain I would know if there was."

Their eyes met briefly. "Good night, Jake."

He didn't move, but instead reached out and took a long strand of her hair between his fingers.

He stared down at it, wrapping it around his hand, feeling the texture. Then his gaze came back to hers, and everything that hadn't been said was in his eyes.

"It's not finished, Revel."

What was he talking about? The anger between them? The mistrust? That kiss?

"I don't know what you mean?" she replied softly, her gaze darting away from his to safety.

307

Then he gently laid the tendril of hair back on her shoulder.

"Yes, you do," he said simply, then added. "Good night, Revel."

They rode out early the next morning and crossed the border into Mexico just after daybreak, Jake was determined they make the small valley he'd spoken of that day.

Once inside Mexico, the land about them gradually changed. They rode through gently rolling hills, following what Jake called the narrow tributary of the Urique River. The foothills lay at the base of the Sierra Madre Mountains.

The land was dry this late in the season, but instead of the barren landscape of the desert, there was knee-deep wild grass that waved in the late summer breeze. It was green and closely cropped near the banks of the river, where wild deer preferred the tender shoots.

The mountains rose before them, a mass of carved granite, with a thick verdant tree line, above which was a jagged, purplish-blue sawtooth range.

Sam Bass and the Comancheros were somewhere up in those mountains.

Late in the afternoon they crossed the small valley nestled in a canyon. In the distance, the sun was like a bright orange ball spiked on the tips of those high mountains. In the cool shadows cast by the peaks lay a cluster of log cabins, snugged against the base of the lower summit.

Long before they rode within shouting distance of the cabins, they passed a crudely fenced pasture spotted with white-faced cattle, rows of trees in a small orchard, and a neatly cultivated field with perfect tilled rows of shoulder-high corn.

A rangy, gray dog announced their arrival, sending the alarm across the entire valley. Chickens squawked in the yard, and in another pasture several mares with half-grown spring colts scattered at the scent of the strange horses. There was something familiar in the half-dozen spotted-rump mares and their smoky dark offspring.

Men, women, and several children emerged from the cabins. The smaller boys were all dressed in traditional mestizo garments, sun-bleached white cotton pants and shirts. The women and small girls wore dark skirts and white blouses. It was a large family, the children ranging in age from the infant cradled in it's mother's arms to young girls rapidly approaching womanhood.

All of them stared with a mixture of wariness and curiosity at the strangers who rode onto their rancho.

The smaller children ran barefoot through soft dirt that billowed up in clouds of dust beneath the horses' hooves. Two older boys, approximately seventeen or eighteen years of age, wore dark, denim pants like the older men. At the corral they watched from beneath wide-brimmed sombreros as another full-grown brother brought a green-broke pony under control.

Two young girls giggled shyly from behind their mother's skirts while they pointed with unabashed curiosity at the two anglos and the Indian.

The older girls came forward with the men, regarding the strangers with a shyness that quickly turned to open admiration as Jake swept his hat from his head in a friendly gesture.

"Jake? Jake Reno?" A heavily accented voice called out as the oldest of the men came forward.

"Is that you, *mi amigo?*" The older man cried in astonishment. His round, sun-bronzed face with the heavy silken, black mustache was split by a gleaming grin.

Jake grinned back. *"Buenos días, Emilio."*

The greeting, obviously familiar to the two men, was apparently a signal that all was well with the strangers. The entire family swept forward in a rush, babbling, shouting greetings; and as Jake stepped down from the

Appaloosa, the woman who cradled the baby hurried over to him, threw an arm about his neck, and gave him a hearty kiss on the cheek.

The baby set up a loud squalling at being caught in the unexpected embrace. The younger children now held back, still uncertain about all the excitement, while the older ones squealed with delight and crowded around Jake and the tall, spotted stallion.

Revel and Broken Hand sat back and watched the emotional reunion. She stared in amazement. Jake had mentioned that he knew of a place to stay, but he hadn't mentioned that he knew these people so well. She listened to bits and pieces of excited conversation shouted in a mixture of Spanish and English.

"I thought you were dead, my anglo friend."

"I almost was—twice." Jake and the man were now standing face-to-face, although Jake was at least six to eight inches taller.

"You probably deserved it," his friend stated bluntly.

"That's what the federal marshal said."

The man called Emilio grunted and frowned. "But I see you are still alive."

"The marshal wasn't quick enough."

That brought a load roar of laughter as Emilio threw back his head.

"You are the same, *amigo.*"

Jake shook his head. "A little older."

"But are you any wiser?" Emilio asked with a thick accent.

"I try not to be," Jake retorted. That brought more laughter as the two men embraced, slapped each other on the back, then stood apart to take a good, long look at one another.

"Your family has grown since I was last here," Jake commented as, with a large smile, he turned to look at all the little faces staring at him.

"How many years is it, my friend?" Emilio asked.

"It's been four years."

310

"Ah, yes. If it has been four years, then you must come and meet my little ones." He wrapped an arm about Jake's broad shoulders and led him over for an introduction to the children who hid behind their mother's skirts.

"This is Pepita. She is almost *cuatro anos*—four years old."

Jake grinned up at Emilio's wife. "I thought you were a bit big the last time I saw you." She playfully slapped his shoulder.

"You be careful of your tongue, if you want supper, Jake Reno."

He placed a hand over his heart. "I came all this way just to eat your fine cooking, Rosa."

"You lie, anglo. But I like to hear you say it anyway. This old man"—she gestured to her husband—"does not appreciate me."

"I appreciate you, *querida*," he objected, "don't you always have a man to warm your bed and a baby in your belly?"

"Arrgh!" Rosa groaned. "He thinks that is the only thing a woman needs. Well, I will tell you. This one"—she held the baby aloft—"is the last one. Tell me, Jake, don't you think eleven children are enough?"

Jake's eyes twinkled as he looked from Rosa to Emilio. "Oh, I don't know. A full dozen is a nice number. And right now, I'd say maybe Emilio is the one who has grown old having all these children. Look at the gray hair he has. While you, Rosa, are as pretty as the day I first met you."

"You are a smooth-tongued anglo. It will do you no good, Jake Reno. I won't listen to it."

Jake laughed, then his face became very somber. "Who is this little one?" he asked, crouching down to peer at a small boy who hid behind Rosa.

Emilio smiled proudly. "This is my next youngest son, Santio. And beside him are the two youngest girls, Maya and Paquita. The baby is my youngest son, Benito. And of course you remember the older children."

They were all introduced in turn. The oldest boys, Pedro, Miguel, and Ricardo were fine-looking young men, almost of age. The three oldest girls were Ana, Margarita, and Elena. They were exquisite, willowy, bronzed beauties who favored their mother with high cheekbones, well-curved mouths, and large, dark doe eyes. Emilio sighed as his oldest daughter nudged his arm.

"You remember Elena, my oldest daughter?" He was obviously very proud of her.

"Of course, I remember. I use to bounce her on my knee. She must have been about twelve when I was last here." He smiled at her warmly. "She always followed me about and wanted to exercise the Appaloosa for me."

Elena's cheeks flooded with color, but she wasn't at a loss for words. "I see you still have him, Señor Jake."

Jake nodded. "He's the best stallion I've ever had. I have plans for him."

Polite, yet openly flirtatious, Elena added, "Then perhaps you would like to see our Appaloosas later. They are very fine animals."

"I'd like that, Elena."

"Daughter," Rosa scolded, "you forget your manners. Jake has only just arrived."

Emilio rolled his eyes. "You can see my dilemma, my friend," he said to Jake. "My daughters are a handful." Then he added in a lower voice as he wrapped an arm about Jake's shoulders. "I must constantly protect them from the young vaqueros who come to buy our horses. They try to steal my little flowers away."

"You should be very proud of your family," Jake declared, and when Elena gave him a long, open look, he added, "and very careful. The last time I saw this one, she was a spindly-legged little girl, running around barefoot with dirt all over her."

Emilio sighed. "Ah yes, but as you see, things change. My daughters have changed. Now they make calf eyes at young men and give me this gray hair." He shook his

312

head as if he carried the weight of the world on his shoulders. Then he smiled up at Jake.

"But you, my friend, have been very lacking in *your* manners." At seeing Jake's surprised expression, he explained, "You have not introduced your *compadres*." Emilio gestured to Revel and Broken Hand, who remained astride their horses, quietly taking in the reunion of the old friends.

For the first time, Revel was vividly aware of how dusty and dirty they all were. It might be acceptable for a man who'd just ridden in off the trail, but it wasn't at all acceptable in a woman. It was especially embarrassing for her because Rosa and the children were simply but immaculately dressed, even the boys who worked the horses in the paddock.

The source of such cleanliness was readily apparent. A long line of freshly laundered clothing was strung out behind the row of cabins. The garments snapped and whipped in the late afternoon breeze. Such a large family obviously kept Rosa busy, but she wasn't about to have her children seem poorly clothed.

Jake made the introductions, and Revel saw the slight confusion over her name, an oddity to these people. Quiet, careful, wary of strangers, Broken Hand merely grunted his greeting. Revel dismounted from the gelding, rubbing dirty, sweaty palms on her pants. Then she swept the wide-brimmed Stetson Jake had gotten her from her head and heard the collective exclamation of surprise as her hair tumbled to her shoulders.

"This is *Miss* Revel Tyson," Jake clarified for his friends.

From the younger children, there was a round of muffled giggles. Revel couldn't blame them, she must look a sight.

The older boys quickly came over from the paddock. They crowded around, greeting Jake with easy familiarity, staring at Revel with respectful admiration.

From behind her, Revel heard a distinctly catty remark

313

from one of the older daughters. It came from Elena, and was directed to her sister, Margarita, in hastily whispered Spanish.

Roughly translated, Elena remarked that only a woman of bad reputation would travel openly with a man she wasn't married too.

In spite of the slight insult, Revel turned and smiled warmly at each of the older girls. Her gaze lingered briefly on Elena. The girl stood beside Jake, gazing adoringly up at him. He seemed not to notice that he was the focus of so much attention.

"There must be many broken hearts in the valley," he said teasingly.

"There are none I care to break yet," Elena answered with a dazzling smile and a subtle widening of those dark doe eyes. It was obvious he was going to have his hands full as long as they were here.

Revel felt a tugging at her pantleg. She bent down to the younger children, and took small, pudgy hands in hers. She smiled and greeted them in fluent Spanish. Their obsidian eyes widened with pleasure.

From behind her came the muffled gasps of their older sisters, provoked by hearing her use of their language. They were deeply embarrassed now that they realized she understood everything they'd said, including Elena's comment—except for Elena.

"You must come inside now," Emilio was saying, "You will have time to clean up. Then we will enjoy a fine meal together and tell each other of the last four years. And you, my friend, will tell me what has brought you back to us."

Three cabins belonged to Emilio and his family. They were made of huge, hand-hewn timbers brought down from the mountains. One cabin was for storage. Supplies of food for the long winter were kept there, along with slabs of beef and pork. When snow fell even at this low elevation, the storage cabin was like a large springhouse, only it was kept cold by the snow.

314

The older boys and the vaqueros slept in the next largest cabin. It was like a large bunkhouse, with beds, a center table and chairs, and it had a porch with an overhang. A huge stone fireplace occupied one wall, for warmth in the winter.

The main cabin was the largest of the three. Emilio, his wife, the older daughters, and the small children lived there. A large kitchen with a stone fireplace and oven dominated the center of the house with several rooms built around it.

The largest was the dining room, which had comfortable overstuffed chairs set at the far end for relaxing after a meal. The stone fireplace opened onto both the kitchen and dining room. In winter, this was a cozy, central place for the family to be together.

The inside walls had been filled and rubbed smooth. Colorful, hand-loomed blankets decorated them in summer. In winter the blankets warmed the floors. These were of planked cedar, also rubbed to a smooth finish.

There was real glass in the windows, each hung with heavy-timbered shutters that would keep out the worst winter storm.

The furnishings were simple but well cared for and comfortable. A long table filled one end of the room. It was here Emilio and his entire family shared their meals.

He and his wife had a room just off the kitchen. The children shared the other three rooms along the west side of the house.

Emilio's second oldest son had just moved out to the vaquero's cabin. Jake was given his room at the far end of the east side.

Revel was given the room Elena had taken after her maiden aunt married and moved to Sonora. During their stay, Elena was moved in with her younger sisters.

Elena held her tongue, making no disagreeable comment now that she knew Revel understood everything she said. But she didn't bother to hide her sullenness as she obediently moved her things.

Revel was aware that she had made an enemy, for reasons that went far beyond the issue of who slept in the extra bedroom.

She gratefully accepted the opportunity to bathe in the small enclosure out behind the house. She wasn't satisfied that her hair was completely clean until she had lathered it twice. That much soap would surely kill anything that had been living in it, she felt.

When she reached for her dirty clothes, intending to wash them also, they were gone. In their place on the small bench beside the wooden tub were sandals, a brightly colored skirt, and a clean white blouse.

The fit was perfect. Revel could only hope Elena hadn't been required to sacrifice some of her clothing. She had unwittingly earned the girl's enmity, but as she'd already guessed that had nothing to do with the room or the clothes. It had to do with Jake.

She walked back into the house, her damp hair streaming down her back. Rosa was working in the kitchen, and Revel offered to help prepare dinner.

Deftly stirring two pots of food that gave off an enticing aroma, Rosa refused aid. She then checked the corn bread in the earthen oven. It was far different from the hard, stale bread Revel had eaten on the trail.

The Spanish names for the foods being prepared were as enticing as their aromas. Carne posada, pollo ensalada, frijoles refritos, enchiladas, and tamales wrapped in corn husks.

Emilio and his wife had a good life. They didn't live extravagantly but they lived well. The cabins were strongly built and immaculately maintained. The animals in the surrounding pastures were healthy and of fine stock. There was an abundance of food, and an abundance of healthy children. Such a place required hard work, but the rewards were many.

One of them was the sticky-fingered infant sitting on the floor and tugging at Revel's skirt. Benito gurgled gleefully and spouted unintelligible gibberish only he could understand as Revel picked him up and deposited him on her lap. He was immediately fascinated with the red-gold light that played through her rapidly drying hair.

"Ah, that is how you may help me." Rosa laughed as she came across the kitchen and cleaned his hands and face with a wet cloth.

"My daughters say he is like a whirlwind. He is always moving and always getting into trouble."

Revel laughed as the baby puffed his bronzed cherub's cheeks and blew bubbles. "He's wonderful and so happy."

"Ah, *Dios*, he is happy now. But you should see him when he is angry," Rosa lamented as she waved a wooden spoon at the child.

"I promise you, if he had been my first child, he would have been the last. He is *un diablo pequeño*—a little devil."

Revel never would have believed it. The infant seemed an angel. Soon she and Benito were making faces at each other and playing peekaboo with a cotton dishtowel.

"So, why do you come here with Jake Reno? Are you his woman?"

Stunned by the bluntness of the question, Revel looked up in surprise. The younger children had obviously not inherited their shyness from their mother. Rosa was polite but to the point, and she was obviously very fond of Jake.

"I am not his woman," Revel answered carefully. "I'm looking for a man. Jake knows where to find him."

Rosa accepted the first statement with a simple shrug, and said, "He is a fool." Then she asked with a frown, "You're looking for someone in these mountains?"

She answered her own question. "I have heard the stories Emilio tells. There was a time when Jake Reno hid in these mountains. That was when he rode with other men."

"Yes, I know," Revel answered without elaborating.

Discussing Sam Bass was hardly necessary.

"*Yo comprendo,*" Rosa answered softly, "I understand."

The silence lengthened in the warm kitchen, broken only by the hiss of cooking food, the occasional clatter of a pot, or the soft gurglings of the baby.

"You mean you really can cook? Have you been holding out on me and Broken Hand all this time?"

Revel looked up to find Jake watching her from the archway. There was amusement in his voice and a strange contemplative expression in his eyes as he glanced from her to the baby she balanced on her lap.

Rosa looked up. "The guest is not expected to cook the food she eats," she reprimanded, but with a smile. Then laying aside her wooden spoon, she crossed the kitchen, scooped up her young son, and thrust him lovingly into Jake's arms.

"But the guest may help with other things. Take my son to his father. A man should have practical experience with babies. It is good for him."

Revel's eyes danced as they took in the horrified expression on Jake's handsome face as he took the squirming baby.

"He's wet!" he exclaimed.

"*Sí,*" Rosa shrugged. "It happens."

"What am I supposed to do now?"

Revel had no practical experience with babies, but even she realized what a wet diaper meant.

Rosa winked at Jake. "I think you can figure that out for yourself."

Revel fully expected Jake to hand Benito back to her or Rosa, or to plop him down on the kitchen floor. It wouldn't have surprised her if he'd refused to have anything further to do with the very damp child who clearly was not pleased with his present circumstances.

To no one's surprise, Rosa's infant son let out a loud squall as he arched his back, fists tightly clenched, face pinched into a huge pout. He was not happy, and he

318

intended to let everyone know it.

To Revel's surprise, Jake tucked the infant into the crook of his arm with practiced ease while he distracted him by providing a piece of soft, flour tortilla to chew on.

"All right, where do you keep dry pants for this little *muchacho?*" Jake asked, while he and the baby carried on a mock battle over the flour tortilla.

Rosa smiled as she went back to one of the pots that simmered over the open stove. She motioned to Revel.

"There are fresh cloths in that basket."

Revel found the clean cloths that would provide fresh diapers when folded. She brought one to Rosa.

"I'm afraid I don't know much about babies."

Rosa laughed. "Jake can do it."

Revel gave him a surprised look.

He shrugged. "I've had a little experience," he said with a sly grin as he chewed on a piece of the flour tortilla. Then he explained, "Besides, someone has to do it. Unless you'd like to try."

She held up her hands in surrender. "Oh no. I might drop him. You go right ahead."

Rosa's older daughters undoubtedly helped her with the smaller children. Any one of them could have taken Benito and changed him, but Jake seemed perfectly content to do it himself.

Or perhaps he was just trying to make a point—the point being that Revel, being a woman, should know how to diaper a baby.

It seemed she was wrong again. With surprising competence, Jake laid the squirming baby down on the wide bench at the kitchen window. He unfastened the large pin that held the diaper together in front, unwrapped the infant, cleansed him with a cloth Rosa provided, and fitted him with a clean, dry diaper.

All the while, Benito kicked his legs and waved his arms, and generally had a wonderful time.

Revel was impressed. "Where did you learn to do that?"

Jake looked up and gave her with one of those rare, dazzling smiles that completely transformed his face and changed the color of his eyes almost to gold.

"Oh, I picked it up somewhere along the way."

"Mama!" Elena exclaimed from the doorway. "What can you be thinking, having our guest change the baby?" She quickly scooted between Jake and Revel and took her baby brother in her arms.

"It is not a chore for a man," she added in a soft, breathy voice as she looked up at Jake from beneath long lashes. "I will take him, and then perhaps you would like to see our horses?"

"What are you thinking, *muchacha?*" Emilio admonished as he came into the kitchen.

"Our guests have just arrived. There will be plenty of time to see the horses. But now I wish to talk with my friend. Be a good daughter; help your mama and care for the baby. Now, go!"

Elena was clearly not pleased that she'd been so cleverly outmaneuvered, but she dared not speak up to her father. She carefully softened her voice and her expression as she carried her brother from the kitchen. "*Sí, papa.*"

"*Ah, Dios,*"—Emilio gazed heavenward—"spare me. A man should have only sons. They are so agreeable." He carried two mugs, one in each hand. Clearly he had other things than the horses on his mind.

"Come, we'll share a drink, my friend." He handed Jake one of the mugs. "It is not often my good friend honors me with a visit. And we still have time before our supper." He looked to his wife.

"When will the meal be ready?"

Rosa waved her spoon at her husband. "If you want your supper tonight, my husband, get out of my kitchen. It will be ready soon enough. Not that you need it." She gestured to his ample girth.

It was clear that Emilio might think he was the one in charge of the household, but actually Rosa carried the greater weight in most decisions—at least she carried a wooden spoon.

"*Ah, Dios!*" Emilio gazed up to the heavens. "Let this be a lesson to you, my friend," he warned Jake. "Never marry a headstrong woman."

Jake's gaze met Revel's over the top of the mug. "I prefer a headstrong woman," he said.

Chapter Seventeen

Revel had seen different sides to Jake, but there were depths she hadn't imagined.

That evening, he enjoyed several drinks of tesquino, the sweet, milky, home-brewed corn beer with his long-time friend, and he and Emilio told uproarious stories of their adventures to the smaller children. Revel learned that the spotted-rump mares and foals in Emilio's pastures came from an Appaloosa mare and a stallion Jake had given his friend years earlier. The horses were highly prized in Mexico, and the pair had provided Emilio and Rosa with good breeding stock for their rancho.

From the men's tales, Revel learned that Emilio had once saved Jake's life. Jake had repaid his friend by giving him the Appaloosas and by making certain Emilio and his family were not bothered by the outlaws he rode with.

The evening meal was served late that evening in honor of the guests, after the younger children had been fed and put to bed.

Broken Hand declined to share the meal. He was uncomfortable among so many people and retreated outside.

Emilio's older sons joined them at the table, while Rosa and her daughters laid out the elaborate spread. But Revel was pleased to see that Emilio waited for his wife and daughters to join them before offering the toast that began the meal.

The food was wonderful. Some of it was very spicy; all of it was delicious. There was a continuous flow of tesquino for the men, a refreshing lemon drink for the women—Rosa and her daughters made it from lemons harvested from their own orchards. The tartness helped quench the thirst provoked by the food.

Lively conversation engulfed the table. None of Emilio's older children were shy, and they all remembered Jake, though it had been four years since his last visit. They flooded him with questions about the Appaloosa stallion he rode, where he had been during those four years, his brushes with the law. He answered every one, carefully avoiding his more serious encounters with the law, including nearly being hanged.

He could have made his experiences grand adventures, could have romanticized his life as an outlaw, but he didn't. Between stories about the colorful people he'd met, he solemnly spoke of the constant threats and dangers, of watching his back because some young gunfighter was trying to make a name for himself.

While Rosa didn't care for the fact that her older sons seemed fascinated by Jake's reputation, she had obviously accepted him long ago as a dear friend whose life had simply taken an unfortunate turn.

Elena watched Jake with adoring eyes. She listened rapturously when he spoke, asked questions. Revel could see that Elena was deeply infatuated with Jake.

Emilio began a story about looking for stray horses in the various canyons that surrounded the rancho, while several other conversations collided with it. It was a noisy, joyous meal, and Revel realized how much she'd missed the closeness of family. How deeply she missed her father.

With Rosa and Emilio and their eleven children all the good qualities of a family were magnified.

Revel sat across from Elena and the other two oldest

girls. Rosa and Emilio sat at each end of the massive table. Their sons sat on either side of Revel and Jake.

Content to simply sit back and enjoy the wonderful food, Revel let the conversation flow around her.

It was a wonderful feeling, and she found herself wondering how much of it had to do with the fact that Jake sat beside her. She looked up as Emilio spoke to her.

"My wife tells me you are here in our mountains looking for a man. I cannot imagine you should have to go searching for any man."

Revel felt color warm her cheeks. "The man I'm looking for is an outlaw."

"Revel is a Pinkerton agent," Jake explained. That brought several curious stares in her direction.

"And you ride with an outlaw to catch an outlaw?" Emilio asked.

"Something like that," Revel answered carefully, "Jake knows the man I'm looking for and the location of his hideout."

Emilio's dark, intelligent eyes narrowed as if he had already guessed who the outlaw might be.

He asked, though Revel was certain he already knew the answer, "And who is this man you seek?"

From the corner of her eye she caught Jake's brief glance. It was impossible to guess his thoughts. Whatever they were, he kept them to himself.

"Sam Bass," she said.

All at once the conversation around the large table ceased. If she had announced the house was on fire, Revel couldn't have gotten everyone's attention quicker.

Rosa's face went pale. She silently made the sign of the cross over her heart and offered up a silent prayer. Emilio's older sons stared at her, a mixture of fear and disbelief on their faces.

Emilio watched her thoughtfully. Ana sucked in her breath and her eyes widened. Margarita stared at Revel, in awe. Then Revel felt the subtle, reassuring pressure of Jake's thigh against hers.

But it was Elena, the oldest daughter, who looked at Revel with barely disguised contempt. "No one goes into the mountains after Sam Bass."

"Quiet, daughter!" Emilio reprimanded.

And Jake explained, "He killed Revel's father."

An unreadable look passed between the two friends. Emilio nodded. "I understand."

It was Rosa who broke the uncomfortable silence at the table as she rebuked her daughters in Spanish for their lack of manners. More serving dishes were passed around, generous portions heaped onto plates, and the conversation was turned to talk of crops, the Appaloosa colts that were already sold for a handsome profit, and the early winter that was predicted.

"Please, Señorita Tyson," Elena invited politely, "you must try some of these." She held out a flat, shallow bowl.

Revel smiled hesitantly. "What are they?"

"They're cactus pickles. Mama makes them each summer. They are delicious."

One of Elena's younger sisters abruptly gasped. There was some commotion going on under the table. It reminded Revel of the time when she and her friends had kicked each other under the table at the private school she'd attended. But whatever it was that had caused Ana to react, she kept silent.

Revel glanced down at the plate of pickles. They did look delicious, and she didn't want to offend her hostess by refusing. She reached out to take a couple. Jake's hand stopped her.

"Revel, don't. Those are hot, pickled peppers; they'll burn a hole through the roof of your mouth."

She looked across the table at Elena. From the very first, she'd known the girl resented her. Of course, it had to do with Jake. Ever since they'd arrived Elena hadn't been able to take her eyes off him.

Elena was cool, her expression full of innocence as she

326

gazed back at Revel with a lift of her delicate dark eyebrows.

"I thought the *señorita* would like to try them."

It was a silent taunt, and Revel knew it. Everyone else, including Jake, had eaten the peppers.

Foolhardy as it was, she wasn't about to let a mere child ridicule her, especially in front of Jake.

She took one of the peppers and bit into it, chewing it carefully. It tasted faintly sweet, with the slight tang common to pickles.

At first she suspected everyone had made a joke at her expense, including Jake.

There was a faint warmth from the seasoning but nothing more. Then, like a sudden burst of fire, the warmth exploded into searing heat.

Her throat constricted, her eyes watered, her skin was unusually warm, and the inside of her mouth was suddenly on fire.

Jake had warned her the peppers would burn a hole in her mouth, and Revel felt smoke would come out of her ears at any moment. But she'd be damned if she'd let any of them know how bad it really was, or how right they all were. Especially Elena, who watched her carefully, expectantly. The girl was actually gloating.

"Are you all right?" Jake asked, as his fingers closed over hers under the table.

"Of course." Revel managed a smile.

Emilio watched her with keen appreciation. *"Es caliente, no?* It is hot?" he asked.

"Just a little." Revel exhaled slowly, thinking of legends about fire-breathing dragons. They undoubtedly originated with hot peppers.

"A little?" Emilio guffawed. He slapped his hand down on the table and set the platters and dishes to rattling. His eyes twinkled and a smile split his face as he turned to Jake.

"Ah, dios, mi amigo. This is some woman! A Pinkerton

327

agent who rides after Sam Bass, and eats hot peppers! The next thing you will tell me, she carries a revolver at her hip."

Beside her, Jake choked slightly. Except that it came out more as a chuckle over the joke Emilio had made about the revolver. Only Revel and Jake knew it was no joke.

"You had better marry this one, *amigo*. Then you will have a fiery woman to warm your bed and guard your back! In no time you will have *diez niños*—ten children—and no outlaws challenging you to a gunfight!" He roared with laughter.

"Emilio!" Rosa scolded in a horrified voice. "Have you no manners before our guests! Such talk is not proper in front of the children."

His laughter increased. "Look at your children, *querida*." He gestured around the table. "Your sons already keep company with beautiful *señoritas*, and your daughters flirt outrageously. You are the only one here who is offended."

His astute observation earned him a look that Revel was certain could have turned most men to stone. Somewhat chagrined, Emilio smiled broadly behind his cup as he offered another toast.

"To the *señorita* who chases outlaws and eats peppers."

It seemed the toasts and the supper would never end. Finally Revel was able to slip out of the cabin for a breath of fresh air. She was certain there was a hole in the roof of her mouth.

The evening breeze had grown cool, with a hint of changing seasons in the night air. But it wasn't cool enough to quench the fire in Revel's throat or mouth. She fanned herself frantically with a lace handkerchief Rosa had provided, dragging in deep gulps of air.

She saw the tip of Jake's cigarette before she saw him. Then he stepped from the shadows at the side of the main cabin and slowly strode toward her. She kept breathing and fanning.

"I apologize for Elena. She's a bit high spirited."

"There's no need"—she quickly drew in some cool air—"to apologize. I made the choice to eat . . . the damn thing."

"I remember the first time Emilio did that to me," Jake explained. "They are a bit hot."

Revel gave him a sidewise glance. That was a complete understatement! So much so that she started to laugh, and her eyes began to water again.

"I thought my teeth were going to melt."

"Here." Jake held out a mug. "This is the only thing that will cool it down."

She looked at the mug suspiciously. "What is it?"

"It's tesquino."

"The beer you were drinking earlier?"

"It'll put the fire out in your mouth. Of course, if Emilio were here, he'd offer you the beer, then the peppers, then more beer."

"The more you try to put out the fire, the more intoxicated you get," she concluded.

He inhaled deeply from the cigarette. "Something like that. It's an old trick of his. That was before I knew what was in the tesquino. It can be deadly stuff."

"As deadly as those peppers? Pickles indeed!"

He gave her the mug. "I don't know what got into Elena. The little girl I remember was always so sweet. She would never have done anything like that."

Revel took a tentative sip of the home-brewed corn beer. It was thick, sweet, and mercifully soothing. "I think that may be precisely the problem."

"What's that?"

She took another drink, closing her eyes as the beer extinguished fire all the way down. It helped soothe her stomach as well. She gave Jake an even look. "She's not a little girl anymore."

"What are you talking about?"

She sipped the tesquino. "She's a woman, Jake. Or at least, she has the feelings of a woman."

"She's sixteen years old, for Christ's sake."

"She *is* a woman," Revel said insistently, in between sips. "Maybe you're not aware of it, but I've seen the way she looks at you—that is not the look of a little girl."

He smiled, amused. "And I suppose you know how a woman looks at a man?"

How had he turned the conversation around like that? Or did it only seem that he had? Perhaps she had imagined it. It must be the beer, she told herself. She sipped cautiously.

"I think I can tell the difference between a girl and a woman," she replied carefully as she finished the sweet, thick brew.

Jake took the mug from her and set it on the fencepost. His shadow blocked the light from the cabin. He was standing so close she could feel the heat from his body, or was it the tesquino?

Revel leaned forward slightly. Her footing was a little unsteady. His arm came about her waist, steadying her, and his fingers slipped beneath her chin, tilting her face up.

"I think I can tell the difference between a girl and a woman too," he said softly, his breath warm against her cheek as he pulled her close.

Sweetness. Fire.

Was it the lingering burn of the peppers or the cooling sweetness of tesquino?

Or was it Jake?

The sweetness poured through her as his mouth slowly found hers. It was the sweet pressure that she remembered from the night before, and like that other kiss it warmed slowly, tenderly, slipping from the corner of her mouth to caress, engulf, and burn.

The night spun into oblivion around them. His body was fiery hot as he pulled her against him, the darkness cool at her back. Hot and cold, fire and ice, sweetness and mind-reeling intoxication.

She tried to blame it on the tesquino, Emilio, even

330

Elena and her sullen, silent dare. But they were not to blame for the fire that had nothing to do with the peppers or the mind-numbing tesquino.

Jake.

From the very beginning it had been Jake—the coldness, the hatred, the anger . . . the passion.

As his mouth took possession and his tongue began a slow, sensual invasion, she tried desperately to remember the hatred. She couldn't.

Revel's fingers closed over his arms, her nails dug into his bare skin, her fingertips sensitized by the soft, golden hair on his forearms.

"Revel."

Her name was hoarse in his throat, soft on his lips. She tried to pull away, afraid of the feelings he stirred in her, afraid of him, more afraid of herself. His hands trapped her, cradling her face with almost reverent need as his mouth moved over hers again and again.

"Revel."

Her name was a sigh as he refused to let her go, trapping her with his mouth—on hers, at her throat—draining the strength from her wildly beating pulse with his lips.

His tongue flicked lightly against the fullness of her lower lip, and she shuddered.

She had been kissed politely by relatives, less politely by young beaus, enthusiastically by a fellow agent she'd once worked with. But she had never been kissed as Jake kissed her now.

His touch was like liquid fire, and she burned.

It was sweetness, and she hungered.

It was seduction, and she was lost.

The night before had been a mistake, just as that stormy night on the desert had been. And Jake knew it. This was a mistake too, and he knew that. And he didn't care.

He was angry, he was scared, he was confused. And he wanted her more than he'd ever wanted anything.

She was soft as a flower in his hands, molten like liquid fire, cool as the whisper of night breezes.

Even as those thoughts registered and he felt her helpless response, he sensed that they weren't alone.

Anger surfaced, hard and volatile. But before he could warn her, protect her from any embarrassment, the gate to the corral that lay between them and the main cabin slammed abruptly, and Revel pulled back from him.

"Jake? Where are you?" It was Elena, and the soft sultriness of her voice was unmistakable.

Revel's gaze snapped to his. Her numbed thoughts and senses slowly focused. She backed away from him.

"I have to return to the house."

"Revel, wait."

"The *señora* will need help with the children." She fumbled for an excuse, any excuse as Elena stepped into the circle of light that pooled from the nearby cabin occupied by the vaqueros.

"There you are," Elena greeted him. She stared in girlish confusion as he went after Revel.

Jake grabbed her gently but firmly by the arm, he pulled her around.

"I want to talk to you."

Revel pried his fingers loose. "I don't think so. Anyway"—she looked around him—"Elena is waiting."

"It's not what you think," he started to explain.

But she cut him off. "It doesn't really matter does it." Then she turned and headed for the house.

Elena's voice carried on the night air, followed by her girlish laughter. That laughter taunted Revel all the way back to the main cabin.

Humiliation burned across her cheeks and through her blood.

How could she have been such a fool?

She didn't immediately enter the main cabin, but circled to the back so she could slip unnoticed into her room.

She tried not to think of what had happened or of that

332

stormy night on the desert. It meant nothing—less than nothing.

In her heart, Revel would have liked to call what had happened between them that night anything but love-making—an attack, an accident, rape.

The problem was, she knew perfectly well that she had wanted it to happen.

Rosa found her just as she reached her room.

"Are you all right, Señorita Tyson?"

"Yes," Revel said, too quickly. "I'm quite fine. *Gracias.* I just stepped out for some fresh air."

"Ah, yes. The peppers or Jake Reno?"

"I beg your pardon?"

Rosa smiled knowingly. "Whatever you believe or think you know about Jake, you are wrong."

"You don't understand. . . ." She was about to tell her about Elena and then thought better of it. Several girls she knew were married by the time they reached Elena's age. Elena was not a child, and what she did with Jake Reno was her own business.

"I understand completely," Rosa informed her with a knowing smile.

"Come. I will fix coffee. It will help clear my Emilio's head after so much tesquino. And Jake could use some when he returns. We will sit, and I will tell you a story." Revel wondered if Rosa knew Elena had gone in search of Jake.

As they relaxed before the dying embers of the fire, Rosa began her tale. Jake and Emilio had become friends when they were hardly older than Rosa's oldest son. Jake was on his own, running with an outlaw gang in south Texas. Emilio was wild and brash. He, too, rode with those same outlaws for a time. The two young men discovered a common love of fine horses.

Rosa lived in Durango, Mexico. She and Emilio were promised to each other although her parents had no idea he was an outlaw. It was after a train robbery, when Jake and Emilio came south to elude the law, that Rosa met

333

Jake for the first time.

She was sixteen years old, no older than her daughter Elena was now.

"How can I tell you?" Rosa was saying. "Jake was so young, *muy guapo*—handsome. His hair was lighter then, almost golden, and he wore it long. And *ojos de verde*—those green eyes." She sighed at the memory. "He can be very charming."

She went on to explain. "I was raised very strictly. My parents would never have accepted it if I fell in love with an anglo. I knew this. Yet, when I first saw him, my heart stood still."

"But you were betrothed to Emilio."

"That is true, and I loved him. But there was something about Jake Reno—something reckless, more reckless than my Emilio. It was as if the fire of the devil burned in his soul. And yet . . ."

Revel looked up as Rosa hesitated and smiled.

"He was the gentlest, kindest young man I have ever known. He has a way with animals. They know he can be trusted. I have never seen him raise his voice or a whip to an animal. And you have seen how he is with my children. He has always been like that. Yet, there was always something very sad about him."

Revel stared down into her coffee. "He is a cold-blooded killer." Was she trying to justify his reputation even to herself?

Rosa nodded. "*Sí.* That is what the law says. It is why he has spent the past eighteen years running, never staying here or anyplace for very long. But Emilio has told me that Jake Reno never shot an innocent man."

"That doesn't give him the right to take the law into his own hands." Revel thought of all the men Jake had killed. The list read like a roster of infamous outlaws. Not one among them was a good, upstanding citizen. They were gunfighters, murderers, outlaws, thieves, cattle rustlers.

"Who among us is to say who has the right and who

334

has not?" Rosa asked, and then she confessed, "I had my doubts about Jake. But that first winter, after Emilio and I were married, there were no more doubts." She began to tell the story of that winter.

"Emilio had big dreams. He wanted a rancho, wanted to raise fine-blooded horses. He had long admired the spotted horse Jake rode. Such horses are highly prized by the aristocracy in the big cities here in Mexico.

"He and Jake went north, into Texas. I did not ask the reason. When they returned, Emilio and I were married, and we came here. They found this valley when they were returning from Texas, and built that small cabin we now use for storage. They had claimed the land. During that summer Jake stayed with us.

"He and Emilio fenced in the first pasture, cultivated the corn field and the orchard, and built the horse shed. This was their land, they were partners."

Revel was fascinated. Everything she knew about Jake indicated he never stayed in one place long enough to make a home. Rosa poured more coffee as she continued.

"When summer came, Jake left to go north for horses to stock the rancho. He was gone for months." She smiled at the memory.

"The corn grew, the small trees in the orchard grew, and I grew." She puffed up her cheeks so that her face was as round as a moon. "Very big, with my first child. By September I was as big as Emilio's horse, and Jake still had not returned." Frown lines appeared on Rosa's smooth face as she recalled that winter all those years ago.

"The winter came early that year. There was frost in the orchard, and Emilio harvested the corn. He built the cabin our sons now use, and we put food in the smaller one. There were several storms and some snow, but then it melted and the days were warm again.

"Emilio began to worry about Jake. He thought of riding north to meet him, but he would not leave me alone. We had three horses, some chickens, goats, pigs, and a mule to pull the plow. As the weather became colder the wolves came down from the high mountains. They were after the chickens and pigs.

"One in particular kept coming around. Emilio was out in the horse shed early one morning when the wolf came. He killed it. The scent must have frightened the horses. One of them trampled Emilio."

"Was he badly hurt?"

Rosa shook her head at the memory. "He was gone for a very long time. I heard the gunshot, and when he did not return, I became worried. I went to the barn and found him on the ground. One of his legs was badly broken.

"It was very difficult, as big as I was, but we got back to the cabin. That night he became very ill with fever. We were completely alone, I was very near my time, and one of the worst storms came that night."

"What did you do?"

"I wanted to take him in the wagon to Chihuahua. It is a long journey, but there is a physician there. Emilio refused. He was afraid for me to handle the horses. So I tried to care for him myself. But I knew his leg was bad. It needed to be straightened, and bandaged. I did the best I could.

"For three days he lay there suffering. It broke my heart. But by then there was no hope of getting the wagon out. The snow was very deep." Her voice became very quiet. "I was afraid Emilio was going to die.

"Late that third night, there was another snowstorm. I had gone out earlier to feed the animals. Somewhere near morning, I heard noises outside. I was afraid more wolves had come down from the mountain. It was Jake.

"He rode all night through the storm to get to us. Emilio was very sick when he got here. He straightened and bandaged his leg. Then he chopped wood for the fire. Late that next night my son was born. I was young and frightened. I had a very difficult time. It was Jake who helped me, Jake who held my son and cleaned him when he was born. We would all have died if he had not been here to help us."

Revel didn't know what to say. Jake could be gentle, she knew that. But she would never have guessed that he'd done something like this.

Rosa went on to explain. "He stayed with us all that winter. He chopped wood, cared for the animals, cared for us. He is the truest friend we could ever have. He has great heart and kindness of soul. Whatever he has done, he has had his reasons. It is not for me to question them."

"A man with heart?" Revel repeated thoughtfully.

"Sí," Rosa said with a knowing smile as she leaned forward and took Revel's hand in hers. "You must always look to a man's heart to know the truth about him." Then she added, "And he has always been a man of honor."

"I was very young then. It would have been easy for a shy, young girl to lose her heart to him—a girl such as myself . . . or my willful, passionate daughter, Elena."

Revel's gaze fastened on Rosa's. She knew.

"Elena is very much like I was, at that age—romantic, easily infatuated, with little understanding of a man. I know her very well. I also know that Jake Reno is a man who has much attraction for women. But he will love only one. It is his way." She waved a finger at Revel for emphasis, like a stern mother admonishing her child. "Remember—only one."

Revel thought of the mysterious Rachel. Memories of her still haunted him. "Perhaps you're right."

Rosa nodded knowingly. "I am right," she said firmly. Then she added, "Do not concern yourself with my Elena. Jake will send her away. I trust him with my daughter, as I once trusted him with my life."

They rose from their chairs together. Rosa walked with Revel to her room. She lingered a moment longer at the doorway.

"I wish you were not going on this journey into the mountains. It will be very dangerous, but there is no better man to have with you than Jake Reno."

"Thank you, *señora*. But I have to go."

"I understand. May God go with you. Good night, Señorita Tyson."

Revel shut the door and leaned back against it, eyes closed. She tried to banish the images of Jake and Elena from her thoughts. She wished she shared Rosa's confidence. In the next instant she was angry with herself. Why should it matter?

There was nothing between her and Jake. He was an outlaw, a man she had saved from hanging and coerced into bringing her here.

He was useful to her for only one thing—helping her find Sam Bass. That was all.

If only that were true.

She was restless. The night was warm and the air was still inside the cabin—Indian summer it was called. That last warm stretch before winter.

The window was pushed open, but very little breeze stirred. Her skin was damp, her long hair hung heavy about her shoulders. She dressed and left the cabin.

It was cooler outside. A fat, full moon hung low and heavy in the inky blackness of the night sky, its glow filling the huge yard with light and shadows.

The dog who had announced their arrival earlier that day sauntered across the yard in the direction of the vaquero's cabin.

A light burned there. Revel caught a few words of the conversation that drifted out on the night air—a mixture of laughter and conversation—as the young men exchanged stories in Spanish. They were colorful tales of fast horses and soft young *señoritas*.

Revel crossed the yard to the corral where their horses roamed about, feeling restless. She saw Broken Hand's vivid paint pony. Evidently the old Indian had returned from his wanderings.

He called the earth and sky his bed and blanket. He undoubtedly slept somewhere nearby, wrapped in his heavily woven poncho.

Jake's stallion caught her scent and wandered toward her. She patted his heavily muscled neck as he nudged her shoulder in greeting.

"You're not so big or frightening, are you?" she asked him. His ears flicked back and forth in response. Revel rubbed the smoke-colored, velvet muzzle.

"I wish *he* wasn't so frightening," she mused thoughtfully. But even as she said it, Revel knew it wasn't Jake she feared. It was herself.

The faint ripple of a girl's laughter drifted on the warm night breeze. It came from the east end of the main cabin, along with a voice Revel recognized.

"Elena . . ."

The name was spoken low, and unmistakably by Jake. Was it an endearment?

A softly response, in Spanish, drifted from the shadows about the house. Revel quickly looked around. She was completely exposed by the bright moonlight that illuminated everything in the yard.

She would be seen if she tried to return directly to the cabin. She quickly darted into the shadow of the horse shed as the voices came much closer.

"Jake . . ." It was said softly, imploringly. "*Por favor*—please."

Revel tried to make herself as small as possible as she heard the faint tread of Jake's soft leather boots, the nicker of the Appaloosa, Elena's whispered entreaties.

"*Querido, por favor.* Do not send me away."

"You should go back now," Jake was saying.

"I don't want to go back. I want to be with you."

Revel could hear the faint, seductive pout in Elena's voice. Then there was silence. She held her breath as she inched her way through the shadows at the side of the shed.

Jake and Elena stood at the corral. They were unmistakable: he by his height, the soft flow of long hair to his shoulders, that wary stance, and the wedge of wide shoulders tapering to narrow waist, Elena by the

339

gleam of bare shoulders above her blouse, her petite willowy figure, the fall of raven black hair.

"*Querido*," Elena whispered huskily as she stretched up on her toes, slipping her arms about Jake's waist, and pressing her slender body against his. Her arms wrapped about his neck, her hands raking through his long hair as she pulled him down to her. Then her mouth was on his, in a long, impassioned kiss.

As Revel fled through the shadows, moving noiselessly back to the main cabin, she carried the image of Jake's hands on Elena's slender arms, their mouths joined intimately.

She felt betrayal, anger—at herself more than anyone—and regret so sharp it was painful. Part of the regret was for Rosa. She had said to look in to a man's heart—it was obvious what was in Jake Reno's.

How could he betray his friendship with Emilio?

The other part of that regret—for herself—was smothered deep inside her by denial.

He was a liar, a user, the worst sort of scoundrel. She had wanted to believe in Rosa's faith in him.

Worse, she had begun to believe *him*.

Anger and pain burned deep in her chest as she stole back into her room. She shouldn't care what he did or who he was with. It shouldn't matter!

It wouldn't matter.

She needed him, but only as long as it took to find Sam Bass. Then Jake Reno would dance at the end of a rope for all she cared.

Chapter Eighteen

Revel dressed early and left the main cabin. She had spent a restless night after returning from her walk. The stars had long disappeared from the sky when she'd finally fallen into fitful sleep plagued by recurrent dreams—the trip to Texas to take her father's body back to Philadelphia, his lifeless face as he lay in that simple pine box, images of Sam Bass staring back at her from countless wanted posters, and . . . Jake Reno.

The vaquero's shouts drew her to a corral. The sun wasn't fully up yet, but they were already at work, moving horses from the paddock out into the pastures to graze, singling out several two-year-olds for training.

She recognized Emilio's broad frame as he called out instructions to his sons. Broken Hand stood beside him, gazing at the fine young horses. He greatly admired the Appaloosa, whose heritage was liked with the Nez Percé Indian tribe in the northern territories.

Revel stepped up to the corral and rested her arms on the top rail.

"They are beautiful."

Broken Hand grunted his approval. "Good ponies, worthy of any warrior."

She gazed to the far end of the pasture. Jake's stallion and her gelding grazed lazily in the early morning dawn.

"I'd like to get started into those mountains. Is there

any chance we could leave today?"

Emilio shook his head. "It was a long, hard ride from the Territories. The horses are tired. It would be foolish to start out without letting them rest."

She knew he was right, still the delay gnawed at her. She was impatient to be after Bass, and the sooner this was over, the sooner they could go their separate ways.

"I know you are impatient, Señorita Tyson, but a good horse is often the difference between life and death out on the trail. It would be a mistake to take tired animals into those mountains."

"You're right, of course. It's just that I'm afraid Sam Bass will get so far ahead of us we'll never be able to find him."

"Jake will find him, if that is truly what you want."

She met Emilio's penetrating gaze evenly. "It's what I want. It's the reason I'm here."

He nodded, almost with an air of sympathy. "I understand what you feel in your heart, *señorita,* more than you will ever know." Then he smiled. "Perhaps a ride on one of my fine Appaloosas would help. I have several. You are more than welcome."

Revel smiled too, gratefully. "I'd like that very much."

"*Bueno,* I will have one of my sons saddle a horse for you. It is a fine morning and I understand your impatience. Follow the base of the mountain to the river. It is well traveled by my vaqueros, there will be no danger."

Beside them, Broken Hand grunted his approval. "I have ridden the trail. It is clearly marked. I will go with you."

"That won't be necessary. I won't go far." Broken Hand frowned but made no further objection.

A half-hour later, Revel rode from the rancho. She saw Elena briefly. She was following her sisters from the house, each girl carrying a large basket under her arm. They were headed for the orchard to gather fruit. Elena's expression was somber, and she walked far behind her

342

sisters. When she looked up, she gave Revel a sullen glare, then turned her head and walked on.

Was it because of last night? Had something happened between her and Jake that she now regretted?

Revel couldn't bear to think about it, so she turned the Appaloosa mare down the trail.

It was a well-worn path, frequently traveled by horses, along the base of the mountain. Emilio had explained that they used this trail to take the horses to greener grass up in the meadows. The horse Revel rode seemed to know the trail well and moved along at an easy gait.

The air was crisp and clear, the sun warmed her back as it rose behind her. As the wind lifted her hair from her shoulders, she could almost forget the cause of the restlessness that ate at her . . . almost.

Jake left the kitchen at the main house and slowly sauntered across the yard. He had waited until everyone left the house before speaking with Rosa. These people were his friends—more than friends. He had no secrets from either Emilio or Rosa. They accepted him for what he was and knew the life he'd lived. He'd felt Rosa should be told about what had happened.

As he had hoped, she had simply laid a hand against his cheek and had smiled at him.

"I trust you, Jake Reno. That is all that is necessary," she had said in that way of hers that conveyed so much more. "It is the *señorita* whose trust you must win."

That last comment had stunned him. But he shouldn't have been surprised. Rosa always understood him better than he understood himself.

Now he walked to the corral, confident that Rosa believed him and would speak with Elena about her behavior.

"Good morning," he called out to Emilio and Broken Hand.

His old friend greeted him warmly. *"Buenos días* to

343

you, my friend, but at this late hour the morning is almost gone. You sleep late and eat well. Before long you will have a stomach like mine."

"It'll take more than that, *amigo.*" Jake answered with a smile. He felt relaxed here, at peace, in a way he hadn't been in years. It could be like this on his own ranch . . . someday.

He gazed out across the pasture. "They're fine-looking animals. You've done well for yourself."

"Because of your generosity," Emilio reminded him, not forgetting how it had all started years ago.

"No," Jake corrected him, "because of friendship. You saved my life—more than once. The horses I gave you were just a payment on a very big debt."

"There is no debt between friends," Emilio responded. Then he pointed across the pasture. "That is what I wanted you to see." He had singled out a yearling.

"Is he not the finest you have ever seen?"

Jake nodded. "Almost as fine an animal as my stallion."

"He is out of the mare who is sister to your stallion. I have been offered five thousand American dollars for him." At Jake's surprised look, Emilio assured him, "I refused, of course. I have plans for that one. He will be the start of a new line of the spotted horses. He will have many fine colts. And maybe I will give you some of these fine animals for your rancho."

"I just might accept your offer," Jake was saying. "I'll be starting with just a few head. That is, if I ever get back there."

The two men stood in silence, leaning against the fence rail, both realizing that dream might never be realized, not with Jake going after Sam Bass.

Jake finally spoke up. "By the way, where is that mare?"

"I let the *señorita* take her out this morning." At Jake's surprised look, he went on to explain. "She came to the

344

corrals very early. I think she needed a ride. I told her to follow the trail to the spring meadow."

Jake nodded. He remembered the meadow. It wasn't far and the vaqueros constantly rode through the area, bringing in the mares and their foals, rounding up the working stock.

He had stopped by Revel's room earlier, but she had already gone. He wanted to talk to her. Too much had been left unsaid last night when Elena had interrupted them. He still hoped to convince her it was hopeless to continue after Bass. They might never find him in these mountains.

"Do you have a horse I could use?"

Emilio smiled slyly and gave Jake a knowing wink. "I believe I could find one. You may use mine. He is not marked as well as most of the Appaloosa, but he can run like the wind. You will need him to catch the *señorita*."

Jake followed the same trail he knew Revel had taken. She had about a fifteen-minute head start on him and according to Emilio she was in a restless mood. He'd said she'd urged the mare to a full run when she'd reached the edge of the rancho. Jake had a pretty good idea of what was bothering her.

The ground along the trail was dry but soft. It was easy to follow the prints Revel's mare had left. Knowing Revel, he was sure she'd go to the farthest point from the rancho—and him.

He held the black and gray stallion to an easy canter, staying a constant distance behind Revel. A good run would give her time to cool down and work through some of her restlessness.

He'd ridden about an hour when he picked up a second set of tracks that cut down from higher up the mountain and fell in behind the prints Revel's mare left in the soft dirt. The second set of prints were from an unshod pony.

Revel was being followed.

345

Jake's senses sharpened as he left the open trail and carefully picked his way through the trees, using them for cover.

His gaze constantly wandered the hillside that rose from the trail, watching for any sign of movement, a reflection. He listened for the alarmed call of a bird or wild animal startled by an intruder.

Several times, he crisscrossed the trail. It took more time, but it allowed him to determine if there were any other riders. He concluded there was only one, and whoever he was, he was staying far behind Revel so as not to alarm her—probably until she got a good distance away from the rancho and any chance of help.

Having made this conclusion about the other rider, Jake spurred his horse on. He had two advantages. He knew these mountains. He'd explored them, hidden in them like only one other man—Sam Bass.

The man he followed wasn't Bass. This rider didn't know these mountains or he wouldn't have kept to the trail. And he didn't know he was being followed—that was the second advantage.

Jake cut a path up the side of the mountain. Emilio's stallion was strong and had good wind. He had obviously traveled these hills a lot; he effortlessly climbed the uneven terrain, cautiously picking his way as he kept up a good pace.

Then Jake saw the rider only a few yards ahead, and confirmed what he had suspected from those unshod prints—Apache. Revel was somewhere further along the trail. Even with her skills as a Pinkerton agent, she was probably unaware she was being followed.

Nothing Pinkerton's taught could prepare anyone for being stalked by an Indian.

He could have picked the Apache off, but a gunshot—any sound at all in these mountains—would carry for miles. Emilio and his vaqueros would hear it, but so would the Comancheros and Sam Bass. And while Jake

346

assumed they were far up in the mountains, perhaps already at the hideout, it was also possible they were close by.

He wouldn't put Revel in that kind of danger. He urged the stallion to a faster pace.

Revel heard it again—the crunch of twigs under a heavy weight—and not too far away. Without halting the mare, she turned in the saddle and scanned the trail behind her, the tree cover along the sides of the trail.

She saw nothing, but still couldn't rid herself of the uneasy sensation that she was being watched. She urged the mare on, but remained alert, listening, watching.

Broken Hand had proclaimed the trail safe. She knew he'd undoubtedly been over it several times since they'd arrived. It was his nature and his livelihood to know the land about him. Still, he could be wrong.

She didn't want to consider that possibility since she had only the small revolver tucked inside her boot. And although she would never admit it to Jake, it had only limited range and use. The pistol Jake had given her was back at the rancho. She had been too restless, in too much of a hurry, when she'd left—too careless.

Up ahead the trees thinned and opened onto the meadow. Once Revel left the tree cover on the trail she would be completely exposed. But if someone was following her perhaps that might be an advantage, for she would be able to see anyone who came at her.

With a tingling sensation vibrating along her nerve endings, she forced herself to remain calm and eased the mare from the trail and out onto the meadow. All the while she listened and watched, glancing casually about her for any sign of her pursuer.

She saw the telltale flash of movement from the corner of her eye. But before it fully registered, before she could react, a shrill whoop split the air. The mare spooked, and it was all Revel could do to keep her under control as she whirled her about.

A single rider on a white and black pony was not more than a hundred yards away from her and was closing fast.

He was an Indian, and the wind was whipping his long, ebony hair about his bare head and shoulders.

In those brief seconds, Revel made out the glistening of dark, mahogany skin, a sleeveless beaded vest, buckskin pants, and wrapped buckskin boots like Jake wore. The hooves of the Indian's horse beat out a frantic rhythm as he closed in on her.

The mare was frightened and fought Revel, making it impossible for her to grab the small revolver without releasing her tight hold on the reins. If she did that, she was certain the mare would bolt.

A second eerie cry split the silence of the meadow as the rider bore down on her. Giving up on the revolver, Revel tried to jerk the mare about in the fleeting hope of outrunning the Indian. The mare danced beneath Revel, eyes rolling wildly as she clamped the bit firmly in her teeth.

As the thunderous roar of hooves descended on her, Revel jerked her head up. In that split second another thought registered: two horses were riding hard across the meadow toward her.

She had decided to throw herself off the spooked mare. But before she kicked her feet free of the stirrups, the white pony slammed into the mare.

There was frantic thrashing and screaming as the two horses tried to separate themselves. A strong arm circled Revel's waist. The smell of dirt and sweat, and a wild-animal musk scent, filled her nostrils as the Indian tried to yank her from the saddle.

Revel screamed and jammed her right elbow hard into the Indian's ribs. At the same time she grabbed the pommel of her saddle and tried desperately to stay astride the mare.

348

Then the air about them shattered with the sharp report of a single shot.

Revel was certain it was a rifle shot. As the two horses finally untangled themselves and pulled apart, winded, blowing and heavily lathered, the Indian slumped forward against Revel.

She saw his wide-eyed expression, the look of disbelief in his dark eyes, the bubble of blood at his lips. He fell forward, his weight taking her with him as his fingers dragged through her long hair in a death grip.

That first wild rush of energy gave way to fear, then panic. Revel screamed as she was dragged to the ground, the Indian's bulk pulling her down.

She thought she heard someone scream her name. That earlier thought of a second rider registered briefly and then was gone because of a more desperate realization.

She was pinned beneath the dead weight of her attacker. Revel fought to breathe, struggled to move, then became frantic to free herself.

Like a madwoman she scratched and clawed to get out from under that body. She leveraged her foot under her and planted both hands against the Indian's shoulder, pushed with all her strength. He slowly rolled off her.

She was grabbed by both arms and roughly hauled to her feet. Her reaction was instinctive. She tried to jerk out of her captor's grasp and reached for the tiny revolver.

"Get away from me!" she screamed. "I'll kill you! I swear I will!"

She was shaken hard. All hope of reaching the revolver gone as her head snapped back. She clawed frantically at her attacker—at his hands, his arms, anything she could reach as he held her by the shoulders. Her hair tumbled over her eyes. Hysteria bubbled up into her throat. She choked it back down.

She screamed, clinging to rage rather than giving in to the hysteria, knowing that would be fatal.

349

She was shaken again. This time her head snapped so hard stars burst behind her eyes and her hair fell back from her forehead.

Her wild-eyed gaze was filled with the sight of the tall, wide-shouldered man. She blinked back confusion and fear, and heard her name called again.

Her shattered thoughts slowly came together as she stared up at him. She wasn't going to die. If that was what he'd intended, she would already be dead. And then the next thought registered—he'd called her by name. She blinked again, sanity slowly returning.

"Jake?"

The bone-crushing grasp on her shoulders eased.

"Are you hurt?"

Before she could answer, his hands quickly moved over her body, checking for blood, bruises, or torn flesh.

Then those same hands were turning her around. Revel pulled out of his grasp.

Like a wounded animal, she backed away from him, her arms wrapped tightly about her. Her breath came in short, desperate gasps.

Jake came after her, gently taking her by the arms. She tried to wave him away.

"I'm all right." She clamped her teeth shut tightly as they began to chatter. "Really, I am."

"No, you're not."

"Please . . . just give me . . . a minute."

He didn't even give her half of one, but closed his arms around her as he pulled her against him.

"You don't have to prove anything to me, Revel. Just let go and give in to the fear. You're entitled to it."

She shuddered as she leaned against him. All at once the wild energy that had driven her seeped from her body. She was so weak she wasn't even certain she could stand if he moved away from her.

Then she began to shake. The tremors slowly swept through her, until she felt she was physically out of control.

Without a word, Jake scooped her up and carried her from the meadow.

He found a downed tree and straddled it, cradling Revel in his arms like a child. They sat there like that for the longest time.

The air was warm, the sun was warm, Jake was mercifully warm—and alive.

She simply lay there in his arms, eyes closed tight, and let the heat slowly warm her ice-cold flesh. There were no angry words, no recriminations or accusations now.

There was only the solid strength of his arms about her, the steady pounding of his heart against her cheek. She felt she could stay like that and never move again.

Strength slowly seeped back into her limp arms and legs. Her heart slowed its frantic beating. It no longer felt as if it would burst from her chest.

She might have dozed. The only thing she was aware of was strength—Jake's strength—as he held her, rocked her, soothed her.

"You're safe," he whispered against her hair. "Just hold on to me."

She wanted to hold on—more than she'd ever wanted anything before. But as strength returned and calm replaced hysteria, reality edged into her thoughts.

When she felt able to, she pushed away from him, shoving back her tangled hair. Each breath shuddered into her lungs. Her voice quavered.

"Is he dead?"

Jake still held her hand, the callused touch of his palm enfusing her with strength.

"He's dead," he answered simply. She swallowed hard.

"I knew someone was following me, but I didn't see him until it was too late to do anything about it."

Jake's voice was unexpectedly soft. "I know."

She took another deep breath. "Who was he?"

There was a long moment of silence, then he said, "It's my guess he's one of the renegades who ride with Bass."

"You're certain?" Her part of the conversation

consisted of phrases. That was all she could manage if she were to hold on to her fragile control.

"There are Indian tribes that wander back and forth across the border. But the markings are definitely Apache. Only renegades travel this far south."

Renegades rode with Sam Bass—it wasn't necessary for him to explain. That much she knew. She frowned.

"The sound of that gunshot will travel for miles in these mountains," she said.

He nodded. "They undoubtedly heard it back at the rancho. Knowing Emilio, he'll send out riders."

Her voice was still none too strong. "Do you think Bass heard it?"

Jake frowned. "Maybe, but it's possible he's nowhere near here."

"Or he could be close and know exactly what happened."

He scanned the high mountains that rose sharply behind them and shook his head.

"Bass isn't close by. He's gone deep into the mountains by now."

She picked up the hesitation in his voice. "But more of his men may be around here."

He reluctantly admitted it was true. "He's a careful man. That's the reason he's stayed alive this long. My guess is, Bass and his men have split up and headed for different hideouts. It's harder to track several small groups of men."

"Then, how will you know where to find him?"

Just by the way she asked, he knew nothing had changed. His voice was hard as he replied, "If he's there I'll find him. But right now, we should get back to the rancho."

Then he added, "We've only got one horse. Your mare bolted and ran."

Revel looked up in alarm. "We have to find her, she means a great deal to Emilio."

Her concern for the mare touched something deep inside Jake. She often did that when he least expected it.

"She'll find her way back to the rancho," he assured her. "In fact, she's probably there now."

Revel slowly stood, holding on to his hand. Her knees felt weak and threatened to buckle beneath her. She hated weakness, in anyone, but especially in herself. As long as she'd known him, her father had never been weak—just like Jake.

"Take it easy," he reminded her as he came to his feet. "I will."

His hands at her shoulders steadied her. "Stay here. I'll get my horse."

Emilio's black and gray Appaloosa stood nearby, perfectly still, loose reins trailing to the ground. Jake brought him over and held his hand out to her.

"We'll have to ride double. If he can carry Emilio, he can carry the two of us." His teasing remark about his friend helped break the tension of fear.

Jake helped her atop the stallion, then swung up behind her in the large saddle.

They rode in silence, the warmth of the sun filtering down through the dense, overhead cover of branches as Jake guided the stallion along a different path. They didn't speak again of the attack or the Apache renegade they'd left back in the meadow. Revel detached herself from the reality of what had happened. She let go of her thoughts and her churning emotions, and simply absorbed the sun, air, peacefulness, and . . . Jake.

His body was like a protective shield about her. His arms surrounded her as he held the reins. The solid wall of his chest was at her back, the steady rhythm of his pulse matching the steady plodding of the horse.

All about them were the forest sounds; the occasional flapping of wings as a bird burst into flight when they passed by, the incessant buzzing of insects, the lulling sigh of the wind in the high branches overhead.

She gazed down at his hands as they held the reins in front of her. They were strong, thickly veined, callused, yet capable of tenderness.

The anger and uncertainty of the previous night were forgotten. The only reality was that Jake had come after her. She remembered Rosa's unwavering belief in him.

She wanted to believe in him too, especially since she was going to entrust her life to this man—had already entrusted it to him.

All the emotions of the night before and of this morning, welled to the surface; anger, confusion, fear, and . . . need.

She *needed* to believe him—needed to believe *in* him.

Tears welled in her eyes, and she bit at her lower lip. Her precarious hold on control wavered.

Jake seemed to understand how fragile that control was. He reined the stallion to a halt, and they sat the horse for long moments while he simply held her.

"It's all over," he soothed. "No one is going to hurt you." He cradled her head against his shoulder. "I won't let anyone do that." As he said this, his mouth brushed her cheek. Revel turned to him.

His lips brushed hers lightly as he said, "I promise."

The feather-soft contact of his warm mouth against hers ignited fire.

She hadn't the strength or the will to fight it and simply let herself drift toward it. As if he were the lifeline and she was fighting to hold on, she opened her mouth to his.

Heat, incredible heat.

She breathed it in. It surrounded her, built within her.

It was as if he were air and she wanted only to breathe; as if he were water and she wanted only to drink.

His thighs wrapped about hers, her bottom snugged against him. Revel leaned back into the solid curve of his shoulder. Her hand lay against his chest. The kiss began softly, tenderly, gradually rousing as it banished the ghosts of fear.

Elena was forgotten. At that moment, Revel didn't want to know what had passed between her and Jake. He was here, and whether she wanted it or not, she needed him. It was all that mattered.

She had known tenderness in his kisses before. There was no patience in her for it now; there was only a driving urgency to taste and be tasted, to touch and be touched . . . to burn and be burned.

Her mouth angled beneath his as her tongue explored. A soft sound of need escaped her.

Jake's roughened hands moved over her in soothing strokes; the hard callused skin of his palms against the skin at her jaw, his fingers tracing down her neck and then fanning across her exposed collarbone.

She sat before him in the saddle, turned toward him as her body strained for closer contact. The muscles of his thighs tautened around hers as desire flowed between them like liquid fire.

His flattened palms eased down the tops of her denim-clad thighs. She arched to feel the heavy muscles beneath the shirt covering his chest, her head thrown back against his shoulder.

As his mouth bruisingly caressed hers, he hoarsely whispered her name. It was smothered as her mouth hungrily found his.

His fingers stroked her knees, then ran back up the length of her thighs to her hips, pulling her hard against him. Even through their clothes she could feel his need as she'd felt it that storm-filled night on the desert.

But unlike that first time, when ignorance had blindly led her, there was no blindness now, and she arched back against him once more as a tightly coiled ache began low inside her.

Jake's hands moved from her hips to her waist. His fingers fanned across her stomach. She could feel the heat of his touch even through the coarse fabric of her denim pants. Then he brought his hands higher still, up over her ribs.

For long moments he simply held her, his fingers stroking the curve above her hip, while his mouth and tongue made identical strokes on her cheek, down the side of her neck, then flicked at the base of her throat where her pulse beat wildly.

"Jake," she whispered with ragged urgency.

At that moment she didn't know if she protested where his hands wandered or where they hadn't yet wandered. In the next moment she knew.

His fingers moved upward, slowly stroking, until his hands covered her shirt-clad breasts. Then he began slow caresses.

He massaged, manipulated, alternately closing his hands over her breasts, then rubbing his flattened palms over the taut, sensitized peaks.

His whispered her name at her throat, his voice thick with needs of his own. Her hands eased down the lengths of his hard-muscled thighs, feeling the contours of tendons and muscles.

It was maddening.

Firmly held before him, she couldn't touch him as he was touching her. She wanted to touch more—wanted to feel bare skin beneath her fingertips as she had felt it that stormy night.

Jake's right hand moved down over her taut stomach, his fingers brushing feather-soft at her waist and running down the front closure of her pants. She shuddered.

He kissed her, his mouth angling over hers as he gently tugged the tails of her shirt from the waist of her pants. His fingers played across the skin at her stomach.

Revel's hands clamped over his thighs as her mouth opened under his.

With a soft cry, she whispered, "Oh God, Jake. Touch me."

In response his hand went under her shirt and she felt that roughened palm cover the bare quivering skin of her breast.

She arched against him, filling his hand. His breath shuddered into her mouth as he held her against him.

That tightly wound coil deep inside Revel tightened even more. At that moment she wanted to be anywhere else but astride that horse—on the ground, in the soft meadow grass—as long as she could feel Jake touching her as he had that night on the desert.

He seemed to sense the need within her as he caressed her breast, rolling that hardened peak between his thumb and forefinger, gently tugging until she was mindless in his arms.

Then his left hand moved from her thigh, to gently stroke the front closure of her pants, and Revel gasped at the sensations his fingers roused. Her eyes were closed, her head was thrown back, as an answering pulse began low in her body.

When he removed his hand, she almost cried out, so pleasurable were the expectant sensations that shivered through her. But then she felt the warmth of his fingers against bare skin at her waist and liquid heat surged through her.

He slipped his fingers inside the waistband of her pants and her breath caught in her lungs.

Every muscle in Revel's body tautened to the breaking point; her stomach muscles quivered beneath the stroking of his fingers, then his hand moved lower still.

She couldn't believe what was happening any more than she could stop it, or wanted to.

Even as his fingers slowly stroked down through soft hair and her natural instinct was to stop him, an even stronger instinct arched her body against his hand.

One callused palm stroked her breast while he gently caressed lower with his other hand, fingertips gently grazing the soft folds of flesh—exploring, teasing—until she forgot everything else except the fire he built with his hands.

He kissed her again and again, his tongue imitating the

stroking of his fingers, until her body raged with fever. Her own hands clamped down over the tops of his thighs as need became a sharp pain deep inside. His fingers once again stroked low, between her legs, and Revel felt the wetness of her own response.

Again and again he tormented and teased, until she was mindless for him to touch more.

"Jake . . ." Her voice was filled with soft pleading.

"Do you want me to touch you again, Revel?"

"Yes! Oh God, yes, Jake. Touch me. Please, touch me."

He responded by caressing low once more, his fingers moving in slow, rhythmic circles, slipping down first one thigh then the other. As he moved his hand up once more, his fingertips brushed the taut, throbbing nub at the center of her body.

Revel gasped. Then, as his fingers stroked down over that hardened kernel of flesh, her breath caught in her throat.

Her body was like a tightly wound spring. Every muscle, tendon, nerve ending focused on his stroking.

Over and over his fingers grazed, stroked, teased. In answer, a hot wetness grew within her. She turned to him, her lips parted, not knowing how to ask. Even as air ached to escape her lungs, Jake's mouth closed over hers as his hand closed over her breast. And then as his tongue caressed her lips, her teeth, and plunged fully inside her mouth . . . his fingers slipped inside her.

Again and again his tongue stroked hers as he stroked into the hot, liquid core of her, building desire until it was a throbbing ache.

Slowly, rhythmically, he invaded her soft wetness, her desire now at a frenzied peak. She quivered. She wanted to pull him deeper inside her, needed him to touch that deepest part of her, to release the ache that tightened until she thought she might die of it.

Still, his mouth and hands made love to her, building

358

her to fever pitch. Jake felt the strain in every limb of her slender body. She was at the brink of fulfillment, and he wanted to give her that even as his own body throbbed painfully.

He took her over the edge as his tongue plunged deep inside her mouth and his fingers drove even deeper inside her hot, moist body. She cried out against his mouth, the muscles deep inside her pulsing wildly.

For long moments afterward, she lay against him. Then as reality slowly returned and along with it, the full knowledge of what they had done, vivid color stained her cheeks. She pulled away from him, fumbling clumsily at her pants and shirt. He gently brushed her hands aside and buttoned up her clothing.

She looked away, too embarrassed to meet his gaze. With even more tenderness, he turned her head back around.

He said nothing at first. Instead he gently brushed her lips with his, an innocent, uninvolved kiss that nevertheless brought a familiar throb of desire. When she tried to pull away again, he pulled her back.

He reached up and brushed damp strands of long hair back from her face and traced her mouth with his finger.

"Look at me," he whispered.

She reached up to push his hand away. "Please, I . . ." When she refused, he forced her to meet his gaze.

"Don't be afraid of what just happened."

"I'm not," she said with faint defiance. She bit at her lower lip. "It's just that I've never done anything . . . like that before." Her voice trailed off as she tried to find the words. "It's not right," she protested. "We shouldn't . . . It doesn't mean anything."

His mouth brushed hers, and even now, in spite of her embarrassment, she began to ache deep inside. "But we both know it's not finished, Revel, whether we want it or not."

She started to protest, and he knew precisely what she

359

would say—that it *was* finished, it should never have happened, just as that night on the desert should never have happened, and would never happen again. But he also knew that she was a magnificent liar.

"Don't say anything." He tasted the bruised softness of her mouth as he pulled her back against him, settling her in the curve of his body.

"Just rest," he murmured against her hair as he took up the reins and urged the stallion through the strand of trees.

Even as she fought it, Revel grew drowsy. In no time at all she heard distant shouts and the loud barking of a dog. Jake gently awakened her.

"We're almost back at the rancho," he said softly with no more mention of what had passed between them.

Revel straightened in the saddle before him, making certain her clothes were buttoned and tucked in. Her hair was a mess, but there was no help for that.

A wild commotion erupted around them as they rode into the yard at the rancho. Vaqueros rode forth astride their horses. Rosa and the children ran from the house to greet them. Emilio crossed the yard from the paddock, his face heavily lined.

He pushed his way through the vaqueros to get to his friend.

"We heard a shot."

Jake nodded. "An Apache followed Revel. He must have come down from the high mountains. I followed them to the meadow."

"He is dead?" Emilio asked, already certain of the answer.

Again Jake nodded. Emilio squinted up into the sun. "You are not hurt, *señorita?*"

"No, I'm fine." Revel managed a wan smile, but her voice was a little shaky. "I knew someone was following me, but I didn't see him until it was too late. I'm afraid I lost your mare."

360

"Do not worry." Emilio explained. "She already has found her way back to us."

"Jake! Jake!"

From across the yard, Elena ran toward them. She had dropped an armful of clean, wet laundry. Fear filled her voice as she reached them.

Jake felt Revel's body go taut against his. He gently tightened his arms about her. It was an unmistakable gesture lost on no one, except perhaps Elena and Revel.

Revel took it as a subtle warning to say and do nothing, and it angered her. Was he trying to silence her, and protect Elena?

Rosa caught her daughter by the arm and whirled her around. *"Silencio, hija!"* she hissed.

"Do not disgrace yourself and your family!"

Elena looked from her mother to her father. Emilio's face was dark as thunder. There was no need for him to say anything to his daughter.

Silence hung over them as Elena turned a tormented gaze on Jake. Then she turned and fled across the yard. Emilio shook his head sadly.

"Mil perdones," he said, both to Jake and Revel. "I beg your forgiveness for my daughter's behavior."

Jake reached down and laid a hand on his friend's shoulder. "It's not necessary, *amigo.*"

Emilio sighed. "She is young and foolish. I promise you, she will not bother you again. But now there are more important matters." His expression became grave.

"We knew before we heard the shot that the Apache renegades were nearby."

Jake tensed. "What's happened?"

"One of my vaqueros returned from delivering a horse to a rancho up in the mountains."

His gaze went from Jake to Revel. "Sam Bass and his men were seen in the high country two days ago."

Revel pushed away from Jake and slipped to the ground. Her voice was much stronger when she asked,

361

"Will our horses be ready to travel in the morning?"

A look of silent communication passed between Jake and Emilio.

"Another day would be better, *señorita*," Emilio suggested hesitantly.

Revel saw the look that passed between the two men and knew precisely what Jake was up to.

"If they're not ready in the morning, I'm prepared to buy horses from you." Her voice was soft, but determined. She briefly glanced from Jake to Emilio.

"One way or the other, I'm leaving in the morning."

Chapter Nineteen

Revel stayed as far away from Jake as possible for the rest of the day.

She busied herself with the children and helped Rosa prepare the evening meal. Late in the afternoon, with the excuse of wanting to see the yearling colts Emilio was so proud of, she went for a long walk out to the grazing pastures.

Emilio's sons and the vaqueros worked in shifts, riding watch along the perimeters of the rancho. The news that Sam Bass and the Comancheros had been seen up in the mountains had set everyone on edge.

The smaller children were fed early and put to bed. The older girls were quiet, whispering among themselves at the supper table.

Except for Elena.

She refused to join her family at supper. Humiliated because of the way she had acted toward Jake, she declared she would rather die than face everyone.

Rosa informed her daughter that as long as she was "going to die" she might as well make herself useful in the meantime.

She gave Elena a basket of mending, ample thread and needles, and informed her that she was "not to die" until all the mending was completed.

Elena retreated to the room she shared with her

sisters, the mending basket she carried piled high with every available shirt and pair of pants that needed a button replaced or the smallest tear repaired.

Rosa winked at Revel, not the least concerned with her daughter's dire prediction of death. "It will give her plenty of time to contemplate her foolishness. That worked with me when I was her age; it will also work with her." Then she confided. "I hated mending more than anything. Elena hates it just as much. But by the time she is done I won't have to worry about doing any until the smaller children are grown."

Revel had very little appetite, although the food was as wonderful as it had been the night before. She accepted the full platter Rosa set before her, pushing food around on it rather than actually eating.

Emilio and Jake came to supper late. Rosa said nothing about their tardiness, but hurriedly brought platters piled high with food that she'd kept warm in the oven.

Revel felt Jake's cool green gaze on her and quickly rose from the table, making the hasty excuse that she had promised the younger children she would tell them a bedtime story.

She carried her plate to the work stand by the washtub, ignoring the questioning looks that passed across the table.

As she fled the house for the horse shed, she berated herself for offering such a poor excuse. Emilio undoubtedly knew his younger children were already in bed, and Jake was no fool.

She could feel his speculative gaze on her all the way out to the corrals. She was avoiding him. She knew it, and he knew it. But she couldn't bear to sit across the table from him after what had happened that morning. And she had no intention of discussing her plans to leave.

Revel wandered through the orchards, then back through the gardens at the rear of the house. She was restless, apprehensive, just plain scared. But there was no turning back now.

Unable to return just yet, afraid Jake might be waiting for her, she pulled fresh, dry laundry from the lines behind the house, folding each piece before placing it into a large basket.

It was busy work, mindless work, and it kept her from thinking about tomorrow, or Jake Reno.

She carried two large baskets of clean clothing into the house. There was only one chore that remained—packing the provisions for the trip into the mountains. She found Rosa in the kitchen.

"It was not necessary for you to do that," Rosa said quietly as she glanced at the baskets piled high with clean laundry.

"I was glad to do it," Revel confessed. "It kept my mind off other things."

"Such as Jake?" Rosa suggested.

Revel sidestepped that issue. She didn't want to discuss Jake with anyone, not even Rosa.

"I'm leaving in the morning," she announced quietly.

Rosa nodded. "That is what Emilio tells me." And then she added, "I wish I could say something to make you forget about going after Sam Bass."

"Don't," Revel pleaded in a quiet voice. "I have to do this."

Rosa nodded sadly. "*Sí*, I know. Just like someone else many years ago." After a pause, she said, "You may have whatever you need, of course."

From earlier experience, Revel knew what food they would need, and she wrapped tortillas and dried beef in pieces of cloth.

She had already spoken to Broken Hand and had told him she couldn't be certain Jake would go with them.

The old Indian guide had accepted that as he accepted everything else, with an impassive expression and a grunt that could have been agreement, disagreement, or neither.

Then he'd simply said. "My destiny awaits me on that mountain. I will go with you."

She knew it was because of the warrior he called Toscaneh who rode with the Comancheros. Whatever his reasons, Broken Hand would help her find Sam Bass.

When the food was packed in the saddlebags, Revel offered to pay Rosa for her kindness, but the woman refused to accept anything from her.

"I will give you something more," she offered, as she took Revel's hand in hers.

"Revenge is a very destructive thing. I have seen it, and I know. Be careful that you do not lose something of greater value in your quest for it, because what you lose you will never find again."

Revel looked into Rosa's wise, dark eyes, wondering at her meaning, wondering if she spoke of Jake Reno.

"Thank you, for everything," she said softly.

Rosa laid a hand against her cheek. *"De nada, hija—* you are welcome. *Vaya con Dios—*go with God. And take this with you." She reached up and unclasped a thin gold chain. A small gold, crucifix dangled from it. She placed it around Revel's neck.

"I can't accept this," Revel protested.

But Rosa would have none of her objections. "You must. It will bring you safely back to us."

Revel fingered the delicate gold cross, knowing she mustn't refuse. Then she said once more, "Thank you. I *will* bring it back to you."

That night, Revel slept soundly for the first time in weeks. She rose before dawn, dressed, and went to the kitchen.

Rosa had left a pot of warm beans at the hearth and soft flour tortillas in a warming pan. Revel wrapped beans in several tortillas, then slipped these inside a small pouch. She gathered the heavy saddlebags holding the provisions, took up her blanket roll, and let herself out of the house.

Several vaqueros talked quietly at the corrals. They had been up through the long night, continuing their vigilant rides into the surrounding hills.

Broken Hand waited for her at the corral. He took two of the saddlebags and secured them to his pony.

Revel's gelding was in the corral, Broken Hand had brought him in from the pasture. She quickly bridled him and threw the saddle blanket across his back. Then she lifted the heavy saddle down from the top crossbar and flung it atop the blanket.

She had become efficient at saddling her own horse, and reached beneath the gelding for the cinch strap, looped it through the saddle ring, then snugged it tight.

Jake strode across the yard.

Rosa had said he would find her here.

Her saddlebags lay against the corral fence. The Colt revolver was in its holster, protruding from one of the bags. The long steel barrel of a Henry rifle gleamed in the gray dawn.

Jake recognized Emilio's scrollwork carved into the wood rifle butt, and smothered back anger.

It wasn't Emilio's fault that she insisted on going after Bass. She could be stubborn and persuasive. God knew Emilio wasn't the first to come up against that lethal combination.

His friend hadn't been able to stop her, but Jake was still determined to talk her out of this.

She was dressed as she had been yesterday, in clinging denim pants, heavy cotton shirt, and the soft buckskin boots he'd given her.

The pants clung to her, outlining every sleek curve and her slender legs. He felt the need build down low in his belly at seeing those pants, remembering the soft skin underneath and the liquid heat of her body.

That, too, was part of what angered him, and drove him to stop her. But he knew better than anybody, anger had never gotten him anywhere with Revel. Rosa knew it too.

She had cautioned him as he'd left the house, saying, "Talk to her, tell her what you really feel, make her undestand."

He could do that. But how could he make Revel

367

understand something he didn't understand himself?

As he watched her saddle the gelding with determined efficiency, he knew he'd never reach her with anger. There had already been too much of it between them.

For the first time in his life, Jake was faced with a situation that couldn't be resolved with a gun. And so, instead, he searched for words.

He quietly stepped beside her as she flung one pair of saddlebags over the back of the saddle and secured them. As she seized the rifle and slipped it into the scabbard, his hand covered hers.

"We have to talk."

She pulled her hand from his and bent to retrieve the second pair of saddlebags.

"There's nothing to talk about."

"I've been trying to get you alone since we got back yesterday. You've been avoiding me."

Revel hesitated, but didn't meet his gaze. Then she flung the saddlebags over the front of the saddle.

"You're right," she said softly, weary of the old anger. "I *have* been avoiding you."

"Do you mind telling me why?" he asked quietly, tying the saddlebags more securely to the saddle, his fingers efficiently manipulating the leather straps. Then he leaned against the saddle and faced her.

Revel went to the horse shed and found the sack of grain for the gelding. There would be little time to allow the horses to graze on the trail.

Jake didn't follow but simply waited for her return— and her answer.

She tied the grain sack to the saddle and met his gaze briefly. "I knew you would try to talk me out of going after Bass."

"There's more to it than that."

She was aware that he was speaking of what had happened between them the day before.

She jerked the leather strings tight. "There's nothing

more to it." Before she could move away, before she even saw him move, his hands were on her shoulders.

"Is this about Elena? Because if it is, then you need to know nothing happened between us the other night. I sent her away. You've got to believe that."

"It doesn't matter," Revel flung back at him, trying hard to control her anger. "None of it matters," she added with quiet finality.

"It mattered yesterday morning." Jake said, every bit as quietly.

She looked away, unable to meet his gaze as she pulled out of his grasp.

"That was a mistake."

"Just like going after Bass is a mistake?" He wasn't going to let up on this. Even as she tried to walk away, he reached out and grabbed her wrist. He twisted her arm and gently pinned it behind her back, forcing her to face him.

Their bodies collided, thigh against thigh, hip against hip, her soft full breasts crushed against the hard wall of his chest.

Need, as hot and dangerous as the anger, flared between them. Revel's head came up, denial caught in her throat even as her body betrayed her.

"It's not a mistake!" she hissed at him. "I want him dead."

"And you along with him?" He bent over her, his face suddenly so close to hers it blurred before her. She could feel the heat of his hands, his lean, hard body, the sweetness of his breath. And she burned—for his touch, his kiss . . . his body.

But even that desire couldn't assuage her desire for revenge.

"I've waited three years for this. It's what I want," she whispered, desperately wanting him to kiss her, knowing it would solve nothing and yet wanting it all the more.

He let her go as suddenly as he'd grabbed her.

Revel staggered and would have fallen into the dust at his feet if she hadn't grabbed at the corral rail for support.

Her every muscle, every tendon ached from the touch of his hands. And within her was an empty, hollow feeling.

She rubbed her bruised shoulder. There was no remedy for that deeper ache—none that she could give in to.

The price was too high for that. She couldn't and wouldn't pay it.

Before he'd crossed the yard from the house, Jake had made his decision. He wouldn't let her go alone. They'd had a bargain from the beginning—his freedom in exchange for Bass.

Now the stakes were higher. He wanted more than his freedom.

"I'll saddle my horse." He spun around so suddenly that the gelding jerked it's head in the air and rolled its eyes.

"That's not necessary," Revel informed him bluntly. "Broken Hand can trail Bass to his hideout. You said yourself he's the best."

"Next to me," he reminded her, then asked, "What about our deal?"

She looked up briefly. "If I get Bass, I'll keep my part of the bargain."

With an oath, Jake smothered back anger. "Do you really believe he'll let you get within a hundred yards of him? Even if Broken Hand can find him?"

She swung up into the saddle. Gathering the reins in her gloved hands, she looked down at him one last time.

"I don't need you."

She kicked the gelding into a canter. Broken Hand waited for her at the edge of the orchard. His old eyes gave her a keen glance, but he said nothing.

She didn't look back.

Jake watched her ride out. He bridled and saddled the Appaloosa.

Emilio stood at the edge of the corral as he rode out. With a knowing expression, he handed Jake his rifle and saddlebags.

"I will send my vaqueros with you."

"No." Jake said firmly. "You'll need every man here if Bass and his men double back. Besides, a few of us can travel faster, and we'll draw less attention." Then he went on. "By the way, a sheriff may be riding through here in the next few days."

"Is this sheriff looking for you?"

"He'd rather have Bass, the reward is bigger."

Emilio nodded and gave him a knowing smile. "But he might also like to collect the reward for you."

"Something like that."

"You could use his help," Emilio pointed out.

Jake shook his head. "In those mountains, he'd be more trouble than help. I don't need Bass in front of me and a sheriff on my tail."

"I understand." Emilio's grin deepened. "I will see to it that he and his men are kept *very busy*—so busy that they won't be able to follow you into those mountains for at least two or three days? And, even then, my men will see to it that they get lost."

"Thank you, *amigo*."

Emilio took hold of the Appaloosa's bridle, his face gone sober.

"You know as well as I, there is only one way this will end with Bass."

Jake nodded. "I know."

"She must mean a great deal to you," Emilio speculated.

Their gazes met, in them the understanding only true friends share.

For the first time, Jake was forced to confront something he avoided—something that opened old

371

wounds that spanned half his life, something that had almost ended on the gallows back in Tombstone.

"Yes," he finally admitted, "she does."

He took a different route up the mountain, not following Broken Hand and Revel's trail, then traversed to the west. Broken Hand was an excellent tracker, but Jake had ridden over every inch of these mountains.

He knew every ravine, every canyon, each fork of the river, every peak and outcropping. More than once, his life had depended on knowing these mountains well enough to find his way through them blindfolded.

Now he sat in cool shade, hidden from the casual eye. He took a drink of water to quench the dryness left by the jerky and tortillas he'd eaten along the way, then packed the canteen away and waited.

He looked up as he heard movement through the brush—the unexpected rustle of leaves when there was no wind. A Stellar jay squawked in alarm from a limb overhead. A ground squirrel stopped foraging for seeds to sniff the air.

"It took you long enough," Jake announced as Broken Hand proceeded almost noiselessly through the brush. The old guide whirled around in the saddle, a knife in one hand, a rifle clutched in the other.

"Damn!" he cursed as he recognized Jake and lowered the rifle. "I must be getting old for you to be able sneak up on me like that."

"You forget," Jake reminded him, "I know these mountains."

Broken Hand shook his head, "It's a bad feeling, having someone come up on me like that."

Jake grinned. "Now you know how the white man feels." Then he asked, "Where's Revel?"

"She'll be along. She keeps up pretty good, for a woman."

"Did you find Bass's trail?"

Broken Hand nodded. "I picked up tracks at the water." Jake knew he meant the river that cut through

372

these mountains and down through the valley. He'd come up the draw from the other side and missed the tracks, knowing he would pick them up ahead.

The Indian grunted. "Even Comancheros need water."

"How many?"

"Seven ponies; three are shod."

"They've already split up," Jake speculated.

Broken Hand nodded. "Just above that rancho your friend spoke of. Seven came this way, the others split into several small parties."

They both knew that Bass rode one of those shod horses.

"That means there are possibly four renegade Apache."

Broken Hand nodded, and then said, "Toscaneh rides with them."

Jake nodded. "I understand." He looked up as Revel joined them. Her stunned gaze met his.

"How did you get here?"

"You forget, Miss Tyson, I know these mountains."

"Does this mean you're coming along?"

"I suppose you could say that."

"I see." She was hot and tired. They'd been riding since daybreak, and she wanted a drink of water, not to mention a few moments of privacy for more intimate needs. She started to dismount.

"There's no time for a rest," Jake informed her matter-of-factly. "If you want Bass, we have to keep moving."

She started to protest, then clamped her mouth shut and sat back in the saddle. Their gazes met briefly.

"Then by all means, let's keep moving," she snapped as she dug her heels into the gelding and sent him on up the trail.

"This way, Miss Tyson," Jake casually called after her as he swung the Appaloosa about and sent him in a different direction. Broken Hand followed, leaving Revel to ride in their dusty wake.

It was midafternoon when Jake finally called a halt. Without bothering to ask how long they would be stopping, Revel scooted out of the saddle and disappeared into the brush. Broken Hand continued to scout on ahead, his keen eyes following the faint tracks left in the soft dirt. Within a few minutes he had circled back.

"They have split up again."

Jake watched the brush Revel had gone into. He turned to Broken Hand.

"Where?"

"A few hundred paces ahead."

"How many?"

"Four go higher up the mountain, three go to the west."

"Are the shod ponies among the tracks you saw?"

Broken Hand nodded and Jake drew his own conclusions.

"Bass is headed for the old hideout at the summit."

"Toscaneh rides with the others." Broken Hand informed him stoically.

Both understood his meaning. Jake nodded. "Then I'll meet you again when this is finished."

When Revel emerged from the brush a few minutes later, she glanced about the clearing.

"Where's Broken Hand?"

"He's gone."

"What do you mean he's *gone?*" she asked as she took down her canteen and drank from it.

"He's gone," Jake repeated, then he explained. "The tracks have split up again. Bass and three of his men have gone into the high country. They're headed for the old hideout."

"What about the others?"

"They took another trail. Broken Hand has gone after them."

Revel's surprised gaze met his. "How could you have let him go off like that? You know how dangerous this is."

374

Jake watched her appraisingly. "I'm glad to see you're concerned. I was beginning to think you weren't. You seem so eager to get everyone killed, including yourself, with this obsession to get Bass."

Her gaze cut away from his. "Of course I care what happens to Broken Hand. He's an old man going against three Comancheros."

"At least one of them is Apache," Jake pointed out, "and he may be old, but he's Indian. That makes up for a lot."

Her gaze jerked back to his. Her voice was quiet. "Is Toscaneh with them?"

Jake nodded. "Yes."

She frowned. "I don't understand. Who is Toscaneh? What does Broken Hand want with him?"

"Toscaneh is his son," he said quietly.

At seeing her startled expression, he went on. "It's called *revenge*. You should know all about that."

"Oh, God," Revel whispered. Then her gaze fastened on his. "What will he do when he finds him?"

"He'll kill him," Jake stated flatly. His voice became hard as he added, "Or he'll be killed."

Without another word, Jake screwed the cap on his canteen, threw the strap over the pommel of his saddle, and mounted the Appaloosa.

As he swung the stallion around and moved out onto the trail once more he called over his shoulder, "We've got a lot of ground to cover before sundown."

Revel scrambled to keep up with him.

Through the remainder of the afternoon, they rode in silence, climbing one invisible path after another up the steep mountainside.

She had plenty of time to contemplate what he'd told her about Broken Hand. It stunned her and left her cold inside.

How could a man kill his own son?

They followed a narrow creek through one twisting mountain gorge after another. At lower elevations they

375

rode through sycamore, cottonwood, willow, and mesquite boskets. The sycamore and cottonwood were aflame with brilliant autumn foliage.

At higher elevations the cold night temperatures had already stripped branches of their foliage. Here the trees looked like pale-limbed women, crowded together, trying to shield their nakedness, only a few remaining leaves dripping from bony-fingered twigs.

A carpet of leaves lay across rocks, boulders, and clear mountain pools.

The glossy faces of beaver broke the surface of the water near a fallen tree, only to disappear again, broad tails leaving ripple trails in the water.

A ring-tailed raccoon stared at them speculatively as they passed by, it's dark eyes glistening mischievously.

Mule deer grazed lazily on wild oxalis and bear's-breech at the water's edge. Even before they picked up the scent of horses and humans, one tossed it's head into the air and sniffed the late afternoon breeze. Then they all bolted up the mountainside in frantic, bounding leaps.

Jake and Revel saw the cause of the deers' alarm—a stout, smoky gray javelina, snorting and rooting through the underbrush.

The horses tensed, and Jake altered their course upwind of the wild boar, not wanting any entanglements with the ornery, unpredictable animal.

That day they made camp at the first summit. It was far too dangerous to continue a treacherous ascent up the mountain in darkness. They had ridden for almost fourteen hours.

Their conversation was guarded. There were too many angry things burning to be said, too many that had already been said.

Jake hadn't given up trying to change her mind about going after Bass, and she hadn't given up trying to explain why she would not.

Because of Rachel, he should have been able to

understand her reasons better than anyone.

He didn't.

And then there was the constant awareness that somewhere out there Sam Bass and his men also made their camp.

As she lay in her blanket roll that first night, Revel found herself listening to the wind, the flutter of an owl in the trees, the lonely cry of a coyote.

Those were the normal sounds of the forest. But she listened for other sounds until her nerves were raw, and her fingers grew cramped from clutching the revolver she kept under the edge of the blanket.

The following day they rose before sunup. She'd slept poorly and fatigue dragged at her. But she said nothing as they rode long into the afternoon.

Every step, every turn in the trail, every rock they climbed around took her closer to Sam Bass—and revenge for her father.

They traveled as fast as they dared, over smooth, rocky river beds, through dense thickets, deep into mountain shadows. The sun was warm, the shade chilled the skin, the air warned of the changing of season.

Because of the pace he'd set, Jake surprised her when he called a halt for the day. There was still at least an hour of light left and she wanted to go on, but he made the decisions out here.

Their camp on that second day was well hidden. He seemed to feel they were safe from anyone stumbling across it.

A shallow, boulder-lined pool provided water. The rock walls of the mountain rose precipitously at their backs, and a thick line of brilliant cottonwood and pine protected them from high winds.

Jake had found this place years earlier. He'd once hidden here while he listened to a posse pick its way over the rocky trail above.

They had ridden for over twelve hours. It was warm

377

and still beside the pool, sheltered from any breeze, but the horses were weary, their heads hanging low as they were unsaddled.

"How soon do you think we might pick up their trail?" Revel asked as she rolled out her blanket.

He didn't answer immediately, then as he hobbled the Appaloosa he said, "We picked it up late yesterday."

She looked up in surprise. He'd said nothing, she'd seen nothing. And she had been watching the trail, what there was of it. Mostly it was rock, loose shale, riverbottom, and hard granite mountains.

"How close are we?"

"The tracks were several days old."

"How many?" she asked, fatigue vanishing.

"Two riders, probably a scouting party. Like I said, Sam is a careful man."

"Do you think he knows we're following him?"

"Not yet. But he will."

Revel's skin was sticky. Her cotton shirt lay plastered against her back. But not from the hot, sweatiness of two days' ride on the open trail. Her skin was clammy cold. It was what Jake had said—*he will.*

Blanket rolls were laid out, along with food for their cold supper. They dared not light a fire and risk having it seen by Bass or one of his men.

The horses were each fed a handful of grain then allowed to graze at the end of short tethers.

Jake took off to scout the surrounding area, as he had the night before.

One moment he was standing over his blanket roll warning her to keep the revolver with her at all times. Then, without a sound, he was gone.

She'd have been a liar if she'd tried to make anyone believe his sudden disappearances and reappearances didn't bother her. If Jake moved that silently, then the Comancheros could move silently too, sneaking up whenever they chose.

It was a disquieting thought.

378

Of course, the advantage was that Jake was also out there. But that thought was less reassuring than it might have been. In spite of everything, Revel still wasn't certain he wouldn't just take off.

The other side to that argument was the fact that he had chosen to come along.

She took the holstered revolver and slung it over her shoulder. If someone came at her, she wasn't at all certain she could handle the heavy weapon.

It was one thing to aim it two-handed, at a stationary target, quite another to unholster it in a moment of fear and aim it accurately.

Revel tied back her hair, grabbed a clean shirt, a washcloth, and soap, and headed for the shallow pool of water. While Jake was gone she might as well make good use of her privacy.

Leaving the revolver on the bank within easy reach, she slipped out of her boots, shirt, and denim pants. She wore a short chemise and pantalets underneath as most ladies' undergarments wouldn't accommodate men's clothing. Someday, she thought, someone is going to make more practical garments for women. She slipped off the pantalets.

The water was cold, lapping around her bare ankles, recalling a time when she was a child and her father had taken her on a summer picnic. There had been a lake and all the children were playing in it. She'd stripped down to her bloomers—at the age of eight modesty hadn't counted for much—and had stood expectantly on the shore.

"It's cold," she had protested to her father.

"Then the only thing you can do is run in and get it over with all at once. Or you don't have to go in at all," he'd said.

His smile had suggested he knew precisely what she would do. That smile had broadened as she'd sucked in her breath, turned back toward the water, and thrown herself headlong into the lake.

That summer was a lifetime ago, Revel thought as the familiar pang of loss struck her.

But the memory of it was special, private, and hers. And now a pool of crystal, clear mountain water was waiting to be conquered just as on that day so many summers ago.

As she had in that distant summer, Revel sucked in her breath, turned toward the pool and . . . carefully waded in, holding her breath as the chill water slipped up her thighs, around her hips, and the hem of the chemise floated about her waist.

Cottonwood leaves gilded the surface of the water. They floated past with abandon like so many yellow-sailed boats.

It was wonderful, exhilarating, cleansing, and chilling to the bone even though the late sun spread heat across the water.

She bathed, sluicing away dirt and sweat and the horse smell. She sank deep into the water, the chemise billowing out around her. It was difficult washing with it on, but she refused to remove it.

Bathing in a mountain pool half-dressed, with Comancheros somewhere out there, was a great deal different than bathing in a mountain pool completely naked.

She lathered her hair with the soap, then rinsed it, glancing back to their camp and the tethered horses, then across to the opposite bank and along the perimeter of the forest line.

It was quiet, peaceful, tranquil. And she was being watched.

She looked up, her gaze scanning the rim of the pool, darting to the camp, the quietly grazing horses, searching among the huge boulders.

She saw nothing.

Still, she felt it—that faint tingling along nerve endings, the sudden chill flowing across her skin.

Someone was watching her.

Her gaze darted down to the revolver, several feet away on the embankment. Her thoughts raced.

If he wanted to kill me, I would already be dead.

Whoever was watching evidently didn't plan to kill— at least not right away.

Could she get to the revolver in time?

She decided against it.

In order to use the gun she had to know where her target was, and she didn't.

Revel took a deep breath. She had to remain calm. Her life depended on it.

Her pulse roared in her veins. Fear dried her throat. She swallowed, took another deep breath.

Then she slowly turned around.

Chapter Twenty

At first she couldn't see him for the glare of the sun off the water.

She glanced to the rocks, through the dense forest line, along the water's edge. There he was, crouched low at the edge of the pool.

He was bare chested, his muscles carving dark shadows on his glistening skin. Lean arms rested on his buckskin-clad knees, buckskin boots encased his feet and calves.

Water trickled from his fingers, beaded across the dark, golden skin at his chest, glistened in the wild mane of hair that hung to his shoulders.

His relaxed position as he stared back at her was deceiving. Every muscle and sinew of his body was tensed in a subtle wariness that suggested he might spring at her at any moment.

There was a predatory power about him that was both frightening and fascinating, a primitive wildness that hinted at a savage danger.

Jake Reno was like a lean, tawny cat—*predatory, fascinating, dangerous.*

When she slowly turned toward him, she reminded him of a frightened doe poised for flight.

Her hair was sleeked back against her head and it fell in

a wet strand down across her shoulders and back. Dark as midnight, it emphasized the honeyed glow of her skin, the wide pools of her vivid eyes, all the hollows and angles of her face.

Then he saw the shift of recognition in her eyes, the relaxing of fists, the sudden clinging of wet fabric to her breasts as she finally took a breath.

The pants, loose shirt, boots, and hat had disguised the fact that she was a woman.

Nothing disguised it now as she stood knee-deep in water, the wet chemise dragging against all the curves and valleys of her slender body.

It covered her almost completely, yet revealed more than it hid by the way it molded to her, sculpting her full breasts, their dark peaks, taut from cool air and cooler water, thrusting against the wet, transparent fabric.

Water sleeked her thighs, beaded across the skin at her throat, glistened on high cheekbones and the fullness of her mouth.

Cool heat.

Desire and regret.

She could consume a man with need for all the things he'd convinced himself he could never have.

Love. Family. Home.

The life he'd left behind years ago—bits and pieces of unfulfilled dreams now obscured by the dust on a gunfighter's bloody trail.

And yet just looking at her made him want.

If they had met in another time and place, everything might have been different.

He would call on her. There would be buggy rides on moonlit nights, summer picnics down by a river. He would bring her flowers.

Jake rose and slowly walked toward her through the knee-deep water. When they stood only inches apart, he reached up and touched her cheek, feeling the wet heat of water beaded on her skin.

Bluebonnets.

There was a high meadow near the old ranch where they grew wild. In the spring they were like a bright blue carpet spreading as far as the eye could see.

He would bring her bluebonnets—armfuls of them— because their color reminded him of her eyes, handfuls of soft petals because they were like her skin. And he would lay her down on thick velvet blue and make love to her beneath the sun and sky and wind.

He wanted all of that . . . he wanted her.

"How do you do that?" she asked softly.

His gaze fastened on the single droplet of water that clung to her bottom lip. "Do what?"

"Sneak up on someone like that."

"You knew I was there." His voice was like soft thunder as his eyes slowly came up to hers.

Eyes that hold and hold back, she thought. "No," she answered softly, a bit breathlessly. "I *felt* something. I thought it might be Comancheros or the Apache. You move like one of them."

"I learned from Broken Hand—how to move without moving, how to see without being seen, how to be in a place without being there." He frowned slightly as his finger stroked the fullness of her bottom lip, captivated by the full curve.

"I didn't mean to frighten you," he whispered.

Her mouth trembled beneath his finger. "You're dangerous, Jake Reno."

"That's why you wanted me."

The words jolted through her. She understood the obvious meaning—she'd saved him from the gallows because she needed him to find Sam Bass.

But a more subtle meaning made her shiver with a deeper, more profound need.

And she answered simply, "Yes, I want you."

The words shuddered out of her as she reached up and wrapped her arms about his neck.

There was no patience in her for tenderness or long, enduring caresses. A raw, naked urgency transfused her

385

body, like a wild, hungering current.

It began two days earlier when his mouth and hands explored and laid claim to all the intimate, secret places of her . . . that rain-swept night on the desert when he first made love to her . . . the first time he looked at her with eyes that reflected back all the empty, barren places in her own life . . . it began here and now.

Her mouth sought the warmth of his in all the ways he'd taught her, beginning with soft touches, tender tastes, then white-hot possession, as her hands plunged through his heavy mane of hair, fingers tangling in the soft gold waves.

Her small mouth angled under his as her tongue slipped inside to explore, assault, conquer, enslave.

Soft sounds began in her throat, then became whispered words as her lips followed her hands down across hardened muscle, down his arms, across his chest.

The danger that surrounded them heightened the danger within them. They were close to Bass, both of them knew it. How it would end, only God could possibly know. But no one who had gone up against Bass had survived.

If they had only these few hours, then she wanted all of him, here, now, before another night, another dawn.

He was like a man possessed by demons as his hands sculpted her body, his fingers slowly memorizing every curve, each indentation, every supple muscle, his thumbs caressing the sides of her breasts; taking her startled sigh of pleasure as the very air he breathed.

The sun played across the water, running it through with golden fire.

There was no shyness in her, only need that ignited and then burned as he pulled her hips hard against his, wanting—needing—her to feel his own need in the hardened thrust of his body.

His fingers wrapped around the thick silk of her hair and he slowly drew her head back, his mouth moving down the arch of her throat, as his other hand moved over her breast. His name shuddered out of her. Her hands clasped his head, drawing his mouth down to her breast.

Through the transparent wet fabric of the chemise, his teeth grazed hungrily over a tautened peak as his hand moved down to cup her bare bottom. His name on her lips became a soft cry.

She brought his mouth back to her as they stood together. Her body was liquid fire, molding his, the taut peaks of her breasts searing him through the cool barrier of the wet chemise.

Even as her sleek, wet tongue plunged into his mouth there was the brief awareness of cool air, then the feather brush of her fingers against his stomach.

Clumsily, uncertainly they played over his flesh, wanting to caress and stroke him as he had once stroked her.

His hands guided hers, and the soft buckskin was pushed aside. His fingers closed over her wrists in almost desperate anticipation as her cool fingers closed over him. And she caressed and stroked as he had caressed her.

Any restraint, any caution that remained vanished at the tender stroking of her fingers. Need ached low in his belly.

Bass was forgotten. The Comancheros and the renegades were forgotten. The past was forgotten. There was only Revel and the wild urgent need to be inside her.

The wet fabric of the chemise separated in his hands. Like a man left in the desert he thirsted, like a wild animal he hungered. He stripped off his buckskin boots and pants, tossed them on the bank. Then his hands slipped under her arms and he lifted her.

"Put your legs around me," he whispered against her mouth.

Mindless to everything except the need that clawed inside her, Revel wrapped her legs around his waist.

The intimate contact burned through them—her full

387

breasts flattened against his chest, his belly pressed against hers, the tangle of golden hair with dark velvet brown, the hard thrust between them.

And then as his mouth angled over hers, he lifted her once more and brought her slender body down over his, gloving him in tight, wet heat.

Revel cried out at the penetrating strength that filled her.

This was what she had longed for ever since that night on the desert. But even as her body molded him, the need returned—sharper, more distinct—and she moved against him, seeking a deeper fulfillment.

Her arms were twined about his neck, her mouth was hard against his, even as her thigh muscles tautened and she thrust down over him.

Everything Jake might have imagined paled in comparison to reality.

She was lean and supple, her body clasping his as he moved within her. His hands cupped her bottom, guiding her over him. Hers clasped his shoulders. Head thrown back and eyes closed, she arched her back, taking him deeper still.

The setting sun shafted through the spires of trees and glinted off her wet body. She was liquid gold in his hands, wrapping about him, enveloping him.

"Jake . . ." His name quivered over the silent water and whispered in the trees. Then she said it again, with soft desperation as she reached the edge.

Her fingers clawed into his shoulders. Every tendon strained. Her startled gaze fastened on his as spasms began deep inside her and her muscles quivered around him.

"Jake!" she gasped as the air shuddered out of her lungs.

"I know." His mouth moved over hers, swallowing her soft cries. "Let it happen. Just let it happen."

She cried out softly against his mouth, and he thrust past her quivering sleek muscles, and burst deep inside her.

For long moments afterward, Jake held her slender body intimately molded over his, his arms closing her against him. Her head was cradled against his shoulder, his cheek rested against her wet hair.

Then he moved deeper into the pool, the cool mountain water, rippling around their fevered bodies. She rolled her head back against his shoulder, her lips moving against his neck.

"What are you doing?" she murmured, a huskiness lingering in her throat.

"I intend to make love to you again," Jake said as his mouth moved softly over hers. They were shoulder-deep in the water now, as her blue eyes fastened on his.

"Again?" she asked, then smiled faintly as she felt him growing hard inside her once more.

"Again," Jake whispered into her mouth as they began to move with each other once more, feeling the cool wetness that surrounded them and the hot wetness he built inside her.

"And again and again and again," he promised, placing feather-soft kisses against her mouth as his body filled hers.

Revel lay cocooned in the blankets. The sudden brush of cool air against her naked body roused her from sleep, as Jake moved away from her side. She was immediately alert.

"What is it?"

She couldn't see him, but she could feel the brief warmth of his fingers as he caressed her cheek, then the lingering heat of his mouth as he kissed her.

"I'm going out to have a look around. Stay here and take this."

The warmth of his fingers was replaced by the cold hard steel of the revolver he wrapped her hand about.

"Jake?" she whispered at the same time she grabbed for the blanket as it fell away from her breasts.

Her answer was the soft sigh of the breeze in the

treetops overhead, the soft lapping of water from the pool.

She was immediately on edge. She should be used to his nightly wanderings, but every time he did this, she was reminded that they weren't alone. Somewhere, out there, Sam Bass and his men made their camp.

How far away?

How close?

She quickly dressed, pulled on a warm jacket against the crisp night air, and sat down to wait, the revolver under her right hand.

Several times she thought she heard the snap of a twig underfoot. The horses roused, snorted at some trailing scent on the breeze, then calmed once more.

Her nerves grew taut.

How much time had passed? Minutes? One hour? Two?

She snugged the revolver inside the jacket. Her eyes ached from straining to see through the darkness. She made out the shape of the horses, the break in the tree line, the glimmer of faint moonlight on the water.

How long had she dozed?

Revel jerked awake. She heard something. Or had she only imagined it?

Her fingers closed over the handle of the revolver inside her jacket. Fear tingled along every nerve ending. Her throat went dry as all her senses strained. Jake had been gone too long.

She heard the faint rustle of a branch, the low nicker of one of the horses.

As she whirled around, a hand clamped firmly across her mouth.

The scream was smothered in her throat.

Terror and a mind-chilling fear gripped her.

"Revel! It's me!" Jake hissed against her cheek.

She twisted out of his grasp and whirled on him.

"I could have shot you!" she whispered angrily.

He held up his hands. In supplication or mock

surrender? She didn't know which.

"I didn't want to walk into camp and have you do just that. A gunshot would bring everyone on this mountain down on us." Then he added, "It seemed the thing to do. I'll have to be more careful next time."

His first words jarred through her fear—*everyone on this mountain.*

"Did you see someone?" she asked with amazing calm.

He said nothing, but rose and turned toward the water.

"Jake?" She grabbed his arm, and her fingers grazed a sticky wetness on his shirtsleeve.

It was then she smelled it—a slight muskiness mixed with the heavier, almost metallic scent of fresh blood that clogged into her throat and brought a slight nausea to her stomach.

Fear rose in her throat. "You're hurt!"

"I'm all right." He headed for the water.

He knelt at the bank and stripped off his shirt. In the soft glow of moonlight that streaked through the trees and across the water, she saw the dark shadow of blood staining his chest. But there was no wound. Then she realized . . . it wasn't his blood.

A cold shudder ran through her.

"What happened?"

"I found one of Bass's men."

It wasn't necessary for him to explain further. There had been no gunshot, and she knew Jake would have acted as quickly and quietly as possible.

She thought of the long-bladed knife he always carried, and shivered again. There was no possibility that the man had gotten away.

"Do you think he found our camp?"

"No. He was too far up the mountain, and this place is fairly secluded." He was silent for a moment before going on.

"My guess is Bass and the others have a camp not too far above. He was merely on a hunting trip; the game is better lower down."

"Then Bass hasn't reached the hideout yet."

She didn't disappoint him. He knew she'd draw the accurate conclusion.

He wished she hadn't, wished he hadn't told her the truth. But Revel was tenacious when she wanted something. If nothing else, he'd learned that about her.

He finished washing out his shirt, squeezed the last of the water from it, and slowly turned to face her.

"No, he hasn't reached it yet."

She was already on her feet and striding toward the horses. He knew exactly what she was thinking.

With a softly muttered curse, he sprang up and went after her.

He grabbed her arm just as she reached for the gelding's bridle. "Only a fool would set out after Bass in the dark." She jerked away from him.

"There're at least two hours before first light. We can cover a lot of distance in two hours."

Bass and his men had no reason to think they were being followed. They wouldn't set out before dawn.

She was right about the few hours of darkness left, and he knew it.

"No!"

She whirled on him. "What is that supposed to mean?"

"It means we'll set out at dawn, just as we have the last two days. We can cover a lot of distance in daylight, and it's too dangerous going after him in the dark. The terrain is too uneven. Your horse could take a wrong step and send you over the edge of a ravine."

Everything he said was logical. She knew that. She also noticed he said nothing about his own horse.

"You're familiar with the mountain," she pointed out, and then added, "That's why I brought you along. I'm not worried about accidents."

She jerked around and efficiently bridled the gelding. Then she reached for the saddle blanket.

His jaw clenched. So, it was down to that—*the reason*

she'd brought him along.

Jake cursed as he shoved her aside. Her words ate at him in ways he wouldn't have guessed.

As she turned on him in surprise, he hauled the saddle blanket from the back of the gelding.

"What are you doing?" she asked, her voice rising in anger.

"Emphasizing a point."

"Which is?" she spat out.'

"Something you just admitted, Miss Tyson." His eyes glittered in the pale moonlight. "I know these mountains—you don't! Without me, you won't find the hideout, and you won't get Bass! We do this my way, or you can just get that sweet little ass of yours down this mountain any way you can—and you can forget about Bass."

"You're forgetting about that pardon you want so badly!" she reminded him, her anger flaring out of control.

He turned on her, the hardened angles and planes of his face reflecting his own anger. "I can stay down here in Mexico till hell freezes over, and no one can touch me."

Her voice softened. "But you don't want to stay in Mexico."

Her words stopped him. She was right and they both knew it.

She took a deep breath as she ran her fingers back through the soft tangle of long hair that only a few hours earlier had been draped over his chest and shoulders as they'd made love. Now that passion had been replaced by the underlying passion that had set her on this deadly journey.

He saw her struggle for control, something very near regret and the shadow of a deep inner sadness in her eyes.

"We both need something, Jake," she said quietly. "With that pardon, you're a free man. The slate will be wiped clean. It'll mean a new life for you. You can go home. Don't you want that?"

He wanted it, with a longing that came from years of running from the law, the loneliness of nameless towns, and the emptiness of an hour or two with faceless whores.

His life had become a shadow, having neither light nor substance; always lived at the edge of darkness because that was safer for the man he had become.

If he couldn't go back, all the dreams he'd kept alive for so long would die. A man could live only so long on dreams. Eventually they began to fade into the shadows and nothing remained.

But there had been something more. In those brief hours they'd shared earlier, he had almost begun to feel alive again.

In that small space of time, he had forgotten the loneliness, the emptiness, and the blood. In those few hours, when they'd made love over and over, the sweetness of her body and the heat of her passion had assuaged all the pain, had brought light to the shadows.

Looking at her now, seeing that closed expression in her eyes, he knew whatever it was he thought he'd found with her had been just one more lie, one more shadow.

"I'll keep my part of the bargain," he said quietly. "I'll take you to Bass. But we do it my way. Is that understood?"

Slowly she nodded. "Understood."

His mouth thinned into a hard line. "And that means we ride at dawn. The horses need the rest—and so do I."

Her reply was a long time in coming.

"Agreed."

"And don't you go riding off by yourself," he added. "I don't want to have to comb this mountain just because you decided to go off alone." His voice was hard as he went on, "You'd get yourself killed, then neither of us will get what we want." He almost spat this out.

After several long moments, she nodded again. "All right. We do it your way."

They rode out at daybreak.

This time, Jake picked up a new trail. Revel guessed he'd discovered it when he'd found Bass's man the night before.

An icy chill hung over them and the mountain. It made the very air ache.

Revel knew it came from many things.

Part of it was the knowledge that Jake had killed a man. She knew his past, and had no illusions about it. But the fact that he was capable of taking a man's life so easily was made sharper, more dangerous, *more real* by knowing that somewhere out there in the wild a man lay dead.

This was not something she'd read about on a wanted poster or in an agency file—*he had killed a man*.

It made her blood run cold.

And, ahead of them, Sam Bass rode through the mist of early dawn. Hunting him down was no longer a purpose, an illusive desire for revenge.

It had become a reality, frightening in it's intensity because they might die.

Then there was what had begun between her and Jake almost the moment they met. It had come to a turning point during the night they'd just spent together.

In those few hours, she'd forgotten about her father's death, her obsession for revenge . . . Sam Bass.

For that short time, there had been only Jake and the feelings he'd brought to her.

But now that, too, lay cold inside her. The things they'd said to each other had seen to that. It seemed there was no escaping anger or words.

Nor was there any escaping the changing seasons that swept down on the mountain with a vengeance.

As if it could sense the cold inside them, the sky wrapped an icy blanket about them, making their warm breath steam in the chilly air. It was a warning that time was short, in so many ways.

They stopped briefly at midday, watered the horses, ate their cold meal, then continued up the mountain.

Jake climbed an invisible path etched into rock and

stone. They traced the rim of a high canyon wall, passed the mouth of a magnificent waterfall in which myriad rainbows glistened as sunlight played on the mist.

The cascade roared like a huge, thundering beast as it fell hundreds of feet into a deep mountain pool.

That night they made camp in the shelter of rocks. Protected from the wind that came up during the night, Revel still felt an aching cold that had nothing to do with the chill air, everything to do with the fact that Jake lay in his own blanket several feet away.

Somewhere in the middle of the night, she was aware that he left camp. She snuggled more tightly into her blankets, her fingers curled over the handle of the revolver.

She stirred sometime later. Something she sensed roused a distant memory.

It was subtle, a scent—a heavy, musky animal smell mingled with the odors of sweat, horses, and leather.

It seeped into her awareness, and she fought her way up from sleep. But it was too late.

A hard, callused hand clamped down brutally over her mouth and nose, smothering her startled cry. At the same time an arm clamped down just under her ribs.

She struggled, she fought. She clawed and scratched. But air was squeezed from her lungs, and the pressure continued at her nose and mouth.

A heaviness made her arms and legs useless. Even as she mentally commanded herself to grab the revolver, she felt it slip from limp fingers.

She couldn't breathe, she could no longer fight.

A gray coldness swept through her and closed around her senses.

Jake!

But it wasn't Jake!

Chapter Twenty-One

Jake Reno crouched low, weight back on one leg, forearms resting on bent knees.

He stared into the dawn.

The sun was an orange ball on the horizon, shrouded by bruised purple clouds over blue-black mountains.

Fingers of light stole across the tops of rocks and made rainbow prisms in ice crystals that hung heavy on tree branches.

They made shadows in the hollows of his face and below the hard line of his mouth.

They reflected off the blade of the knife he clutched in one hand, and the small gold crucifix that dangled from the other.

Revel had been wearing it. He'd found it in the rocks where he'd left her.

Jake slowly stood.

In the cold dawn, he resheathed the knife and dropped the crucifix into the pocket of his shirt.

He left Revel's saddle hidden in the rocks. Then he swung his own atop the gelding and cinched it. The saddlebags were tied behind.

With efficient fingers he rechecked the load in his rifle, the Colt at his left hip. Then he swung astride the gelding.

He found the trail in the cold hard-packed ground.

The air was cold, his breath a thin, white vapor as images out of the past froze in his mind. Another winter day, not unlike this one.

A fourteen-year-old boy stood in the middle of a field, dressed in a thin shirt and pants. He wore no hat, no coat, and his shirt was torn and soaked with blood that dripped from the wound on his head.

He stood weakly, propped over the handle of a shovel, the spade thrust into the hard-frozen earth. His breath came in short, painful bursts of steam as he thrust the shovel into the ground again. Again and again. Scraping out four graves.

It was bitter cold, and tears streamed down his face, blinding him, freezing on his cheeks. Weakened from the loss of blood, he closed the last grave. But still he refused to quit. He staggered across the ranch yard, past the barn that was nothing more than smoldering ash, to the burned-out shell of the ranch house.

Inside he found his father's Navy revolver that he was never allowed to touch. He shoved it into the belt holding up his pants.

All the horses except one had fled. His vision blurred by tears and blood, the boy pulled himself atop the spotted horse that remained.

He slowly turned the Appaloosa about. He rode south, turning his back on childhood and innocence.

His heart was as cold as the winter season that blew down out of the Wind River Mountains.

No matter how long it took, he would find the men who had murdered his family and taken Rachel. No matter how long it took.

"No matter how long," Jake repeated as he turned the gelding, heading higher on the mountain, trailing the Appaloosa behind.

He followed that single set of tracks until they disappeared in the snow that began to fall lightly.

After crisscrossing the trails that cut through the mountain he picked them up again. He had lost valuable time, but it was critical that he knew which trail Revel's captor took—critical that he be certain one of Bass's men had her.

That second day, snow covered the tracks. A half-dozen times he found them, only to lose them again. They traveled slowly, one horse burdened down by two riders, the sudden weather change, the grueling terrain.

Midafternoon of the third day, they were joined by another horseman, and the pace picked up. Jake drove the gelding hard, pushing him past his endurance, riding long after dark until the trail became too perilous.

His only consolation was that if he was forced to stop, they, too, must stop.

He ate little and never slept. He couldn't afford to have those same men come upon him as they had come upon Revel.

Fatigue and cold fury were a lethal combination. He alternately sharpened the blade of the knife he wore at his belt, and rechecked the load in the Colt.

Old fears eroded caution, ate at the fear that churned inside him. He wanted to keep going, ride right in and get her back.

Once, caution had extracted a high price.

But he knew these men. They were brave in numbers, ruthless at best, bloodthirsty at their worst. If he found them and rode into their camp, there was every possibility they would kill Revel without the least hesitation. It was a game—a deadly game. And Revel's life was the stake.

In quiet moments when he was forced to stop because of darkness and the horses, all the old questions ate at him.

Did they know who she was?

He doubted it. Revel was smart enough to realize that revealing she was a Pinkerton agent would mean her death. The Comancheros had taken particular delight in killing several agents in the past, including Revel's father.

Were they taking her to Bass?

Their trail headed steadily southwest into the deep

399

canyons of the high mountains—the general direction of the old hideout. If they cut directly south through the mountains, in the next day or two he would have his answer and know their exact destination.

The last question was the hardest.

Was she alive?

He had to believe that she was. The deeper imprint of one of the shod horses indicated it was carrying a heavier weight than the other—possibly that of two riders.

It was logical that they would keep her alive, at least for now. Any woman provided amusement and entertainment on the trail, if she wasn't too much trouble. But a beautiful woman was a prize, offered up to El Jefe, the leader of the Comancheros.

A bitter taste rose in Jake's mouth at the thought of Revel being taken to Sam Bass for his pleasure, but it meant that she hadn't yet been harmed or violated.

As a bitter wind came up on the mountain, he pulled his hat low over his face. He would let the horses rest for a couple of hours, then set out again. The last tracks he'd picked up had indicated the riders ahead of him were just as weary. He couldn't afford to let them get any farther ahead of him. *She* couldn't afford it.

Late in the morning the next day, Jake had halted beside a roaring creek. He walked slowly to the gelding. The animal trembled violently, its sides heaved, lather foamed across its neck and withers. It had been a hard climb up a steep grade all morning long. The gelding could go no further.

Jake removed his saddle and saddlebags and swung them atop the Appaloosa. Then he cut the gelding loose so it could find its way back down the mountain.

He led the Appaloosa on a traverse course across the mountain, following the tracks of two horses—one overburdened—both sliding badly in the loose shale on the steep grade.

Then he lost the tracks once more, but he knew where they led. Just past midday he found the mountain pass.

The trail picked up again at the other end. The tracks headed due south.

"*Puta!*" the Comancheros shouted, as Revel was dragged back from the edge of the stream.

It was difficult enough trying to drink with her hands bound in front of her. Her face was streaked with water. Now she lost her balance and fell to her knees, unable to break her fall.

Her hands hadn't been untied since she'd been taken captive. She imagined how she looked. Undoubtedly muddy. But she didn't care. The worse she looked, the greater the chance these two would leave her alone.

She managed to drink water by making a cup of her hands. But it was awkward and the Comancheros grew impatient with her. Now, water soaked her pants and shirt, and hair was plastered to her cheeks.

The rest of it hung in a tangled mass down her back. The wind blew it into her eyes, it fell into the water before her. She couldn't brush it, she couldn't even push it back. They were suspicious of her every move.

Puta.

She understood the word. It was Spanish for whore.

It was used to humiliate, to belittle her. But there was a greater implication—how they intended to use her when they reached their destination.

And what was their destination? Were these two of Bass's men?

She knew the direction they traveled—first southwest, then directly south—but she had no idea of the location of Bass's hideout.

Did Jake know she was gone?

That was foolish, the fatigue and pain must be getting to her. It had been three days. Of course, he knew she was gone.

Did he care? She had no idea.

Revel slowly stood. She gingerly moistened her

bruised bottom lip as she met her captors' gazes, loathing in her glare. The pain was a reminder that she was still alive. She clung to it.

Would he come after her?

As she staggered, weak from hunger and fatigue, she almost laughed at the notion.

The answer was simple—no.

Why should he help her?

He'd made it clear from the first that he wanted no part of Bass, the Comancheros, or her.

The openhanded blow drove her to her knees. Her cheek burned and her head throbbed from it, but she threw back her head and glared defiantly at her captor.

He took her by the arm and led her through the soft mud from the newly melted snow to the horses. He practically threw her atop the horse, then swung up behind her.

He was slightly built, unlike his companion, so a horse could more easily carry the two of them. His clothes were dirty and he had black hair, and, except for the growth of beard since he'd captured her, he was clean-shaven. He was young, perhaps younger than she was.

She silently named him "the boy."

His companion was dark-skinned and filthy. It was difficult to tell whether he was Spanish or Indian. It was enough to know he was a Comanchero.

His long black hair was unkempt and hung about his shoulders in greasy clumps. A heavy beard covered most of his face, but his eyes were cold, emotionless, and black as death.

In Revel's mind he was *ojos negros*—"black eyes."

Giving them both nicknames helped her focus her bruised thoughts. Were they Bass's men? Was Sam Bass the one they referred to as El Jefe—the chief?

It made sense. The man who had attacked Teresa was called El Jefe.

She clung to the saddle horn as the horse lunged across the stream. They set a grueling pace, traveling all day and

402

most of the night. She was certain no one could keep up with them.

Not even Jake Reno.

Jake knelt in the slush and mud created by the slowly melting snow. There had been sun most of the morning, but even now clouds built overhead. There would be more snow before nightfall.

He removed his gloves, tracing the print in the mud with his bare fingers.

It was well formed, although snow would cover it by morning. It was made by a soft-soled boot without a heel, and it was small, not much bigger than . . . a child's.

The small perfect boot print altered in his memory and became the outline of a slender, bare foot.

He'd been riding for hours, but here the dirt was soft, his horse's hooves leaving tracks beside those small, perfect ones.

Jake swung out of the saddle, wincing against the pain that throbbed in his head.

He should have gone for the sheriff, but the sheriff was at least a two days' ride away from the ranch. By the time a posse could get on the trail, the men who'd killed his parents and brothers would be hundreds of miles away.

No, he'd been right to come after them himself. He drew a strange comfort from having his father's Navy Colt in his belt as he crouched down to look at the tracks.

They were small, slender, and were made by bare feet.

That meant that Rachel was alive.

Jake swung back into the saddle. Now he knew for certain they were headed to the old hideout. Revel was with them, and at least for the time being she was alive.

He pushed the Appaloosa as hard as he could, but the trail through the canyon was rugged. By nightfall he was forced to rest the stallion or risk losing him. Without the Appaloosa he had no chance of getting to Revel.

He rested, but didn't sleep. If he slept, he dreamed, and he didn't want to face the ghosts of the past.

403

He had no appetite for a hot meal, though he built a small fire in the shelter of some rocks where it wouldn't be seen. Instead he ate hardtack and stale bread, and washed them down with water. Then he sat before the fire, cursing every minute and hour that he was forced to delay.

His eyes stung from the smoke and from bone-wearying fatigue. Fear and that old familiar pain ate at him, along with the impotent fury that had driven him for over half his life—driven him to kill seven men.

He'd thought he was through with that when Charlie Trask died. And as far as Rachel was concerned, he was. He had his revenge.

But now, he saw it happening all over again. And the image of Rachel's sweet face loomed in his memory.

Too late—he'd been too late to save her from rape and a brutal death.

He couldn't let that happen now—he couldn't lose Revel.

The cold steel of the rifle was reassuring beneath his hand.

At dawn, he continued on and discovered the Comancheros had also stopped to rest. They had pushed their horses almost to the limit, alternately carrying a double weight, but they were smart enough to realize, as he did, that without horses they had no chance of surviving in these mountains, much less of reaching the hideout.

He found their abandoned camp in an old cliff dwelling just after midday. The remains of their campfire were still warm. That meant he was only a few hours behind them.

Revel was exhausted. It had been four days since her abduction by the Comancheros. In the interchange of conversation—part Spanish, part English—she'd picked up one thing, the name of Sam Bass.

These *were* Bass's men, and they were on their way to the hideout Jake had spoken of.

After all this time she would finally come face to face with the man who murdered her father—as a prize to be used as Teresa had been used. And then what would her fate be?

She had refused to confront it, had been unwilling to accept that it would end this way. But anger, bitterness, and fear twisted deep inside her as she faced the reality that she would end up dead at Sam Bass's hand just like her father.

She had told Jake countless times that was a possibility, but she hadn't *really* thought it possible. The hatred had been too strong, the desire for revenge too deep. And now, as she glared back at her captors, she still refused to accept that she would die this way.

They had stopped at the summit of the gorge. They had been climbing for most of the morning since leaving the abandoned cliff dwelling where they made camp the night before.

Revel had constantly watched the gorge below them as they had climbed, hoping against hope that Jake might have followed. She had seen nothing. And it took a great effort to smother the feelings of despair that threatened to overwhelm her.

She had no reason—or right—to think he would come after her, or even care that she was gone. But every time she forced herself to face that harsh reality, another reality seeped back into her fragmented thoughts—the reality of that night on the desert when they had first made love, the ride back from the meadow when he'd made love to her with his mouth and hands, and that night at the mountain pool when he'd made love to her over and over.

Oh, God, Revel thought. How can I think it meant anything. It was just something that happened and is now forgotten.

Except she couldn't forget. She knew the ways a man

405

and woman came together. For some, there was passion. And for others, like Teresa, it was a violent act that left hidden wounds which became hidden scars and never went away.

Her hands shook as she accepted the canteen of water that was offered. She kept her eyes downcast.

So far neither man had touched her, other than to shove her around or drag her off the back of the horse. But it was always possible that one of them would take it into his head to do more.

From the very first she'd realized what she must do. Her hair had become tangled and matted from dirt, the wet snow, and blowing loose in the wind.

She made no attempt to untangle it or brush it back from her face. Nor did she make any other effort with her appearance.

She had seen her reflection in a frosty pool of water just that morning. Dirt was smudged across her face—she had added to the effect by getting mud on her neck and clothing. Even when it became warm in the afternoon as they climbed the mountain, she did not ask to have her hands untied so she might take off the heavy buckskin coat she'd worn since the night she was abducted.

It was thick, oversized, and hung misshapen on her slender frame. She did nothing to change the illusion it created, nothing to draw attention to herself.

She drank water sparingly, taking only what she needed to wet her mouth and throat. Moments of privacy were nonexistent. When they were absolutely necessary, she was tied to the end of a short rope and allowed to go into the brush. But she constantly feared that one of the men might follow her. That was why she drank as little as possible and made few trips into the brush.

She thought many times of leaving some kind of marker at intervals along the way, just in case Jake did come after her, but she dismissed the idea. She was too closely watched, and there was nothing she could leave behind.

Now the one she had nicknamed Black Eyes grunted at his younger companion that they should be on their way.

Revel had learned not to provoke him. He was an impatient, surly man with a volatile temper. He became violent at the slightest provocation.

When she moved a little too slowly, he lunged at her. He spat several curses at her in Spanish, and shoved her toward the horses. She got away from him and scampered in the direction of their mounts.

He followed and grabbed hold of her hair, jerking her around.

Revel cried out, her hands going to her hair. As she raised them, the front of the jacket gaped open.

Her captor shouted something unintelligible at her as he seized her by the front of her shirt, the fabric tearing as he pulled her toward the horses.

Revel gasped as chill air hit her bare skin, and she desperately tried to cover her exposed breasts.

With sickening awareness she saw the abrupt change in her captor's look—brutal anger had been replaced by brutal lust. His eyes glistened as he came at her and tore away the rest of her shirt front. Revel tried to get away from him, and fell to the ground.

"Compadre!" his companion shouted to him. "El Jefe will not be pleased if you abuse the girl. You know he likes to be the first. He will be displeased if you touch her."

Black Eyes hesitated as he seemed to give consideration to what his companion said. His barrel chest heaved, his breath hissing out between stained teeth as he stared at his friend.

Revel frantically pulled the remnants of her shirt together, then reached up to close the front of the coat. Her hands froze at the buttons.

Only inches away from her right foot, a long knife lay

407

in the mud, it's blade gleaming dully.

Black Eyes must have dropped it as they struggled.

His back was toward her as he faced the other Comanchero. She swallowed hard, her gaze fastened on the knife.

"She is only a whore!" he argued with his companion. "A whore is for the taking."

"Not before El Jefe has seen her," the other reminded him.

The conversation was the usual mixture of English and Spanish, most of which Revel understood. She learned that they thought she was alone. They didn't know about Jake. She also found out that she was being taken to Bass for his own use.

"Bueno," her attacker spat out disgustedly as he threw the torn remnant of her shirt into the mud.

"I will not touch her now. But when he is through with her, then it is my turn." He still held her hair with one hand, and he twisted it, pulling her head back so hard the muscles in her neck cramped.

He leaned over her, his breath hot and sour.

"We will have our time, *señorita*. Make no mistake about it. When El Jefe is through, you are mine." He shoved her away from him, and snarled at his companion that they should be on their way.

As the two men gathered their canteens and weapons, they both momentarily turned away from her. Revel scrambled for the knife, and quickly thrust it down into her left boot.

When the Comancheros returned to the horses she was already astride and gave the appearance of meekly waiting for them. Once more she kept her head bowed and her eyes averted.

Now she had a weapon. And, God help her, she would use it.

The tracks that rose from the bottom of the gorge

disappeared among the rocks.

Jake doubled back a half-dozen times, wasting precious time, as he searched for the trail to pick up again.

He finally found it along the ridge.

They had evidently stopped here. The tracks all ran together, and it was impossible to make out whether one of them was the lighter, smaller impression made by Revel's soft leather boots.

It was also impossible to determine how long they'd passed this way. One hour? Three? Or more?

He'd lost valuable time doubling back to find the trail, and it ate at him.

Then he saw it, the soft fluttering of fabric as the late afternoon wind came up along the ridge and caught it.

Jake picked it up, twining it in his fingers.

It was a long strip of plaid fabric, the kind found in a man's shirt. But the plaid was distinctive, and he recognized it as he stared at the black and red square pattern.

An old pain knifed through him, and time slipped away. His vision blurred, from the wind or the pain remembering brought. Now the fabric that fluttered at his fingertips, was a pale pink gingham.

He'd been following those men for four days. He found the fabric. It was part of Rachel's dress—the dress she wore the day those men rode onto the ranch. Then he found Rachel.

She was laying on her side, much like he'd seen her countless times in bed at home when she'd pretended to be asleep. Only now she didn't move when he called her name.

She didn't answer, she didn't stir at all.

He knew she was dead even before he turned her over, her skin cold and lifeless beneath his fingers.

Her pale blond hair was tangled and matted. Her face was bruised and bloodied. But the bruises didn't end there. She had been badly abused, in ways that made Jake retch violently.

Then he cried. He cried with the pain of loss, of anger. He cried with impotent rage for what the men had done to his parents, his brothers, and . . . Rachel.

And then he wrapped his sister in his shirt and took her home, the hem of her bloodstained gingham dress fluttering against his hands as he held her.

Jake's face was stark as he looked into the setting sun. His features were gaunt from relentless tracking, too little sleep, and too many memories. But his eyes burned with a predatory hunger.

Once, a long time ago, other men had taken from him. He'd hunted them down one by one and killed them. But he'd been too late to save Rachel.

The setting sun pierced his cold green eyes as he swung astride the Appaloosa and took up the relentless pace. The plaid fabric of Revel's shirt was wound around his hand as he clutched the reins.

She made him angry, she made him laugh. For a small place in time, she made him feel alive again.

He'd lived with death too long. He wouldn't rest until he found her.

Revel was slumped forward in the saddle of the Comanchero she called Black Eyes.

They had been riding since early dawn.

Now, as their pace slowed, she looked up through a matted tangle of disheveled hair. Another mountain rose before them, all jagged peak and hard granite.

A bone-chilling weariness ached through her.

How much farther?

This peak looked impossible to climb. At certain points it loomed over them, almost completely vertical.

She expected Black Eyes to rein in the weary horse, and send his young *compadre* on ahead to scout out an accessible route. But he pressed on, cutting a circuitous path east around huge boulders and granite slag.

The wind blew at their backs, the clouds ominous overhead. It would snow before nightfall. That reality only added to Revel's misery.

She had harbored the small hope that Jake might follow them. But the route Black Eyes followed couldn't even be called a trail. And the snow that had fallen intermittently throughout the past days would obliterate any tracks the horses left.

As her hopes of rescue slowly faded, Revel tried memorizing distinctive landmarks or unusual formations of rock they passed.

After this much time on horseback, she doubted they were headed for Bass's hideout. That meant when they eventually did reach wherever it was they were going, she knew what her fate would be.

The knife was still snugged inside the leg of her boot. When an opportunity presented itself, she would escape.

Her hand closed over the pommel of the large Mexican saddle as the horse shifted unexpectedly beneath them. Black Eyes' arm snaked around her waist with the pretense of steadying her.

Revel glared at him over her shoulder and pushed his hand away from her. She might have been swatting at a bothersome fly that always returned . . . until it was killed.

Her disgust and anger made him laugh.

"Save you spirit, *señorita*. You will have need of it when you meet El Jefe." His sour breath seared her cheek and she tried to pull as far away from him as possible.

"You will meet soon enough," he predicted.

Instead of continuing east, he cut the horse sharply around a huge cluster of boulders, carefully guiding it between the two largest ones. They were forced to duck their heads as they passed through.

Revel stared in amazement at the small valley spread out before them. They had passed through that small opening in the rocks as if passing through a doorway.

As soon as they emerged on the other side, she heard the distinct sounds of a rider approaching.

Her head snapped up, and her gaze fastened on a young man with lean features and sandy brown hair.

411

"*Eh, compadres!* It's about time you got here!" he shouted in greeting.

He looked familiar to her—the square chin, the high forehead, and the hard eyes that were an unsettling pale color, neither blue nor gray, but cold like shards of ice. The hollowness of his sunken cheeks was emphasized by the slant of prominent cheekbones and the slash of the scar that ran from his eye to his jaw.

Revel looked up into the eyes of a cold-blooded murderer who had never felt remorse for the men, women, or children he'd left dead, a man whose reputation for killing was matched only by his reputation for brutality . . . Sam Bass.

Chapter Twenty-Two

Revel was dragged from the saddle and shoved to the floor inside a crudely built, one-room cabin.

The dirt floor was hard and cold. There were places where she could see fading daylight through gaps in the log walls where mud caulking had dried and crumbled.

The single window was covered with a rawhide skin. The door was sturdily built. But the crossbar to prevent anyone from entering had been removed.

Heat for the small cabin came from a stone fireplace, but it waged a losing battle with the wind that seeped through the gaping cracks in the walls.

A long table stood in the middle of the cabin. Dried food was crusted on the metal plates that littered it, and scraps lay about on the floor. Several bedrolls rested against the far wall, and a pile of animal skins filled one corner, a pile of blankets another.

The stench of rotting food, stale hides, and woodsmoke pervaded the air, along with bone-chilling cold. All washed over Revel and only added to her misery.

She felt as dirty as the cabin looked. Worse, as she looked at those hides, she could feel her skin crawl at the thought of the bugs infesting them.

She was stiff and sore from riding nonstop for five days. Her cheek was badly bruised if pain was any indication of its appearance. And her situation was bleak.

Only God knew where she was, let alone whether she could escape and find her way back through the mountains. And winter was fast closing in.

It had snowed as they'd ridden deeper into the mountains, and although it had stopped, the air carried that familiar cold bite she'd come to know while living in Denver. There would be more snow, and none of them could get out.

And there was Sam Bass.

With her fingers, she traced the reassuring hardness of the knife through the soft leather of her boot.

He was the reason she'd come to these mountains and risked so much. She wouldn't leave until she accomplished what she'd come for.

She gnawed at the taut strip of leather that bound her wrists. Above all, she had to stay in control, she mustn't let her situation overwhelm her. Instead, as she furiously worked at the leather binding her wrists, she evaluated her situation.

As they'd ridden into the tiny valley, she had counted seven men, including Bass and the two Comancheros who'd brought her here. She had spotted two in the rocks above, rifles cradled in their arms as they watched the entrance to the valley.

Another had ridden out with Bass, on his way up to relieve one of the spotters. The last one was an Indian, perhaps an Apache. He'd taken their horses when they arrived.

She was acutely aware that she was the only woman, and she knew that sooner or later those men would want their turn at her.

By the supplies of food, and the stack of wood she'd seen at the back of the cabin before being thrust inside, they planned to stay a while. But how long that might be she couldn't guess.

Futile as it might seem at the moment, Revel's plan was to get a weapon, get to Bass, and get out of there. Not a difficult task if she'd had the cavalry with her, the posse

414

that had followed them from New Mexico territory, or Jake Reno.

But she was on her own.

She'd wanted Bass, no matter what it took to find him.

"Well, I certainly found him," she muttered to herself as she looked about the cabin. It occurred to her that deception was the only thing that could work in her favor.

For all the Comancheros knew she was some helpless woman they'd abducted, as they had done many times. The fact that she wasn't might work in her favor. It could also work against her if they discovered the truth.

Her thoughts raced as she moved about the cabin, taking careful inventory. It was too much to hope there might be a gun somewhere.

She was right. There were no weapons, but she found a few other things she might use.

Although she hadn't been able to untie the bonds at her wrists, she had loosened them. The trick, of course, was to keep that a secret for as long as possible. But now, she had a certain amount of leeway.

She quickly stuffed a metal fork inside a boot and hid a small pouch of what appeared to be cayenne pepper inside her jacket. She also found matches, some string, and a box of shells left open on the table. She took several, also slipping them inside her boots.

If they searched her, she was dead.

Her head came up in alarm when she heard conversation just outside the door, and she scurried back to her place by the hearth.

The exchange, muted at first, soon punctuated by angry words—spoken in Spanish. She recognized Sam Bass's voice and Black Eyes heated response.

"*Estúpido!*" Bass shouted at the Comanchero, and he continued in Spanish. "Why did you bring her here?"

"I thought she might be interesting entertainment. It has been a long time since some of the men had a woman. And she's not bad looking."

"You fool! Did you think she was just wandering around by herself out there?"

"I told you," Black Eyes responded, "there was no one else. She was alone."

"Without a horse?" Bass flung back at him.

"There were two horses, but she was the only one there. She put up a struggle, and I didn't want to bring an angry husband down on us. It was probably some fur trapper."

"Imbecile!" Bass spat back at him. "Does she look like a fur trapper's woman?"

There was a moment of silence, and Revel found herself straining to hear Black Eyes' reply.

"Who else would be up in these mountains this time of year? It wasn't a posse. No posse would travel with a woman."

Bass grunted some vague reply, then asked, "What about the horses? We need fresh mounts. Now someone will have to ride double with the damned woman."

"I told you," Black Eyes reminded him in a babble of apologetic Spanish, "there was no time to take the spotted horse."

"*Qué es esto?*" Bass's voice suddenly changed to a low whisper that Revel could barely hear through the thick door even as she moved closer.

"What are you talking about? What spotted horse?"

"There were two horses," Black Eyes explained, and Revel could almost see him shrug stupidly.

"Sancho watched them while I took the woman. One of the horses was smoky gray and white with small black spots across the rump."

"You're certain?" Bass's tone changed from anger to cool speculation.

"*Sí*, the spotted horse. I remember because I have not seen many of them."

"There aren't many of them," Bass admitted. Then he went on to explain, "The spotted horse is the pride of the Sioux Indians. There are only two ways a man comes by a

416

horse like that—killing for it or receiving it as a special gift from a Sioux war chief."

Revel decided perhaps he wasn't quite as stupid as he looked. "You know a man who has such a horse?" Black Eyes asked.

There was a moment of silence that sent fear tingling down her spine. She slowly backed away from the door. Bass's voice followed her.

"Yeah, I knew such a man. But it was a while back."

Revel listened hard for Black Eyes' next question and Bass's reply, but the heavy wood door was thrown back hard and a cold wind swirled into the cabin along with Sam Bass. Black Eyes stood like a menacing shadow behind him.

Revel stood at the hearth, holding the loose end of her bonds taut between clasped hands. She couldn't afford to have them find out she had loosened them.

Bass slowly walked toward her.

Everything she knew about this man was etched in his hard features—ruthlessness, coldness, cruelty.

This was the man who'd killed her father, then escaped.

She didn't flinch or step back, didn't cower or look away, though it took all her will to stand still.

She forced herself to meet his gaze squarely, steadily, with a look that betrayed none of the fear that clawed it's way into her tight throat.

Implicitly she understood that Sam Bass had little regard for cowardice or weakness of any kind. If a man like him had regard for any human quality, it was strength.

For long moments he simply stood there looking at her, as if he could see the answers to his questions in her unwavering stare. The minutes dragged out, drawing the tension taut as a bowstring, until the very air about them seemed to quiver with anticipation.

Still, Revel refused to look away or betray, by even the smallest gesture, the fear that churned in her.

When Bass spoke at last, his voice was just as she'd imagined it—low, dangerous, like the hiss of a snake.

"What are you doing up in these mountains? *Who are you?*"

Three simple words, yet the answer to them could spare her for a few hours or immediately seal her fate. With a man like Bass, it would all end the same.

Would a lie help? Did she dare tell him the truth?

In the end she chose half-truths.

"I have friends in the valley. They raise horses there."

"Horses?" Bass repeated speculatively as he slowly reached out to touch her jacket where it closed at her neck.

"What kind of horses?"

Revel knew he was curious about the Appaloosa. Had Jake ridden an Appaloosa when he was with Bass years earlier? ·

"They raise Appaloosa."

"I know of a man who used to ride such a horse. But that was a long time ago, and he's dead now," Bass said, a trace of a question in his voice. "There were two horses when my friend took you. Who rode with you?"

"A vaquero from the rancho," Revel answered carefully. "We were looking for strays."

His pale eyes narrowed. "Appaloosa strays, high in the mountains." His tone suggested he thought it unlikely as his fingers brushed the front of her coat, stopping at the top button.

Revel mentally cringed from his touch. It was all she could do not to show any of the loathing she felt.

"I don't think so," Bass said suspiciously. "You're anglo. Not many anglo women come to Mexico, and none come into these mountains."

"I've told you," she insisted, "I was with friends." And then she said something that was more truth than lie. "My father was killed some time ago, and I came here"—she hesitated—"to put the pain of his death behind me."

No sooner had she said it than his fingers closed over the front of her jacket and he jerked her toward him.

"I think you're lying!" he hissed.

Hatred, more powerful even than fear, exploded in her veins. If she could have reached the knife at that moment she would have stabbed him with it and felt nothing more than if she'd killed a crazed animal.

Which was what he was. He scavenged, he killed, he destroyed. Mercilessly, without regret, without any shred of remorse or trace of human decency. So he deserved to die.

"I told you, we were looking for horses," she repeated, startled by the sound of her own voice. It was emotionless, as cold as the air that whipped through the open door of the cabin.

"*Jefe!*" the urgent cry came from outside. The Comanchero who'd ridden out with Bass to meet them ran into the cabin.

"What is it?" Bass snapped, his cold eyes never leaving hers.

"Joaquín's horse!" It was shouted in Spanish, but Revel understood.

Bass's gaze cut from hers angrily.

"What the hell are you talking about?"

"His horse!" The alarmed explanation, once more in Spanish. "It came back alone. Joaquín is gone!"

Bass's gaze snapped back to Revel's, and those cold eyes were like slivers of ice as he stared at her, trying to see more, trying to understand something that made him uneasy. But she returned his stare, hiding her hatred and loathing.

He shoved her away from him, and she fell to the dirt floor.

"This isn't finished between us," he warned. "I have a lot more questions, and you'd better have the answers." Then he whirled around and yelled to the Comanchero and Black Eyes in a furious mixture of expletives and orders.

419

Revel scrambled to her feet and followed them. She caught a brief glimpse of the riderless horse. It was badly lathered and trembled violently, and it was dangerously skittish, lunging away from the men who surrounded it.

Then she saw the red stain that streaked the saddle and the horse's withers—blood.

Before she could see more, the door was slammed in her face, and she heard the distinct sound of a heavy crossbar being dropped into place.

She was locked inside the cabin.

Revel furiously worked at the leather thong binding her wrists. It loosened once more, and she pulled it off with her teeth. Something was wrong, very wrong.

What had happened to the man they called Joaquín?

Once her hands were free, Revel made an even more careful inspection of the cabin. She needed a way out, but as she'd discovered earlier, there was only the window, thick rawhide nailed over it, and the door, now barred. She immediately ruled out the door. That left the window as the only possibility. She could easily cut her way out, but to do so in daylight was worse than dangerous, it was foolish.

The loud shouting and cursing outside ceased, and Revel whirled around just as the door opened. The young man, Sancho, came into the cabin.

His arms were laden with firewood. He glanced at her unbound wrists, but said nothing.

"El Jefe wants you to build a fire and prepare the meal. There is food." He gestured to the cloth sacks and saddlebags piled in the corner.

"Is that right? Well, El Jefe can go jump off a cliff before I'll lift a finger to do anything for him!" Revel retorted, her tone bringing the boy's gaze up to hers in alarm. He crossed the cabin.

"*Silencio!*" he hissed as he reached out for her.

Revel recoiled instinctively from the anticipated blow that never came. Instead he seized her wrists.

She thought he meant to bind them again, and she tried to jerk away.

"*Alto!*—Stop! Do not risk your life unnecessarily, *señorita.*"

"What do you care?" she flung back at him in English not willing to betray that she understood everything they said among themselves. "You brought me here."

"*Sí, es verdad.* That is true, but it was Manuel who took you from the tall man who rides the Appaloosa."

Revel went very still. "What are you talking about?"

He gave her a long look, then shrugged. He obviously felt it made no difference if he told her.

"I saw the man who rode with you. He is not from one of the ranchos, yet he rides the spotted horse. I have heard stories."

"What stories?"

He looked down at her wrists. In a gesture of kindness he rubbed the welts the leather bonds had made.

"I will tell El Jefe you will prepare the evening meal. You must cooperate if you want to live."

Revel almost laughed out loud. "We both know what he intends to do with me." But she wanted more, she wanted answers.

"What stories have you heard?"

Sancho glanced nervously to the door, as if he expected Bass to come through it at any moment—or perhaps someone else. He obviously thought he had already said too much. He shook his head and turned to leave.

On the grueling ride to this place, he was the one who had shown her some compassion.

He gave her water. *He* persuaded Black Eyes to let him stand guard over her when she needed privacy, and then let out the rope that became her tether a little further to make certain she had that privacy.

And more often, *he* was the one who rode with her, surprising her with his concern, and secretly whispering

421

encouragement to her.

Now, Revel grabbed at his arm, drawing on that compassion. "What is so special about this man?"

Sancho turned back and said quietly. "He is the only man El Jefe has ever spoken of in that way."

"What way?"

"With fear," Sancho answered simply. Then he added. "It was a long time ago, but the man El Jefe feared rode a spotted horse. And he knew of this place."

Jake.

It was impossible, yet she wanted desperately to believe it.

Time. It came back to that.

If Jake was out there, he was alone against seven—no six—men.

She shuddered as she thought of the horse that had returned covered with blood. If Jake was responsible, and she still had no way of knowing that, the killing reminded her of the man who had been sentenced to hang in Tombstone.

Outlaw . . . bank robber . . . train robber . . . murderer. Dozens of crimes. He was rumored to be guilty of all of them. Because he once rode with men like Bass, he had a reputation as a cold-blooded gunfighter, but the men he'd killed were all outlaws, the same men who raped and killed Rachel, the men he had methodically tracked down.

No one could prove any of the other charges against him.

Who was she to find fault with him when revenge was what had brought her here?

"Will you cooperate, *señorita?*" Sancho pleaded. She looked up at him. If Jake was out there, her cooperation would buy him some time.

She needed to believe he was out there. It was her only chance of getting out alive.

Of course it was possible that Sancho was wrong. Something else might have happened to Joaquín.

422

But who else was out there besides the Comancheros and Jake?

"I'm not a very *good* cook," she confessed.

Sancho smiled, and for the first time Revel saw how very young he was.

"*Está bien, señorita.* That is all right. These are not *good* men."

She smiled at his remark. "I'll give it a try."

He nodded as he went to the door. Then he hesitated. "Do not make El Jefe angry. He is a cruel man." He went out and slammed the door behind him.

Revel was brought water, which she put in the huge kettle over the fire she built at the hearth. She found tortillas, dried beef, beans, and canned fruit.

The water was soon simmering. Thank God, she thought, for the help I gave Rosa back at the rancho.

She soon had tortillas steaming in a covered pan, and a mixture of beef and beans simmered in another pot. She added some of the cayenne pepper she'd found, along with salt and some crushed herbs, though she had no idea what they might be.

Then she went to the door and listened. She heard the sounds of horses and riders, but they came from some distance away. She rattled the latch at the door. When there was no immediate response or curse shouted at her, she concluded that Bass considered her safely imprisoned and hadn't put one of his men outside.

Still, she watched the door and listened for any intrusion as she sat before the stone hearth and carefully bathed. She washed as much of her body as she could reach without fully undressing. She even managed to work the fork she had found through the tangles in her hair. It was a crude comb, but at least the effort made her feel better. And it was amazing how good the hot water felt.

If she lived through this, she swore she was going to soak for a week in a tub of soap and water. But at the moment it was wisest not to draw attention to herself.

423

She buttoned her shirt and then put her jacket back on, even though it was warm inside the cabin. She would die before she would remove it again. It gave her a lumpy appearance, which for the time being was her only defense against these men.

She put the food, such as it was, on the table, and hoped they choked on it. Then she retreated to the far corner of the cabin as Sancho led the other men in for the evening meal.

There were three of them. Bass came in a short while later. That meant two of the men were still out in the surrounding mountains, looking for Joaquín.

Revel crouched down on her heels, arms wrapped about her knees. She tried to make herself as inconspicuous as possible.

Outside, it was dark and the wind had come up. As the door to the cabin was slammed shut behind Bass, a blast of icy air gusted to the hearth, sending cinders and ash swirling about the cabin.

The cold air cut through everyone in the room. It carried the sharp bite of snow and the even sharper bite of something dangerous.

After supper, the men began drinking, and Revel's fear sharpened. Sober they were dangerous, drunk they would be animals.

Sancho seemed to sense her apprehension. He glanced at her several times, then quickly looked away. When one of the men called out for her to put more wood on the fire, it was Sancho who quickly stood and built the blaze back up.

When a joke was made about "doing women's work," he simply shrugged and went back to the table.

He was offered more tequila, but Revel noticed that when he drank from the bottle it always seemed as full as when it had been handed to him. He passed the liquor on with a good-natured remark.

The men all drank from the bottle. When it was empty another was brought out. The fire burned low again, was rebuilt, and roared back to life as they drank through the night.

They were loud, laughing at jokes told in Spanish and English. But all too quickly the laughter turned boastful, then belligerent as the Apache unsheathed his knife and made some guttural challenge to Black Eyes.

The table was shoved back under the window at the far wall, and as the distance to the other side was paced off, other knives were brought out. It was apparent a contest had begun.

Revel was only able to make out part of what they said as they roared challenges back and forth.

The Apache gleamed with sweat brought on by the warm fire and the tequila as he grunted and stepped forward to take his turn.

Like the others he'd had a great deal to drink, and he staggered, off balance, drawing a roar of laughter from the others. The look in his eyes was dangerous as he spat at them. Black Eyes immediately seized his own knife and lunged toward the Indian.

Sam Bass stepped between them. With a few words, he calmed them down. They would settle their differences by throwing knives at the wall, not each other.

As the contest began, Sancho slowly moved toward Revel.

It was soon apparent that Black Eyes and the Apache, although roaring drunk, were fairly evenly matched.

The air was filled with the sharp *thwang* of a steel knife being thrown, then the dull thud as the tip embedded in the log wall.

"Be careful that you say nothing to anger any of them," Sancho warned under his breath. "It could be dangerous for you."

Revel looked up in surprise at the steadiness of his voice and met his even steadier gaze. He wasn't the least drunk. Anger simmered in her.

"You're the one who kept giving them tequila," she hissed, careful that no one saw their conversation. She caught his brief smile.

"And I plan to give them even more. If they drink until they pass out, they cannot harm you."

"And I suppose I should be grateful for that?" Her anger was evident.

"Perhaps." He nodded. "You are the prize for the winner of the contest."

She felt her skin go cold, but her fingers traced the reassuring edge of the knife inside her boot. She would kill anyone who came near her, and then she would kill Sam Bass.

"Why do you care what happens to me?" she asked, partly in fear, mostly in anger.

Sancho crouched low several feet in front of her, with his back toward her.

If any of the others glanced their way, it would seem that he had merely found an out-of-the-way place from which to watch the contest. He spoke carefully, whispering to her in low tones, his lips barely moving.

The muscles in his young face tightened as he appeared to watch his *compadres*.

"I am weary, *señorita*," he said softly. "Weary of the burning, the looting, the killing.

"And I am weary of the blood on my hands that I can never wash away.

"I want to go home."

She had no idea where his home might be, but she understood what he was saying.

He didn't have to be kind to her. He could simply treat her the same way Bass and the others did.

But he hadn't. And she believed him.

He was so young, seventeen maybe eighteen years old at the most. But more years were etched into his face.

He had seen and done things that would remain with him for the rest of his life. And now he simply wanted out.

But they both knew there was only one man who had ever ridden away from Sam Bass and lived to tell of it.

426

She wanted to reach out and touch him, to offer some comfort, but to do so would have risked both their lives. So she simply offered him the only comfort she could.

"*Yo comprendo, mi amigo.* I understand," she said softly.

His head came up slightly as she responded in his native language. Then he frowned.

"Who are you, *señorita?*"

"You wouldn't believe me if I told you."

He turned to her briefly, his dark brown eyes searching her face. His look was long and penetrating.

"I think I would."

She smiled slightly, knowing she could trust him.

"I'm a Pinkerton agent." Her smile faded. Her eyes were cold as they met his. "I'm here to get Sam Bass."

Chapter Twenty-Three

It was late. Black Eyes and the Apache were beginning to weary of their game.

Sancho continued to provide them with a constant supply of tequila, and their speech was now slurred as they hurled taunts and curses at one another.

Sam Bass left the cabin several times. Each time he returned his expression was darker, his mood more dangerous. He shoved Sancho aside when he was offered the tequila, knocking the bottle to the dirt floor.

That immediately brought a howl of complaint from Black Eyes. He had become surly and unpredictable as the game continued. Now he wanted it to end. He whirled on the Apache who stood beside him, making a slashing motion with his knife and barely missing the Indian.

"The game is over, *compadre!*" He snarled making *compadre* sound like an insult. Though these men rode together, it was clear there was no bond of friendship between them. They would just as soon use their knives on each other as throw them at the wall.

"I win!" Black Eyes declared as he hurled the knife one last time, then staggered on his feet.

He crossed the cabin, removed his knife from the wall, and shoved it back into the leather sheath at his ample waist. Then he turned and looked to the far corner where Revel had taken refuge in the shadows.

He drew the back of his arm across his wet mouth, as if his appetite had been whetted.

"The *señorita* is mine!" he announced loudly.

Bass was the one who enforced the crude code of rules these men lived by. He gave the orders and they followed them. That had been established long ago.

Now Bass returned to the cabin once more.

The door slammed back on its leather hinges, and small flakes of snow swirled around him.

"You fools!" he bellowed in Spanish. "You're fighting over a woman, and two more men are missing!"

Almost immediately they all seemed to sober up. Sancho stood closest to Revel. As she started to her feet, he waved her back.

"What are you talking about?" Black Eyes grumbled at Bass. He cast a glance toward Revel, obviously thinking he might still collect the prize for beating the Apache.

"Marquez and Billy have been gone too long," Bass said. "They should have been back hours ago."

"They're probably in the shed with the horses." Black Eyes showed little concern, but his dark eyes took on a feral gleam as he watched Revel.

"They're *not* in the shed," Bass informed him. "Get your horse," he ordered.

"What are you talking about?"

"You're riding out with me. We're going to check the lookouts. I don't like this."

"But it's started to snow," the Comanchero protested.

Without the least hesitation, Bass drew his gun and aimed it straight at Black Eyes.

"I give the orders. Or have you forgotten?"

Clearly, Black Eyes wanted to say more, wanted to challenge Bass. But he checked his anger, and Revel released the breath she'd held, disappointed. It would help if they killed each other off.

"You ride, or you die," Bass said coldly.

Black Eyes wasn't that much of a fool. He knew Bass

too well, and wasn't about to challenge him further.

"*Eh, amigo!* Of course, I will ride with you. Our *compadres* are probably warming themselves by a fire at this very moment." He chuckled in a too-obvious attempt to break the tension that filled the cabin. "And then who will be the fools, eh?" he asked, laughing jovially.

He seized his hat from the table and took a thick serape off the pile of blankets.

"I will saddle my horse," he told Bass, then left the cabin.

Revel was silently grateful. She was safe for now. But when Black Eyes returned, sober, there was no telling what frame of mind he would be in—or what her fate would be.

Bass turned and spoke to the Apache and Sancho. "Get your rifle," he said to the Indian. "Keep watch outside. And you"—he looked over at Sancho—"watch the woman. If she makes a move, shoot her."

"*Sí, Jefe,*" Sancho assured him. "I will make certain she causes no trouble."

While they were gone, Revel tried to sleep. She was exhausted, and knew she was safe as long as Sancho was nearby, but each little sound made her start, certain that Bass and Black Eyes had returned.

As more time passed, she became convinced they would come back at any moment. She grew restless, snuggled in blankets in her corner. She watched Sancho as he put more wood on the fire.

He had probably saved her life. She knew he wanted to leave Bass and the Comancheros. But could she persuade him to do it now, before Bass returned?

"Would you leave if you could?" she asked quietly as the wood snapped and crackled at the hearth.

He looked up, youth filling the lean contours of his face.

"No one ever leaves alive."

"You could if you wanted to. I'll help you."

431

"Bass has killed every man who tried to leave. He would not hesitate to kill me."

"There's only the Indian right now," she reasoned. "We could take the horses and go into the mountains."

His dark eyes pinned her. "You said you came for Bass. You would be willing to leave without him?"

"No," she answered honestly. "I still want him dead."

Sancho was doubtful. "There have been others who tried to kill him, and he always escaped."

Revel thought of her father. "I know." Then she added, "But we could do it. Before it's too late. While the others are gone."

"They'll come back," Sancho argued. "Billy and Marquez probably just got caught in the snow."

"And what about Joaquín?" Revel asked. "Was he caught in the storm too?"

He shook his head, obviously remembering the blood on Joaquín's horse. "No. I do not think he will be coming back."

"If you stay, it could happen to you," she argued. "Get me a gun. It's your only chance to leave Bass once and for all." He clearly was not convinced; his fear of Bass was too great.

"Are you really a Pinkerton agent?"

She nodded. "Yes, I am."

"Then why are you alone."

Revel saw no reason to lie to him. "The agency doesn't believe Bass is still alive. But I didn't come here alone. You saw horses the night you abducted me."

He nodded as he remembered.

"The man I came with used to ride with Bass," she explained. "He knows this place."

Sancho's eyes widened. "The one with the spotted horse."

"That's right."

"Then he is the man Bass fears."

Again she nodded. "Yes, and he's out there right now."

432

He had to believe it, so she could convince him to give her a gun.

Sancho's expression clearly indicated he did believe her, and he was afraid. "What will he do?"

Revel had always thought a lie was an act of desperation. At the moment she had no idea where Jake was, and she was very desperate.

"He's on his way here, right now. You must let me have a gun, Sancho. It's the only way."

He hesitated, and their last opportunity to leave disappeared.

It was almost dawn when Bass and the Comanchero returned. Sancho jumped to his feet as the door was thrown open. Bass pushed his way inside, Black Eyes right behind him.

"Get the woman!" Bass ordered the Comanchero.

Sancho stood between them. "What is it? Where are Billy and Marquez?"

Bass stared past him to Revel, his eyes cold and ruthless. "There's no sign of either of them—and no sign of a camp." Then he concluded, "They never made it to the lookout point."

"What could have happened?" Sancho questioned nervously. Then he suggested, "Perhaps they became lost."

Bass's eyes narrowed. "All I know is that it all started when you brought her here. You were followed, and they're picking us off one by one. It's all because of her. They want her back."

He continued staring at Revel. "Bring her outside."

"What are you going to do?" Sancho asked.

"If they want her so bad, let them come get her, on our terms."

Revel was dragged from the cabin. It was barely dawn. The sky was a cold, misty gray, blanketing the valley in layers of ominous clouds. A light snow began to fall.

433

"Get a rope," Bass ordered as he followed them outside.

Wide-eyed, Revel stumbled and fell as Black Eyes dragged her mercilessly through the mud. She scrambled to her feet as she fought him. From the corner of her eye she saw the Apache run toward them with a rope.

Dear God, what were they going to do?

"Tie her." Bass pointed to a makeshift hitching post near the shed.

"And get her out of that jacket. I want to see what they want so badly."

Revel tried to pull away as Black Eyes grabbed the front of her jacket. She heard Sancho argue with Bass even as she fought the Comanchero.

"You're wrong," he pleaded with Bass. "No one followed us through the pass. It would be impossible, you said so yourself."

Bass whirled on Sancho. "There were two horses when you took the woman. Who the hell was with her?"

Sancho looked back at him helplessly. He dared not admit what he suspected. It was too dangerous for the woman.

Revel's jacket was stripped off her. She winced as Black Eyes bound her wrists and snugged them tight to the hitching post.

Cheated of his prize the night before, he knew there would be no reward now. He reached out, and crudely pinched her breast.

She turned burning eyes on him as she cried out and tried to kick him.

He grabbed her hair, twisting it viciously about his hand and jerking her head back so hard she thought her neck would snap.

"*Puta!*" he spat out. "I was right about you. Now you will know what the Comancheros do with worthless women."

"Burn in hell, you son-of-a-bitch." Revel flung the curse at him in Spanish, and felt a brief moment of

434

satisfaction at knowing he understood every word she said and was now aware that *she* had understood every word he had spoken.

"Get on with it!" Bass ordered. "Then we'll see just who this man is."

Revel gasped as Black Eyes seized her by the back of the shirt collar. He separated the fabric with his knife. She felt the cold, deadly blade against the skin at her back, then heard the rending tear of the shirt. It lay open across her back.

"No! Don't do this." Sancho once more tried desperately to save her. "The woman must mean a great deal to them. Perhaps we could ransom her."

Bass turned on him. "I don't want money. I want the man who followed you here, and I want him dead." He turned to Black Eyes.

"Do it! I want to know what it will take for him to come out of hiding."

Black Eyes took great pleasure in slowly coiling the lethal leather whip where Revel could see it.

She swallowed convulsively as she clamped her teeth together. She wouldn't scream, and she wouldn't cry out. By God, she wouldn't!

Bass had killed her father, but she wasn't afraid of him. And she wouldn't break.

She heard it the instant before she felt it—that eerie, sighing sound that seemed to sting the air before it stung the flesh. She reeled with the blow. It felt as if her back was torn open.

She tried to breathe, tried to fight back the tears. There was no need. She was absolutely paralyzed by pain.

The second lash came before she recovered, then a third. It cracked through the air like a rifle shot.

Like a rifle shot.

Slowly, recognition seeped into her numbed brain.

It focused her frozen brain. Revel jerked her head up, forcing herself to think. She *had* heard a shot.

Another crack cut through the piercing cold wind. But

435

it wasn't the whip. With each, new cut of the lash there was new pain. Black Eyes took a great deal of pleasure in using that whip, striking a different place each time.

But he didn't strike her again.

More loud cracks filled the air—gunfire.

Then there were wild shouts, the thunderous pounding of an approaching horse.

Bass shouted orders to his men. The Apache fled across the yard to the horse shed and stole inside, the tip of his rifle protruding slightly.

Black Eyes' whip hung suspended in the air for a brief moment. At Bass's command he dropped it and drew his pistol.

Sancho was several feet away from Revel, watching, powerless to stop the beating. Now he ran to her.

More gunshots filled the air amid the staccato beat of a horse's hooves on the hard-packed earth. A single rider raced toward the encampment.

Bass and his men returned gunfire, aiming several shots at the rider, before Bass screamed at his men to stop.

"It's Billy!" He cursed at them. "Hold your fire!"

The horse was frantic and heavily lathered. It's sides heaved as if Billy had made a desperate run down the hillside. The Apache ran out into the yard and made a grab for the reins to stop the wild-eyed animal.

"What the hell happened?" Bass shouted to Billy as he ran across the yard. Billy remained silent.

Sancho tried to offer Revel what comfort he could. She trembled from pain, exhaustion, and hatred.

"Get me a gun!" she whispered desperately to him. "Can't you see something's wrong?"

Sancho hesitated. He stared past her to Bass who was walking over to Billy's horse. The pain was excruciating, but Revel turned and looked over her shoulder, desperate to know where Bass, Black Eyes, and the Apache were.

If only she had a gun.

But now there was one more of them with the return of the man called Billy.

She fought back dizziness, and the pain from the welts on her back, as she stared at the horse and rider.

As Bass reached the horse, he shouted, "Goddammit, Billy! What the hell is going on? Where have you been? Where's Marquez?"

A puzzled frown creased Bass's hard features as he stepped up to the horse.

Revel guessed the truth almost at the same instant Bass realized it.

She saw the unusual slump to Billy's shoulders as he sat motionless in the saddle. His hat had been jarred loose by the ride and looked as if it was about to fall off his head. He made no attempt to salvage it. His expression was emotionless.

But it was something else that made Revel go cold inside.

His eyes stared fixedly ahead, without glancing to either side.

She recognized that look just as Bass did, though the others were still confused.

It was the look of death.

Bass snarled as he reached up and took hold of the front of Billy's thick coat. The outlaw wobbled in the saddle, like a puppet held only by strings. Then his coat gaped open and the bloodstained front of his shirt was visible.

As if someone had cut him loose, Billy sagged, then fell forward across the front of his saddle. Bass jumped back. He cursed and yelled to the Apache.

"Get him down!"

"*Madre de Dios!*" Black Eyes exclaimed. "We killed Billy!"

"Shut up, you fool!" Bass snarled. "We didn't kill him. He was already dead." Then his voice lowered with an emotion less easily understood than anger. But Revel

437

knew it—it was fear.

Beside her, Sancho started forward.

"It's happening," she whispered desperately. "Don't you see? There's someone out there. Sending Billy back like that was a message to all of you." When he hesitated, she pleaded once more.

"Get me a gun!"

Before he could answer her, a volley of shots came from a completely different direction, followed by the hoofbeats of another horse.

Revel knew that whoever the rider was, this would be her only chance. She had no idea who was out there, but she intended to take full advantage of the situation if she could.

"They're coming in! If you don't help me now, you'll all die."

Sancho stared as another horse raced into the encampment.

A quick glance at the stiff posture of the two riders astride told Revel the two men were Joaquín and Marquez. They were as dead as Billy.

Sancho also understood and quickly made his decision. He whirled back to her. Panic erupted as Bass and the Apache both took cover from new gunfire.

Neither Revel nor Sancho were aware of Black Eyes.

As Sancho turned to untie her, the Comanchero shouted to him, his gun drawn.

"*No, mi amigo*," he spat out. "The woman stays where she is!" He fired at his young *compadre*.

Revel screamed as she jerked around, pulling free of the hitching post. She was so weak from the beating that her knees buckled. Then she saw the stunned expression on Sancho's young face, that moment of truth as blood spread in an ugly stain across the front of his shirt.

He collapsed beside her.

"No!" she cried out in angry denial. Then she was grabbed from behind. Black Eyes fingers were brutal as they dug into her arms, pulling her to her feet.

She slammed her elbows back into his ample gut, then twisted away from him. He grabbed her by the hair, and she dropped to the ground. His hand closed over the collar of her shirt, and he tried to pull her up.

But Revel turned on him, tossing the pouchful of cayenne pepper into his face. He jumped back, coughing violently. His eyes immediately began to water, and he wheezed and sputtered. Wrists still bound, Revel crawled back to the boy, hoping desperately that he was still alive.

"Sancho!" she cried out as she half crawled, half ran to him, gunfire exploding around her.

She fell to his side, tears streaming down her cheeks as she stroked his face.

"Can you hear me? Please!"

He was sprawled on his stomach. He turned his head toward her, and his eyes fluttered open, long sooty lashes shading eyes dulled with pain.

"Señorita Pinkerton?" he whispered in a weak voice.

"I'm here," she reassured him as she looked around frantically. She had to get him to safety.

"Take this." The words came in deep, labored gasps. He pulled his hand from under his prostrate body. His revolver was clutched in his fingers. He thrust it at her.

"Take it, *señorita!*" And then the air rushed out of his lungs and lifeless eyes stared back at her.

Even as she took hold of him and shook him, she knew he was gone.

"Puta!" Black Eyes recovered and came at her.

Revel grabbed Sancho's revolver and turned on him, driven by rage—over the beating, the countless times he'd hurt and humiliated her, and because of Sancho.

She brought the revolver up in both hands as Jake had once taught her and, without the least hesitation, pulled the trigger.

Struck at close range, Black Eyes staggered backward. Then he dropped to the ground.

"Revel! Get outta there!"

She heard her name and that familiar voice. But she

didn't believe her ears. Then, as he yelled at her again, she realized it was true.

Jake.

He fired several rounds from the rifle and sent the horse charging down into the encampment.

The numbers were against him, so he had to rely on the element of surprise, and then on confusion. In only a few precious seconds, Bass would figure everything out and all hell would break loose.

He'd waited for just the right moment, knowing that as long as they were inside the cabin, and Revel with them, any attempt to get her out would only get her killed.

He'd seen his opportunity when they all came out, but still he was forced to wait. Rage tore through him as he watched Bass give the orders and saw the Comanchero follow them, tearing away the fabric of Revel's shirt. He watched helplessly as she was whipped. He couldn't afford to have them know he was there, not yet. Or he'd get them both killed. He hoped she would keep her wits about her when all the excitement started.

As chaos erupted, he saw one of the Comancheros shoot his own man and then turn on Revel. Jake knew he could never get to them in time to help her.

The next thing he knew, the Comanchero lay dead at her feet.

Now he rode into the encampment and opened fire. The Comancheros reacted just as he knew they would.

Bass and the Apache scattered for shelter and immediately began to return fire. As he made his move, Jake kept Revel in constant sight.

He was caught in a crossfire between the shed and the cabin, and swore violently as a bullet tore into his right thigh. He reined the Appaloosa hard, and half slid, half fell to the ground.

He ran for cover at the same time he yelled at Revel, and saw her head toward the cabin. He headed for the side of the horse shed.

"Damn!" He knew she had seen Bass go in that same direction. The little fool was going to get herself killed.

Jake leaned against the outside wall of the shed. He was vaguely aware that warm blood seeped down his leg, but he forced himself to concentrate on the man he knew was inside that shed.

When he first found the hideout there were seven men, including Bass. Now there were only two—the Apache and Bass.

There was a lull in the gunfire. He took advantage of it and moved along the side of the shed.

It was a three-sided structure built to shelter horses in the summer. There were slight gaps in the walls where light shot through. But on this side, firewood was stacked high, providing protection.

Jake approached the back corner, trying to guess the Apache's next move. He looked up as he saw a shadow on the ground.

A shot was fired. It came from the roof.

He hit the ground and rolled to the side as another shot dug into the dirt where he'd stood only a moment before. He lay on his back and raised his rifle, firing continuous blasts into the roof of the shed.

When the chamber was empty, there was complete silence. Then there was a dull thud as the Apache collapsed to the roof, rolled off the back of the shed, and landed on the ground only a few feet from where Jake lay.

The Indian was dead.

Jake staggered to his feet. Now only Bass was left. And as Emilio had said, there was only one way this could end.

He limped around behind the shed, approaching the cabin at an angle and from the side. He carefully reloaded the rifle.

When he was halfway across the yard, the door was thrown open. He saw Bass standing in the shadows at the doorway.

Jake swore as he saw Revel with him.

441

She stood slightly to one side of Bass, one arm twisted behind her back. The barrel of Bass's revolver was pressed against the side of her head.

"Kill him!" she screamed to Jake, then winced as Bass pulled back on the hammer of the revolver.

"Hello, Jake," Bass called out. The greeting was anything but friendly. "I figured it was you when one of my men told me about a man ridin' a spotted horse. Only one man I know owns a horse like that. Trouble is, I thought they hanged you."

Jake stopped, pain pulsing through his wounded leg. If he went any closer, he knew Bass would kill her. He was calm, relaxed, his eyes cool as green ice as he watched every move Bass made, every blink of an eye, every breath he took.

"As you can see, they didn't," he replied casually.

The smile on Bass's face hardened. "You always did have more lives than a cat. What's this make it? Twice, three times you got lucky and escaped the law?"

Jake smiled—a dangerous smile. "I lose track."

Bass broke out in a cold sweat. "Well, maybe you'd better start countin', cause you may just have run out of luck—and lives."

"I don't think so," Jake answered. Then he said quietly but no less threateningly, "I came for the woman. Let her go."

Bass shook his head. "Uh-uh, nothin' doin'. She's my protection until I get outta here." Still, he looked intrigued as he pressed the tip of the revolver against Revel's head to make his point.

"She looks like a scrawny piece to me, not your style, Reno."

"Yer right," Jake agreed with a casual shrug of his shoulders, and immediately received a murderous glare from Revel.

"But there's a little bit more to it than that. You see," he added casually, as if they were discussing the weather or the price of beef, "the lady and I have an agreement."

Then he went on to explain so there would be no misunderstanding on Bass's part.

"When I fulfill my part of the bargain, she'll fulfill hers."

Bass had always liked Jake in a careful sort of way. He'd thought they were a lot alike, and he'd learned to respect him—and his speed with gun.

"What can she do for you?" he asked out of curiosity.

Jake knew Bass as well as he knew himself.

He watched him like a hawk. He would only have one chance at him.

"Well, you see, she's the reason Virgil Earp didn't hang me in Tombstone," Jake explained with a shrug, as if he were casually conversing with an old friend.

Bass frowned and looked skeptical.

"That so?"

Jake nodded. "That's right. She made a deal with me."

He saw Bass's fingers shift around the handle of the revolver, the faint glisten of sweat at the edge of his hand.

"What kind of deal?"

Jake gave him a steady look as he saw curiosity turn to wariness.

"She offered me a full pardon if I found you."

Amusement, confusion, bafflement all appeared on Bass's hard face.

"What the hell are you talking about?"

"A full pardon," Jake repeated, and he added, "In exchange for you."

Bass laughed nervously, but his eyes remained cold.

"That's the damnedest thing I ever heard of. How the hell can she do that?"

Revel felt the sudden tensing of the fingers around the wrist pinned at her back. She could almost sense the cold fear that began to pour through Bass. Then he laughed again.

Jake shrugged. "Kinda makes you wonder, doesn't it?"

Bass shifted uncomfortably. Revel could feel his uncertainty. Then she gasped as he jerked her arm up

443

high against her back. Pain shot through her shoulder and brought tears to her eyes.

"As I recall, you turned outlaw in the first place over a woman," Bass speculated. "Ain't that right?"

Revel saw the muscles in Jake's face go rigid when Bass made that obvious reference to Rachel, the woman Jake had once loved and been unable to save.

"That's right," Jake said quietly—too quietly. "And I'm not leavin' without the lady, so put the gun down."

"And if I don't?"

Jake brought the barrel of his rifle up, and aimed it at Bass's head.

"Then I'll have to kill you," he said without the least hesitation.

Bass grinned, but it was a hollow expression. "Do you think yer good enough to kill me before I kill her?"

"Why don't we find out?"

Jake appeared to watch Bass with unbroken concentration, but he was also aware of the play of emotions in Revel's vivid blue eyes. They widened with a mixture of fear and doubt.

Bass laughed nervously. "Maybe I'm faster."

"Maybe," Jake said, although both men knew it wasn't true. It was a game of bluff. Jake held the winning hand, and Bass knew it.

"All right," Bass finally conceded, "I'll put down the gun. Then you can have the woman, and we'll just forget this ever happened."

Jake watched them both as Bass slowly brought the revolver away from Revel's head and dropped it at her feet.

Then he saw what he had been watching for—the look of alarm that sprang into her eyes, the sharp intake of breath. These warned him that Bass had tricked him.

Revel felt the subtle shift of Bass's weight as he tossed his revolver to the ground. Then she felt something else as he released her arm—the painful scrape of cold steel against her raw back. The rifle between them.

"Jake! Look out!" she cried.

Bass shoved Revel away from him, at the same time he brought the rifle up.

A roar of gunfire filled the air as both men fired.

Bass was thrown back against the wall of the cabin by the blast from Jake's rifle.

Revel watched in horror as Jake reeled backward and fell to the ground.

He fought to get up, the barrel of the rifle wavering as he aimed a second shot at Bass.

Bass's breathing was labored as he leaned heavily against the front wall of the cabin. Blood was spreading across the front of his coat. His lips thinned with pain as he pushed himself away from the wall with great effort and slowly staggered toward them.

He raised his rifle and took aim at Jake.

A single blast shuddered through the chill morning air.

Chapter Twenty-Four

A spiral of gunsmoke faded on the chill wind as Revel slowly lowered the revolver, Sam Bass's revolver.

She had wondered countless times what her thoughts would be at this precise moment—her only thought was that she couldn't let him kill Jake.

Sam Bass stared back at her in disbelief as the coldness of death spread through him. He brought his fingers away from the second bullet wound at his chest, now covered with blood.

"Who the hell are you!" he screamed at her, death bubbling into his throat in a mixture of blood and spittle.

Revel kept the revolver aimed at him. Her fingers ached she clutched it so hard. And she said what she'd lived three years to say to him.

"My name is Revel Tyson. I'm with the Pinkerton Detective Agency."

"Yer a damned Pinkerton?" Bass screamed in disbelief.

"That's right."

"All this—because you're a Pinkerton?" he was dying and because of a woman.

"No, not just because of that." She took a deep breath, fighting back the emotion that choked her. "This wasn't for the agency, and it wasn't for me. I did it because of my father!"

He staggered toward her, shaking his head as he fought the pain, the weakness, and death.

"Who the hell is your father?" he gasped, blood seeping through his fingers as he clutched his chest. His face was contorted, but he fought to remain standing, his skin pale, his eyes already glazed.

"You may remember him. His name was Matt Gibson!" It was important to her that Bass remember, that he know the reason he was dying.

"Matt Gibson. At Red Rock," he gasped, unable to believe yet knowing it was true.

She saw recognition along with death in those cold blue-gray eyes. And then Bass began to laugh, a crazed, hysterical sound that was drowned in the blood at his throat.

"Not even those damned Texas Rangers could find me," he whispered as he staggered another few steps forward. Then, as he half ran, half fell, he tried to grab the gun.

Revel took a small step backward as he grabbed the front of her shirt. She pressed the tip of the revolver against his neck as his weight dragged at her. If she had to, she would shoot him again. But he slowly crumpled to the ground. He stared up at her in confusion and disbelief.

He choked out, "Not even . . . the . . . Rangers . . ." And then he collapsed, his sightless eyes staring up at the sky.

The strength seemed to seep out of Revel, and she almost fell as her knees buckled. She slowly walked away from Bass's body. His revolver, the same gun that had killed her father and countless other men, dangled from her numbed fingers.

Then she thought she was going to be sick. Nausea churned into her stomach, aching cold swept through her, and her back throbbed. It was as if she were numb to all feeling at one moment, then it came washing back over her the next.

"Revel, are you all right?"

She felt the unsteady pressure of a hand at her shoulder. She spun around.

"Oh my, God!" She put an arm around Jake's waist as he swayed against her, and felt the warm blood soaking his shirt.

"You're hurt!"

Jake gave a short, ironic laugh. "Yeah, I guess the son-of-a-bitch was quicker than I thought. The idea was to shoot him and then get the hell outta the way."

A frown knitted her dark brows together. "Damn you, how can you make jokes at a time like this?"

"You can either listen to my jokes or my swearing. Which is it going to be?" As he looked down at her, he smiled in spite of his pain and brought a hand up to touch her face.

"I asked whether you're all right."

Tears flooded her eyes as her fragile hold on control threatened to crumble. It was ridiculous for him to be asking, with a bullet wound in his side, but she couldn't get the words out to tell him so. She nodded, sniffled, and held on to him a little more carefully.

"You're one helluva Pinkerton agent." He winced from pain.

"And you're one helluva fool," she shot back at him. It was easier to banter with him than it was to stand there and have him touch her like that. "And if we don't get you bandaged, you're going to be one helluva dead fool. You're bleeding all over the place."

"What do you suggest?" His voice was thin.

"The cabin," she said without hesitation. "I can find something in there to use as a bandage." She placed his arm over her shoulders, then stopped.

"That is, if it's safe. There's one more—the Indian. . . ." Her voice rose in alarm. She hadn't seen the Apache since the shooting began.

"He's dead," Jake whispered as he leaned heavily against her.

Revel looked up at him with somber eyes and tried to make light of what they'd just been through.

"I see. I guess it was a good idea to bring you along. I knew you'd come in handy."

"Revel . . ."

She looked up in alarm at catching his tone of voice. "What is it?"

"Can you shut up long enough to get me inside? I'm bleeding all over the place."

"Don't push it, Reno. I just might decide to put another bullet hole in you."

He chuckled softly, his breath warm against her forehead as he leaned on her and they slowly walked to the cabin.

"I'll be careful what I say from now on. I think I can only handle two bullet holes in one day."

Revel's hand came up in alarm as they stepped through the doorway.

"Two?" She helped him to the pile of blankets and serapes in the corner, and when he collapsed on it she saw the patch of blood at his thigh. Fear raced through her.

"Damn you, Jake Reno." She cursed softly. "You weren't supposed to get yourself killed over me."

He grunted as she carefully turned him over onto his back. His breathing came in short, hard gasps. A sheen of moisture broke out across his skin from the effort of getting this far.

"It seemed"—he smiled up at her, those green eyes, glinting wickedly—"like . . . the thing to do . . . at the time."

Her fingers trembled as she gently pulled the tails of his shirt from his pants.

"A helluva lot of good getting yourself killed will do either of us."

"Ah, Revel, the way you talk somebody could almost think you care what happens to me."

She looked up as she ripped open his shirt. "I suppose that *would* be a mistake."

450

"Yeah, a big one. I'm no good at feelings, Revel."

It was a subtle reminder, and her head came up again. Her eyes met his, then went to the wound at his side.

"I'll try to remember that," she said stiffly. She swallowed hard and pulled her hands back.

"I don't recall you having any trouble touching me the last time we were together."

"I don't remember." She lied, simply because it was the easiest thing to do at the moment—a moment when he had just reminded her he was no good at feelings.

"Then let me refresh your memory," he said softly as his hand slipped behind her head and he drew her to him. In spite of the pain, his mouth hungrily sought hers.

Revel's response was immediate, equally hungry, and damning for all her brave words. She started to object. Jake took advantage, his tongue slipping between her softly parted lips to plunge inside.

That intimate contact roused more intimate longings as Revel felt desire knot deep inside her. She gently pushed him back onto the blankets, taking the sweet, hot, masculine taste of him with her as she drew away.

"I think you remember," he said softly.

She ignored him, as she rose and began to search the cabin for the supplies she would need. "I have to get you bandaged. But that bullet will have to come out first."

"It's already out."

She turned back around, and Jake explained. "It passed clean through, but I think I've got some broken ribs."

"How can you tell?" she asked with a worried frown. A bullet hole was one thing. Broken ribs were an entirely different matter.

He gave her a wink that she found maddening for a man in his condition.

"I've had a few in my time, although none from a bullet before."

"I see. It was probably some barroom brawl."

"Once or twice," he admitted. "And once a horse

451

kicked me. I didn't see that one coming."

"I'll just bet you didn't."

He grinned at her in that maddening way of his.

Revel found several clean shirts in the wide-sleeved style Mexicans preferred. Their size suggested they might have belonged to Sancho. They would do for bandages, and one would replace her own torn shirt. She put water on to boil, and tried to make Jake as comfortable as possible.

When the water was ready, she cleaned the double wound, at his side and low at his back.

"You're lucky that bullet passed through."

He grunted in pain as she helped him sit up.

She placed a clean heavy pad over the wounds and then bound them. She continued winding wide strips of fabric around him, from his waist to just under his arms to protect his broken ribs.

"You're right. I didn't fancy trying to dig it out myself." He leaned against her shoulder.

"There are a few things I *can* do," she reminded him. She didn't need to mention that she had finally killed Bass.

He brushed his fingers against her lips. "I suppose you could do just about anything you set your mind to."

"Of all things, dig a bullet out yourself," she muttered half in disgust, half in disbelief.

"It's been known to happen on occasion."

Her skin went pale at the thought. "You've actually removed a bullet yourself?"

"You do what you have to, Revel," he said. And then he became very solemn. "Remember that. It may save your life, sometime."

She frowned as she gently settled him back on the blankets. She found a knife and started to cut his pantleg. His hand stopped her.

"Just get the bleeding stopped and bandage it."

"That bullet has to come out. I *really* can do this."

He shook his head adamantly. "It's too deep, Revel. It

452

would take too much time—time that we don't have. I'm better off if we leave it in."

"And take the chance of blood poisoning? Don't be ridiculous." When she tried again to cut the cloth of his pants, his fingers closed over her wrist with surprising strength for someone who had lost so much blood.

"We don't have time," he repeated with less patience.

"What are you talking about? We're safe here. We'll take the time. Then when you're better—"

"No! You don't understand. *We don't have time.*" His eyes closed and he seemed to be gathering his strength.

"The weather is going to close in on us. If we get caught here, we'll die here. Bass knew that. It's why he was only stopping here before going deeper into Mexico. This place was only meant as a temporary hideout."

"But . . ." Even as she started to protest, she thought of the gaping cracks in the walls of the cabin. It was true, this place would never protect them from a heavy winter storm.

"We can't stay here. We have to get out, now." He lay back on the blankets.

"You'll bleed to death if you try to ride a horse."

"I'd rather bleed to death atop a horse, than freeze to death here."

Those crystal green eyes burned into her. Even wounded as badly as he was, Jake Reno could be formidable—and dangerous.

The weakness in his voice now was deceptive. "We've got to leave before the next storm hits, or we'll be stuck here."

She nodded, agreeing because she had put her life in his hands once before and he hadn't failed her. Besides, deep down, she knew he was right. She had felt the change of weather in the bite of the wind. This was high country, not unlike Colorado. Only fools allowed themselves to be caught in unfamiliar territory when the weather changed. And it would be brutal up here, even in this sheltered valley.

453

But how foolish was it to leave with Jake in his present condition. With that bullet in his leg, it would only get worse. The question was, could they make it down without killing him?

She finished bandaging Jake's leg, knotting a tie off above the wound for a tourniquet.

"You'll need something to tighten that with," he reminded her weakly. Revel found the fork she had hidden inside her boot.

He smiled at her. "Do you always keep forks in your boots?"

She smiled in spite of their desperate situation. She knew pulling a fork from her boot must seem ridiculous.

"I thought I might have to use it as a weapon."

"That would have been something to see."

She nodded. "I guess we will do just about anything if we're desperate enough." She smiled. "I would have used it on Bass, if I had too. Or Black Eyes." Her voice had become hard.

"Black Eyes?" Jake asked.

She met his gaze, then looked away.

"He was very fond of whips."

Jake's eyes darkened. "I had to wait until they were distracted."

"I know. It's all right."

His fingers closed around hers. "No, it's not. As long as I live, I'll never forget what it was like seeing him do that to you."

Revel pressed her fingers against his lips.

"It's over."

He kissed her fingertips. "You'd better get something on those marks."

"I'll see if I can find something as soon as I get you bandaged."

When Jake was finally resting, she searched the cabin. Now that she was able to move about freely, without her hands tied, she discovered several things they would need to take with them.

There were boxes of shells, matches, and tins of dried food. As Jake had said, Bass had no intention of spending the winter there. It was only a place to rest the horses before he and his men headed deeper into Mexico to escape the law north of the border.

She found a small tin of something that resembled animal fat and applied it carefully to the areas of her back that she could reach. Then she pulled on one of the small shirts she'd found.

Her jacket was still outside, and she needed to see to the horses. She closed the door quietly behind her.

Seeing the bodies that littered the camp stopped her. They were an eerie sight. But she quickly walked past Sam Bass and Black Eyes. The bodies of the three men Jake had encountered earlier lay several feet away, where they'd fallen when Bass had ordered them cut down. She saw the Apache behind the shed when she tied up the horses, including Jake's Appaloosa.

Her first thought was that Bass and his men should be buried. Her next, more rational thought was that was an impossible task. She had to leave the outlaws where they were, except for Sancho.

She knelt beside him, and stroked the jet black hair that tumbled cross his forehead. He had died trying to protect her.

Tears slipped down her cheeks. He was so young. All he'd wanted was to go home. And she would have seen that he did.

Now this was as close as he would get to home.

Revel found a shovel in the shed. She worked until she had blisters on her hands and she cursed herself for having forgotten to look for a pair of gloves.

When she was through, the sun was high in the sky. Her back throbbed, but she refused to stop until the task was done. She dragged Sancho's body to the crudely dug grave and rolled it in. When freshly turned soil was mounded across the grave she collapsed onto her knees. Tears slipped down her cheeks.

"Good-bye, friend."

She kept the fire going, preparing food they could take with them, and she filled canteens with water from the spring she found behind the cabin, knowing Jake would want to leave as soon as he awakened. Then she sat before the fire and dozed, a loaded rifle in her lap, Sam Bass's revolver in her hand.

More than once she considered leaving Jake there with plenty of firewood, water, and food, and riding out for help. But she knew it was foolhardy. If she succeeded in finding her way out—and there was no guarantee she could—she might never find her way back again. Then Jake would be left there to die. That she would not do.

"We need to ride."

Jake's voice was weak but coherent. Revel's eyes came open, and she met his dark green gaze. She nodded.

"Everything's ready."

She knew as she helped him leave the cabin he would never let on how much pain he was in, so she simply didn't ask. She learned to judge his limitations by the silence that drew out between them.

The sky was clear, the weather warm, when they left that afternoon. Behind them lay that isolated cabin, the bodies of six notorious Comancheros—including the infamous Sam Bass—and a single grave.

They led two extra horses, packed with extra food, water, furs, blankets, and anything else Revel thought it best to take with them, including firewood. They had weapons, and Revel was taking Bass's revolver back to the authorities as proof they'd found him.

It was at least a six-day ride back to Emilio's rancho. If bad weather set in it would take longer, and the only shelter they would have at night was what they could find along the way.

Jake rode ahead, following the trail only he knew, taking them down a different way than she had come in.

They rode four hours that first day, and she was

grateful they were forced to stop for the night. She didn't think Jake could have gone any farther, and she silently wondered if he would be able to go on the next day. More than once she thought of turning back. But she knew he would never allow it.

That night they made camp amid the rocks, sheltered from the wind that came up. Revel settled Jake into a bed made from the thick furs, then built the fire and made dinner.

He woke briefly, ate, then dozed off. But he slept fitfully. He was in pain, and she had nothing to give him to ease it. Mercifully, his skin was cool and there was no fever.

They started the next morning at daybreak. Jake seemed better, but she knew that was precisely what he wanted her to think. Every hour in the saddle took its toll, even though she constantly checked his bandages, and tried to soften the ride by padding his saddle with the skins.

She wanted to shorten the hours they rode each day, convinced it would be easier on him. But he pushed on as long as there was even a glimmer of daylight, as if he burned to get off the mountain.

Revel hoarded the precious, dry wood packed on one of the horses, scavenging for firewood each night. If bad weather set in there would be no dry wood on the ground.

She fought back her nagging doubts about Jake's ability to survive the ride down the mountain. But that night, as they sat before the fire, she asked him to make a detailed map of the trail that would lead them down.

On the third day after they left the hideout, a light snow began to fall. It continued throughout the day, blanketing everything in crystal white softness that was deceptively beautiful. Actually it presented a threat—it covered familiar landmarks.

The horses stumbled and slipped, and Revel wanted to stop just after midday, at least until the storm passed.

457

The snow was almost knee-deep and the horses were tired. Jake refused to stop, but relented a bit, slowing their pace.

As the day wore on, Revel worriedly watched him. He slumped forward several times, but always caught himself and straightened in the saddle.

Even in his condition he set a relentless pace. But near dusk, when he would have normally pushed them on at least another hour, he made no objection when she stopped. Instead the Appaloosa continued on ahead slowly, picking it's way through a stand of trees.

Revel slipped from the saddle as she watched. Something was wrong.

"Jake." There was no response.

She ran to him.

When she reached the Appaloosa, Jake didn't look up, he didn't even stir.

"Oh, God. No!" Panic squeezed her heart as she unwrapped the thick skins thrown over his legs and hands. Then she felt warmth, and when her icy-cold fingers brushed his, he finally stirred. His eyes opened, but they were heavy lidded and recognition was slow in coming.

When he spoke, it was in a vague, incoherent mumble, and she was certain he called out for Rachel.

This affected Revel in ways she hadn't expected, making her throat tight, cutting at her heart. She told herself she had always known he loved only one woman, and she strove to recover her composure as she slipped the reins from his hands and looped them over the Appaloosa's head.

"Where are we?" he asked, an odd, glassy sheen to his eyes. Revel fought back the fear that choked her.

"We just made camp," she lied, quickly deciding they would go no farther that day. "It'll be all right, Jake. I promise you."

The fever had begun.

458

Even before she got him down off the Appaloosa and helped him to the crude shelter she was able to find, she could feel it through the thick furs. It was the one thing she had prayed would not happen, and the thing she was least capable of handling.

She had no medicine, only water, heat, and clean bandages.

Dear God, what was she to do?

Revel did everything she had done on the previous nights. She made him as comfortable as possible, then checked his wounds.

The bullet hole at his side was closed and dry. There was no sign of infection. The broken ribs she couldn't see or fix, so she simply rebound them. But it was the wound in his leg that scared her the most.

It was badly swollen and bluish purple in color. The bleeding had stopped after that first day, just as he'd said it would. She had removed her fork tourniquet before they'd left and had padded the wound with a thick bandage.

Now the skin surrounding the wound was feverish, the heat spreading throughout his body. She didn't have to be a doctor to know it was blood poisoning.

She said nothing to Jake as she applied hot compresses. They seemed to help. The wound opened up, and she was able to remove some of the fluid that had built up. Then she put on a fresh bandage and tried to make him comfortable. She found him watching her with feverish eyes.

"You and I both know what it means."

Revel started to deny it, then decided against it. From the very beginning, she and Jake had been brutally honest with each other, about everything.

"You'll make it," she said stubbornly.

"Revel—"

She cut him off. "We won't discuss it."

"We have to."

459

"No! I won't."

He reached out with surprising strength, his fingers clamping around her arms. He shook her.

"I'll make you listen."

She knew the easiest way to make him shut up was simply to let him have his say. But when her eyes met his they were stubborn. He smiled faintly at that all-too-familiar look. His fingers relaxed.

"You may have to go on alone." When she started to protest he laid a finger against her lips.

"It's blood poisoning, there's no denying it. If you know anything about it, you know fever is only the first sign. It'll get worse. I may even get delirious. If that happens I won't be able to sit a horse, much less get you out of here."

"We'll get out together."

"Why are you being so mule-headed?" he asked. "You have what you wanted. It's over now."

"I . . ." She started to say that none of that mattered any longer. She'd realized it when she'd shot Sam Bass.

The only thought in her mind at that moment had been that she couldn't let him kill Jake.

But Jake would never understand that because he didn't feel what she felt. He never had. He couldn't, he loved only Rachel.

So she simply said, "I promised you would have that pardon." Then she added softly, "I always keep my promises." She looked at him for a moment. "That pardon won't do you much good if you're dead."

"You can be the most stubborn woman," he said weakly.

She smiled at him, and he caressed her cheek with his fingers.

"You once told me I'd never find Sam Bass."

"You almost got yourself killed doing it."

"But I found him."

"Meaning?"

460

She cupped his hand with hers holding it against her cheek, feeling the heat that burned through him.

"It means I'm not leaving you on this mountain."

He gave her a long, steady look. "It may come to that, Revel."

"No, it won't."

But in the morning, he was worse.

Chapter Twenty-Five

Jake's fever was out of control. His skin was so hot and dry it seemed to Revel that he was burning up. And she was afraid. She had never been so afraid.

The truth she'd confronted when she killed Sam Bass surfaced again—she loved Jake.

Regardless of the fact that he didn't feel the same way about her, she loved him. And she couldn't bear it if he died.

She was determined to get them both down off the mountain, and refused to accept any other possibility. But first she had to get his fever down.

His eyes were glassy. He took hold of her wrist as she put more blankets on him. His mouth and throat were dry, his voice was raspy; but for the moment he was coherent.

"You've got to get out of here," he whispered, trying to raise himself on one elbow.

If she argued with him, she knew instinctively it would only make things worse. So she lied.

"We can't leave right now."

Confusion clouded those green eyes bright with fever. She didn't give him time to object.

"One of the horses was limping when we stopped last night."

"Cut him loose and take the others."

For a man who bordered on being completely delirious, he was amazingly argumentative.

"No, we need all the horses. I want to give him a little longer to rest. Besides, I can't pack all the provisions on the other horses."

"Revel!" His fingers painfully squeezed her wrist. She wrenched free, and he hadn't the strength to fight her.

"You little . . . fool. You'll get yourself killed if you don't . . . leave."

"We'll go in a little while. You're better this morning." She lied again as she placed a cool, wet cloth on his forehead. It wasn't enough to cool his entire body, though.

He tried to push the cloth away, forcing her to tie it across his forehead.

"Broken Hand . . ." he mumbled, obviously thinking that Indian was with them.

She kept up the lie. "He'll be back later," she said. "He's ridden on ahead to mark the trail."

Jake nodded as the restlessness from the fever receded. "He can get . . . you . . . out."

"I know," she soothed. "Just rest."

Soon he seemed to doze once more, and Revel quickly got to work.

She packed snow inside several skins, then wrapped them about Jake's body. When he stirred, she forced broth down him. She'd made it from dried beef and herbs.

Gradually the fever lessened. His skin lost that fiery parched look, and he seemed lucid when he awakened. He looked around.

"What time is it?"

Again she lied. With the thick cloud cover he had no way of knowing or remembering that first light had been some hours ago.

"It's early. We can get started now." She began to unwrap the snow she'd packed about him. The bandages were clean. The one at his side was dry. She changed the one at his thigh.

"You can't keep this up," he said softly.

"I can keep it up longer than you can. And you're in no condition to argue with me. Now, c'mon, let's get going."

"What if I refuse to get in that saddle?"

He wasn't delirious. He was perfectly coherent. She needed him that way to get him atop the Appaloosa. What she didn't need was an argument.

"You'll only slow things down a little, and probably hurt yourself in the process," she said with a stubborn shrug. Then she grew serious. "If I have to drag you to that horse with a rope, I'll do it." Her voice rose in anger. "And if I have to tie you to the saddle, I'll do that too."

"One way or the other, you're coming with me!"

Their gazes met, one stubbornly determined, the other bright with fever.

He gave in, but as she turned to pack the last of their supplies, he muttered under his breath, "For now, I'll do it."

Revel heard it, even though he thought she hadn't.

They rode for three or four hours. Jake was coherent enough to realize that it was early afternoon, not early morning as she'd said. When he brought that to her attention, she didn't bother to answer him.

Just as she had suspected, the fever returned late in the afternoon, but she tied him in the saddle in order to keep going.

She constantly forced him to drink water. It was impossible to pack him in the snow-filled skins unless they stopped. And each time they did pull up to rest, she feared she wouldn't be able to get him astride the Appaloosa again.

It made her ache to see him bent over the saddle horn that way. If he were fully conscious the pain from his broken ribs would be excruciating, but they had to go on. She secured a thick roll of skins and blankets across the saddle in front of him, and then simply let him slump forward, curled over them.

Their situation seemed hopeless, but late in the

465

afternoon as she led the Appaloosa and the two pack horses along the trail indicated on the crude map, there was one bright moment. It quit snowing, and the clouds overhead began to break up and scatter.

Later, as the sun was going down and stars began to emerge, along with a full moon, Revel made a critical decision. They wouldn't make camp that night, but would continue on.

She was taking a terrible risk, she knew. If she missed one landmark, one familiar rock or turn in the trail, it would be disastrous for both of them. It might be hours before she discovered her mistake. But stopping for the night meant another delay in getting off the mountain, and Jake might not survive it.

For the first time since her father died, Revel prayed.

Early evening was the most difficult time. The moon wasn't up yet, and little light came through the trees.

She slowed their pace, but was forced to stop and double back more than once to make certain she was following the right path.

When she discovered a landmark just as Jake had drawn it, she was happier than a miner finding a gold nugget. She wanted to shout for joy, but was too weary.

Jake had lost consciousness several hours earlier. Perhaps that was best, for the fever burned through him.

It was now a race against time, the elements, and the mountain.

And the wolves.

She heard them in the distance, their bone-chilling call piercing the cold night air as the moon came up over the trees. The horses heard them too and became skittish.

She checked the revolver to make certain it was loaded and placed it just inside the front of her thick coat. Then she shortened the leads of the horses. Jake didn't stir, but remained slumped over the Appaloosa. She pushed on.

The most difficult thing was staying awake. She was so tired she ached, but she knew if she gave in to fatigue for just a moment they could easily stray from their course.

466

And the wolves were at their backs. Several times Revel stopped and listened.

Sound was deceptive in the forest. It echoed off mountains, disappeared through trees, then echoed back from another location. It was difficult to determine where it began. The only thing she was certain of was that those frightening cries and howls were louder, closer.

She watched the shadows that surrounded them for any sign of movement.

The wolves were very close now and may even have picked up the scent of the horses. As long as she and Jake were out in the open, they were fully exposed and vulnerable to anything that came at them. And the fading light put them in even graver danger.

Throughout the night they followed the course of a mountain stream. In spring, with the runoff, it would become a raging creek, but now the carved-out banks were covered with fallen timbers and fresh snow. Revel had been looking for a spot to camp, and she finally found one that provided perfect shelter. The creek bank rose eight feet at their backs, water was in front of them, and the massive trunk of a downed tree provided a barrier from any approach upstream.

She tied the horses securely to the tree, and before she went back to get Jake down off the Appaloosa, she built a huge fire using the dry wood she'd packed on one of the horses. She laid out the rifle nearby and shoved the revolver into the waist of her pants. Then she went back for Jake.

He hadn't moved.

She worked quickly, untying the ropes, uncertain how she would ever get him back astride if he didn't regain consciousness. He slumped to the side, then slowly slipped to the ground. If he were conscious the pain would have been excruciating.

It took a great deal of effort, but Revel finally dragged him to the fire. She had spread out dry furs and blankets alongside it, and she wrapped him warmly.

He still hadn't awakened, and fear clutched at her heart. But as she lay her head against his chest, she heard the light rapid beating of his heart. Lying there with him, her arms wrapped about him, Revel gave in to the tears she'd fought back for days.

"You have to live. Damn it, Jake Reno! You have to." She looked up at him and caressed his heavily stubbled cheek, remembering other moments with him. Gently her cool lips brushed against his fevered ones.

"I can't lose you."

When Revel stirred sometime later, it was just beginning to get light. There was no wind, not even a gust of breeze. The last few stars were fading overhead. It was completely, perfectly calm, silent, still. And a frisson of fear tingled along her nerve endings in silent warning.

They were not alone.

She sat up in alarm, her hand closing over the revolver. The fire had burned low and she carefully added more wood, building it back up. Jake was no better, but he was no worse either. He slept on.

Revel gathered the blankets and furs more snugly about him as her gaze slowly took in the gray perimeter of the camp, swinging across the water to the other embankment, to the fallen tree, and then downstream.

She saw nothing at first. Everything was muted in shades of gray, shapes were indistinct.

Perhaps it was the sky that gradually grew lighter, outlining shapes of trees and rock. Or perhaps it was the glowing firelight that reflected back from golden eyes across the stream.

She wasn't certain which she saw first—that fierce, shaggy shape or the feral glow of those eyes. But they were there. Wolves.

The horses snorted and moved nervously as they picked up the scent. Then there was heavy panting punctuated by deep-throated growls, and gleaming teeth flashed in the firelight.

The first one boldly stalked across the water,

approaching from upstream. Revel raised the gun. As the wolf came at them, she fired.

The first shot plopped in the water, but the blast from the revolver was enough to halt the wolf midstream. Its head was low as it found the scent, lips pulling back over long fangs.

Revel grabbed for the rifle. She made out a half-dozen shapes in the growing light. If they attacked in a pack as she had heard they often did, there would be no time to reload.

She considered cutting the horses loose, perhaps using them to draw away the wolves. But there was no guarantee the pack would follow, and there was the nagging fear they had also caught the scent of Jake's wounds.

She'd heard tales about wolves—that they would hunt down a wounded man. And if she turned the horses loose, their last hope of getting down that mountain would be gone.

Then the first wolf came at them again. He was large, shaggy, and heavily built. He snarled as he edged closer through the water, seeming to sense her vulnerability. The others crowded the far bank.

As the wolf came closer, Revel raised the revolver and took careful aim. When he raised his head and lunged, she fired.

The blast caught him in the chest and he went down, thrashing in the water. The other wolves scattered retreating, their noses lifted to the air as they picked up the scent of fresh blood.

Several of the animals paced the far bank, lured by the human and animal scents, yet wary. One approached tentatively several times, and Revel fired into the pack with the rifle. She heard a sharp yelp, and they scattered again, looking back at her warily.

Singly and in pairs, they repeatedly tried to cross the water. Revel's nerves grew taut as she tried to stay calm. She picked her shots carefully, bartering for time and better light for her target. Again and again she fired into the pack, until the rifle was empty. And again and again, one wolf became braver than the others and tried to find a way to get to her.

The pack circled to the high embankment behind her. They attempted to cross the fallen tree. They lunged and splashed in the water only to turn back when she fired at them.

Revel kept the fire built up, in the hope of driving them away. She fumbled at the nearest saddlebag, but there were no boxes of shells, and she silently cursed herself for not paying more attention to what she'd brought from the horses.

How many bullets had she fired? How many were left in the revolver?

She glanced back up, looking at those indistinct shapes that moved restlessly back and forth on the other side of the stream. There were at least three or four others that now lay still in the snow and at the water's edge. But she was exhausted and scared to death. Her hands shook as she held the revolver.

"No!" she screamed at the wolves. "I won't let you have him. Do you hear me? Do you? I won't! Get out of here!"

She fired into them, scattering them once more. Then one separated from the pack and lunged across the water.

Revel was on her knees. She stared wide-eyed as the wolf came straight at them, as if it could sense their helplessness. She fired, but the revolver clicked with a sickening, empty sound. She threw it down and grabbed a stout piece of firewood. She pushed herself up as fear poured through her veins.

All thought stopped. She refused to think of what it would feel like to be torn apart by the wolves. Her fingers ached as she clutched the log and placed herself between Jake and the pack.

As the wolf leaped, there was a sudden hiss through the

470

air and a sharp yelp of pain. The wolf fell into the water only a few feet away. It twitched and spasmed, its tongue lolling between deadly fangs. Then it jerked and lay perfectly still, impaled on the gleaming shaft of an arrow.

Revel's head jerked up, her eyes wide, the wood still clutched in her hands.

Slowly, a long, shadow separated from the others and came toward her. Revel backed away in panic at this new threat. Then she blinked in confusion as the shadow stepped into the light from the campfire.

Broken Hand knelt beside the dead wolf. Then he looked at the other carcasses that littered the ground and floated in the water. He grunted his approval.

"Not bad, for a woman. Especially a white woman. But you should still learn to carry a knife."

The old Indian fired several more shots, and the remainder of the wolf pack scattered into the forest.

As recognition sliced through her fear, Revel stared in amazement at Broken Hand. And then Emilio and several of his vaqueros stepped into the circle of firelight.

"You have been gone a long time, *señorita*. We were very concerned. When we saw your campfire, I knew which way Jake had chosen to come down the mountain." Emilio looked across the fire to Jake, huddled in the blankets. He immediately went to his friend.

"How bad is it, *señorita?*"

All the emotions, the desperation, she'd held back these past days washed over Revel as she knelt beside Jake. Tears coursed down her cheeks, and she wiped at them furiously.

"He was shot twice. Once in the side, but the bullet went through. I think his ribs are broken. But the wound in his thigh is the real problem. The bullet is still in him." She wiped tears again, but more came.

Emilio gave hasty orders to his men, and then he took Revel aside.

471

"We must get him to the rancho." She nodded, fighting for control.

"How long has he been like this?"

Revel tried to remember how many days it had been since they'd left the hideout.

"Today is the fourth day." She clutched at Emilio's heavy coat. "Will he live?"

He smiled at her as he pulled her into his arms to comfort her.

"We will make him live, eh, *señorita?*" But something in his voice failed to drive away the fear she'd lived with the last four days.

With Broken Hand's help, Emilio's vaqueros built a travois—a platform made from animal skins bound between two trailing poles—to transport Jake. Thick furs would protect him from the cold at the same time they cushioned him from jolts and bumps.

Broken Hand and Emilio checked Jake's wounds before setting out, assuring Revel that she had done all she could. It would have been unwise to remove the bullet; he could easily have bled to death.

It began to snow again as they continued down the mountain. They made their way quickly but carefully with Jake, still unconscious, on the travois.

Revel had spoken only briefly with Broken Hand, to convey her gratitude. He had merely grunted some vague answer, uncomfortable with her tearful "woman's ways" as he'd called them.

Later when she asked Emilio how he found Broken Hand, he revealed it was the Indian guide who had found them, already on their way up the mountain. Broken Hand had come upon the Comancheros he'd gone after. Emilio told her they were all dead.

Revel stared at the Indian, wondering at the kind of man who would kill his own son for honor, then risk his life for a friend. She found no answers on that long ride down, only fear that it might all have been for nothing. Jake was near death.

They didn't stop to rest, but rode through the night and reached the valley late the next morning.

Everyone on the rancho was somber and quiet as they returned.

Rosa quickly gave orders. Pots were put to boiling to prepare bandages, meals were prepared for the weary vaqueros. The smaller children huddled in corners, staring wide-eyed as their mother became a whirlwind of activity. When Rosa set about mixing some strange concoction in a kettle on the brick stove, no one dared interfere—no one except Broken Hand.

He pushed his way into the kitchen, drawing curious stares from everyone. Ignoring them all, he approached Revel and grabbed her hand.

He placed a leather pouch in her palm. "Crush the leaves and mix with the juice from this." In her other hand he placed what looked like a leaf from a cactus plant.

"Bind it to the wound when the bullet is removed. He will not lose the leg." Then he turned and left them all staring after him.

Rosa inspected the dried leaves in the pouch. "The Indians have ways with medicine. And I know this cactus. I have heard it has magic healing powers."

Revel was very near the breaking point. "I don't know about magic, but I trust Broken Hand. We'll use it. It may be the only chance Jake has."

Rosa agreed, although she refused to allow Revel to help her remove the bullet.

"You are tired. You will be no help to me, or him. What if your hand should slip?"

"I won't leave him," Revel stubbornly announced.

"Very well, then you may help hold him down. And Emilio too. We will need him if Jake should awaken."

Jake didn't awaken, he remained unconscious through everything.

Rosa easily found the bullet. It lay very near the bone. She removed it, careful not to cause any more damage as

473

she did so. But even as she closed the wound with precise stitches, working tirelessly in the light from several lanterns, and then applying Broken Hand's strange, green salve, there was no certainty Jake would live.

Fever from the poison ravaged his body. He alternately burned and then was cold as ice. Twice Revel was certain he was gone, and each time he fought his way back, clinging to her hand.

She sat with him, she spoke to him, she held on to him, somehow sensing that if she let go, he would slip away from her.

Shadows lengthened in the room. It grew dark outside.

Several times, Rosa tried to persuade her to rest or eat. She refused.

It continued that way for two days. Rosa was fearful for Revel's health, but no amount of argument could persuade her to leave for even a few hours' sleep. Revel lost all track of time.

And so when she suddenly jerked awake, she had no sense of reality or what day it was, or even of the hour. She only knew that the hand beneath hers was cooler. Jake's entire body was cooler. He still didn't respond when she spoke to him, but his color was better, his skin not so drawn and parched.

She wept as she kissed him, and then lay her head at his shoulder as she sat beside him.

Rosa found her like that, exhausted, and finally sleeping. She had Emilio carry her to Elena's bedroom, where Revel slept for almost twenty-four hours.

Revel was dazed and confused when she awakened. Slowly her memories of the last several days came together. She rushed from the bedroom, her only thought of Jake.

As she reached the doorway, she saw Elena leaving the room across the hall. She caught a brief glimpse of Jake in the bed before the door was closed.

He was asleep. The heavy growth of beard was gone

from his face, and his color was better. Elena glanced up briefly, her dark eyes filled with many emotions. In her hands, she clutched a shallow basin, soap, and a shaving brush.

Her clean clothes and glossy hair, her exquisite face, made Revel painfully aware of her own disheveled appearance. She had refused to take any time for herself since they returned. Now she realized how dreadful she must look, in torn and filthy clothes, with dull and dirty hair carelessly pulled back.

"How is he?" she asked, one hand going back to smooth wild tangles of hair that had come loose.

Elena gave her a long look from head to foot.

"My mother says he will live."

Revel felt a flash of anger at the girl's closed dark look, but she smothered it back.

"Has he awakened yet?"

Elena brightened. "*Sí,* earlier this morning. When I was with him." Her meaning was all too obvious; her feelings for Jake were still strong in spite of her parents' disapproval.

"*Ah, bueno!*" Rosa said happily as she came toward them. "You are awake at last." She took Revel's hand and gently stroked it.

"You had me very worried. I was afraid I would have two invalids on my hands." She turned briefly to Elena and asked her to finish her chores. Then she led Revel to the kitchen. She immediately shoved a warm flour tortilla filled with meat at her.

"Eat. You must build up your strength."

"Is he really better?"

"Yes, much better. There is still some fever, but it is less each day. I would never admit this to anyone else, but that salve I made from the leaves the Indian gave you has worked a miracle. The wound is less swollen."

Revel was so grateful she was overcome by emotion. She bit her lower lip and closed her eyes against tears as she shielded her face behind her hand, trying to regain her composure. She felt Rosa's gentle touch on her shoulder.

"It is all right to cry. We came very close to losing him."

After several moments, Revel looked up again. "But he will recover?"

Rosa nodded. "In time. The wound at his side heals rapidly. He has three broken ribs, but they, too, will heal. The leg will take longer." She looked down at her hands, her expression solemn. "I pray the medicine will take away the infection and that he will not lose his leg. Only time will tell. But he will live."

Revel's heart tightened. When the infection had set in she'd known the risk. She quietly wept at the thought that Jake might still lose his leg. Rosa put a comforting arm about her shoulders.

"You must not blame yourself. Jake made his own decision to go with you. He has always made his own decisions."

"But it is *my* fault. If I hadn't been so determined to get Sam Bass . . ."

"You did what you had to do, just as Jake did. You accepted the risk, just as Jake did."

"But he came after me—when Bass's men took me."

"Then he was willing to accept the risk for you," Rosa said softly. "You cannot blame yourself for his decision." She stroked Revel's cheek. Then her expression changed and her smile returned once more.

"Now you must eat." She shoved the meat-filled tortilla at Revel. "Then you must wash—everything. You will want to see him, but I will not allow you to see my patient dressed like that, or . . ."—she made a face and held her nose in mock horror—"smelling like that."

In spite of the tears that still came too easily, Revel laughed. She picked at the filthy, torn shirt she wore, and had to agree. She smelled of dirt, sweat, horses, and other things she couldn't possibly identify.

She smiled with embarrassment. "I think you're right."

Rosa nodded vehemently as she kept a good distance from Revel. "I know I am." She added, "The water for your bath is already prepared. I've had it boiling for two days." Then, as if on second thought, she suggested, "Take the tortilla with you. I usually do not allow anyone to take food from the table, except perhaps the vaqueros when they are so busy with the roundup. But I am willing to make an exception. At the moment, you smell and look worse than the vaqueros." She waved a wooden spoon at Revel, shooing her in the direction of the storage room off the kitchen that served as the bathing room.

As soon as Revel took one bite of the tortilla, she discovered she was famished and quickly finished it. Then she undressed and slipped into the tub. She winced as lukewarm water met the sore flesh across her back. Rosa brought another bucketful of hot water from the huge kettle in the kitchen. One look at Revel's back and she muttered, *"Madre de Dios!"*

The bucket thumped to the wood floor. Rosa took a cloth from the nearby bench and, over Revel's protests that she could bathe herself, carefully washed the angry welts at her back. She asked no questions as she finished, but handed Revel the cloth.

"Soap. And brush." She pointed to the nearby bench, then gave firm orders, no doubt sharpened on her several children. "Wash everything—twice." Then she scooped up Revel's clothing and headed for the door.

"I am going to burn these," she announced. Revel stopped her with a cry.

"Not the boots!" she pointed to the soft buckskin boots that Jake had bought for her.

Rosa inspected them with a knowing smile. "Very well. I will have them cleaned. But I do not understand why you should want to keep them." The teasing look in her eyes suggested she knew perfectly well.

Revel bit at her lower lip. "They're very comfortable—and very useful."

Rosa nodded and gave her a wink. "*Sí*, I understand." Then she added softly, "I am very glad you came back to us safely."

As she said that, Revel recalled the last time Rosa had spoken of her safe return. Her hand went to her neck. She had completely forgotten about the small gold cross. It was gone.

"Oh, Rosa, your cross! I must have lost it up on the mountain!"

Rosa simply smiled at her. "It's not important. The only thing that is important is that you and Jake have returned."

"But it was yours," Revel protested, a soft catch in her voice. "I intended to return it to you."

"It was a gift, a symbol of my hopes and prayers that you would return safely—and you have. It served its purpose." Then Rosa looked at her with mock severity and commanded, "Wash!"

She closed the door behind her. When she returned a short time later, she held a clean white blouse and a richly embroidered skirt, like the ones she and her daughters wore, in one hand, a small carved bowl in the other.

"I have burned your clothes. You will wear these. And I have brought something for your back." With great gentleness, she carefully applied a pleasant-smelling salve to the angry welts that still covered Revel's back.

"They will heal quickly now," she announced, and then as if Revel were simply one more of her children, she instructed her to dress. "We will eat when you are ready."

When Revel emerged a little while later, Rosa approved the transformation.

Revel's skin had been scrubbed until it glowed bright pink, and her hair was still wet from several washings.

But the most dramatic change was the blouse and skirt. It had been so long since Revel had worn women's clothing that the feel of the skirt lightly brushing her bare legs took some getting used to. Rosa had adamantly refused to return the boots until they were thoroughly cleaned, so Revel wore woven sandals.

The one tortilla had barely taken the edge off her appetite. As she stepped out of the steam-filled bathing room and into the warm, scent-filled kitchen, Revel's stomach complained loudly.

"Sit," Rosa ordered, even though it was several hours until the evening meal. She put a large plate piled with food in front of Revel.

"First I'd like to see Jake."

"He is still asleep. You can do him no good if you faint away from hunger, even if you do smell better. Now, eat!" Rosa commanded in a tone Revel had heard her use on her children when they misbehaved.

It would be rude to refuse. Still, Revel was determined to eat quickly. It had been days since she'd had a solid meal, and her appetite reflected that. It was almost an hour later when she finally pushed back from the table in the kitchen, unable to take another bite.

Rosa looked at her with a smug, satisfied expression on her pretty face.

"Now you may see him, unless, of course, you think you should take a walk first. My Emilio eats like that, and you see how big he is."

"It was wonderful, Rosa. *Muchas gracias,*" Revel said, feeling a warm drowsiness slip through her. "I had almost forgotten what real food tastes like."

As she turned to go to Jake's room, Rosa handed her a tray. On it were a tea made from herbs and a delicious smelling hot broth.

"He has been awake a few times, and he must eat something if he is to regain his strength."

Revel took the tray. *Gracias,* Rosa—and to Emilio

also—for everything. But especially for being his friends."

Rosa reached out and stroked her cheek. "You are his friend also. Emilio has told me what happened up on that mountain. Jake would have died without you." Her look became very wise. "I think you are more than his friend."

Revel swallowed back the emotions that tightened in her throat.

"*Sí, es verdad*," she answered in Spanish. It was true. However, she knew Jake could never love anyone but Rachel. "But it doesn't matter," she said softly as she turned to Jake's room.

She sat with him for hours. He roused occasionally, but only when the fever abated. It was less severe now, the worst of it seemed to be over.

During the times when he seemed more lucid, Revel carefully cradled his head and spooned some of Rosa's broth into his mouth. Then he slept again.

His wounds were healing. The bullet hole in his side was neatly closed, covered by only a light bandage. Heavier bandages were thickly wrapped about his waist to protect his broken ribs so they could also heal.

The infection that had swollen his thigh to almost double its normal size had abated. No longer were there angry streaks of red on purplish-blue flesh.

The bandage at this wound was changed frequently, however, with fresh salve applied each time. Revel thanked Broken Hand for the remedy that seemed to be working such miracles. And she silently prayed that Jake would not lose his leg.

In those quiet hours as she sat with him, Revel had a great deal of time to think.

She had finally had her revenge, and she had the proof she needed—Sam Bass's distinctive black steel revolver with the gleaming burlwood handle etched with notches. One for each law man and Pinkerton agent he claimed to have killed.

The men who had ridden with Bass were all dead. It wasn't the end of the Comancheros, but the largest band of them was now gone. Revel claimed no responsibility for that. The credit was entirely due to Broken Hand and Jake.

Jake.

She owed him the greatest debt—one that could never be fully repaid. He had saved her life, and had made it possible to avenge her father's death. She couldn't have done it without him. She realized that now. But the cost was high.

As she sat beside him, holding his hand, she realized that she had very nearly gotten them both killed because of her need for revenge. And she remembered that moment up on the mountain when she knew none of it mattered any longer—when the only thing that mattered was the fact that she loved Jake Reno and couldn't bear to see him die.

She owed him so much . . . loved him so much. For reasons she understood and for those she didn't.

Perhaps it all came down to the fact that everything she'd been trying to find for so long—was so certain she would have when Sam Bass was dead—she'd found with Jake.

She had changed. Her feelings and emotions had changed. Revel knew she would never be quite the same.

"All because of you, Jake Reno," she said softly in the quiet room, silent except for his breathing.

Yes, she owed him a great deal. And she intended to repay that debt, just as she'd promised. That was partly why she had to leave—to make certain Jake got his pardon. It also had to do with what had happened between them.

She loved him, but never once had he spoken of his feelings for her. Never once had he said the words she needed very badly to hear. Whoever Rachel was, he had loved only her. There was no room for anyone else.

It was over, done with. They were too different from

481

each other, their lives were too different. It would never work.

Her hair fell about them in a soft veil as she leaned over him, and her mouth closed over his.

She kissed him, tenderly, deeply, cradling his face between her hands as a single tear slipped down her cheek and spilled onto his. She kissed him good-bye.

Chapter Twenty-Six

Revel walked down the steps of the Arizona Territorial governor's office in Prescott, and crossed the plaza at the center of town. In her reticule she carried a hand-drafted copy of the full pardon the governor had just signed for Jake.

Her next stop was the *Miner*, to see its editors, Mr. Beach and Mr. Marion. The *Miner* was the only daily newspaper in the Territory and enjoyed a large circulation and equally large influence. She gave the editors the story of the year—the death of Sam Bass, crediting Jake Reno, outlaw, for his part in Bass's demise. She also mentioned that because of Reno's assistance to the Pinkerton National Detective Agency, the Territorial governor had granted him a full pardon.

This was the best way Revel knew of quickly spreading the word of Jake's pardon.

When Mr. Beach and Mr. Marion had their story, she went to the local Wells Fargo dispatch office. She sent a copy of the pardon to Marshal Virgil Earp in Tombstone, asking if he would see that Jake received it.

The following morning, she left her hotel and boarded a Concord stage of the Southern Pacific Mail Line for the half-day ride north to the railhead of the Atlantic Pacific Railroad. From there, she would travel east and then north to Denver.

It was time to go home.

The weather was cold that early November morning as she waited for her train, promising snow before the day was out and recalling her journey into the mountains of Mexico.

It was almost a month since she'd left. In all that time there had been no word from either Rosa or Emilio, nor was there any place where they might have sent a letter or note to her.

It had taken her over two weeks to make the journey back to Tucson. Broken Hand had ridden with her, insisting Jake would want it that way. When they had parted, the Indian guide had mumbled something about maybe riding south again, and Revel hoped he had. She'd had no parting words or messages for him to pass on to Jake when he saw him again. She hadn't known how to say what she felt, or what purpose it would serve.

It had taken almost another two weeks to see the governor. First he was out of the Territory and she was informed it might be better to come back in a few months. Revel adamantly refused to be put off. Instead, she contacted Mr. Beach and Mr. Marion at the *Miner* and informed them she had an exclusive story for them about Sam Bass.

At first they were skeptical. But when they saw that legendary burlwood-handled revolver there was no longer any doubt she indeed had a story they wanted, but on one condition. First she had to see the governor.

Within two days of his return from Washington the governor had bowed to the power of the press and Revel was sitting in his office relating everything to him. And, as promised in their first meeting, he granted Jake a full pardon.

Now, as the train pulled up beside the railway platform, blowing steam from its boilers, a chill wind blew at her heavy skirts. That was something else she had to get used to, the confinement of woolen skirts, shirtwaists, and form-fitting jackets.

Her hair was twisted into a thick mass topped by a velvet hat in the same shade of hunter green as her skirt and jacket. Her feet were encased in thick-heeled button-top ladies' boots. But inside one of the newly purchased valises, along with her newly purchased clothes, were the soft, leather buckskin boots she had once worn crossing Indian territory and the mountains of northern Mexico.

"Ticket, ma'am?" the conductor called out as she started to board.

"Yes, of course." Revel handed him the ticket she had just purchased, and he led her through to a leather upholstered seat.

"I see you're going on to Denver. Is that your home?" he asked congenially.

She smiled hesitantly, and then simply said, "Yes."

"Well, have a pleasant journey, ma'am." He politely touched the bill of his cap. "Maybe you'll come back to us someday."

The way he said it made her look up—*come back to us.*

Her smile became wistful. "No, I don't think so. But thank you, anyway."

The conductor nodded. "You just let me know if you need anything," he said before he went to assist other passengers aboard.

Revel looked out the window to the nearby mountains, and the silvery glimmer of the Verde River, remembering other mountains and a crystal-clear mountain pool. It seemed a lifetime ago.

"No," she whispered, "I don't think I'll be coming back."

She traveled to St. Louis, and from there to Philadelphia for a visit with her aunt. After two days she knew she had been right in deciding to return to Denver and her work there—that is, if she still had a position with the Pinkerton Agency.

Her aunt was a dear, sweet lady, but they were very

485

different people. She had never understood Revel's decision to join the agency after her father's death, and for the entire two days Revel was in Philadelphia, her aunt alternately lectured, pleaded, or tried to shame her into staying there.

"After all, Revel, the life your father led was dangerous and unpredictable. He was never there for you when you were a child. And I've had the most dreadful time explaining to my friends where you are and just what it is that you do." Her aunt paused only briefly for breath before continuing her tirade. "And, of course, it's what killed your dear mother."

That was it. That was the straw that broke the camel's back.

As far as Revel was concerned, that last remark made many things clear. Her aunt had never understood that her mother would have died any way, that her mother's death had had nothing to do with Revel's father or his profession.

And much as she respected and loved her aunt, Revel simply could not live Addie's kind of life. She was certain that inside of a week, immersed in her aunt's schedule of society parties, teas, balls, cotillions, and coming-out parties, she would go stark, raving mad. She might have been raised among the Philadelphia Main Line, but she had no more in common with them than a prized Appaloosa stallion did with carriage horses.

What was there to discuss with them?

"Yes, your gown is perfectly lovely, my dear. Oh, by the way, I shot a Comanchero to death down in Mexico."

Or . . . "Of course I'd love to come to tea Thursday afternoon, and I can tell you all about the notorious Sam Bass. He killed my father, you know, but I followed him down to Mexico. I was abducted, almost raped, competed for in a knife-throwing contest, and horsewhipped. Then Mr. Bass came after me, but I killed him.

". . . How did I do that? With a gun of course. I've become quite good at it too. I'll have to show you sometime."

And on the occasion of someone's betrothal:

"My dear, how fortunate you are. Of course, he's the most eligible man in Philadelphia. I just know you'll be very happy.

"By the way have I told you about Jake Reno. He's an outlaw. I spent a month and a half with him, alone out on the trail in the Territories and down in Mexico.

"He's the most dangerous man I've ever known . . . trustworthy, brave . . . tender, handsome . . . and we made love."

". . . No, he didn't force me. It just happened. No, more than once. There was the time on the desert when we were caught in the flash flood. And then there was the time astride a horse—no don't be silly. He touched me—in so many places—and then he made love to me by a mountain pool, all night long, and again in the morning. And my dear, I wanted him never to stop."

". . . Where? Someplace in Mexico, I think. If he's alive."

"No, I'm certain I'll never see him again. You see, he's in love with someone else."

Perhaps she could have lived with the silliness of society women if it hadn't been for Jake Reno.

She had no regrets about what had happened between them, but falling in love with him had changed her. She was less tolerant of the pettiness in other people's lives, and wanted none of it for herself.

Or perhaps it was the fact that her journey through the Territories, Indian country, and the wilderness of northern Mexico, had somehow changed her.

She felt confined in her aunt's elegant Clarington Court mansion, ill at ease in satin gowns, restless at the endless rounds of theater, parties, opera going, and balls.

More than once she imagined what everyone's reaction might be if she appeared at the opera in one of her finest satin gowns and buckskin boots, or instead of stepping daintily into her aunt's elegant carriage, if she leaped astride one of the horses, skirts flying, and rode to an evening gala.

That would certainly set Main Line Philadelphia on it's very proper ear.

She might have put up with all the rest of it, if the aching loneliness hadn't haunted her, if she hadn't felt she'd lost something as vital to living as the air she breathed.

Perhaps she was running away, deciding that she had to leave after only one week, but Revel simply knew she couldn't stay in Philadelphia.

She didn't know what she wanted, she only knew she didn't want that kind of life.

Once before, when her father died, she had gone to Denver. Her life had become real there, more grounded, more honest. And she had a purpose there—at least she hoped she did. Returning to Denver, of course, meant a confrontation with William Pinkerton about taking off after Sam Bass. But going back was the one thing she was certain she wanted.

Her aunt was absolutely beside herself when Revel announced that she was leaving, but Revel had been through all this before, three years earlier.

It was easier this time. The decision itself was easier. Perhaps that had something to do with a nagging suspicion she had. At any rate, the day arrived. Her aunt wept pitifully at the train station, declaring she had no idea how she would explain Revel's second disappearance to all her friends. Then when she discovered that all her pleading, weeping, even guilt couldn't dissuade Revel, she quickly hugged her and instructed her to write often.

As Revel boarded the train, she knew she had made the right decision.

A week later as she stood in William Pinkerton's office at the Denver headquarters of the Pinkerton National Detective Agency, she had reason to doubt her decision.

"You, young lady, have a great deal of explaining to do!"

Jake stood at the window of the cabin, watching the vaqueros herd mares and yearling colts into the pastures for winter grazing.

Frost lay across the yard between the paddocks and the cabins, gleamed off fence rails, and left a slick sheen on the watering troughs.

As the spirited yearlings ran, their breaths gusted clouds of steam on the frosty morning air. He caught sight of the Appaloosa stallion tethered at the corral fence, waiting patiently.

"You are impatient to leave us," Rosa said softly from the doorway.

Jake turned carefully, balanced on one foot and the crutches Emilio had made for him. He was thin, almost too thin, his body only now beginning its slow recovery from weeks of fever and from the second operation on his leg.

It hadn't healed as Rosa had thought it should, nor had Jake recovered as a man of his strength should. She had had Emilio send for the physician.

It was a three-day trip, and by the time the physician had arrived, Jake had once more been close to death.

He'd recovered slowly after the second operation, and now he was forced to use crutches. Rosa knew it bothered him not to be able to walk or ride, but he never complained.

"I've stayed too long."

She crossed the room and looped her arm through his, smiling up at him warmly.

"You are welcome to stay forever, you know that. Emilio has often spoken of how it could be if you stayed. He would like it very much. He has missed you. We have all missed you."

Jake patted her hand affectionately, the hand that had

489

cared for him during his long convalescence. He kissed the glossy black hair smoothed back from her face into a tight bun.

"It's not an invitation that I turn down lightly, *hija*." He'd always called her *little girl*. He still remembered her as that young girl he first met almost eighteen years ago when he and Emilio were barely old enough to shave. She had been beautiful then, she was beautiful now. And a dear friend to him.

"But it's time. I need to go."

She nodded. "The rancho in the Wind River Mountains?" she asked, knowing how often he'd dreamed of going back if he straightened out his life. Now the Señorita Pinkerton had made it possible."

The Indian had returned from north of the border with the news that Jake had been given a full pardon by the Territorial governor, just as the *Señorita* had promised.

"It's a beautiful place, Rosa." He smiled. "Almost as beautiful as it is here. And a friend of my father's is keeping some horses for me. I can go back now. It's what I've always wanted. The stallion will provide good breeding stock to get started."

"So at last you are finished with the past," she said softly. Emilio had told her long ago of Jake's earlier life. Like the *señorita*, he had wanted revenge. He had found it, had been willing to pay the price for it. Because of the *señorita*, he now had a second chance at life.

Jake looked down at her, something unreadable darkening his green eyes.

"Yes, I suppose I am finished with it now."

"I wish you would wait just a little longer. How will you manage?" Rosa lamented. "Perhaps you could wait until spring to leave, when you have had more time to heal."

"I've had enough time. Broken Hand and his magic potions will take care of me, if I need help."

Emilio pulled the buckboard around in front of the cabin. Jake's Appaloosa was tied to the rear, his saddle and gear packed in the back. It was a reminder that he wouldn't be riding astride to the ranch in the Wyoming Territory.

Rosa laid her hand lovingly against his cheek. She had tried to put some flesh back on his bones the last few weeks, but there were still hollows at his cheeks, and a dark, haunted look behind his eyes that she felt certain had nothing to do with his long recovery.

They had spoken very little of the *señorita* after the fever was finally gone, but before that, he had spoken a great deal about her in dreams and delirium.

For the first time, since Rachel, Jake Reno cared deeply about a woman. When he finally awoke, free of the fever, he had asked for the *señorita*. And when Rosa had explained that she was gone, something had changed in him.

He seemed to close in on himself. The long recovery began but he ate little, said little, and when he was strong enough, he hobbled to the windows that faced the mountains.

At first he sat, then when Emilio gave him the crutches, he stood for long hours, staring at those distant peaks, as if he might have lost something there and was searching, trying to get it back.

Rosa was not fooled. She knew it had everything to do with the *señorita*.

Now, as she heard Emilio stamping the frost from his heavy boots she said her farewells to Jake, then pressed something into his hand.

He opened his fingers and looked down at the small, gold cross.

"I found it in your clothes when she brought you back to us," Rosa explained quietly.

"Keep it," Jake said gruffly. "It belongs to you."

She shook her head adamantly. "No. I gave it to her."

He stared down at the shining gold cross. "I found it after Bass's men took her. She must have lost it when she tried to fight them off."

491

"I gave it to her in the hope that it would bring her back safely to us. And in a way it did." Strong in her beliefs, Rosa was convinced of that.

"Perhaps you should return it to her," she suggested. And for just a moment she saw the light change behind those solemn green eyes as Jake looked up at her.

Loneliness and inner pain were reflected there, along with other emotions so intense Rosa felt them as well—desire, need, and love.

"The wagon is ready," Emilio called out as he walked into the large room, looking questioningly from his wife to his friend.

"Have you persuaded him to change his mind, *querida?*" he asked hopefully.

Rosa shook her head and gave Jake a secretive smile. "No, my husband. It is time for him to go."

Emilio and two of his vaqueros rode north as far as the border at Sonora. They said their farewells there, as only life-long friends can—not good-bye at all but "Vaya con Dios. Go with God. *Hasta luego.* Until we meet again."

At the border, Jake and Broken Hand caught the stagecoach line north to Tombstone, trailing the Appaloosa and the paint pony behind. He wanted to make certain the pardon was legitimate, that he wouldn't turn around in some backwater town and find himself taken in and hanged for that reward money.

Virgil and Wyatt Earp were glad to see him, and congratulated him.

It was true. Just as she'd promised, Revel made certain he had a full pardon from the Territorial governor. Virgil gave him the signed copy, and assured him that every lawman in the Territories had been made aware of it.

And there were frequent articles in the *Miner* and the *Territorial Gazette* about the tracking down of Sam Bass, three years after the Texas Rangers claimed to have killed him at Red Rock in Texas.

Jake was now a free man. And there was one more surprise—the reward money for Sam Bass. Revel had insisted he be given the money—ten thousand dollars.

"Somehow I thought this would go to that sheriff out at Las Cruces. He trailed us into those mountains, but a friend of mine managed to get him lost."

"Oh, he tried to get his hands on it," Virgil assured Jake. "He talked long and hard about how he was the one who tracked Bass down. But that little Pinkerton gal set everybody right. And she had Bass's revolver."

"You talked to her?"

"Yeah, I wrote a letter for her to take to the governor."

"How was she when you saw her?"

Virgil and Wyatt exchanged looks. "She was just fine, I suppose. Although Wyatt thought she seemed different somehow."

"Different? How?"

Wyatt shrugged. "I don't know. All quiet like, the way gals sometimes get. Not like before when she came in here like a ball of fire, real feisty and determined to have her way about things."

Jake remembered how she could be when she got like that. "Did she say where she was headed?"

"Denver, I think," Virgil answered thoughtfully. "Said she had work to do. And that's where she was from originally."

Jake nodded. "Yeah, I suppose that's where she headed. She got what she wanted."

Virgil added, "And you got what you wanted—that pardon."

"What will you do now, Jake?" Wyatt Earp asked.

Jake felt the smooth gold of the small cross in the pocket of his coat.

Had he gotten what he truly wanted? What was really important?

"I think maybe I'll head up north toward the Wyoming Territory."

"It's mighty cold up there, this time of year," Virgil pointed out.

"Yeah, but there's a place up there I've been trying to

493

get back to. With this"—he held up the pardon—"I can go home now."

They said their farewells.

Broken Hand was waiting for Jake as he hobbled out of the marshal's office.

"I thought you might have decided to head back to Fort Buchanan. I hear the Army still needs scouts."

"Bah!" Broken Hand grunted in untypical Indian fashion. "I'm getting too old for that. It's too dangerous out there with every young buck Apache renegade looking to take himself a scalp. Let the Army find the renegades themselves."

"Will you go to the reservation?" Jake asked as he blew out a streamer of cigarette smoke.

"No reservation!" Broken Hand snarled, a deadly gleam in his eyes. "They kill the Indians on those damned reservations."

Jake smiled faintly. "I hear there's a spread up north in the Wyoming Territory. Some crazy fool plans to raise Appaloosa horses up there."

Broken Hand grunted again as his dark skin wrinkled in a thoughtful frown.

"It will be a long trip," he grumbled.

"Very long," Jake agreed.

"You might need someone to take care of that stallion of yours."

"He gets a little feisty since I can't ride him."

Again Broken Hand nodded. "Is there a lot of work to be done?"

"A lot. The main ranch house was gutted out by fire years ago. But the walls are still standing. We'll need to rebuild corrals and paddocks. We may need to build a barn."

"That's a lot of work for a broken-down Indian guide and a crippled outlaw," the old Apache was never one to say other than exactly what he meant.

"Yeah, it is. But we'll have help. I've the promise of

494

friends when I get back there. It's a blood promise from an Indian war chief."

Broken Hand seemed to have made his decision. "Unlike the white man, you can believe the promise of an Indian. I think I will ride north with you."

Jake simply nodded and offered the old Apache a cigarette.

The next morning as Jake and Broken Hand left the hotel, they passed a milliner's shop.

A young woman stood admiring something in the paned-glass window. For just a moment there was something about her that reminded Jake of Revel.

Maybe it was the way she held her head. Perhaps it was her dark hair, which as he saw when he approached her, wasn't as thick, or silken like Revel's. And it didn't have those hidden fiery lights running through it.

The young woman looked up, obviously surprised to find a man standing in front of a lady's shop. She smiled at him shyly and he saw that she wasn't at all like Revel. She wasn't as fair, the shape of her face was different. It didn't have high cheekbones or a softly curved, full mouth.

And she didn't have those remarkable, deep blue eyes that had a way of looking far inside him.

As she turned and walked on down the boardwalk, Jake glanced in the window to see what had caught her fancy. He saw an elegant lady's hat.

It looked out of place in a town like Tombstone. Undoubtedly it was the latest fashion from St. Louis or some other big city.

Made of soft gray velvet, it was shaped like a man's small derby, with a curved brim all the way around and a wide, blue satin ribbon circling the crown.

But what caught his attention was the cluster of small, blue silk flowers attached to the brim in front.

Their deep blue color reminded him of *bluebonnets*.

When the morning stage arrived, Jake and Broken Hand boarded for the ride to the railhead.

With the reward money, Jake bought tickets on the Atchison, Topeka and Santa Fe train. The Appaloosa and Broken Hand's paint pony were loaded into one of the cattle cars.

They were headed north.

It was bitter cold outside. The windows of hotels, shops, and restaurants were frosty. The high-altitude Denver air was crisp, filled with the soft flurry of snow.

Closed carriages churned the newly fallen fluff to slush. Even though it was midday, light pooled golden on white drifts outside offices and business establishments, and voices drifted on steamy breaths as patrons dressed in fine wools and heavy velvets left their fashionable luncheons at the Brown Palace Hotel or Blandings.

Cattlemen in Stetson hats and rawhide leather jackets mingled on the snow-covered streets with gentlemen wearing the latest in silk vests and overcoats from the East.

Revel rounded a corner just ahead of Operative Sammy Noonan, holding her skirts out of the slush and mud.

"Miss Tyson, wait!"

"We'll lose him. Mr. Pinkerton said we were to stay with him. He went down this alley."

"If you say so." Sammy ducked down the alley and slowly walked the length of it.

Just as they reached the end, they saw a shadow. They flattened themselves against the far side, and waited.

"Let me go first," Sammy said, edging past her. "Mr. Pinkerton was specific about that. I hope you didn't bring that revolver."

"No, I didn't bring it," Revel assured him, then added,

"I couldn't get it into my reticule. Honestly, it wouldn't be so difficult keeping up with him if I could wear men's clothes."

Sammy gave her an amiable grin. "Mr. Pinkerton was sure angry the first time you tried wearing those buckskin boots."

"It's far more practical than sneaking down streets dressed like some society matron."

"Well, as far as I'm concerned, you looked great in those pants." When Revel raised an eyebrow, he looked sheepishly away. "You know what I mean, Miss Tyson."

She smiled at him. "Yes, I know what you mean. But I certainly hate chasing footmen wealthy ladies suspect of lifting jewelry from family safes. I wonder when Mr. Pinkerton will be satisfied that I've served my penance and give me a real case to work on."

Sammy gave her a rueful look. "I'd say tracking down Sam Bass is just about all the case anyone could want for an entire lifetime."

"Yes. Unfortunately Mr. Pinkerton considered it a personal quest. Now he wants to teach me a lesson by restricting me to the cases no one else wants."

By the expression on Sammy's face, she knew she had hurt his feelings. He'd been put on the same case but for other reasons.

He was the newest operative and had the least experience. Somehow William Pinkerton thought they couldn't possibly get into any trouble on a simple case like this.

She tried to reassure him. "Don't worry. You'll graduate to harder cases soon enough."

"But what about you?"

"Oh, I think I'll have to be content with stolen jewels for a while," she said as she smoothed her hand down over the waist of her skirt.

"Well, Mr. Pinkerton certainly didn't mind the agency taking credit for tracking Sam Bass. I think he was unfair about that."

"It was the only thing he could do, Sammy. Officially, I wasn't assigned to the case. Unofficially, I stepped on a few toes and broke a few rules. Actually, I suppose I'm fortunate he was willing to let me off with an unofficial reprimand."

"Yeah, I suppose. But golly, think of it. Sam Bass!"

She hated to dampen his enthusiasm, but they were on a case of their own.

"There he goes, into the back of that restaurant. The owner could be the shill. C'mon, lets go." Revel lifted her skirts again and quickly walked down the alley, Sammy right behind her. As they reached the back entrance to the restaurant, he stepped in front of her.

"I'll go first, just in case there's any trouble." He grabbed the knob and pushed open the door.

Light poured out into the valley, along with welcome heat from the kitchen and a mixture of scents and aromas. The sign over the back entrance, for deliveries, declared it was Kaminski's Polish Restaurant. Within, spices and the aroma of pungent meat mixed with the heavy scent of cooked fat. The smell hit Revel like a thick blanket, smothering her and making her nauseous. Her skin went clammy cold, and she became dizzy. She grabbed at the door for support.

When she didn't immediately follow, Sammy stopped and looked back.

"Go!" she ordered him. "Stay with him or you'll lose him."

"Will you be all right?"

"I'm fine," she lied, fighting back the nausea as she covered her mouth with her hand.

"Don't let him get away!"

As Sammy turned and ran after the suspect, Revel whirled back out into the alley behind the restaurant and was promptly and thoroughly sick.

Thank God, I'm alone, she thought as she finally quit throwing up. The chill air helped. She scooped fresh

498

snow from a window sill and patted it against her face.

She had thought she was done with being sick—just a discomfort of the stomach, she'd told herself. It was common in the winter; people were frequently sick. But not continuously, not for three months.

As she ate a handful of the fresh snow, letting it melt to cool, refreshing water in her mouth, she admitted what she had known even in Philadelphia—she was going to have a child, Jake Reno's child.

"Revel?" Sammy popped back out into the alley. "Are you feeling better?"

"Yes, of course. Did you find him?"

Sammy beamed. "Not only him. I found his shill and one of Mrs. Mainwaring's ruby earbobs. I had the owner go for the constable. They took our friend out the front." He gave her a closer look.

"Say, you don't look too well."

"I'll be fine, Sammy. And you did an excellent job."

"You deserve all the credit, Miss Tyson. I never would have thought he was the one. All this time, I thought it was the butler."

She smiled at him as her stomach finally settled down. "They always think it was the butler. We'd better get back and file our reports. I think this will get you a field assignment." She congratulated him.

"And maybe now Mr. Pinkerton will give you better assignments too." He beamed.

"Oh, I don't know." She smiled softly. "I think maybe I should work here in Denver for a few more months. It'll do me good. Maybe Mr. Pinkerton will even let me work closer to the office."

Sammy looked at her strangely. "Well, of course, if that's what you want."

She nodded. "I think it's what I need."

They were congratulated by everyone in the outer offices upon their return to the three-story building owned by the Pinkerton National Detective Agency.

When Sammy told of catching the thief, he went into great detail, making a great fuss over Revel's participation.

Then Mr. Pinkerton's personal secretary informed them that their employer was in his offices. Mr. Pinkerton had asked to see Revel as soon as she returned. Several field operatives were present, taking care of the endless mundane paperwork that always accompanied a case, when this request was made. They were all aware of how close Allan Pinkerton came to discharging her, and they had all spoken in her behalf. It was no small accomplishment, tracking down a man even the Texas Rangers couldn't get. But their employer was a stickler for rules and proper procedure. It was the only thing, he insisted, that separated his operatives from criminals.

Now an apprehensive quiet fell upon the office.

"Thank you, Mrs. Adams." Revel carefully put away her reticule and hung up her cape. She read the unspoken question on their faces and wondered if Mr. Pinkerton had had a change of heart and had decided to discharge her after all.

She smoothed back her hair and lifted her chin slightly as she knocked lightly at his door and let herself into the spacious office.

"Good afternoon, Revel." Pinkerton greeted her warmly, causing her to frown. "I understand you've broken the Mainwaring case. Excellent work, but then I was confident you could do it."

"Thank you, Mr. Pinkerton," she replied hesitantly.

"Please, sit down." He gestured to a chair across from him. He was a large man and seemed to take up the entire width of the desk he sat behind, propped back, stroking the end of his mustache.

"Of course, there will be the usual commendation. But I was already thinking in terms of your next assignment."

"I see," Revel replied with even greater confusion.

Word usually spread quickly about a solved case, and Mr. Pinkerton was always aware of everything that went on.

At times it seemed the walls had ears. It wasn't because he eavesdropped, it was simply that he was a very thorough and meticulous man, especially about the reputation of the firm that carried his family name.

Since he'd brought the subject up, she decided to take it further.

"Actually, I was considering your earlier suggestion that it might be advisable for me to handle cases closer to the office rather than field assignments."

"I see," he said thoughtfully. "We can discuss that later of course, but I want to discuss a particular case right now. I have a client in my private office. We've discussed his case at great length, and I believe you are the only agent to handle it."

She glanced to the side door leading from Mr. Pinkerton's suite. He rarely conducted business in his private office, only in extremely delicate situations. Its separate entrance allowed someone to come and go without entering the outer offices.

"Well, of course," she said uncertainly, wondering if she would be able to accept the case or if she would be forced to refuse and reveal her reason to Mr. Pinkerton. Although, as the weeks passed, that would become obvious.

"Very good," Mr. Pinkerton smiled in a fatherly way. "He's waiting now. I've already told him your qualifications. You can discuss the case in my private suite."

She stood hesitantly. "Certainly. Thank you, Mr. Pinkerton."

"Not at all, Revel." Then he stopped her. "By the way, I don't think I ever mentioned in my anger that I do understand your reasons for going after Bass. I would have done the same thing if I'd been in your place."

Revel felt as if a weight had lifted from her. She had always cared a great deal for Allan Pinkerton, and she had feared she'd lost his friendship, he had been so angry with her when she'd returned.

"Thank you."

She crossed the office to the private suite and let herself inside, closing the door behind her.

It was like a sitting room, with elegant, richly upholstered furnishings—high-backed, overstuffed chairs, a settee, two side tables—all clustered before a fireplace with a handcarved mantel.

The only exception to the intimate furnishings was the large, wide desk that was an exact duplicate of the one in the outer office. It was obscured in darkness against the far wall. Rich, burgundy velvet drapes framed the high windows. It was a masculine room.

A fire burned at the brick hearth, and the drapes were drawn at the windows to keep out the cold. The only other light came from a single lamp resting on one of the tables. Other than that the room was full of late-afternoon shadows.

She frowned, wondering if Mr. Pinkerton's *special client* might have chosen to leave. She didn't see anyone in the room and turned back to the outer office.

"Miss Tyson."

She spun back around, looking into the dark shadows at the desk.

"I'm sorry. I thought you might have left."

When there was no immediate reply, her frown deepened, but she slowly approached the desk.

"Mr. Pinkerton informed me that you are in need of our agency."

Again there was only silence. If Mr. Pinkerton hadn't already approved the case and the client, she might have been uneasy. Perhaps it was merely the delicacy of the case that made the client so reticent to speak out.

"Of course, we will help you in any way we can. But I would like to know something about the case."

There was a slight stirring from behind the desk, and a

shifting of shadows as the mysterious client came around the desk. There was something odd about the way he moved. Then he sat on the edge of the desk, not more than two feet away from her.

When he spoke, his voice was a gruff whisper.

"I'm looking for someone."

Revel was faintly disappointed. Missing persons cases weren't particularly exciting work. She'd handled several in her first year as an operative and had found them boring. Still, Mr. Pinkerton had insisted she take this case, and she wasn't in a position to refuse.

"Very well, we'll need the usual background information, of course. Can you tell me something about the person you're looking for?"

The slight hesitation made her wonder if the client's circumstances were somehow painful. Then, still obscured in shadows, he spoke again in a whisper, but softer now so that she was forced to lean forward to hear him.

"She's young—and very beautiful."

Revel listened politely, mentally taking notes that would be put down on paper later.

"Go on."

"She's very refined, elegant—a lady."

"I see." That might explain any number of problems, and the necessity for discretion.

"She's very well educated, always knows the right things to say. But she swears worse than some men."

Revel's brow wrinkled slightly. The lady, whoever she was, was a mixture, a mass of contradictions.

"She likes fine silk dresses." He reached out, almost as if he might touch the sleeve of her dress; then he withdrew his hand. "But she's been known to dress like a man and wear pants and boots."

"I see. Please go on." For the life of her, Revel couldn't explain why this conversation was beginning to make her uneasy.

"She can be very stubborn and headstrong, even when

503

she's wrong about something. She's also the most generous, bravest, most passionate woman I've ever known," he continued to whisper.

Revel was beginning to understand his meaning. There was something almost sad the way he described this woman. He must love her a great deal, she thought. She dreaded asking the next, rather delicate question.

"I'm sorry I have to ask this, but it is necessary," she apologized. "Is there a man involved in her disappearance?"

Her client's silence seemed to give her that answer. Then, after several moments, he said,

"I hope to God there is."

No longer a whisper, that voice was gruff, full of emotion, and dearly familiar.

Revel was stunned and started to step back, when the mysterious stranger reached from the shadows, his arm slipping around her waist as he pulled her toward him.

There was no time to react, to escape, much less to think. She was pulled full-length against him, the silk of her gown crushed against the soft wool coat across his chest.

Even as her thoughts reeled and her senses screamed to deny what had haunted her dreams for months, his mouth found hers.

Fire—all the places inside that ached with cold emptiness were ignited.

His lips crushed over hers, with a hunger that was frightening. As her lips parted beneath his, half in question, half in surrender, his tongue slipped between like white hot velvet.

He pulled her closer, taking her weight against him as he sat at the desk, while his other hand plunged into her hair, desperate to pull her closer. He would have pulled her inside him if he could.

"Jake!" Her voice was a ragged whisper as their lips parted, caressed, and then came together again.

504

He kissed her cheek, her temple, the soft wing of her eyebrow, and then the delicate sweep of lashes at her closed eyes. He trembled with the need that poured through him, and the effort to maintain his restraint.

What if she pulled away? What if she walked away again?

He hungrily traced the angle of that perfect, high cheekbone, gently flicked his tongue at the curve of her ear, stroked the line of her jaw to her neck, tasting sweetness and heat. His fingers spread across her shoulders, easing down her slender back.

He wanted to feel her naked beneath him, hot and liquid over him.

Any doubts that he should have come wavered the moment he saw her, were obliterated the moment he touched her.

His hands caressed her back, ran down the lengths of her slender arms, then back up over the sweep of her bodice. As his fingers spread across the silk over her breasts, he heard her moan softly.

"Why did you leave me?" he whispered against her mouth, her small tongue wrapped around his. She was breathless when she angled her mouth away from his.

"I had to—" His lips trapped hers. "You didn't need me anymore . . . didn't want me . . . Rachel . . ." She hadn't meant to say it, and the moment she did, she felt him pull back from her. And she knew she was right. But as he brought his hands up to cradle her face and search her eyes, his expression was fierce, angry.

"What has this to do with Rachel?"

Oh, God. She ached for his kisses, his arms, for the feel of him moving inside her even as his child moved inside her. But she couldn't live with the ghost of another woman between them, whether he thought he could or not.

"You loved her . . ." she whispered softly as tears pooled in her eyes.

505

"Of course, I loved her."

"You spent seventeen years of your life tracking down the men who killed her."

"Just as you tracked down the man who killed your father." His hands tightened about her head.

"It's not the same," she cried out, wishing with all her heart that she didn't want him so, didn't love him.

"Yes, it is," he insisted. "We both did what we felt we had to do. What I felt for Rachel has nothing to do with what I feel for you."

"How can you say that? I've seen the way you look when you talk about her. She's not dead to you, not really. You loved her," Revel repeated, her heart breaking all over again. "You're still in love with her, and I can't take her place."

Jake's hands trembled as he held her.

"What are you talking about? *In love with her?*" he shook his head in confusion. "Yes, I loved my sister, but there's only been one woman I've ever fallen in love with, and I'm losing you. What can I say to make you believe it?" Despair thickened in his throat.

"Your *sister?*" Revel whispered in disbelief. "What are you saying?"

As he held her, Jake slowly began to understand. "You thought I was in love with Rachel, as a woman?"

"Yes, of course."

Jake slowly shook his head, a small ironic smile twisting his handsome lips.

"Rachel was my youngest sister. She was twelve years old when the rest of our family was killed by an outlaw gang. They left me for dead, but I went after them. Knowing she was still alive was the only thing that kept me going. Then when they killed her, I knew I had to finish it."

"But I thought—"

He silenced her with a finger at her lips. "You were wrong, *querida*. I love you. That's what I came here to tell

506

you, even if you didn't want to hear it. I didn't know it myself, until Rosa made me see it." He reached inside the pocket of his coat and retrieved the small gold cross.

"She said you were to have this. She gave it to you once."

"The cross! I thought I had lost it," Revel exclaimed with joy. "Where did you find it?"

"At the camp after our last night together on the mountain, when Bass's men took you."

She looked up into those crystal green eyes, seeing all the love, hope, and desire that she'd felt these last months reflected back. Then she noticed something else for the first time.

"You've grown a mustache," she exclaimed. "I didn't even notice when you kissed me."

"I thought it might help if I changed my looks just a little. I was afraid there might be some fool out there who didn't know about that pardon and might come gunnin' for me."

She leaned up on her toes and brushed her mouth against his. "I like it. I like it very much. Oh, Jake!" she wrapped her arms around his neck and held him tight. "I love you so much. I was so afraid you were going to die. Then I knew you would live, but I had to leave, and I was afraid I would never see you again."

He pulled her hard against him, trying to absorb the sweetness of her, the heat, the life and vitality that were so innately a part of her. His hands slipped down her back to her bottom pulling her in to him, molding her soft curves against his hardened body.

His hands encircled her waist as his mouth closed over hers again, his tongue making love to her in all the ways his body wanted to.

They slowly drew apart, and Revel's gaze carefully inspected what she could see of him. He was thinner, but he seemed to have fully recovered from the bullet hole in his side and the broken ribs.

507

Then her gaze wandered lower. He had been sitting on the desk the entire time. As soon as she knew it was him, she'd been afraid to look at his leg, expecting the worst.

Her heart leapt. His leg was whole and complete, though carefully braced against the edge of the desk. And beside him a cane rested. He could walk.

But even the worst wouldn't have mattered to her. She would take Jake Reno as he was. Still, it would have mattered to Jake, would have affected the plans he had for that ranch in Wyoming.

Jake was taking his own careful inventory, his thumbs gently caressing the silk dress at her waist. His questioning gaze met hers, and she realized that what she might have been able to conceal from everyone else, she couldn't conceal from someone who had known her so intimately.

She nodded. "I'm going to have a child." She bit her lip, uncertain of how he would greet such news, and hated herself for it. She'd never known herself to be so unsure, but then, she'd never had a child before.

"I'll understand if you're not pleased about it. It's just that I didn't intend . . . that is, I'm not familiar with ways to prevent these things from happening. . . . Oh God!" she muttered, completely mortified.

He raised her face so that she was forced to look at him. "Not pleased?"

"It's not exactly what you expected," she acknowledged. "And I am perfectly able to take care of myself."

"Oh, I fully realize that, Miss Tyson," he said with a smile. Then he added, "There really isn't any way to guarantee these kinds of things won't happen."

"There isn't?"

He shook his head. "No, there isn't."

Now Revel was curious. "But what about women like Lilly. I mean, they do it all the time. How do they keep from having babies?"

The lines about Jake's eyes and mouth relaxed as he chuckled.

"I'd forgotten just how outspoken you can be. Lots of times women like Lilly have babies. They're usually sent off to live with someone else. Sometimes a woman can't have babies, or something happens so that she can't."

"Oh." Revel gave that some thought. "But you had no way of knowing that I wouldn't have a baby when we . . . that night on the desert . . . and again in the mountains. . . ."

His voice became thick all over again with memory—and need. "You mean when we made love together?"

"Yes."

"You're right," he said softly. "But it didn't matter. I wanted to make love with you then, just as I want to make love with you now, and the way I'll want to make love with you tomorrow."

"Then you didn't care if I had a child?"

"Oh, I cared very much. But I didn't think you cared. And when you left the rancho without even saying good-bye . . ." His green eyes were especially bright. "I'd never loved anyone like that, until I loved you. You gave something back to me. Maybe it was my life, maybe it was my soul."

"I almost got you killed," she pointed out in a small voice.

"I'm willing to forgive you for that," he said magnanimously; then his hand spread low over her stomach. "But you have to promise to give it back to me, with this baby."

"I see."

"No, I don't think you do, just yet Miss Tyson. The fact is I came here prepared to ask you to marry me. I've decided against it."

"You have?"

"Yeah, I'm just going to *tell* you, so that even you will understand. You're going to marry me—today if possible. If not then, tomorrow. But it will make it seem a little more respectable over at the hotel tonight if we are

509

married. And you're going to Wyoming Territory with me."

"Is that right?"

"That's right."

"What if I refuse?" she asked stubbornly.

"Which?"

She shrugged. "Marriage or Wyoming, or both."

Jake leaned back on the desk. The light in those green eyes had changed to something that promised it would be dangerous for her to refuse.

"One way or the other—married with baby, unmarried with baby—you're going with me." He reached out, catching her off guard, and pulled her to him.

"And if I still refuse?" she teased.

"Then I just might throw you down on the floor right now and make love to you until you change your mind."

The blue of Revel's eyes deepened with desire.

"In that case"—her voice became husky with desire—"I think I'll refuse."

Jake's hands swept up over her breasts, and his fingers stroked across her bodice until she shuddered with needs of her own.

Her fingers plunged through the heavy silk mane of his hair, and her mouth opened under his. She pulled back, running her tongue along the soft brush of his mustache before slipping it between his lips once more.

And she whispered, "At least for now."

Author's Note

Sam Bass the notorious bank, stagecoach, and train robber was supposedly gunned down by U.S. Texas Rangers, and died at Round Rock, Texas on July 21, 1878.

In a volume of the Arizona archives, there is reference to an incident which happened some time after.

A man by the name of Ben Waters knew Sam Bass and claimed the man he saw riding south out of Tombstone in early September, 1878, was none other than the infamous outlaw leader.

As he recounted, "There was no mistakin' that fancy burlwood-handled revolver Bass always wore." Afterward, rumor had it Bass died somewhere in the Sierra Madre Mountains of Sonora, Mexico.

Unexpected bits and pieces of information found in some long-forgotten volume on a dusty shelf are the things stories are made of. Ben Waters believed he saw Sam Bass alive and well, and headed for Mexico.

SURRENDER TO THE PASSION

LOVE'S SWEET BOUNTY (3313, $4.50)
by Colleen Faulkner

Jessica Landon swore revenge of the masked bandits who robbed the train and stole all the money she had in the world. She set out after the thieves without consulting the handsome railroad detective, Adam Stern. When he finally caught up with her, she admitted she needed his assistance. She never imagined that she would also begin to need his scorching kisses and tender caresses.

WILD WESTERN BRIDE (3140, $4.50)
by Rosalyn Alsobrook

Anna Thomas loved riding the Orphan Train and finding loving homes for her young charges. But when a judge tried to separate two brothers, the dedicated beauty went beyond the call of duty. She proposed to the handsome, blue-eyed Mark Gates, planning to adopt the boys herself! Of course the marriage would be in name only, but yet as time went on, Anna found herself dreaming of being a loving wife in every sense of the word . . .

QUICKSILVER PASSION (3117, $4.50)
by Georgina Gentry

Beautiful Silver Jones had been called every name in the book, and now that she owned her own tavern in Buckskin Joe, Colorado, the independent didn't care what the townsfolk thought of her. She never let a man touch her and she earned her money fair and square. Then one night handsome Cherokee Evans swaggered up to her bar and destroyed the peace she'd made with herself. For the irresistible miner made her yearn for the melting kisses and satin caresses she had sworn she could live without!

MISSISSIPPI MISTRESS (3118, $4.50)
by Gina Robins

Cori Pierce was outraged at her father's murder and the loss of her inheritance. She swore revenge and vowed to get her independence back, even if it meant singing as an entertainer on a Mississippi steamboat. But she hadn't reckoned on the swarthy giant in tight buckskins who turned out to be her boss. Jacob Wolf was, after all, the giant of the man Cori vowed to destroy. Though she swore not to forget her mission for even a moment, she was powerfully tempted to submit to Jake's fiery caresses and have one night of passion in his irresistible embrace.

Available wherever paperbacks are sold, or order direct from the Publisher. Send cover price plus 50¢ per copy for mailing and handling to Zebra Books, Dept. 3506, 475 Park Avenue South, New York, N.Y. 10016. Residents of New York, New Jersey and Pennsylvania must include sales tax. DO NOT SEND CASH.